MAP

LEBONATH JAS

Look for The Continuation of the Dragonhorse Chronicles:

Dragonhorse Rising (Book 1)

Conscience of the King (Book 2)

Peace on Another's Terms (Book 3)

A Lopsided Colorwax Heart (Book 4)

Spirit in Motion (Book 5) *(Coming Soon)*

Visit our website at

www.dragonhorserising.com

And for this Author's Peter Aarons Books:

Glory Days (Book 1)

Another Man's Wife ~ A Love Story (Book 2)

Home Again Home Again (Book 3)

The Converging Objects of the Universe (Book 4) *(Coming Soon)*

Oh, Baby! (Book 5) *(Coming Soon)*

Visit our website at

www.peteraarons.com

Showandah S. Terrill

A LOPSIDED COLORWAX HEART

BOOK FOUR OF
THE DRAGONHORSE CHRONICLES

SHORT HORSE PRESS

This book is a work of fiction, and any references to historical events, real people or real locales are used fictitiously. Other names, places, characters and incidents are products of the author's imagination, and any resemblance to actual events or locales or persons, living or dead, is purely coincidental.

Published 2022 by Short Horse Press

Dragonhorse flags and chevrons are the original artwork of Edwin M. Pinson
Book design and Shorthorse Press design by Jeremy T. Hanke
Maps and incidentals by Showandah S. Terrill, ***et al***
The text for this book is set in Times New Roman, 11 point
Manufactured in the United States of America
Library of Congress Control Number 2022914484
ISBN: 978-1-7342194-8-7 (hardbound)
ISBN: 978-1-7342194-9-4 (ebook)

A LOPSIDED COLORWAX HEART

"Land created by El'Shadai is never cursed
but by those who inhabit it."

-Ardenai Gideon Morning Star

This book is dedicated to

Every person with a tomato plant on the balcony

Herbs on the windowsill

Every gardener

Every homesteader

Every small farm and family dairy

Every person who cares where their food comes from and acts accordingly

CHAPTER 1

Ah'ria Konik Nokota, Military Governor of the Lebonathi Worlds, felt the weightlessness of awakening from a vivid and protracted dream. He rolled his head to one side, and managed to open his eyes, first one, then the other, expecting to see his hetaera beside him. She wasn't...wherever he was, which wasn't at all where he remembered being. He managed, "Hmmm," and realized his voice was rusty. His mouth was parched, his throat was raw. He felt like he'd been hit with a polo mallet and fallen under a running pony. He closed his eyes and poked gingerly around in his head for information.

He remembered stalling, trying to get one more thing done, until his heat cycle became unbearable – arriving at the apartments set aside for him on the Jocundome barely in control of his sanity, insisting over and over that whomever this hetaera was, she wasn't prepared for what he was about to inflict on her, and Ah'ren telling him not to worry, which was a ludicrous thing to say given the circumstances.

And then, from the dimness of the ithyphallic chamber a figure had emerged to take his face in her hands and whisper, "Nik, Beloved, it's me. It's Swift. You're safe." With a groan that mingled relief with need, he had given himself into her keeping, and most of what had followed had been the usual painful and exhausting blur.

But this…was not where he had been. The pain was not sexual; the blur was not familiar. Swift was not there, nor the bed, the priapic bench, the apartments, for that matter. He rubbed momentarily at his forehead as he did when he was puzzled. Something brushed his shoulder and he realized it was a tube – that there were enterodermal jacerei on his forearms pumping something into his veins. His chest hurt. His head was throbbing. The small of his back ached mercilessly. He couldn't smell grass, but he opened his eyes wider and patted around, just to make sure he wasn't lying on the ground with an amused polo pony and three disgusted teammates standing over him.

"Nik?"

He rolled his head the other way and looked into the worried face of the Thirteenth Dragonhorse. "Ardi?" His voice was raspy and reverberated in his skull. He sucked momentarily on his bottom lip and managed to generate some moisture.

"How do you feel, my friend?"

Konik closed his eyes again. Breathing was such an effort. "I have no idea. Disoriented. Where am I?"

"You're in the sanecere on the Jocundome," Ardenai said, and while he sounded worried, he also sounded a little peeved. "Precious Equus! You didn't think it necessary to tell anyone what your body puts you through during a Dragonhorse cycle?"

"For me, they're all Dragonhorse cycles," he muttered. "The last two or three have gotten progressively worse. Maybe the next one will kill me and I'll be shed of them."

"Well, you've already cleared that particular chevron," Ardenai responded, still intent on the governor's face.

Konik caught his breath and his eyes widened with alarm. "What does that mean? Where is Swift? Did I hurt her? Why am I here?" He coughed from the dryness in his throat, and the jacerei band bit into his forearm as he brought a hand up. "Shit!" he snarled, "What's going on, Ardenai?"

"Calm down," the Firstlord soothed. His hand closed over Konik's, but the man looked no less distraught.

"I ask you again…."

"Swift is fine. She and Ah'ren went to find something to drink. The only person who's hurt, is you. Why didn't you tell someone what your heat cycles are like? Maybe we could have headed this off. We nearly lost you, my friend."

"Sorry to have worried you," he said, looking more at the wall than Ardenai. A sudden and vivid image filled his head – a boy of fourteen, trying to glue together the fifty discrete pieces of his grandmother's favorite vase. Which piece went where so the pattern made sense? He tried for a deeper breath that ended in a groan. "Eladeus, I feel half dead."

"Funny you should mention that," Ardenai drawled. "Remember when you told us you thought maybe being tortured by Eridu had made your heart rhythm feel a little off kilter?"

Konik gave it some thought, and half-nodded against the pillow.

"Well, you were right. You're here because your heart gave out. This heat cycle did kill you, Governor. You are here by the grace of the Wisdom Giver, the quick thinking of Swift, and the skill of our friendly serpent physician."

"What?" Konik gasped. Those pains in his chest had been his heart and not that damned crossbow bolt through his breastbone? Why was he bothering to act surprised? He'd known it was his heart…hadn't he? He tried for a deeper breath. The beeping monitor grew more insistent.

"You're supposed to be calming him down, not winding him up," said a growly alto with laughter in it, and an exceptionally tall, stunningly beautiful woman walked into the room. "Nik, Beloved, are you feeling better?" she asked. She gave him a lingering kiss on the forehead and perched like a long-legged bird at the foot of his bed.

He was trying to figure out how to answer Ah'ren's question when a smaller, softer woman came into the room and sat beside him opposite the Dragonhorse. "Swift," he said, and it was a sigh of relief.

"Hi there. Welcome back," she smiled. She took a sliver of ice from her drink and extended it between thumb and forefinger. "Let this melt on your tongue," she said, and pushed his heavy silver forelock into place with practiced fingers. "Better?"

He closed his eyes and forced a deep breath. It had become a habit to rub at the spot where Sarkhan's crossbow bolt had shattered his sternum, and now his fingers told him he was…encased in something. It was unyielding, and hard enough to click when his fingernails hit it. Just his trunk. He could feel his thighs, see his arms. "Start talking," he growled. "One at a time or all at once. But talk. Now."

"Look at me," Swift said, taking his hand. "Nik. Look at me. I'm fine. You're fine."

She gave his hand a squeeze and he felt himself relaxing into her. That quiet, unruffled voice went back ninety years, from one miserable, half-conscious heat cycle to the next, and the face, usually just a blur in his memory, was lovely when he really looked at her. Sweet, smart, and slightly sexy, with ophidian eyes an unusual shade of bright spring green and a soft, smiling mouth with a strong chin, neatly framed by honey brown hair pulled back at the crown and flowing over her shoulders in the manner of most Equi women. It was pleasant to have her close.

The sensation caught him off guard, and sent a shiver of guilt up his spine.

Swift sensed his discomfort and paused a bit before continuing. "The Firstlord told you your heart stopped, didn't he?"

"Um hm," he replied, realizing he'd drifted for a minute. He was so tired, and he ached all over. He still wondered if he was dreaming.

"Well, the good news is, you're here. You made it," she said. Before he could ask, she added, "The bad news is, your heart failed permanently. Pythos spent hours wrapped around you and couldn't resynchronize it. The shell you're in is currently integrating your new heart with your other bodily functions. It's Androtech, from your own tissue. Once the shell is off you won't know it's not the heart you've always had."

He bit his bottom lip to stop the shock from registering on his face.

Another piece of the precious vase crumbled in his hand. It couldn't be fixed. His grandmother was going to cry. "But it isn't my heart, is it?" he said quietly. His heart was gone. First his eyes, now his heart. Gone, like his beloved wife.

Ah'ren read his face. "The heart that belonged to Ah'davan, is buried with Ah'davan," she said. "Teal crafted a beautiful box which she holds in her hands. We didn't disturb her rest. Kehailan did it using scrambleshaft technology, and you know how good he is."

Konik nodded, not trusting his voice or the possibility that his lips might tremble. He could see her kind and beautiful face, hear her laughter, and now she held his heart in her hands. Just for a moment – just a moment – he wished she embraced all of him in her hilltop casket. He opened his eyes again.

"Well, this is the heart you have now, and this one has got to last," Ardenai said in his best, matter-of-fact teacher's voice. "In order for it to do that, you cannot go through another heat cycle like this."

"And I was so looking forward to it," Konik muttered. "I love those things." His eyes closed and he fought the urge to sleep.

Ah'ren smiled and gave his leg a little pat. "Most of what is happening to you is because you are heavy with Dragonhorse blood, and when they rise..."

Konik's eyes came open. "Stop. Right there," he said. "We've had this conversation, Wren. You've told me what happens to certain people when a Dragonhorse rises. What do you mean I have Dragonhorse blood? Me, personally? Direct Dragonhorse blood? No. Not me."

"Yes you. But not the Twelfth Dragonhorse. Not Kehailan. Not his line." She hesitated, trying to figure out how to say something she knew he was not going to like in the least. Wondering if he was up for it.

He scowled. "I can see it in your face, so you might as well spit it out."

"The Ninth," she grimaced. "Kabardin."

"Oh...perfect." There was a lengthy silence. He was spawn of the most hated man in Equi history. Despite himself he had to laugh, which made him cough and clutch his aching head. "It was my understanding that the Great House put forth a concerted effort to breed his genes out of existence three thousand years ago," he managed, gasping for air. "I thought Sarkhan was crazy when he said he was related to Kabardin – the *true* line of Dragonhorses." His eyes widened. "Oh, Precious Equus, don't tell me I'm related to Sarkhan. Please."

"Full brothers," Ardenai droned, and the look he got from Swift made him jump and shut his mouth despite the obvious joke.

"You are most certainly not related to Sarkhan, nor was Sarkhan related to the Ninth Dragonhorse," Swift said, peeling her eyes off Ardenai. "That was all part of his lunatic family fantasy. But Kabardin had a very smart daughter who went off to Lycee and never came back. She changed her patronym, moved to a sparsely populated corner of Viridia and quite inadvertently married the son of a keeplord in the direct line of Timor, the Fifth Dragonhorse. I suppose you could say they were cousins of the remotest sort, and so, then, are you and Ardenai, since Timor's line was later brought back in. Point being, that's how, despite the best efforts of the Great House and Mountain hold, Kabardin's blood is still in play and coursing with all its fire through your veins and a very few others, most of whom we think we have now tracked down."

"Explains a lot about me and the things I struggle with, doesn't it?" Konik said, almost to himself, and the humor faded from his eyes. "Explains a lot about my grandsire's behaviors, and my mother's. And now this, too, will come down upon my daughters and my grandchildren."

Ardenai winced. "I wish you would let go of that whole thing with the Telenir, Governor. Nobody holds it against you, but you."

"The Dragonhorse is right," Swift said. "Now take a deep breath and try to relax. Get your heart rate back down or you'll be awake in this contraption for a week instead of the prescribed twenty-four hours."

"Of course. Time enough later for explanations," Ah'ren said, nodding agreement. "Right now I think Nik needs to sleep and get his strength back. We need to go and let you recuperate." She unfolded off the foot of the bed and extended her hand to her husband. "Dragonhorse?"

"I'll meet you outside," he said. "I'd like a word alone with Konik."

Ah'ren dropped him a respectful nod. Swift rose from her spot, and as she exited into the sunlit garden, she gave Ardenai a glance that told him his crown and kingdom would not save him if he upset the governor. He gave her a reassuring smile and bowed as Swift closed the tall glass door behind her, leaving the men alone.

The Firstlord took a deep breath and blew air through his lips, his usual preface to a touchy subject. "You know, Nik," he ventured, "I could set my head against yours and that whole nonsense with the Telenir and Calumet and the dust-up with Sarkhan, would just be..."

"Gone. I know," Konik responded with some irritation. "And when someone brought it up to me and I gave them a blank look, how would that go, exactly?"

"I wasn't going to say, 'gone', for one thing. I can buffer those memories to where they don't slap you so hard. You have enough on your mind as it is trying to orchestrate the governance of a couple planets and deal with Ah'davan's loss. Nik, you were dead there for a while. Literally dead. You've been unconscious for most of a week. Something has to give somewhere. You could at least let me try."

"I'll think about it," Konik said in his soothing purr, but Ardenai was not deceived. He gave the man a lingering kiss on the forehead, and gave Swift a nod and a wink in passing as he departed with his wife.

Swift assumed the chair Ardenai had vacated and the gleam in her eye made Konik chuckle. "He's really a very dear man, and a very good friend," he said. "He carries the weight of the Affined Equi Worlds and the Seventh Galactic Alliance on those young shoulders. The last thing he needs is his military governor flat on his back in bed."

"You'd be less useful if you were deceased, wouldn't you?" she sniffed.

Konik let the comment pass. "You said twenty-four hours. What happens in twenty-four hours, provided I'm a good boy and do as I'm told?"

"Pythos cracks your shell. Twenty-four hours after that, I get to take you back to your apartments, where you will be much more comfortable, and so will I, so behave yourself, Governor." She smiled then, and patted his hand before offering him another piece of ice from her drink.

While it melted on his tongue Konik thought about her – what he actually knew about her – the time they had spent together over many years and under what circumstances. "I've known you so long," he said, "and I hardly know you at all. No matter where I was, when I needed you, there you were. How disruptive has that been for you? I feel like I owe you a hundred apologies for how you've been pulled away from your life, and how I've treated you. The fact that I come to you half-crazed, and the second I regain myself I take off again. I don't suppose you've ever seen me in a normal moment, and yet here you are for me. Who am I, that I deserve such devotion?"

She settled back in her chair and fixed him with those brilliant green eyes. "I have seen you more than you think I have," she smiled. "I'm never very far away and I never have been. You are my first and only charge, Nik. My only assignment from Mountain hold."

He scowled, wondering what Mountain hold had to do with it. He needed to ask that at some point. He closed his eyes for a bit, then opened them and smiled at her. "All other questions about worthiness aside, what do you do with most of your life? I know you don't just wait for me. Do you have a family? A husband and children?"

"Promise you won't laugh," she grinned.

"Promise."

"I'm a cardiologist."

He laughed of course, then groaned, pressing a hand to his temple, and she shook her head with a look of mock disgust. "I'm also a paleopathologist. Mostly a cardiologist. Mostly a children's cardiologist, actually. And I am single."

"So, when I decided to stay and become governor of the Lebonathi worlds, you…?"

"Came with Ah'ren when she was sent as a companion wife for the Firstlord. I got your apartments set up the way I thought you'd like them. Well, actually they're our apartments, as I live there whether you're there or not, unless you want me gone for some reason, so I decorated for both of us. When I was done with that, I established a practice here on the dome. One of my passions is juvenile nutritional cardiopathy, and the Lebonathi are fascinating in that respect. I'm here to keep you company, Nik. Just as a companion," she added hastily, "You may live with me as little or as much as you desire, and in any capacity you choose. Or I can move out. Your choice. No hard feelings."

Konik was frankly amazed. "After the way I've treated you, you're willing to do that?"

"One of the things we need to discuss is the disconnect you have between what your brain thinks you do when you're in heat, and what your body actually does. You've never hurt me or mistreated me in any way, though you obviously think you have."

"But…I do go crazy."

"Sort of, to tell the truth, but not in the way you think you do. You might have frightened your wife, but you would never have hurt her, despite the fear that you would." She paused, watching the grief flicker in Konik's eyes.

He was realizing all those times, all those weeks over the years that he had spent with Swift, he could have been safely with his beloved wife. Ah'davan had been his sexual trainer and many years his senior in age and experience, and yet he had feared for her in his presence. How hard that must have been for him – for both of them – how deeply ashamed he must be for a condition that was not and had never been his fault. Perhaps now that could be changed. Now that it didn't matter to him anymore.

"I'm so sorry you lost her, Nik."

"Me too," he said quietly, and in a minute or so the tears receded. "Why do I ache all over?"

"Probably what we gave you to help mitigate your heat cycle. Had to get the adrenalin out of your system to fix your heart, you know. That was a serious jolt to your muscles."

He gave that some thought. "Do I want to know what we were doing when I collapsed?"

"Probably not," she laughed. "I have to go for a bit. I have polo practice, and I want you to get some sleep, Governor. When I come back, we're going to start putting your stomach to work so Pythos will let me take you home in a day or two." She kissed his forehead, slipped him one more piece of ice, and left him alone.

He laid there awhile, staring out into the sunlit garden with its butterflies and flowers and contemplating her words. Home. Where and what would that be, exactly, and with whom, and would it be so unbearable if it were with Swift? Again, he felt a bit of a jolt. Why was she making him feel this way? It was too soon – much too soon. There was a minute of contemplation, then a mental shrug. He'd been married as an adolescent barely out of childhood. Married his entire adult life. His only frame of reference was as a married man. It was only natural to think of this woman in those terms.

He thought about doughty little Anchoress Ensharra and wondered how she was doing after her bump on the head. Now there was a woman. Smart, valiant, feisty and funny. Made his heart flutter just a bit. Lifespan of a gnat. How many more people could he bear to lose? He wondered about it for a few seconds. How cowardly, he thought, to put fear of loss over desire to love. He thought about the cadaverously thin Lebonathi who had dropped to his knees and said, "You saved us." What was that worth? How many of those men had been fully accounted for and their families found? The comment that he'd been unconscious for a week finally penetrated. He'd been unconscious for a week, out of his offices for three days before that. He had paperwork to do and wondered if anybody was keeping up with it. Priestess Ah'nis's priorities and affections lay in other directions, but Ah'ren would have followed through with whatever time she had to spare.

Beautiful Ah'ren – she of the brilliant mind and the gentle, laughing spirit – sent from Mountain hold as wife and adviser to help the Firstlord navigate an interposing campaign on a world so out of balance it seemed a caricature of everything the AEW stood for. The people were passive consumers of an unconscionable culture which left them hungry and haunted by fear, yet they shrugged and shuffled on. Medicine was practically nonexistent except for the barbaric practice of albinizing any child whose parents could afford it. Schools were religion-oriented and excluded girls, technology was a patchwork shamble. There was no water, no food with any essential nutrients in it except what the AEW had brought with them, the male priesthood was out to destroy any headway the Equi could make in any arena. Arena? Polo field? Swift played polo? Polo. Konik took a deep, untroubled breath and found himself pounding downfield, the surge of a fast horse under him, the long, easy swing of his practiced right arm. The whistle of a custom-made mallet splitting the air.

"Oh no!" Teal exclaimed, but his steadying hand wasn't quick enough, and the irreplaceable pot of finish hit the floor and spilled everywhere. "Oh no." He was so tired he could hardly think, his fingers were nicked in a couple dozen places, Gifting-night, which kicked off Celebration of Storms, was two days away, and the hammered dulcimer for Ah'rane was not finished. "And now it's not going to be," he snarled, and fought the urge to throw the micro-detailing knife and the last of the treble tuning pins after it.

He'd asked Pythos to bring the instrument back with him, and the old dragon had managed it despite having its unsuspecting recipient on the same small vessel with him. Now Teal had spilled the instrument lacquer – very old, very rare. Why hadn't he put the stopper back in while the piece he'd finished dried? He was so close. The last two tuning pegs still to be whittled. He'd even bribed Ardenai into restoring the intricate paintings on the soundboard. "No. Not again," he said, taking a deep breath. "We are not going another year with this hanging over our heads."

He let Dragonhorse Thirteen know he was on the move, grabbed the empty lacquer jar, locked the door on the little room he'd borrowed from Anchoress Ensharra next to her shop, and set off for the Street of the Bells, Ancient Sector. Basement. That's where Naram had said an old man named Kish resided, and Ellsbeth and Company had confirmed it. Kish, whose great-grandfather had repaired pipe organs and upon whom Ardenai had hung his hopes for repairing the huge organ in the great church nearest the capitol. Apparently, Kish was building furniture these days with his sons and grandsons, and if he was building it, he was likely finishing it. Because he was as ancient as the sector in which he resided, he just might be using a traditional lacquer.

Even dressed in loose trousers and an old muslin tunic, hair knotted at the nape of his neck, Teal garnered looks and nods, and despite his gentle voice and ready smile, people moved out of his way. His tall, powerful frame and raven-dark hair made him stand out amongst the small, pale Lebonathi, and he was immediately identifiable as Master Captain of the Interposing Forces. Some loved him, some did not, but almost everyone knew who he was and either respected or feared him for one reason or another. This day he seemed to be on a personal mission as he threaded his way through the crowded, evil-smelling byways, and they viewed him with less than their usual suspicion.

He got directions twice before finding himself on yet another dim subterranean street in front of a shop that had windows opaque with sawdust and a weathered sign overhead announcing,

TRADITIONAL HANDMADE FURNITURE.

He let himself in and followed the sounds of saws and hammers to the workroom at the back of the space. Four men looked up, the noise ceased, and a small, slightly stooped figure stepped forward, clutching a finishing hammer and peering at him from under bushy white eyebrows.

"Are you Kish?" Teal asked, nodding respectfully.

The old man moved closer. "My name is Kish," he said. "How may

I serve you, Master Captain?"

Teal wasn't sure the man had heard him, and wondered if he should raise his voice a little. He glanced up at the others, and one of the men grinned and tapped his ear, answering the question. "Ahimsa, I wish thee peace," he said, making the traditional Equi gesture before grasping Kish's forearms. "I have had a foolish accident and spilled what little instrument finish I had left. I am hoping you have something that will suffice."

"My idiot grandson Esha told you I'm deaf, didn't he?" the old man queried. He had a voice like sandpaper, but his eyes were sharp, and he studied Teal carefully as he spoke. "He likes to eavesdrop on my conversations. It's his idea of a joke and he doesn't think I know he's doing it. You needn't speak like you're shouting across a city street, Master Captain. I can hear you just fine. I have brains enough to wear ear protection."

"Apologies," Teal said, crimping a grin.

"Where are your soldiers?" the old man asked, looking around Teal toward the door.

Teal was puzzled for a moment. "I am not soldiering today. Today I am but a restorer of old instruments."

"You do know the flamen have put a bounty on your head?"

"I do."

"And yet here you are."

"Because I need traditional finish and I spilled all I had. Yes. Can you help me?"

Kish chuckled, then held out his hand for the jar, pulled the stopper, sniffed the contents and dabbed at the remnant with an exploratory finger. He rubbed it between thumb and forefinger, sniffed it again, and stood thinking. "Let me show you what I have," he said. "It's not an exact match, but it might suffice. What are you building, if I may ask?"

As they walked to the side of the workroom and the old man gestured him into a chair, Teal told him about the hammered dulcimer that had belonged to his mother-in-law's grandmother. Ah'rane had such wonderful memories of it – of her grandmother playing and singing, and teaching her to play, as well. The dulcimer had been badly damaged in a roof collapse which had killed the grandmother. It had been carelessly stored in the trauma which followed, and left moldering under an old horse blanket in an unused section of a huge barn for over a hundred years. Teal, who had heard the story many times, had sleuthed around Pinecliff keep, found the instrument and spent three years trying to restore it in his spare time. Now, with victory in sight, he'd gotten careless and set himself back.

"Sometimes the little setbacks can be the most frustrating," Kish nodded, rummaging around on the packed, well-ordered shelves. "I don't see what I'm looking for here," he said. "If you will excuse me for a minute I'll look further back. I may have to concoct something." He gave Teal a brief nod and disappeared through a doorway.

Teal looked around, then rose and went over to where the other three men had been working. "My name is Teal," he said politely. "I did not mean to take you from your tasks."

"I am Temen," said the older man. "My sons Ashte and Esha. We are at your service."

"And I am at yours," Teal smiled, grasping their forearms in the manner of Lebonathi greeting. "This is a beautiful bench; may I touch it?"

The youngest man nodded; the one who had tapped his ear. Teal rubbed his hands on his trousers to remove any oils, then stroked the piece in a practiced gesture that was almost a caress. The wood was raw yet, and gold in the light, smooth as ice and tightly grained with no knots or figuring. "What kind of wood is this?" he breathed, sniffing his palms. There was no identifying fragrance, but in the gesture the men saw the nicks, cuts and calluses of hard-working, capable hands, and relaxed with their visitor.

"We do not know," said Temen. "There is no available timber anymore except for the date palms, of course, and their wood resembles cork more than anything. This wood we retrieved from a broken mushroom cart brought from the tunnels last year."

"All this beauty hidden in those terrible conditions," Teal mused. A thought struck him. "Do you have any of this left as it was when you got the cart?"

"We didn't get the whole cart, just the wood," Ashte said, "and I think we've used every scrap. Wood is so precious."

"I can just imagine," Teal nodded. "I wonder if all the carts are made from this same timber." He had been wondering what he could offer Kish in exchange for the lacquer. What if all the carts, all the trays and frames were made from this amazing stuff? How could he not have noticed this? "Excuse me for just a moment," he said, and stepped to one side, tipping his head slightly to the right and concentrating as he pinched one of the crys-tels around his neck. *Kehailan?*

I am here. Are you in trouble?

No, not at all. I know this sounds strange, but can you possibly get a scrambleshaft lock on one of the mushroom carts?

There was a pause, and Teal could sense his nephew's amusement. In a few seconds he responded. *Cutter says he can capture the image of those nearest the mouth of the southern tunnel. What would you have us do?*

Can you scramble one to sit three feet in front of me?

Again, there was a pause. *Yes. It's not exactly in pristine condition, and you know it's going to stink.*

I do know this. Please ask Cutter to stay close for a few minutes, just in case we need to get the thing out of here.

Of course. Coming your way in three, two, one...

At that moment Kish appeared from the other room, carrying the jar. He was saying, "I think this is very close," when there was a slight ma-roon shimmer, a soft whumping sound, and where there had been bare floor, there sat a bedraggled mushroom cart. It was larger than it had looked in the tunnel, and it definitely stank, but it was also definitely made of wood. Solid wood. Kish put the jar on the workbench and stared with the others.

"Sorry for the abrupt appearance," Teal said. "I get excited about wood. Is this what that," he pointed to the bench, "looked like before you planed it?"

Temen grabbed a saw, Ashte another, and they began cutting at each end of the cart. The first few strokes told them this part of the cart was spongy punk, but the sawdust was the right color to be the wood in the bench. The second set of cuts bit solid wood, and the men smiled and nodded at one another as they lifted the board. "This is it," Temen said, eyeing the end-grain.

Teal turned to Kish with a respectful nod. "Will you accept this as payment for the lacquer?"

"Of course," the old man smiled. "I would have given you the lacquer for the pleasure of your company, but I am overjoyed to have the cart."

"And I am pleased that you should have it," Teal replied. "It would be a tragedy to have all that wood lost when the tunnels are repurposed."

"How many carts are there?" Esha asked, and Teal did not miss the gleam in his eye.

"Some," he said. "When I have a few spare minutes, I will be back to speak to your father and your grandfather about their proper disposition. For now, I must advise you not to approach the tunnels. They are unsafe. They are also extremely well-guarded."

The young man nodded, and Teal could sense his disappointment. A fortune gained and lost in a few seconds. Unfortunately, anything of any real value carried the potential for riot. This was a time for cooler heads to prevail. "I will see that you receive a good share as a finder's fee," Teal said consolingly.

Kish thanked him, handed him the stoppered jar, and Teal made his way to the door before turning at a remembered question. "Has someone spoken to you about the possibility of fixing the pipe organ, the carillia, I think you call them, in the great church?"

"Carillon. Yes," Kish replied. "Two males and a female came to see me. The female was smaller with brown skin, the two males had yellow-orange skin, slanted, wide-set eyes. Their heads were shaven with a wide..." he gestured, "strip down the middle and inkings on the sides. Big people. Said they had been sent by the Thirteenth Dragonhorse."

"They were," Teal affirmed. "Amberian troopers on special assignment. Ellsbeth, the female, is Demetrian. What did you tell them?"

Kish looked for a moment at the floor. "Nothing," he said. "I couldn't understand what they were really after. I thought maybe they were trying to trick me into saying something bad."

Teal turned and walked back into the shop, sitting casually to make himself more accessible. "Please tell me what concerned you about their visit," he said. "Were they rude or threatening in any way?"

Kish shook his head. "No. I…they were not rude, Master Captain."

"Kish, I'm not interrogating you, but I am responsible for their actions. If those who represent the Affined Equi Worlds are projecting a hostile image, I need to know so I can instruct them not to do that."

The old man shook his head. "They were polite, but their request worried me."

"There is no need for concern. They were sent by Ardenai Firstlord because Regent Naram had heard through who knows who that your grandfather, or great-grandfather, could make beautiful sounds come out of that old instrument. Ardenai was hoping that you could, as well. That's all. All Equi love music, and we are fascinated by that carillon. We just want to fix it so everyone can enjoy it."

Kish was quiet for a long moment. "To make music on such an instrument is punishable by death," he said, barely above a whisper. "The flamen say it is sinful, that it is the sound of the witch world. The music to which the witches dance while sinners scream and burn. They say the first notes would strike the city deaf and the fires of the witch world would rage in the streets."

"They lie," Teal replied, but he kept his voice low and reassuring. "Their so-called witch world is populated, not by witches, but by trees of many kinds. Some which shed their leaves to raise their branches in prayer to the snow-filled skies, some which keep their leaves all year around. Carefully harvested, they will make beautiful lumber for furniture and other necessary things. The skies and the water are blue and clean and the rain is nourishing and pure. It is a place of great blessings, not evil. I know. I live there in a tent by the river."

"No matter how much I believed that, I would never repeat it," Kish said warningly, "nor will I ever raise a finger to repair or play that carillon. To do so would mean death, either by the hand of the Gods, or the hand of the flamen. In either case, I would be equally dead and my family hungry and homeless. Those who displease the flamen are turned out. Their homes are seized, their goods, their livelihood. No one is allowed to sell or give them food or comfort. They are counted among the dead."

"I understand," Teal said with an acquiescing nod. "We will speak of it no further and I will tell the Amberians not to bother you again. With your permission, though, I will return to speak to you about the mushroom carts and the lumber which they contain. I would like your help in seeing to its proper dispersal, if that's acceptable to you."

"Of course," the old man said, and his eyes were sad as he walked Teal to the door again. When his back was to the others he whispered, "I'm sorry," and Teal knew Kish was unsure of someone in his household. "Be careful, Master Captain. They say they will throw you in for the wild animals to rend, and they will do it."

"Thank you for the warning," Teal said quietly. "Ahimsa, I wish thee peace." With that he turned and strode away, carrying the pot of lacquer.

Konik was freshly bathed and sitting up in bed, enjoying a hot cup of cinnamon orange tea and relishing the ability to scratch his ribcage or anything else that itched, when a thin Lebonathi appeared in the doorway and bowed respectfully. "Bona!" the governor exclaimed, setting aside his teacup. "Come in my friend, and welcome. What brings you?"

Bona shuffled in on his mutilated feet and bowed again at the bedside. "I was sent by the others to see how you are getting along," he said with some embarrassment. "We had heard you were injured, or sick. Some even said you were dead. That made us very sad, so I was sent to discover the truth of it."

"And now you see that I am doing very well," Konik smiled. "Please, sit down and visit with me for a bit. Have some tea. Tell me, how goes life on the great farming ships?" Bona hesitated, and Konik pointed firmly to the chair next to the bed. "Sit," he said, and Bona did so, keeping his eyes on the floor. "Give me your hands in friendship. Yes, now look at me and tell me how you are enjoying being a real farmer, Bona."

The man looked up, cautiously at first, then with more confidence as he saw Konik's genuine enthusiasm. "It is a whole new life," he said. "We are learning to treat the soil as a living thing, with care and kindness and an eye to the future. Every day there is something new to see or do or practice, and every night there is enough food for everyone, and all the light we want, or all the darkness, all the warmth of a blanket or the coolness of a walk in the park. We laugh. We are safe, Soft One. The children do not fear us, nor the women. We do not fear one another. Those who care for us and guide us live amongst us, speak the truth to us and do not threaten us. We are…all the same. Even those who do not want to be there, are learning to be content. We are all the same."

As he paused to catch his breath, face filled with the words he spoke, Konik realized Bona was not an old man at all, but a fairly young one, terribly scarred inside and out, beginning to recover the joy of being alive and a sense of who he was. "Have they found your children?"

"Mine, no," he sighed, "but the sons of others, yes, and the wives and daughters. Almost every day families are restored. The schools are bursting at the seams with Menorquin and Lebonathi boys and girls, too, and we adults go at night and learn all kinds of things. Whole families have basket meals in the park, or go together to the pools to splash, and many are learning how to swim. It is fun, and it pleases the Menorquins, who say they are all fish at heart. Even, a few at a time, they are taking us to Lebonath Tras to see its wonders, so we know what a planet should look like! It is a whole new world, and you have given it to us."

Konik squirmed. "All of us, Bona – the Dragonhorse, the Master

Captain, the anchoress of the ancient city – all of us are trying to put all of you in a position where you can work hard and earn back your worlds. Surely nothing is given, and most assuredly not by me."

Bona smiled and shook his head, and again he looked young. "You may tell me that a thousand times and yet will I see you kneeling at my feet, releasing my shackles, supporting me with your arms, standing in the water with me, bathing me with your own hands, washing away not just the filth, but the fear. In that alone, you gave me a whole new world, and until the day I die, I will worship you, Soft One, and nothing you can say will change my mind."

"Then I shall bow to your stubborn streak and say nothing," Konik smiled. "Which crops do you most enjoy tending?"

"I love them all," Bona replied, "but above all else, I love to tend the bees!"

"Wonderful!" Konik exclaimed. "No skill will be more valuable than that. Tell me all about what you have learned and what you do with our tiny kinsmen each day."

Bona was still talking and Konik was smiling and asking questions when there was a movement in the doorway and Pythos appeared. He caught the governor's eye, and Konik nodded his direction. "Physician Pythos," he said by way of greeting and introduction. "Bona, this most ancient and respected fellow is the reason I'm able to sit here and talk to you. I'm pleased that you are here to meet him, as I think he can be of benefit to you, as well."

Bona turned in his chair, and only Konik's warm and confident words kept him from running – or screaming – or both. Pythos was a dragon. A huge serpentine dragon. He was dressed in long, emerald green robes which brushed the floor as he walked on what must have been legs, as he rocked from side to side rather than slithering. His long tail trailed behind him, and Bona could tell by its slight twitching that it was helping him keep his balance. His arms were short and branch-like, and his hands and fingers resembled the fronds of a fern. Bona managed a nod.

"Thee iss a brave individual," hissed the old doctor. "I am pleassed to meet thee."

"Bona represents the community of Lebonathi farmers," Konik said as Pythos toddled up beside him. "I have been enjoying his company very much this afternoon."

"I should go," Bona said hastily, and both Konik and Pythos shook their heads.

"Thee iss welcome to sstay," Pythos hissed. "I will be but a minute with thiss one."

"I would like Pythos to look at your feet," Konik said, and glanced up at the old doctor. "They've chopped off his toes."

"Thine, and otherss, as I undersstand," Pythos murmured. "I think perhapss a weighted prossthessiss iss in order to help thy gait. I will ssend for thee when I have a proposal."

"I will come," Bona said, and rose with a respectful nod. "But for now, I must go. There is work yet to do before supper, Soft One. I am glad to find you alive and on the mend. And, thank you for your words just now." He smiled at the governor's quizzical expression. "The community of Lebonathi farmers." He tasted the words and said them again. "The community of Lebonathi farmers."

"And so you are. I will be up to see you soon," Konik smiled. "Tell everyone, all your fellow farmers, thank-you for their concern."

Pythos watched Konik as he spoke – the handsome young face and the striking silver hair – the stunning blue eyes that were beginning to show signs of life again. A strong man returning to health. When Bona had gone, Pythos bent over and flicked Konik gently in one ear with his long tongue. "And thee, my good man. Thee sseems in better sspiritss, and much better without thy sshell. Thee did not enjoy the opportunity to experiencce a turtle'ss world?"

"To my lasting chagrin, no. I cannot say I appreciated the cultural exchange," Konik chuckled. "Turtles must not itch very much."

Pythos released a hissy giggle, then sat quietly, holding both Konik's hands in his own until the governor began to drift. He could hear laughter, and his grandchildren ran toward him, bundled in their winter coats and carrying their ice skates. There was a sense of gliding – forward, backward – so easily, steadying them as they learned to skate with him, one on each side, laughing as Addie called to them across the ice.

"Thee iss healing niccely," Pythos said, and Konik's eyes snapped open. "I am going to let thee go home to thy apartmentss and thy companion thiss afternoon." He fixed Konik in a draconic gaze and drawled, "Which iss not to ssay that thee iss a free man, Governor Konik. Thee will remain under housse arresst for at leasst another week, and under Sswift's wing for at leasst another month. Thee may have Kehailan or Ah'ren bring thee the tiniesst bit of work to keep thee occupied, but thee iss not to usse the sscramblesshaft ssystem jusst yet. Iss thee lisstening?"

"I am listening," he said respectfully.

"Eat, ssleep, walk, sswim, make love, all thee wantss, thesse thingss are good for thee. Thee may watch polo practisse, thee may not practisse polo. If thee iss a good and obedient hatchling, thee may go back to work nexsst week. Are we agreed?"

"We are agreed," Konik smiled. "I will do as you ask."

"Under Sswift's capable thumb, I'm ssure thee will," Pythos nodded.

When Swift arrived an hour later, he was dressed and sitting in the sunshine on the patio, enjoying the butterflies and feeling quite his old self. She was wearing a soft green blouse that matched her eyes and brought out the gold in her hair, and Konik spent a long minute just looking at her. Then he rose and offered her his arm. "We have never had any normal time in a normal place," he said. "I believe I can now offer that to both of us, if you are interested."

"I am," she said, and slipped her arm through his. "And I know where we live from here."

CHAPTER 2

"You know that went out over every telegenic device on the planet, and probably the Seventh Galactic Alliance," Teal observed, swirling the wine in his glass and holding it up to the light.

"Be that as it may," Ardenai responded, trying to get comfortable in his chair and making a little humming sound out of what had started as a groan. "Celebration of Storms is not Celebration of Storms without polo the first week. The fact that we were not all that practiced did not diminish the gesture."

"I'm sure those Equi far from home appreciated it," Krush soothed, "and the Lebonathi went absolutely crazy over the sport."

"Especially the part where the Thirteenth Dragonhorse landed on his ass," Teal drawled, still studying the wine.

"I wish that's all I'd landed on."

"Served you properly. If you'd been paying more attention, it wouldn't have happened."

"Yes, well if I'd been playing the position I'm used to playing it would have helped, Master Captain."

"Then why did you say it didn't matter which position you played?"

"Because I didn't think it would," Ardenai muttered. "And we did win."

"It was a comedy of errors. We only won because we made fewer of them than the Amberians. It was definitely not good polo, nor how the game is played amongst people who are supposed to be experts. We have given the Lebonathi an altogether false impression of an ancient and sacred sport."

"Boys," Krush said, holding up a hand, "We laughed. That's all that matters. We're together, the women have blessed us with a beautiful table, and we are being summoned to dinner even as we speak. After that, there are presents. By next week – or maybe by the time Ardi can straighten up all the way – nobody is going to remember who fell on whose ass, and whatever else one fell on." He paused and considered his next words. "You do need to remember to get that stick out of the way, Son, or you're going to be singing soprano."

"Thank you," Ardenai muttered, ratcheting himself out of the chair. "Thank you both for your invaluable insight and assessment." He straightened up with all the dignity he could muster and made his way to the table in front of his snickering companions.

"Seems odd to be celebrating the storms and snows of our world in a setting such as this," Kehailan said, gesturing to their encampment under the trees with one hand and taking a steaming platter from his grandmother with the other. "Blue sky above us, river placid beside us, warm air around us. My only complaint is that staying in pavilions makes hiding presents difficult." He speared two stuffed alcibus rolls off the platter and passed it to his grandfather.

"You're the captain of a huge stellar ship," Gideon laughed, "and you couldn't find a hidey-hole?"

"I'm reflecting the concerns of others," his brother grinned. "Grandmother, Ah'din, Ah'ren, this is absolutely wonderful, thank you. And you, Grandsire," he said, looking across the table at Krush, "Thank you so much for putting your own concerns on hold to come and spend time with us. Pythos, thank you for bringing everyone. Everyone, thank you for coming."

"It has been so far worth the trip," Ah'rane laughed, and went on to talk about her meeting with the city engineers, who, as it turned out, had the title but little in the way of expertise. Kehailan nodded and said that had been his experience with the technicians as well.

Pythos made note of the fact that nothing was new in medicine on the planet's surface. "If our beloved governor had been on the ssurfacce instead of the Jocundome when he had hiss heart attack, he would be altogether dead."

"He looked good at the polo matches this morning," Criollo said. "He was with quite a lovely woman, too."

"His hetaera, Swift," Ah'ren said. "For the moment she's also his doctor, jailer, keeper and fetcher."

"He didn't look to be suffering much," Criollo grinned. "He did look to be in pain at some of the fouls and fumbles."

"When he's back playing the position he's supposed to be playing, we will be well-nigh unstoppable," Ardenai said. "I invited them to dinner, but apparently Physician Pythos here has told him he can't use the scrambleshafts for a week."

"I want to be very, very ssure that hiss ssystem iss fully integrated before he sscrambless it. One doess want one'ss partss to arrive in the ssame sspace they formerly occupied."

"Good point," Ah'din said, passing a steaming platter of greens to Krush. "I must say, even the things I've learned from Ensharra speak to the past. Oh, they've adapted some things, and discovered a few things rather, it seems, by accident than design. It's as if the whole planet is stagnant."

"Which is why it seems fragmented," her husband said. "Wherever they were when the lights went out, that's where they stayed. The question is, what happened?"

"It's like the stone age with buses," Gideon said. "They're doing the same moronic, destructive things they've done for centuries because they aren't smart enough to figure out how to do anything else."

"They were mighty once," Criollo said a little defensively. "That city, the planetary capital, is still beautiful." He eyed his sire and his uncle across the table. "I'd like the chance to explore it."

"All in good time," his father smiled.

"Who knows," Kehailan said, "maybe your storm gift will be a magic horsehide. You can explore from above and pick out what you most want to see in what order."

"No hints!" Pythos bawled, spraying a mouthful of sugar melon in all directions. "If thee cannot keep thy peacce thee must leave the table, Captain."

Kehailan burst out laughing and the table with him, and they were still snickering from time to time and throwing out false hints to annoy Pythos as the plates were cleared and the family gathered in their usual gift-giving circle.

This day it was under the trees with grass at their feet rather than the main hearth at Sea keep with snow falling, and it made Ah'din a little sad until Teal's arm came around her shoulder and his lips caressed her temple. "I am so blessed to have you here," he whispered. "My wife. My life. Thank you for coming."

"We must remember with love and positive thoughts those who are not with us today," Krush said. "Our beloved Io, who seems to be doing well in her deep sleep, and whose babes grow stronger by the day."

"And Jilfan," Gideon added. "We don't know whether he wanted to be here or not, but we do know that right now he's not getting to make a lot of choices."

"Well said," his grandsire nodded. "Dragonhorse, thine is the authority. What shall the order be?"

Ardenai looked a little startled and shook his head. "I am Firstlord of the worlds of Equus, not the master of this house. That title, and that honor is thine, Sire."

"Then I defer to the eldest amongst us, and that is the order in which we shall go," Krush smiled. "Pythos?"

"It wass I who drew Jilfan'ss name, and Jilfan who drew Ardenai'ss name. By that processs, I have gifted the Firsstlord with the beautiful Ah'ren as hiss companion wife." He smiled at the two of them where they sat together. "And I do have a ssmall ssomething for each of thee, as well. I made them as we traveled to and fro." He held out two small boxes, one in each hand, saying, "They are the ssame."

The boxes were opened to reveal clips for heavy tresses, intricately woven of black horse hair and bearing the seven chevrons of the Firstlord in silver-grey. "These are stunning," Ah'ren breathed, and Ardenai smiled and nodded. "Thank you," they said together.

The clips were duly passed and admired, then Pythos nodded to Krush, who said, "I had the honor of drawing the name of my golden-eyed grandson, whom I treasure with all my heart, and whose presence has enriched my life this past year to the point where I cannot fathom being able to give him anything that would adequately express that." He slapped his thighs and rose from his chair, saying as he walked toward the big Equi clipper at the edge of the trees, "Nevertheless, I shall try." He returned with a two-foot square box, which he placed on Gideon's lap. "Something for us to do together of a snowy evening," he said.

Gideon opened the box and stared into it. It was full of odd shapes and rusted parts, cleaning tools and oils. He looked more closely, gently stirring the collection of...wheels...and what appeared to be metal boxes and track, and then he realized what it was and burst into tears.

"It's a train!" he managed. "It's a Lionel train, like the one I used to visit at the museum when I was little!" He put the box down and threw himself into his grandsire's arms, eliciting a grunt from the impact and squeezing the man until he could hardly breathe. "Oh, thank you, Krush! Thank you, Grandsire. Thank you so much! It will be the most beautiful train in the world when we're through!"

Krush rocked him a bit and Kehailan muttered, "Well, the rest of us are unhorsed or I miss my guess. Thanks, Grandsire."

"No problem," he grinned, giving Gideon a last squeeze and nodding to his wife. "Ah'rane, my darling, you are next."

"And I had Io," she sighed. "When I found out Io was not going to be here and Ah'ren was, I was both sad, and overjoyed. I was also flummoxed. Jewelry isn't something one wears in the field to any extent. Bringing something like an heirloom quilt, would be more burden than gift, and I don't know you well enough yet to do much beyond that. Then my beloved son-in-law mentioned something in the course of a conversation that I thought might please you, by helping you bring joy to someone else." She walked to the pavilion she shared with Krush and returned with a tube roughly thirty inches tall and a foot in diameter, which she handed to Ah'ren.

The girl removed the top, looked inside and looked up smiling. "It's a rohanth bush," she said.

"And not just any rohanth bush," Ah'rane smiled. "It's one of Ah'davan's. You had said you wanted to plant one on her grave. From this bush, can come many more, Ah'ren, and we hope that your kindness in marrying our son, even though he was a stranger to you, will return many joyous years from that one selfless act."

"You could not have given me anything that would please me more than this," Ah'ren said, and leaned momentarily into her husband, "except your blessing to marry the Dragonhorse, and you gave me that the day we met. Thank you, so much."

Ah'rane smiled, accepted a hug from her new daughter-in-law, and thought a moment before gesturing to the next person. "Ardenai, you have Teal by a smattering of days, so it's your turn."

"I was lucky enough to draw the brother Eladeus gave me when my sister got married," he said, turning in his chair and laying a hand on Teal's forearm. "We've been best friends for almost ninety-six years, and fifty-seven of those years we've been kindred, as well. I have asked you to give up so much to be my closest adviser, Brother Mine. You even said a few seasons back that you didn't think you'd find time to make wine this coming year. So..." he rose rather creakily from his chair, went into his pavilion and returned with a bottle of River keep wine. "...I thought I'd better get you some help." He handed the wine bottle, which by its weight was empty, to Teal.

The Master Captain looked puzzled, and studied Ardenai's face, but there was no hint of what was coming. He uncorked the bottle and removed a sheet of paper with the seal of the Thirteenth Dragonhorse at the bottom of the page. As he read it his expression changed from puzzlement to wonder, and his jaw went slightly slack. "Really?" he said at last.

"That's a copy. Your sire got the original."

"What is it?" Ah'din asked. "We're dying of curiosity here."

"My sire...has been relieved of his duties as ambassador to Taraxia and is returning with Ah'clare to Equus and River keep, as Master Vintner to the Great House!" Teal rose and gave Ardenai a careful hug, whispering, "Thank you so much. Thank you so much."

There was a round of applause and Ardenai eased himself back into his chair. "This was not done higgledy-hop just for the sake of friendship," he said. "Vanner told me after a council meeting several seasons ago that he wanted to retire from the job and without doubt Gidran is one of the best vintners of which Equus can boast. The fact that I could do something nice for someone I love in the bargain made it all the better. I wanted them to be here today, but your mother is still wrapping things up at school. They will join us when they can." He grinned and nodded to Teal. "Kinsman, the gifting honors are now thine."

Teal flashed his slow, beautiful smile in Ah'rane's direction. "When I was eight, you let me hold Ah'din for the first time. When I was forty-three, you let me hold her permanently. Even though both of us were really too young to marry, you trusted us, and you guided us. Thank you. I have been so lucky with my family, and you, Beloved, some of your memories of family happenings are not so good. Some of those memories are of great sadness and loss. I hope to assuage one of those with my gift." He rose, went to the pavilion he shared with his wife, and returned with a large, sheet-draped object, which he placed in front of his mother-in-law.

Ah'rane stood up, carefully removed the sheet and just…stared. "It was your grandmother's," Teal said softly, and for the second time that day, someone burst into tears. He reached into the back pocket of his trousers and produced the wooden hammers. "I couldn't find the originals, so I carved these," he said. "I didn't have a pattern, so they may or may not work."

By that time Ah'rane had her arms around him, had kissed and thanked him a dozen times, and asked him a dozen questions which he was attempting to answer and laugh at the same time. "We will have a long time to talk," he said, "and I will do my best to tell you the odyssey of the hammered dulcimer. For now, play us something and tell me if it's properly tuned."

"This is the first song my grandmother ever taught me," Ah'rane sniffed. She wiped her eyes with the backs of her hands, and beginning slowly and carefully as she re-taught herself, she played the Naming Song. "Because my granddam said The Creator Spirit should always come first," she smiled as the notes died away. "Thank you, Son."

"My pleasure." Teal sat down and nodded to his wife. "Your turn, My Love."

"So it is," she laughed. "My special person this year is none other than our beloved physician." She, too, rose and returned with a bag, which she handed to Pythos. "You so rarely get to go home to Achernar, where it's warm enough for you, and you've often said your tail gets cold on Viridia in wintertime, so I made this for you in hopes of solving that." He opened the bag and extracted a very long, hand-woven tube of emerald green wool. He studied it a moment and began his hissy laughter. "You're agile, but you may have to have help putting it on," Ah'din chuckled. "It's a single piece which goes first over your tail like a stocking, then step into it with your feet, pull it up and insert your arms into the long sleeves, and secure it at the neck as you do your robes. It stretches, so it should stay nice and tight for you. Only the tail and the neck will show when you are wearing your robes, like long underwear."

"I sshall be one ssnug old ssnake indeed," he said, and flicked her with his long tongue. "No one but thee could have made thiss for me, and I will wear it gratefully and often when we are home again."

"And I will chase tree toads for you for a full season if you'll let me watch you put it on," Krush laughed.

Ah'din resumed her seat and looked questioningly from Kehailan to Ah'ren. "The oldest of the youngest?" she said.

"That would be me," Ah'ren smiled.

Kehailan gave her an apologetic smile. "I know you're next, Wren, but I kind of assumed...."

"And you would be incorrect," she twinkled. "I, too, have had time in my travels for some handwork. I do not have a specific person this year, but I do have a specific something to share." She rose, went into the pavilion closest and came back with two tubes. She handed one to Ah'rane, saying, "Like your half-brother, who is also your beloved son, you were fostered. These are your true bloodlines. Obviously, this is not public knowledge." She handed the other to Teal, saying, "And you, Master Captain. A study of this will reveal some of the oldest bloodlines on Equus, those of the water-fowl, which should explain why certain requests have been made of you." Both scrolls were intricately done, beautifully illuminated, complex and extensive, and the entire family was fascinated by them. "Probably better studied when we are not already in motion in another direction," Ah'ren said, beaming at the profuse thanks and smothering hugs. "Now it's Kehailan's turn."

"Well," the captain began, "I sort of wasn't joking about the magic horsehide. I got Criollo, and since we both have feelings for Lebonathi women, I've arranged to take a week off, either all at once or a few days at a time – Criollo's choice – and Criollo and I are going to spend all day every day learning everything we can about Lebonath Jas and its people – dusty libraries, moldy records, old maps, dangerous prowling, enlightening exploration – I have arranged to have a shuttle at our disposal, but we will travel however we need to go. If you wish you can bring one or more of these people along, but this is going to be our week together to gather information and expand our understanding." He gestured out with both hands and smiled at his younger cousin. "That's it, Kinsman."

"Wow," Criollo breathed, and his face was wreathed in smiles as he stood up to hug Kehailan. "Best gift, bar none! I can hardly wait! How soon can we go?"

"We'll talk about that later," the captain smiled. "After all, it's our week together."

Ardenai sighed and closed his eyes for a moment. The boy whom everyone had for years called the pouting prince, angry, moody, selfish, rebellious – had turned into this strong, loving, intuitive man, captain of his own ship and master of his own emotions. Ardenai, too, felt like saying, *best gift of all.* He caught Teal smiling at him and knew his pride was sticking out all over. He quickly veiled his thoughts more deeply and watched as Kehailan gestured toward Criollo.

"I got my grandsire," Criollo said. "I've listened since childhood to him telling the Legend of the Wind Warriors, and singing or whistling the Legend of the Wind Warriors, and since I love books so much, I thought… well, maybe I've already said too much." He rose, went to the clipper and returned with a slightly bulky, one by two-foot package which he handed to Krush. "I made it myself," he said shyly, and it made him sound very young despite being in his fourth year of final form.

Krush opened the package to discover an oversized, hand-bound book with a tooled, horsehide cover. "This is beautiful," he said, running his hands over the leather. He opened it, and said, "Ohhhh, look at this! All done in calligraphy. It's the legend, and the poem, the music it's set to, and even some of the research your father and your uncle did to uncover the truth of the Telenir. Criollo, this is a princely gift."

"And it's not finished," Criollo smiled. "I still need to hear the final part of the story, about the priestesses saving Equus and starting the legend to hide what they were doing. But I can work on that around the table while you and Gideon restore that train of his."

"It's a date," Krush said, and handed the book off to be passed around as he hugged his grandson.

"Last, but not least, as the old saying goes," Criollo said, and gestured to Gideon.

"By process you must know I got Ah'din, who was the one I wanted to get, and here's why." He, too, went to the clipper, and returned with a good-sized wooden box which he placed in her lap. "I didn't understand what this name-drawing was all about until Ah'brianne and Criollo explained it to me, and I was excited to get you, because you were so kind to me right from the very first day I came into the family. I also came into this. The first part by accident, the rest by design. Open it and see what you think."

Ah'din did so, and discovered a neatly pigeon-holed interior, each rectangle holding a medicinal plant, clay, stone or piece of bark, along with its identification, properties, and how it was used in traditional medicine. "I know you know all that already, and you probably have all that stuff, too, but it was fascinating for me. The Eldest, Chirion, when he was coming back to Canyon keep with us – he showed us so many things and told us how to use them, and…Ah'brianne said you would like it."

"For once Ah'brianne understated something," Ah'din laughed. "Gideon, I love this! Look at all the work you went to!"

"Chirion helped me make the box while we were all at Mountain hold," Gideon said, not wanting her to think he'd done more than he had. "I am the apprentice in a family of artists."

"This is the best gift of them all," Ah'din said firmly, handed the box to her husband, and rose to hug Gideon. "It is both practical and beautiful and I am very grateful."

"And now it iss time for admiration, and explanation at our leisure," Pythos announced, uncoiling from his chair and heading toward the table where everything was being displayed.

"And dessert," Krush amended.

"And music," Ah'rane laughed, stroking the dulcimer and blinking away fresh tears.

When they were all fully engrossed with admiring gifts and trying not to spill holiday puddings on anything, Ardenai leaned into his sire and murmured, "I am intrigued by your acquisition of what is obviously a rare and valuable museum piece."

Krush hooked an arm through his son's and steered him slightly away from the others toward the noise of the waterfall. "Rare, yes," he admitted, "but completely unrestored, thus reducing its actual value, luckily."

"I am no less intrigued," Ardenai grinned. He watched patiently while Krush's eyebrows considered and discarded a series of responses. Finally, the eyebrows were still.

"Since you are my only son, I shall deign to tutor thee. First, of course, one must determine where best to find such an object. In this case, Declivis. Then, one must enlist the aid of one or two people who have a certain...flexibility in their acquisitional fiber. One must be ready to barter in the coin of the realm for the item one wishes to acquire, and then find an appropriate and secure method of delivery."

"Let me see if I can translate this," Ardenai snorted. "You used your influence as a prince of the Great house to get a museum on Declivis to admit they might have an extra train in their archives. Knowing you, it was probably the museum Gideon used to visit – the Museum of Transportation. Then you recruited Hadrian Keats. No, you don't know him well enough. You recruited Winslow Moonsgold, and he recruited Hadrian Keats. How am I doing so far?"

"Amazing," Krush intoned. "Seriously, that train was for sale. Perhaps not on the active market, but it wasn't purloined in any sense of the word. Dr. Keats says hello, by the way, and I do know him fairly well. Now."

Ardenai just shook his head and laughed. He wondered if Hadrian had said anything about the research he was doing, but this was definitely not the time to ask. Any questioning would have to involve the simple, shocking explanation that Ardenai wanted his son to function sexually, as any boy who would soon be a young man should be able to do – that Keats was actually a prisoner of sorts, for a crime of sorts, with an exact moment his sentence would end. *'Oh, I get it. This is about fixing Gideon. The day his pecker stands up and spurts little towheaded, fox-eyed grandkids for you, I walk, don't I?'* In a flash his mind was racing, unbidden, through the first year of his reign – Calumet and before – finding Gideon, marrying Io, killing Sarkhan, losing Ah'leah...

"Ardi?"

"Sorry," he smiled, but the humor had gone from his eyes and his father was quick to notice.

Krush put an arm around Ardenai's shoulders and they walked a little further apart. "Something on your mind, Dragonhorse?"

Ardenai shook his head. "Not really. I guess. I haven't spoken to Io for a couple of days and I'm feeling a little guilty about having a good time when she's not here to share it."

"You do understand that she can't hear you," Krush admonished. "She's asleep, as was her wish, not yours. She chose her present path, not you. It's perfectly acceptable for you to enjoy your entire day and evening without checking in with Ah'riodin." He looked at Ardenai's face and huffed with annoyance. "Guilt over Io, because even with her in a crèche pod, you're afraid she's figured out a way to keep score. I love her, but I swear – and as much for her sake as yours – I wish you'd never married the girl."

"Me too," Ardenai whispered, and the self-loathing which flooded his features made Krush instantly regret his words.

"I'm sorry," he groaned. "Ardi, I'm so sorry. It's none of my business."

"Of course it's your business. You're my father and I need your help," Ardenai replied, lowering himself with a grimace onto the sandy beach beside the waterfall. The sun was setting, making orange, rippling streaks across the face of the river and up the gentle slope of the bank to where they sat. Ardenai was quiet for a while, staring at the moving water, enjoying the feel of his father's shoulder against his. That unwavering support. He knew he could say whatever he needed to.

He took a deep breath and just started in motion. "She says she's been in love with me her whole adult life, and I think maybe that's the problem, or part of it. She may have been ready for marriage, but I sure wasn't. Mild flirtation, maybe. Some time to transition. I already had so much going on...." He trailed off and thought some more. "I'm still shocked and sickened by what I did with and to her. Ah'ree and I raised her. It felt like she was my daughter, my child, and suddenly I was having sex with her? Every time I try to explain to her that I loved her like a daughter, which part of me still does, she gets thoroughly pissed off, brings up the same old things…." Again, he was quiet.

"I love her so much. She is so perfect in so many ways. She's a brilliant tactician. She's a wonderful Primuxori. In that, I couldn't have done better if I'd searched a lifetime for a partner. If only she could relax with our relationship enough to let me work through that incredible transition from foster father to husband, and she just can't, or just won't. Either way, it's exhausting."

The sun slipped over the horizon and the water went dark before he spoke again. "Io is, historically, so many other things than a wife. I have a great deal to contend with where Io is concerned, plus I'm trying to learn to rule wisely and well. And then, along comes Wren, who is the perfect wife and working partner. How fair is that to Io? I begged, Sire, I begged Ah'krill not to make me take a second wife. It's just not in my nature. She said she wouldn't."

"I don't think she did," Krush said. "I think Ah'ren is strictly the will of Mountain hold and, to be perfectly honest, Pythos. I think he's far more powerful than we give him credit for, and I think he forced you into marrying Io for his sake, and her sake, more than yours. He was afraid for you. I understand that. An Imperial Dragonhorse cycle could have killed you without some serious help, and he knew it. But, number one, he could have helped you himself with quelling potions, and you and I both know he could. He could have forced you into marrying Ah'nora or someone else. Anyone else. Marrying someone who was High Equi would have spared you a whole lot of grief. But he chose Io instead. He knew Io was in love with you and he wanted to please her. Now, he feels guilty because he knows she's of two minds, you're not happy, and, like magic, there's Ah'ren." Krush raised his eyes from the sand and turned his head enough to look at his son in profile. "You'll not convince me you don't love Ah'ren. I've never seen you so happy – ever – not even with Ah'ree. Wren is good for you and you know it."

"Of course I do. Of course I'm in love with her, she's perfect. I just said that. We may have been relative strangers, but her role was clear to her, my role was clear to me. We understood what we were to be to each other, what our function was to be together. The exact opposite of Io and me in every single respect. Wren is more mature than Io. No, Wren is more stable, I think. More predictable in that, while she may bring it up for discussion, she's not going to blow up in my face over something I unwittingly said, or did, or thought. She knows who she is and what she wants. She knows what is real and what is not, what is possible and what is not. She even came with an exit strategy in case Io just won't accept her." Ardenai turned and met his father's gaze. "I know I just met her, but I cannot bear the thought of losing her, Sire. You're right. I am so happy with her. Yet I adore Io. I value Io. I have loved her since the day she was born. If she fights me over Ah'ren..."

"She's not fighting you over Ah'ren," Krush said in the firm, quiet voice he usually reserved for recalcitrant horseflesh. "She doesn't even know about Ah'ren. You're fighting you over Ah'ren."

"Now you sound like Teal."

"Your chief advisor? The soft-spoken one who has been married to your sister for nearly sixty years? That Teal?"

Ardenai hunched up and resisted the urge to say something really nasty. "Yes, him. The perfect man with the perfect wife. The perfect love story. You know as well as I do that if he was asked to share board, bed, and bodily fluids with a second wife, his heart would do things to him that would make Nik's collapse look like a case of the hiccups. So, I suppose it's me. It's all me. Placid, hyper-reasonable little Ah'riodin isn't going to say a word, and preparing myself in advance just in case she does, is foolish and futile."

"Are you going to pout? Because jumping to self-pity is not your best strategy here."

"Fine. Here's the truth, Sire. I know, practically to the minute, when Io is going to wake up, because in addition to what her health may be, whether or not our babies are alive or dead, regardless of what kind of mood those factors put her in, and me, for that matter, I have to tell her I have another wife. The one I told her I wouldn't marry. The one it's going to be obvious I'm in love with and do not want to be separated from. I, the Great Me, the Thirteenth Dragonhorse, absolute ruler of the Affined Equi Worlds, maker of dozens of important decisions every single day – I have no idea what I'm going to do, what I'm going to say, how I'm going to respond to having two wives. Who sits where? Who sleeps with whom and when? Do we all live together? What sorts of questions do I ask which wife? I'm terrified spitless!

"I'm in love with both of them, which seems immoral in the first place. I've been put in a position that no other male on Equus has had to occupy for seven hundred years, and I'm going to be in that position for another hundred and forty-nine, give or take. I've been raised by my mother and father to be loyal to a single mate and forced by tradition and decree to have multiple wives. Only one of us is even remotely prepared for that, and that's Wren.

"I'm afraid Io is going to start screaming and accusing, and I'm not going to have the time it takes to get her to come around. I have eleven planets to govern, one to colonize and another to assimilate. I'm going to go with the wife that's the better, easier partner and not my wildly popular Primuxori, because that's what's best for Equus, and frankly, for me. So, pardon me if it seems like I'm pouting."

The silence was longer and the sky grew as dark as the water. "Hmmm," Krush said at last.

There was another protracted silence. "I was kind of hoping for more than that, Sire."

"A man has to think, and you have to let him do that," Krush said. He stood up, brushed the sand off his trousers and gestured toward the sound of singing and the dulcimer. "I'll get back to you."

"Thanks for listening," Ardenai said quietly. "And…one more thing."

"What is that, Son?"

"I can't get up."

Krush gave Ardenai both his hands and eased him to a standing position. "Better?" Ardenai nodded, brushing sand off his clothes. "Maybe you should let your sister or Pythos help you with that."

"It's a bruise. I'll be fine to play on Hoplegyr. I'll put some ice on it when I go to bed."

"I'll remember to wear earplugs," Krush drawled. "Nobody puts ice on his nethers."

Ardenai snorted with amusement. He also re-thought the ice. His father was usually right about such things. "I only wish Nik was able to get on his horse."

"How is Nik by now? Really. I know Pythos let him go back to his apartments on the Jocundome. I know his hetaera is still with him, which is pretty unusual, isn't it?"

"It would be if she wasn't also a cardiologist. Pythos is right. If Nik had been on the surface, and if she hadn't been with him, he'd be dead. He's still really fragile, not that he'd ever admit it. He's bored, and twitchy. Mostly, he's Nik."

"I knew him when he was just a boy. His sire and I were friends – played some polo together before you ever came along, traded around some horses over the years. Nokota was a nice man – scared of his father-in-law and for good reason." Krush's mouth turned down in appraisal. "I never cared for Konik's grandsire. He was into hitting horses, and boys. I saw him knock his grandson down more than once. Nik was a nice boy, too, very gentle. Soothing voice and easy hands. Horses loved him."

"And so did the girls," Ardenai noted. "He's the only man I've ever known more oblivious to female attention than Teal." A thought caused him to turn to his father in surprise. "You – mother, that is – got a rohanth bush from Ah'davan's garden on Anguine II! How did you do that, or did you just say that's where it was from as part of the backstory?"

"No, that's where we got it," Krush responded, raising his voice a little as they got nearer the singing, "Ah'rika had several she'd started in her hothouse from the original bushes. We contacted her and she said she was happy to give us one, so we picked it up on the way by."

Ardenai stopped just outside the lantern light and stayed Krush with his hand. "Did she, or Ah'nia say anything about their mother, or their sire? Konik is so sure they hate him."

"And they're afraid he hates them," Krush muttered. "Things do not go well when we make assumptions rather than communicating. Come on. I want to look at my book and dig into that box of train parts with my grandson. We can talk about the governor tomorrow."

CHAPTER 3

Teal stopped humming. "Relax, I've got you," he said soothingly. "Pretend like you're face-up on a priapic bench. Plant your feet flat on the floor. Just like that. Now I'm going to straddle your legs, bend my knees, feet flat, and I'm going to squat down until our working parts touch…like this."

"Eww. Teal, this is obscene – ouch – why don't I remember this part from when I watched you and Bonfire dancing? Does she really let you grab her…you-know-what like this?"

"It's going very fast and there's music. And yes, she does. It's part of the dance and if I let go with you in that position, you'll find out my un-welcome hand is all that's keeping you afloat. Now hush, and relax. Let your body follow the contours of mine, just melt into me, and you're going to go backwards between both sets of our legs with me on top of you." Teal began humming again. "Relax," he sang, "It's a mating dance. Just let yourself bend under my weight as though we're making love. The Phyllans do this naked."

"My back will NOT bend any further!" Ah'ren managed, her foot slipped, and she and Teal went down in a heap on the gym floor.

"Sorry," Teal laughed, getting his elbows under him and his weight off his sister-in-law. "Ah'ren, you're just not relaxed enough for this."

"If I were any more relaxed, I'd be asleep," she retorted, "What I'm not, is a mammalian dough-twist."

"Sis, if you can't bend over backwards far enough to look out between your own legs, this is not the dance for you," Teal said as he stood up. He offered her a hand and hauled her to her feet. "I won't hold it against you if you decide this is all too much for your level of expertise."

"What a cad you are," she sneered. "First you tell me my horse just isn't on a level with yours and cannot possibly win a race, which of course, he does, and rather handily, I might add. Now you're telling me my dancing just isn't on a level with yours? Well, I won the bet fair and square, so get your instruction up to an acceptable level, because we're going to be at this until you do."

"Fine," Teal said, trying not to laugh at her teasing. "But if you break something, or I accidentally break something on you, there will be no whimpering, understood?"

"Fine."

"Speaking of broken, how is our Sovereign Lord this morning?"

"Much better. He finally let me put a warm poultice of calendula and telarepere on the worst of the bruising. Maybe tonight he'll do the same for me."

"I know a couple other Phyllan dances. Would you rather learn one of them?"

"No." She stuck her lip out and looked away, crimping a grin.

"I chose the gym on Dragonhorse Ten…well, actually it's now Dragonhorse Phylla, which would make it Dragonhorse Nine, for a reason. Captain Dannis said she can spare us a few minutes and we can go through this for you in slow motion. I think it would help if you could see how one part flows into another…so to speak."

She looked around, then back at Teal. "Marion really doesn't want this beautiful brand-new ship back?"

"Apparently not. He loves Belesprit, which is also pretty much brand-new. Bonfire is happy, so the trade is done. It was easier to repaint the number on the ship than to discompose a core crew that's just getting used to working together. They'll flesh out the crew with Phyllans as they become available. Everybody seems happy, which is a battle won right there."

Ah'ren sighed and plopped back onto the floor, pulling her knees up and wrapping her arms around them. "Everybody but me. Am I really not going to be able to learn this? Because I really wanted to."

"It's not the learning," Teal said, sitting beside her, "it's the doing. If we focused on flexibility exercises for a few weeks first..." he paused and thought a moment. "Are you actually able to gain flexibility, or do you have built-in limitations?"

"I have a perfectly normal body, Master Captain, just like yours – except that I can't bend over backwards and put my head through my legs, which, by the way, is decidedly not normal. But you and Ardi can both do it. Did you practice when you were children?"

"Not specifically. Ah'din can do the same thing." There was a movement in the doorway and they looked up to see Criollo and Gideon walking across the floor toward them. "Good morning, boys," Teal smiled. "What can we do for you this fine day?"

They glanced at one another and Criollo ventured, "We'd like to go down to the surface and look around a little."

Teal felt the tenuousness of the request. "Depends on the planet."

"Jas," Criollo said. "It will be all right. We're both bigger than the average Lebonathi."

"No. I'm sorry." Teal said firmly. "Size has nothing to do with it. It's not safe."

"With harness?"

"And half a squad of Amberians, maybe. And I can arrange that in a day or so." He sensed their disappointment and stood up. "Would you like to ride with the science teams? I can arrange to have Marion Eletsky drop you with one of them."

Criollo put on a face and Teal just shook his head. "You can explore anywhere on Tras you would like. You can go to any one of the farm ships and explore. Gallios invited you to do that. You can go and explore some of the venues on the Jocundome. But I will not risk you down there in the streets of the old city – There are too many people, and too many things can happen too quickly."

Gideon put a hand on his cousin's arm and said, "I would really like to go and explore the Jocundome. All we've seen are the polo fields. You said you wanted to talk to the governor, and so do I. Let's get that out of the way. We can go to the surface later."

Criollo gave him a grudging nod. "I suppose," he said, but his face was not happy. "How do we get over there?"

Teal neither snickered nor smiled condescendingly at his son's expression. As a boy he'd hated it when people did that to him. "Are you wearing a crys-tel necklace?" He asked. Criollo nodded. Teal reached inside his tunic and looped a finger through his own chain. He slid the small crys-tels, selected one of bright yellow, and handed it to the boy. "Put this on yours," he said. "If you touch it and state where you want to go, it will send you there, along with anybody you're touching, so be careful. You may keep that. I'll get another."

"Thank you," Criollo smiled, gave his father a hug, and left with his cousin in the direction of the scrambleshafts. "We'll see you at dinner," he called over his shoulder.

"Said crys-tel will also get him to the surface of Jas, but you know that," Ah'ren grinned.

"I do," he replied. "They'll be fine. I've been thinking – what if we reverse positions? You can grab my, you-know-what, and go over on top of me. If you can support my weight at the other end of the motion."

She eyed him to see if he was teasing, but his face said he was not. "How much do you weigh?" she asked, wondering just how intimate she really wanted to get with this. Maybe learning the Phyllan Wolf Dance wasn't such a great thing to win after all, but the race, had been wonderful.

"Two hundred and thirty-two pounds. Anyway, if we do this, and if Bonfire tells me it isn't breaking some sacred taboo, you're bending forward and I'm the one bending back. Let's try it just for fun." He was reaching for Ah'ren to continue their lesson when his body jerked slightly. His head tipped toward his dominant right hand and his deep green ophidian eyes lost some of their focus. In a few moments he said, "I'm sorry, I must go. They're shooting at each other up north near the city of Tholen, and I need to get up there. Probably another water fight. Can we pick this up at a later time?"

"Absolutely," she smiled. His long strides were already carrying him toward the door when she called, "Teal, be careful."

"I'll see you at dinner," he called back, and disappeared into the corridor on his way to the scrambleshaft.

"I'm not saying you have to marry somebody tomorrow," Swift said soothingly. "I know you just lost Ah'davan. I know you need time to grieve. What I'm trying to convey is that it would be a nice gesture of bonding and acceptance if you considered marrying a Lebonathi female. Sometime. *Some* time, Nik. You seem very fond of Anchoress Ensharra, who is a lovely woman, and you could…" the look stopped her.

"I could what, kill her during one of my heat cycles?" Konik growled. "I'm sure that would go over well, and what a delightful way to display my obvious affection for her. I will not bother to deny the attraction, you're too perceptive for that. But – BUT – Ensharra is already forty years old. Her life is half over, given her genes and probably her state of health." He tossed aside the document he'd been studying and gave Swift his full attention; something he should have done the second he realized where the conversation was headed. "Even if she did survive my hypersexuality, I'd be a widower again in forty years with another ninety years of my own lifespan left to go. That means I could probably bury two or three more Lebonathi wives besides Ensharra. Let me think about how much I'd enjoy that." He paused and sighed. "Self-centered bastard that I am. Besides, how is marrying a Lebonathi anymore an indicator of acceptance than anything else I've done and will continue to do?"

"Now I've upset you," she said. "We should talk about this when you're stronger, and when you're not in heat."

"I'm plenty strong enough to get back to work, I'm not in heat, and I'm not upset," he purred.

She leaned forward and ran her finger along his hairline from temple to earlobe on the left side. "Then why is this little vein standing up?"

"You're annoying, you know that," he said, catching her hand. He pulled her over to land in his lap, and began kissing slowly up the side of her neck. "You're also irresistible."

"Governor Konik," she murmured, "Do you ever think about anything but sex?"

"Of course I do," he said against the side of her neck. "I think about food. I think about polo."

"You are well rounded, then." she said, sliding her hands over his shoulders. "I was worried."

"No need, Mistress. I wouldn't be bothering you with this at all, but my doctor insists."

The tinkle of a bell announced visitors.

"Hold that thought," she smiled, kissing him lingeringly on the lips.

In a few minutes she reappeared in the garden with two boys, a tall, handsome Equi child in his mid-twenties, and a striking blond teenager with brilliant gold eyes. "This is Criollo," she said, gesturing to the darker lad, "and you know Gideon already."

"I do," Konik smiled, standing to greet them. "Both of you, welcome!"

"Criollo has come to speak with thee," Gideon smiled. "I am content to watch the fish and breathe in the fragrance of this garden."

Konik grabbed a stack of papers off the chair across from him and gestured Criollo into it as Gideon sat on the rim of the fountain and tickled the water to attract the swimmers.

"Ahimsa, I wish thee peace," Konik said, making a desultory pass of his right hand, which still held the papers, over his left. "Please, sit down." He looked for a spot to put the papers and ended up adding them to an already sizeable stack beside the fish pond. "How can I help you?"

The boy looked slightly uncomfortable for a moment, then started with a rush. "I love old books! I love history, and my father says you know where to find some dusty old professors with some equally dusty old books. I would like to find them myself if you would be kind enough to help me. Oh, sorry. My father is..."

"Master Captain Teal," Konik chuckled. "You have his face. Along with a good dollop of your grandsire, Krush. So, you are a lover of musty lore, are you?"

"The fact that there are libraries left at all, and something left of the university? That is phenomenal," Criollo breathed. "Just to see the books and meet the people who have been through so much." he paused and thought for a moment about what he wanted to say. "I think it would add depth to a past that most Lebonathi don't know they have." He shrugged slightly and spent some time watching the fish Gideon had attracted while Konik watched him without seeming to. "We're here for a while, you know," the boy said, picking up the conversation. "All of us. And my uncle asked each of us to choose a project. I should say he asked Gideon and me to choose a project. My mother and my grandmother know what they want to do and are already about it."

"What is that?" Konik asked. Intense, this one, eyes alight with the prospect of adventure, and at the same time thinking beyond it as best one could at this age. Perhaps he'd be a strategist like his brilliant sire. For now, he was an infectiously excited boy, but soft-spoken. Again, like Teal.

"My mother is a doctor, and she's working with your friend, Anchoress Ensharra, studying medicinal herbs and wild foodstuffs, at least as I understand it. It seems to be convolving as it develops. My Granddam is a Friction Analysis Engineer, and she's trying to take the internal combustion engines out of all the buses and trains and replace them with sun-cell technology. So anyway, Gideon and I were asked to choose a project, and I want to bring some prestige back to books, to having books, to wanting to read books, not fearing books. Even if all I get to do is dust shelves, or listen to the stories those old professors have to tell, I will have gained depth in my knowledge of the Lebonathi!"

Again, there was that excitement that made Konik want to get out of his chair and go with the boy, back to the depths of the old city and the crumbling university he'd explored one afternoon. "Why are you so interested in Lebonathi history, or is it just the books that fascinate you?"

"They go together, don't they?" Criollo responded. "I mean, when you think about it. It's more than just how they're bound and what kind of paper they used, it's the words inside that shaped the minds that shaped the world before books became redundant and spoken ignorance replaced written wisdom."

Their conversation was interrupted by Swift, who brought cool drinks, a tray of snacks, and tidbits for Gideon to feed the fish. Konik thanked her and gestured to the chair beside him. "Please, join us. This young man shares your passion for books. Swift is my friend and hetaera of many years." She took a seat, and leaned forward, much as Criollo was doing. "Criollo would like to see the university library restored to its former glory, or at least get it on its way."

Swift smiled. "The goal of a man who plans to stay, if you don't mind my saying so."

Criollo looked a little startled, almost guilty. "What makes you say that?" he asked.

"Boys on holiday who choose a short-term project usually paint a wall or clear debris from a corridor. One of the long-term goals of the interposing forces is to restore and eventually integrate the educational system. Therefore, I assume that you, too, are thinking long-term."

"It's complicated," Criollo sighed, and took a bite of nectar bread to give himself time to think. "I would love to stay. The girl I want to marry is Lebonathi. Lebonath Tras is beautiful, and I could see us making our home there and..." he took a chance and blurted, "one day I could see myself raising children from our blended cultures. Maybe even being governor, like you."

Konik laughed and nodded. "I think that's a wonderful goal," he said, reaching over to give the boy's knee a brief pat. "I will happily start training you right now. Job security for you, peace of mind for me – the perfect plan."

"Except that I am the only son, the only grandson, of two of the premier winemakers on Viridia, perhaps on all of Equus. My sire and my grandsire expect me to make wine – on Equus – and I have given them no reason to think I'm not all in favor of that. It would be unfair at this point to suddenly decide I want to do something else."

"Have you mentioned any of this to your sire?" Konik asked, holding out a speck of nectar bread for a huge orange and yellow butterfly. The insect lit on his finger and began working the tidbit with its front legs, antennae moving slowly and gracefully, seeming to listen to the conversation.

Criollo shook his head, eyes fixed on the butterfly. "I worship my sire, Governor. I have done enough to disappoint him as it is. My inattention is in good part responsible for this whole probative interposition. Not honoring his profession by following it myself, would be the ultimate betrayal."

"Probably in your mind more than in his," Konik responded, still watching the butterfly and keeping his breath at a distance so as not to disturb it. He turned his attention to Criollo and smiled. "I'm sure if you are patient and apply yourself to your aspirations, they will become apparent, along with the proper time to mention them to your parents."

Gideon, sitting slightly behind and to one side, rolled his eyes in sympathy and shook his head.

"Just say it," Criollo sighed, "I know you're thinking it."

"If you're talking to me, I've already said it," Gideon responded. "Your sire didn't do more than flinch when you said you were going to marry Jasreth. Somehow, wanting to serve these people instead of making wine, doesn't seem quite as shocking as that, at least to me. As a matter of fact, it seems noble, and your father exudes nobility. I just can't see why you think he won't understand you not wanting to make a profession out of what is an avocation for him in the first place."

"He tolerates the whole idea of me marrying Jasreth, because I'm still a colt. It's a childish whim. Leaving Viridia, leaving him, and my mother – and now Gidran is going to be back? No. I'm destined for River keep and the vineyards."

"If all goes as planned, you're going to have a baby sister later this year. She may be just a lingering kiss right now, but she could be a winemaker," Gideon reasoned. "My father will sire more children. You will sire children. There will be winemakers in the family. You, on the other hand – you, could become the premier vintner on Lebonath Tras. Surely that would please your father and fit in with your long-term goals."

"Absolutely," Konik chuckled. "In any case, knowing more about your lady's people will serve you well. If you end up serving them as a career, you'll be a chukka to the good. I'm going to be back in my office on Dragonhorse Thirteen tomorrow. Come and see me, and we will work out a schedule that suits both of us."

"And when you head down to that dusty old university library, let me know, because I want to come along," Swift said. She turned and looked at Gideon. "We know what your cousin wants to do for his project while he's here. What do you want to do?"

Gideon sighed and shrugged. "Everything. That's my problem. The microbial studies are fascinating – reseeding microbes into the soil? How amazing is that? Seeing how things that grow on Equus will grow here and what those ramifications might be? Just exploring, looking at potential farmland and pastureland? Along with that, I want to help Ah'ren with her mapping and laying out of the keeps. My grandsire is going to assist her, and I'd love to listen to their reasoning as they work out this puzzle. They're both so smart. I would learn so much about mathematics and agriculture and probably distribution economics.

"And I'd love to find some signs, no matter how ancient, of the animals that are now in stasis, and how they lived. Maybe get to the surface and meet some of the colts my age. What games do they play, what do they do?" Then his eyes really lit up. "Those abandoned continents with their cities and towns and farms! The flamen say they are cursed, that the people who lived there burned when the witches' fire swept over, and to go there is to die. We have to know that's not true. Land created by El'Shadai is never cursed but by those who inhabit it. What all was left behind in those cities and on those farms that can help us reconstruct where they veered off track so we can help them build a more sustainable way of life? What did they grow, what kinds of animals did they have? The research is endless."

"And in that research, you've now joined your cousin's endeavors," Konik said. "You'll have things to do together as a joint project, and I am happy to help both of you." He paused a moment and studied Gideon. How much he had changed over these last seasons – definitely taller, broader of shoulder. Piercing topaz eyes, heavy white-blond hair long enough now to be caught up in the traditional Equi overbraid. The abused and neglected child had become every inch a prince. No wonder Ardenai was proud. "No desire to follow your sire around?"

"Not really. Even as much as I love being with him," Gideon admitted. "I do plan to sit in, but as far as being able to actually help, which is supposed to be what the project is all about, I don't think I could do that."

"Don't be too sure," Konik said. "Ardenai has told me a dozen times how much he values your counsel. I know he will be pleased if, in all the other things you want to do, you find a little time for him and his work."

"I will do that," Gideon smiled. "And I would like to see what you do, as well. It looks," he said, gesturing at the piles of documents, "like you're already back in the game."

It was Swift's turn to roll her eyes, and Konik laughed. "Keeping a work horse from work just confuses him and makes him nervous. Many of these are from document recovery efforts. The Lebonathi developed the ability to record things with reasonable sophistication, but lost the ability to preserve them. I'm just getting a smattering for now."

"My brother says you're moving your offices to the Jocundome," Gideon said. "This looks like a good start."

"Several of us are moving," Konik affirmed. "Dragonhorse Thirteen is an Imperial Stormclass Tactical Cruiser, so are her sister ships. If they are needed somewhere in a hurry, two governors, our cartographer and the Dragonhorse himself would find themselves without a functioning office. We're going to keep the Governance Chambers intact so we have an absolutely secure facility, and one we can easily move if we need to, but for the most part we will be in a secure facility here." He pointed a finger at Criollo. "Now there's something you can help with right away."

Criollo nodded and grinned. "I'll add you to the queue with my sire, my uncle, and Ah'ren." He stood up and bowed respectfully. "Governor, we have taken enough of your time. We should go."

"It was a pleasure," Konik smiled. "I'll see you tomorrow."

Criollo nodded and turned to go when Gideon said, "I'll be right there. I have something I promised I'd deliver in secret to Governor Konik."

Swift smiled and gestured Criollo toward the garden gate. "We'll be over here when you're ready," she said.

Gideon reached into the pouch on his hip and withdrew a rather battered envelope about six inches square. "We stopped on Anguine II on the way here, because…anyway, it's a long story."

Konik stiffened just enough for Gideon to sense it without seeing it. "You have my undivided attention," Konik said. "I'd like the long version."

"Of course. My granddam, Ah'rane, got Io's name in the Celebration draw, but since Io isn't here, she wanted something for Ah'ren. I guess Teal had mentioned in some conversation that Ah'ren wanted to plant a rohanth bush on your wife's grave, so Ah'rane contacted your daughter Ah'nia, who said your daughter Ah'rika is keeping in your ancestral home and that she had some beautiful, well-rooted but reasonably small rohanth bushes that she'd started from Ah'davan's originals." Gideon smiled a little apologetically. "With me so far?"

Konik nodded, folding his arms to steady his hands, which he realized were beginning to shake. "I am," he said.

"Anyway, Grandmother contacted Ah'rika, who is a delightful woman by the way, and she was overjoyed to send along a rohanth bush for Ah'davan's gravesite. Now, we're back to the point where we actually stopped to pick it up," Gideon grinned. "We stayed awhile and visited, of course, being we had womenfolk with us, and they did the whole tour of the big hothouse, and fussed forever over which rohanth bush to bring, and talked about all those things women seem to talk about, and my grandsire visited with your son-in-law, and we looked at horses and talked about the latest improvements in intergalactic communications, because apparently that's what Eriskay does.

"When we came in to warm up and have a bite to eat before leaving, your grandson got me by the hand and took me to his room, and we sat down at this little table you made for him, and he got out his colors and made this for you." At that point, the envelope changed hands.

"He said I was to give it to you without anybody knowing, because you two hadn't had any secrets for a long time and he wanted one because he missed you." He could see Konik's eyes beginning to fill, and broke his gaze to give him time to recover. "I also have something I promised I'd deliver from Ah'rika, though she wasn't sure you would want it." Gideon took a deep breath, and put his arms around Konik, giving him a lingering hug. "She said, 'Give my sire this hug, and tell him I love him,'" he whispered. He dropped his arms and met Konik's eyes, just for a moment. The governor was visibly shaken, and Gideon didn't want to embarrass or distress him further. "I'll probably see you in the morning," he said, nodded respectfully, and followed his cousin out the garden gate onto the broad, cobbled avenue.

Konik lowered himself into a chair and willed himself to stop trembling. He turned the envelope face up and found, carefully scribed in green colorwax, which was Nokota's favorite, a large, rather lopsided heart, and the words, *for Niknik from me.* He ran his hands over it for a few moments, seeing, not the envelope, but a bright little face with an infectious grin. The paper inside was carefully folded, and Konik suspected Gideon had helped with that part. There were hearts, and horses, a house and flowers. Seven colorfully dressed and coiffed stick people stood in a row, waving – five big sticks, two little sticks. All of them were smiling, all of them had a big blue tear covering part of their face. There was an orange lithoped stick, as well, with a jaunty tail curving over its back and a rat in its mouth. The eighth stick was lying down in front of the stick with blue hair, eyes closed, smiling and holding a flower. In big letters across the bottom was a single word: L O V E. Konik doubled over and sobbed.

He was vaguely aware that Swift was sitting beside him, rubbing his back. All he could see were the sticks, seven in a row, none standing separately. Ah'rika and Eriskay, Ah'nia and Tokara – and on each side of the blue haired stick, firmly holding his hands, six-year-old Nokota and seven-year-old Ah'sienna, whom, Nokota had correctly noted, favored pink dresses. Even the rat was smiling.

Konik sat for a long time after he quit crying, first with his forearms on his thighs, watching the fish without seeing them, then with his head back, long legs stretched out in front of him, eyes closed, breathing steady as the knots in his chest, then in his soul, begin to relax. Swift said nothing. She sat close until he assumed a more relaxed position, then left him alone with his thoughts.

As it grew darker and cooler he rose rather stiffly and walked across the garden to the spot where a ribbon of water spilled gracefully into a private, wooded grotto. He was hungry, but he was also a little chilly, so he opened the doors to their bed chamber, tossed his clothes casually in one corner and stepped back out into the warmth of the pool. He sat, chest deep on a smooth, narrow stone and relaxed, enjoying the bird calls and the quiet splashing of the water.

He must have drifted, because he realized Swift had joined him without seeing or hearing her do so. He held out his hand and she glided over to sit astride him. He groaned softly with pleasure and his breath quickened a little as he kissed her where neck met shoulder. She kissed him back and as he swelled inside her, she murmured, "I see you held the thought."

"I did," he replied, pushing up with his hips and down on the tops of her thighs. "Thank you for putting up with me today, and in general. Precious Equus that feels good."

"I think you do, too," she replied cryptically. She slid her hands down his flanks, sank her teeth in his collar bone, and no more was said for a long while.

Teal dropped the clipper below the perpetually angry orange haze and surveyed the ground beneath his shadow. "This is the Imperial Equi Clipper Arcessitus. Dragonhorse Amberia, what is your perspective?"

"This is Ulric Hamar. You're right on course. They're just at the base of those hills ahead of you. You should begin to see smoke. Cut your speed by half in three…two…one. And…."

"…There they are," Teal muttered. "Barking mad, all of them." He pivoted slowly on a small, sleek wingtip, letting himself spiral downward for a closer look. He felt like he could lean out of the cockpit and touch the ground, yet there was no indication that the participants were aware of him. "Probably too bent on killing each other to look up," Teal said aloud. "What are you doing? Why are you fighting? There isn't even a water pipe nearby." He engaged communications again. "Ulric, are you there?"

"I am."

"Can you come down here?"

"Ship and all," he chuckled, "or just me?"

"Just you, at least for now."

In a minute or so the big Amberian captain was standing next to Teal, running his palms down the sides of his roach, and staring at the scene below. "What do you want to do?" he said finally.

"Watch. Wait. Let them sort each other out," Teal replied.

"Not my first inclination. We could send a pulse from one of the platforms that would knock all of them on their asses. Maybe they'd stop this nonsense."

"Or maybe they'd take it underground, or take it out on innocent people," Teal said. "They seem bent on killing each other, so let them. Maybe they'll leave everybody else alone."

"You could put it in their heads to stop fighting," Ulric suggested. "Why haven't you done that? Seems like that would be the Equi way."

Teal raised a dark eyebrow and let the comment sink in. "Making wise choices for them teaches them nothing about making wise choices of their own accord. If this is to be a Tribute World, it needs to have a thinking population."

"So far not in evidence."

"Have you done a DNA scan of this group?"

"Yup," the Amberian nodded. "He's not there."

"Kraa," Teal muttered. "He's got to be somewhere."

"Most probably dead and, if he's lucky, buried. Bona said he hadn't seen his son for how long?"

Teal shook his head and scowled. "He doesn't know. As far as we can figure out it's been at least three, maybe four years. Men didn't last on the carts longer than that. Bona said they chopped his toes off within the first few weeks because he kept trying to get away, and the doctors think they've been healed about three years."

Hamar sucked air through his teeth and grimaced. "Chopped his toes off. Ugh! It's a miracle he didn't die of infection in those filthy tunnels. He's got to be a very strong individual for all his fragile appearance. You almost died, and you're strong as a horse."

"Agreed," Teal muttered, looking at the wide, pale scar forming from his wrist nearly to his elbow. "I had people who cared, and people who knew what they were doing, or I would be dead. Luckily Ardenai didn't decide to go to work and let me sleep in." They watched the battle for a few minutes in silence, then Teal added, "Dozens, hundreds of those men had been mutilated. How is it possible that they survived? I should ask Bona if someone tended to his wounds."

Hamar nodded, but his mind was on the struggle below. The dust from the pulverized earth was the same malevolent hue as the sky, and it formed a blinding, choking haze through which Teal and Ulric watched the contest, which progressed seemingly without any kind of organization or leadership. From time to time someone was dragged from the melee and dumped to one side, but nobody rushed to tend the wounded. "Look at them," he said with a gesture. "How can they see? How can they breathe? What in kraa are they doing?"

"It almost feels like a game," Teal said. "A bloody, violent game. I half expect a horn to sound or a whistle to blow, and they'll all go to the sidelines for tea."

"Lebonathi Fungus Kombucha, more likely. Have you tried it?"

Teal rolled an eye Ulric's direction and shook his head. "Yummy, is it?"

"It's effective," Ulric chuckled. "Stronger than their fermented water, but somehow not as nasty." He sobered and went back to staring at the battle. "These people were on the brink of space travel – interstellar exploration – and look at them. They're fighting with the kinds of weapons my people were using against invaders eight thousand years ago. Rocks, clubs, firesticks, splatter cannon, knives, flamethrowers. The deadliest weapon down there is a crossbow, and it's not well made. What in the name of Ahura happened?"

"If they were allied with the Nargas, why don't they at least have more advanced Nargawerld technology? The closest I've seen to a modern Narga surface weapon is that little pultronel Eridu used to shoot Kehailan. The Royal Guard has a few of them, not many."

"Probably gifted to the Most Wise Lord Eridu from a Narga official. A tease to get them to buy more," Ulric said, parking one hip on the arm of the command chair. "Do you think they'd notice if we went down there and had a looksee?"

Teal looked dubious. "Have you seen that scar on the governor's chest? I was there for that battle, and I know what an arrow can do at close range. Primitive weapons wielded with deadly intent, are no less deadly than anything in our arsenal."

"I wonder how many of those people down there are children, playing at being grown-up? I swear, it looks like a thoroughly disorganized game being played by large five-year-olds."

"It does," Teal muttered. "I wonder if it is." The Amberian gave him a quizzical look and Teal turned from the screen to look at him. "My wife has a theory that because there is very little complex nutrition in the food, the people have become less intelligent. From the looks of things, they've been reduced to morons."

The Amberian nodded. "That would explain a great deal, wouldn't it?"

There was a sudden *thunk* against the side of the clipper and both men burst out laughing. "We're under attack," Teal snickered. The forward viewing screen revealed a lumbering field piece, being loaded a second time. "It's funny," said the Master Captain, "But it's also unacceptable. My first inclination is to kill all of them, but it's hard to get answers from the dead." He looked at Captain Hamar, who was twitching with anticipation. "Have your ship grab the cannon, and we'll grab her crew."

"I suppose," Hamar groused. He activated communications, and in less than five seconds four men stood gawping at the bare spot where their field piece had been. In another five seconds they were standing in front of Teal and Ulric.

For a few startled moments there was silence. Master Captain and Fleet Commander assessed their captives. Not albinized. Laborers, probably. Not country folk. There really weren't any of those to speak of. Simple men, and, from their wide eyes and open mouths, terrified. Men who knew they were completely at the mercy of their captors – a huge orange savage with inkings from the back of one hand, up his arm, across his shoulder, up his neck, across his skull and his forehead, and down the other side – undecipherable, tribal, primitive. The slanted eyes seemed not to blink at all, the smile ominous and hungry. The other one nearly as big, eyes like a poisonous snake, and a face that was all too recognizable as the Master Captain himself. They realized in a breath that they were dead men. Their filthy faces went from terrified to sullen. They sank to the floor, folded their legs, dropped their heads, and waited.

When they looked up, their captors were sitting cross legged in front of them. "My name is Teal," said the gentle voice. "Would you like a drink of water?" He extended a cup and a pitcher, and gestured for them to take what they wanted.

"It's poisoned," one of them hissed. "Don't touch it."

The youngest, who was just a boy, began to cry softly.

The man nearest the pitcher picked it up, poured himself a drink, and downed it. "Thank you," he said. "My name is Eshkar. I'm Anchoress Ensharra's brother."

"Traitor!" the first man exclaimed. "You had us fire on this ship on purpose! You knew this would happen!"

"I had hopes," Eshkar smiled. "I couldn't very well pass up the opportunity to get their attention. If you had been listening to what my sister has been saying, and watching what these people have been doing, instead of listening to the flamen, you would know the water is clean and the words are true, Aga, so get that look off your face."

"You are possessed of the devil!" Aga shrieked. "Your home is forfeit! The lives of your family, your wife, your children, your parents! Dead! All dead!"

"Interesting," Teal said, "given that you are all apparently prisoners at this point. No one knows but the four of you what Eshkar has told us."

"If we live, they will know!" Aga snarled, and Ulric laughed. The snarl stuck and suffocated in Aga's petrified throat.

"You really can't think very well, can you?" the Amberian said in a conversational tone. "What about you two?" he asked, looking at those who remained silent. They wouldn't even make eye contact. The youngster was wiping his nose on his ragged sleeve, leaving a trail of slime and a clean spot on his upper lip.

"Let's split them up," Teal suggested. "You take Aga and the silent duo to your ship where you can separate and interrogate them. I'll keep Eshkar and see if he is who he says he is. Don't let them make contact with anyone."

Ulric nodded, glanced up at the screen and jerked his chin to point. "Look," he said.

There was no fighting. Everyone was standing, staring up in the direction of the vanished cannon and crew. "They probably want their field piece back," Teal chuckled. He touched a spot on the console and his voice blanketed the fighters below. "I am Teal, Master Captain of the Interposing Forces. We were fired upon. That was a mistake. We now have prisoners who will be held accountable for their actions. If you are wise, you will quit your positions before we drop that cannon we borrowed."

By the time he'd touched the console again to deactivate voice mode, the fighters were already dispersing into the settling dust.

"I'll be in touch," Hamar said, stepped against Aga and jerked the two silent men to their feet. Teal caught Eshkar by the elbow and pulled him out of the pattern, there was a swirl of maroon and blue, and the two of them were alone.

"Come with me," Teal said and led Eshkar to the back of the clipper, where he pointed to the lavage. "Wash your face and hands, thoroughly," he said, and watched to make sure it was accomplished.

Eshkar washed slowly – face and hands, then arms and neck – obviously relishing the feel of the water and breathing deeply of the clean, soapy fragrance. "You don't believe me," he said, accepting a towel.

"What I believe is not important," Teal said. "Come with me, please." They went back to the main console and Teal led him to one side where there was a dark, soft pad about eight inches square. "Spit in your palm." Eshkar gave him a questioning look, then did as he was told. "Now put your hand, palm down, right there." He pointed to the pad. The man followed orders, then accepted the chair Teal gestured him into, and contented himself with a pitcher of water.

Teal sat at the console and tapped a small, lighted space. "Belesprit, this is the IEC Arcessitus. Doctor McGill, are you available?"

The screen engaged and Timothy's smiling face appeared. "Doctor Teal. I am, indeed. How may I serve the Great House this day?"

"Please check the sample I just sent you against what you have on record for Anchoress Ensharra, will you?"

"Of course," McGill said, and the screen went dark.

"Amazing," Eshkar breathed. "Absolute control without knowledge or intimidation."

Teal gave him a rather startled look. Apparently not all Lebonathi were dolts. "We'll talk when I know who you are," Teal muttered. "And what your intentions are."

"That's fine with me," Eshkar said, "as long as Aga doesn't get loose and let the flamen know what I did. My family will be dead before I can even begin to go to their rescue, and others will die with them."

The screen brightened. "Filial match," McGill said. "Your spitter is Ensharra's full brother. Hopefully he's not trying to kill you."

"Not at all," Teal smiled. "He's sitting right here beside me. Timothy McGill, this is Eshkar. We are going to need to collect his family and friends, and I do not have room to do that with my ship."

"Which is very nice, by the way. Sister to Dominus and Regence, I presume?"

"Yes. But newer," Teal grinned. "Is Captain Eletsky able to join the conversation?"

There was a momentary pause, and Marion's face appeared. "Master Captain Teal," he smiled. "Good to see you. How may we serve the Great House of Equus?" Teal explained, Marion nodded. "We will stand by to receive whomever needs to come," he said.

The clipper wended its way toward the city of Tholen, and, guided by Eshkar's knowledge of streets and buildings, they began to search for his family amongst the myriad life signs. "What if just taking us was enough to trigger their arrest?" Eshkar fretted. "They're so quick, and so deadly."

"Even if the flamen have arrested them, we can simply pluck them out of their grasp. We have been working for some time on being able to penetrate any of the materials forged on this world, and we've accomplished that with most of them. Not all, but most."

"Shouldn't we just go down there?"

"Why?" Teal asked, and Eshkar heard the suspicion in his voice.

"So, you know who I am, but my motives still escape you," he sighed. "I don't know how to convince you, Master Captain."

"You don't have to," Teal said quietly. His head turned slowly and the green ophidian eyes stripped Eshkar where he stood. "Feel that?"

There was a quick, dull pain in Eshkar's head and he nodded, ducking slightly to one side and closing one eye until it let up. "You're in my head, I assume. You said you could do that – all of you."

"And I'm especially good at it. I hear Lebonathi thought patterns whether I want to or not. If you mean us harm, you've hidden it well."

"You invaded my private thoughts."

"You shot at me. We're even. Now tell me why you think we should go down there."

"I feel helpless up here! Down there I could at least confront anyone who is trying to take my family!"

"And remove all doubt of your defection. How much more quickly would they move at that point?" Teal tried to look casual and sound comforting, but he remembered all too well what had been done to Brak – the broken bones, the beating, the severed thumbs – all because Eridu thought Brak might have been involved in helping Ardenai and Konik escape from the glastaline fighting dome. He slapped the console and Ulric's face appeared. "Captain, I think we need a diversion, just in case they're going house to house looking for Eshkar's family. Can you put troops on the ground?"

"I would LOVE to put troops on the ground!" Ulric exclaimed.

"Good," Teal chuckled. "I'll disable all the vehicles. You bring the Dragon's Teeth to just above the height of the highest building and disgorge as many troops as you can muster into the city square. Make your presence felt. Make it known who you're looking for, but don't tell them why. That will split their focus and give us time to scramble as many as we can find of the family."

"Done, Master Captain. I will keep a channel open for you at all times."

"Thanks," Teal said, and turned back to Eshkar. "We are going to do our best, but there are no guarantees. Your family we can identify by their familial signatures. Your friends, not so easy. Where should we begin to look for those who concern you?"

"On the ground," Eshkar said through his teeth. "In their homes. In their shops! They are innocent people who are completely unaware and unprepared for what's coming! Holding me here is a death sentence for them! Please, let me find them for you."

"Oh, fine," Teal muttered, "but if you get mortally wounded down there don't die until I can say I told you so." Again, he tapped the console. "Belesprit, please take over the rescue, and send me a pilot. I'm going to the surface with Eshkar."

"You don't have to do that!" the man exclaimed, but Teal was already striding to the equipment locker.

"Put this on," he said, "under or over doesn't matter. It's a harness that will let them jerk us out of there if we're hit, hurt, unconscious or dead."

There was a swirl of blue and maroon and Oonah Pongo appeared, stepped off the small scrambleshaft platform and gave Teal a quick hug. "Consider your ship in good hands," she grinned.

"I'm glad you're here," Teal muttered, kissing her forehead. "Much could go wrong quite quickly."

"I have you," she said, and handed him a small item. "Tim says to take a portable spit pad."

There was a momentary pause and Teal grinned. "Tim's a genius."

Within a few seconds they were scrambling into a dark and cluttered storeroom in the basement of a crumbling stone building. There was light from a narrow window at the far end and Teal stood still until his eyes adjusted, then gestured and Eshkar crept forward, looking sharply from one side to another and picking his way around boxes and equipment. Near the door he paused, and Teal jerked his head to one side. "Footfalls," he whispered.

The door opened, and into the wedge of light stepped a girl of eighteen or so. With no sound at all Teal had his hand over her mouth and his lips against her ear. "Don't scream," he whispered. "I'm a friend of Eshkar's." The girl nodded, and Eshkar stepped from behind a stack of boxes. The girl relaxed, and Teal took his hand off her mouth.

"They're after you!" she hissed. "They've already taken Papa. What did you do, Eshkar?"

"Later," the man said quietly. "Who else is here, Sura?"

"Just Papa and me. Mother is at home, so is Drenna. They're tearing the streets apart, looking for all kinds of people from four different families. What are they going to do? What are we going to do?"

"You're going to spit," Teal said quietly, and the girl remembered that he was behind her. When she turned and saw who it was, she nearly passed out. Teal put a hand on her shoulder and held out the pad. "Spit now," he said. "Faint later."

"Just do it!" Eshkar snapped, and she did. Teal momentarily closed his eyes, and the girl was gone. "What?" Eshkar hissed. "Where did she go?"

"Belesprit. Anybody related to her is now being collected, including Papa. I hope you can see how quickly this is going to become unwieldy. We will send back anyone who wants to go, but in just a short time we will have hundreds of people to deal with."

"This family is my main concern. The others should be safe."

"I should have asked earlier," Teal grimaced. "Do you actually have a wife, or was Aga spouting hatred in general?"

"I do have a wife," Eshkar said, and the realization crossed his face. "She's not related to me by blood. Your ship won't find her!"

"Depends," Teal said. "Do you have children?"

"No. Not yet. Our first child is coming in a couple of months."

"Then you are correct. We'd best get to her. We can scramble there very quickly if you have a physical address."

When they arrived in the dingy, subterranean corridor the door was already ajar, and from inside a woman's voice was crying and pleading. "I do not know!" she sobbed. "Truly I do not know. He closed the shop and went as he was ordered to do. He said it was to play war games. That was early this morning. I have not seen him since. Please, Sir. I do not..." there was the sound of a slap, and despite Teal's attempt to grab him, Eshkar leaped snarling into the room to face eight men with weapons.

"You would touch my pregnant wife with your filthy hands?" he yelled, and in the next second, he was gone. A second after that, his wife vanished, as well. The men stood there in shock for another moment, and in that moment Ulric Hamar materialized, grinning with anticipation.

"At last!" he chortled, "A fistfight!"

Teal stepped in from the corridor and gave Ulric a disgusted look as the first Lebonathi made a lunge for them. "You came alone? Really?"

"No," Ulric laughed, "I came with you!"

By then the men had recovered, and Teal rolled to one side as a knife whistled past, just grazing his ribcage. "Oh, all right," he said, wading in. "But just for a few minutes. I have work to do yet today, and I promised I'd be home by dinner."

"Ah'clare Teal Gidran, just look at you!" Ah'din said, hands finding her hips as she stood up from the patch of forest greenery where she and Ensharra were working. "You look like you've been in a brawl. Have you been rolling in filth of some kind?"

"How you talk," he grinned, catching her around the waist and kissing her despite her protestations and wrinkled nose. "I engaged the enemy, and made off with treasure. I hope."

"I hope it's enough to make up for the way you smell, plus the battered knuckles and the blood on your tunic." She looked more closely and her eyes clouded with worry. "It's torn. Teal, that blood is yours."

"Just a scratch. I was yelling at Ulric instead of paying attention." He turned and nodded toward Ensharra, giving her one of his charming smiles. "You are looking much better, Anchoress. Are you feeling better as well? Concussion all healed up?"

"I am and it is," she grinned, rising to join them and patting gently at the bruise still evident on the side of her face. "Little yellow yet, but fading. And how did you spend your day, Master Captain, other than brawling and rolling in filth?"

"The brawl was but a small part of it," he said, and his wife began to chuckle as she studied his face.

"You look like Mikilosh with a barn rat. Out with it."

"Well, if you must know so soon, I met someone who says he knows you, Anchoress, so I took a chance and brought him here with some members of his family. If they disquiet you in any way, I will remove them at once and forever."

Ensharra was immediately sober and concerned and Teal wondered if he'd done the right thing in bringing Eshkar, his wife and parents here to Lebonath Tras. Perhaps it would have been better to take Ensharra to them on the Jocundome, or Dragonhorse Thirteen. Concern showed in his face, as well, and Ensharra came to stand beside him and take both his hands in hers.

"What?" she asked.

"Let's sit." Teal parked himself on the grass with the women in front of him, and thought for a minute. "After you take your vows and become an Anchoress," he began, "do you ever see your family again?"

"Yes," she said. "You can. There's no rule against it."

"Did you ever see yours?"

"For a while, the first five years or so," she said, studying his face as he looked at her. He was not just concerned. He was worried. It showed in the slight scowl and the way his jaw worked as he spoke. She sighed and ran one hand through her light brown stubble of hair. So many years of having her head shaved. Strange not to have it so. "Things were bad, much like they are now. The flamen were still killing anchoresses. We were considered witches, or worse. I was sixteen when I took my vows – just out of my teens when I stopped going to see my family. My younger brother was just a baby when I became an anchoress, and six or so the last time I saw him. I loved watching him go from a baby into a little boy, and he loved having me come home. So did my mother. But my papa and my older brothers decided I was going to get everybody killed and after a while, I didn't go home anymore." By now she was thoroughly frightened, partly by the questions, partly by Teal's expression. "Please," she said. "Teal, what has happened?"

"Everything is fine," he soothed, patting her hand. "Wait right here." He stood up and walked the hundred feet or so down the sloping bank to where he'd left the clipper on a wide spot beside a small tarn. He opened the door, made a beckoning gesture, and four people crept slowly out, two men, two women. Even at that distance, Ensharra recognized her parents. She was on her feet and running to them before they'd cleared the ship.

Teal turned and walked back to where Ah'din was standing, watching the reunion. She held out her hand to him and smiled. "The Master Captain is unsure of his decision."

"The Master Captain is," he agreed.

"They all seem happy to see one another."

"And they'll stay that way until they realize that they've been uprooted, that their way of life, their day-to-day activities, everything they owned and worked for, is gone. Oh, we can collect a few of the physical accouterments, but the rest of it? That, we cannot replace."

Ah'din patted his arm without taking her eyes off the anchoress and her family. "I've been to Ensharra's home and so have you," she said. "It's one tiny, unventilated room with no light but the single burner she cooks on and the single, obscured window up over her head. No running water. No lavage, just a pot that she has to carry and dump in the sewer when it's too full to use any more. Her only beautiful possession is the pillow her grandmother made. And she says she is lucky to have such a comfortable place to live. A steaming, rat-infested hole in a crumbling, crime-ridden city. How can what you are offering them not be better?"

"Because what they have is all they know, and our definition of better may not be theirs." Teal said. He smiled and kissed her temple before pulling her back down on the grass beside him. "Remember when we were first married and Ardenai asked you to make a home for all of us at Canyon keep?" He asked.

Ah'din nodded. "I do indeed."

"That was his first time being sent to Terren as Ambassadorial Magistrate, and that's when he met Ah'ree and brought her home for a visit. And of course he brought her parents, so she'd be properly chaperoned. And all of them came out to Canyon keep, our ancient home that is but a pebble on the windswept reaches of forever."

"That is how her father described it, isn't it?" Ah'din nodded.

"Um hm. Her mother was terrified of going outside for fear of getting lost or being devoured by some marauding beast, terrified of getting lost inside the house, terrified of the bathing pools because the house might collapse while we were bathing. Afraid of the food because she'd seen the manure in the compost pile, and the soil on the vegetables before you washed them in...*that* water out of *tha*t river."

"Her father was afraid of the horses and revolted by the smell," Ah'din chuckled. "I remember asking them if they'd like to go riding, and they looked at me like I was drooling mad." She smiled and made eye contact with her husband. "They did come around after a while and gave Ardi and Ree their blessing, but I guess I see your point. So, what are you going to do with them? Stone Spring?"

Teal shook his head. "Oh no. Those scientists have spent their lives caring for the plants we rescued. I don't want anybody near them who might wreak havoc for whatever reason. I think, for now, guest quarters on Dragonhorse Thirteen. Then, maybe, one of the farm ships. Kehailan can keep an eye on them without seeming to, and there's nothing they can really get into or damage. So," he said, standing up and offering Ah'din a hand up, "I should be on my way. Would you like to come with me? We can eat with Kehailan, or even go to our apartments on the Jocundome for the evening, if you'd like."

"I have plants to process," she said apologetically. "I'm sure Ensharra is much too preoccupied to help me, and that's as it should be. I'll be at Stone Spring for a good part of my evening and I'll probably eat there. You do what will serve you best, Sweetheart. For all my teasing, you do look tired."

"Tell you what," he grinned. "I'll have these good people transported to Dragonhorse. Ensharra can show them around as well as I can, and Kee will be there to help her. I will take a bath, which you are more than welcome to share with me, and then we will process those plants together. How's that?"

"Why Master Captain, I think it's a brilliant plan. Especially the bath. I'll scrub the places you can't reach, and I do want to take a look at that scratch, just to make sure."

Teal leaned forward and kissed her lingeringly on the lips. "I'll let Stone Spring know we're coming," he said. His eyes went back to the five people standing by the clipper, and Ah'din could see the strategizing, the weight of office that she never saw when he was at Canyon keep. The first tingle of homesickness made her shiver a little.

"High altitude. It's cool," Teal observed. He sighed quietly and squeezed her hand.

CHAPTER 4

Gideon and Criollo, each with an armload of Ah'ren's maps, nodded politely to the Lebonathi coming toward them in the ship's main corridor, and received a curt nod in response as he brushed past. "I see Naram's still alive," Criollo whispered, nearly in Gideon's ear, and Gideon snickered in response.

"Our sires are probably still arguing with the governor over which one of them gets the pleasure of killing him."

"He looks angry about something," Criollo observed, turning the corner toward the scrambleshaft platform. "I wonder what's wrong this time."

Gideon looked momentarily at Naram's retreating back then stepped up onto the platform ahead of his cousin. "I'm sure some lucky person is about to find out. Dome Administrative Offices, please," he said, and a moment later they were standing in the entresol gardens of a sunlit, fan shaped building. "Why is it," he muttered, juggling the rolls in his arms, "that people, no matter their job or station, build up so much stuff? How can all these papers and rolls and cases be irreplaceable?"

Criollo just shrugged as best he could and muttered something about affluence under his breath as they headed for the doors which opened into Ah'ren's chambers. Her space on Dragonhorse Thirteen had been very nice. This space was spectacular, as were most spaces created by the Papilli. It was large and airy, seeming almost transparent, though that was an illusion of the light. With a high, multi- faceted ceiling and softly glowing walls, it felt like part of the gardens outside. Mostly, it was efficient. Meticulously designed, like all things Papilli, for optimum usefulness and ultimate pleasure. A place to think, and create.

Gideon hadn't seen his father's chambers yet, but he was hoping they'd have this same ambiance. The man needed a sanctuary. He was still trying to create a code that would allow Equi ships to detect the glastaline domes. He was trying to find a way to get around the flamen and their hate-filled rhetoric without killing them, which to Gideon seemed an unnecessary courtesy. He was debating with Teal, Ah'ren, Konik, Anchoress Ensharra and Priestess Ah'nis about how best to deal with a huge, poverty-stricken population in a small area. He was also preparing for their first planet-wide inspection, trying to choose venues that would give him the most information on more aspects of more subjects than Gideon could even fathom. And always, at the back of Ardenai's mind, *tap, tap, tap,* the rhythm of the respirator surfacing in his eyes – especially when he was tired – the fruitless, unrelenting worry about Io and the twins.

A few days before, Gideon had been in his father's office on Dragonhorse, taking a turn at talking to Io…at Io…when a serpent physician had appeared on the screen and asked to speak to Ardenai. First Ardenai was told to rejoice, that his wife carried twin girls, one slightly smaller than the other, both very active. Then, before the grin could assert itself on his face, the doctor had gone on to say that there was a change, and not for the good, in Io's condition – her ability to carry and nourish the babies while keeping herself well-nourished as well. He had asked the Firstlord – just in case, of course, no need to worry yet – but if they needed to save the mother or save the babes, which should they choose?

Ardenai had stood there for a few moments, as a stunned man does before he drops, and then looked at the screen and the Achernarean physician. "You must fight to save all of them," he had said, "even if it means losing all of them. I will not choose between my wife and my daughters, and you must not ask me to." The physician had nodded, vanished, and Ardenai had collapsed into a chair like his legs were broken. There had been no tears, no words. Gideon had stood behind him, hands on his shoulders for what seemed a long time before the Dragonhorse rose silently and went back to work. Gideon wondered if Ardenai had said anything to anyone about expecting twin girls. He doubted it.

"Gideon, just dump those maps and let's get going," Criollo said, and Gideon realized he'd been standing still, staring at nothing. "Are you all right?"

"Sorry. Yes, I'm good," he replied, rolling the maps out of his arms onto a large table at one end of the room. "One more load should do it and we can have lunch."

They went back out to the entresol and the scrambleshaft pad, stated their destination as Dragonhorse Thirteen, and materialized in a dim and dusty subterranean field of enormous proportions. The air was like the slap of a hot, wet towel, and the realization that they were being jostled by boys of various ages left them momentarily stunned. "What did you do?" Gideon exclaimed.

"Me?" Criollo retorted. "You're the one who..." He stopped, realizing that whatever jostling had been going on had now ceased, and that they were being studied intently by a dozen or more dirty, hostile looking Lebonathi children – some their age, some younger.

There was another swirl of maroon and blue, and a very small, startled boy appeared, still holding an armload of materials bound for the new offices. "Oh no," he said, "Oh no, oh no. I have taken a very wrong turn, haven't I? Yes, I have. How did I do that?"

In an instant Criollo and Gideon ceased to exist and all eyes went to the newest arrival. "It's a rat!" one of the boys yelled. "It's a talking rat!"

"Catch it!" someone yelled.

"Kill it!"

The boy's eyes got big and his mouth dropped open as he looked around. "Rat? Where?" The realization hit him. "You mean me? I am NOT a rat!" he exclaimed. "I am a Taraxian! My father is Ambassador Dahman! I am Jobie! I am not a rat!"

The cry went up, "Catch it! Grab it!" and the stampede was on.

"Get him up!" Criollo shouted, and Jobie found himself swung amid a flurry of his father's documents, onto the shoulders of a tall, blond youth about his own age who then spun to face the oncoming mob.

"Just hold on!" Gideon shouted. "We don't want to fight with you. There's been a scrambleshaft malfunction, that's all. Go on with your game and pretend like we're not here."

Apparently, rat-boy was not fair prey after all. The boys stopped and surveyed the two big strangers who were protecting him. "As long as you are here," said the largest boy, "we might as well find out if you can hold your own in a fight."

Criollo looked nonchalant. "Take our word for it when we tell you we can. What are you playing, anyway? Is that a ball you're holding?"

"A ball?" Jobie exclaimed, leaning over Gideon's head for a better look. "A game? That scrambleshaft malfunction is the best thing that's happened to me in weeks! Quick, what are you playing and what are the rules? We need to get in a round or two before they get the scrambleshafts fixed!"

Being thoroughly worried and having already lost valuable time due to the same scrambleshaft problems which had landed the boys on the surface of Lebonath Jas, Naram steeled himself for the pleasantries which preceded any dealings with the Equi hierarchy and knocked on the jamb of the Firstlord's open door.

Ardenai looked up, smiled and rose as he beckoned Naram inside. "Regent Naram," he said, brushing his right hand over his left in ancient greeting, "Ahimsa, I wish thee peace. How may the Great House serve you this day?"

Naram accepted the chair and the cold glass of cinnamon orange tea which was immediately beside him, sweetened to his liking. They'd known he was coming. He took a deep breath to quiet himself, nodded his thanks to the server and asked in the calmest tone he could muster, "Did you have

Akadia transferred somewhere?"

Ardenai's smile faded. "No, why?"

"When I went to see her yesterday, I couldn't find her, that's why," Naram replied.

"Those ships are huge," Ardenai said, rolling his glass between his palms. "She could be out and about on business of some kind. I wouldn't worry just yet."

"Well, I am!" Naram snapped, banging his drink down on the corner of Ardenai's desk. "The Menorquins keep very close tabs on who comes and who goes, and this morning they still couldn't account for her."

"They keep tabs on who comes and who goes if they are associated with the tunnels. Nobody else is required to wear a tracker, and a thousand people a day move on and off those ships. Hopefully you're worried for nothing, but let's check." Ardenai tipped his head slightly to the left, toward his dominant hand, and in a few moments Konik stepped into the room and nodded to Naram.

"Still alive, I see," Naram sneered.

"Yes. Sorry to disappoint you," the governor replied. "What's this about someone missing?"

"His friend Akadia," Ardenai said. "She has been assigned to the farm ships, and Naram hasn't been able to find her for a couple of days."

"That's not good," Konik muttered. "Did you ask them to check for a scrambleshaft signature?"

"Of course I did," Naram replied. "They're having problems with the equipment, and apparently so are you. It took me two tries to get here. I need to find out where she is!"

Konik saw the genuine worry and let the snappishness go by. After all, it was Naram. "This is my first day back on the job, and I've not seen anything that isn't written in big, purple letters. If it's been two days, maybe the offices of Priestess Ah'nis know something."

In another long minute Ah'nis swept into the room, blonde hair piled atop her head in the fashion of the Eloi, pale green robes brushing her ankles.

Her haughty expression said she was not particularly pleased to have been disturbed. She nodded curtly to Konik and Naram and looked expectantly at Ardenai without sitting. "How may I serve you?"

If the Firstlord was offended he hid it with a chuckle. Everyone knew these two powerful people had their own treaty. "We gave sanctuary to Naram's friend Akadia a few weeks ago," he said. "She was given work aboard the farm ships, and now Naram can't find her there."

"Really?" Ah'nis said, "She should have been back by now."

"Back from where?" Naram asked, alarm standing in his nearly colorless eyes.

"She said she wanted to go home and see her family. Perhaps retrieve some personal things that had meaning for her. Things she wanted for her children."

No one in the room had ever seen Naram so much as turn a hair, and now he went from alarmed to stricken. "Why would she do something that crazy? Why didn't you stop her?"

"She was excited to share the news of her pregnancy. She wanted to see her family. She was not in any way a prisoner. I couldn't have denied her passage even if I'd wanted to, which I didn't."

Now Ardenai was alarmed. "You didn't give her an escort?"

Ah'nis drew herself up and looked frostier than usual. "Need I say again that she is a free woman?"

"In a hostile environment," Ardenai retorted. "Freedom and safety go hand in hand, Governor. Thank you. You may go."

Ah'nis tossed her head and swept out, pointedly not acknowledging any of the men in the room, who were all on their feet and out the door behind her. "You might want to take a runabout," she said over her shoulder, "the scrambleshafts are sending people to random destinations this morning." She paused, her posture softened, and as the men caught up with her she added, "If you are worried then I am, too. I will come with you."

Ardenai's arm went around her shoulder and he kissed her temple without slowing much. "Absolutely not," he said gently. "Too many women depend on you, not just Lebonathi. Stay here. Stay in touch. We may need you." She nodded, and they continued at a dogtrot in the direction of the launch bay.

"I hope you know where we're going," Konik muttered. "That's a huge city down there."

"Of course I know where we're going," Naram snapped. "I just hope your overcomplicated, underperforming technology can get us there."

Ardenai just shook his head. What a time for the scrambleshafts to have problems. Moving day for the offices, and now this. He had time to wonder who was stranded where, but not long enough to worry about it. Even as he was launching Dominus he was talking to Cutter, trying to figure out how to focus a scrambleshaft anywhere close to where they needed to go. "Do you think if we get close enough it will make a difference?"

"It should," Cutter said, but his tone was not encouraging. "Get right over top of where you want to be – just above the rooftops – and try scrambling. But harness up just in case. That way I can find you and yank you out when things are working again."

Ardenai just snorted and went to get scrambling harnesses. Fifteen minutes later they were hovering above one of the older sectors in what was already an ancient city. It was not policy to scramble into or out of populated areas, but in this case they shoved weapons into their utility belts, locked arms so they'd all end up in the same place, and found themselves on one of the dank, sweltering subterranean streets. Naram looked around, got his bearings and said they were close to where Akadia's family lived.

They began walking in the direction Naram indicated, and became immediately aware that people were shrinking away from them, then looking over their shoulders when they had passed. "That's odd," Konik said. "I thought we were through that stage for the most part."

"That's not all that's odd," Ardenai grimaced. "Do you smell that?" Konik shook his head, but a few seconds later his nose caught the stench. They looked at each other and began to run with Naram close behind.

They were too late, of course. Akadia was dead, and had been dead long enough to stink – stripped naked, eyes bulging, hanging by her neck in a public space with the word, WHORE, carved into her blackened forehead. People were just…walking by…eyes averted, pretending she wasn't there.

"Eladeus help us!" Konik snarled, spinning around to scan the corridor. "What is wrong with these people?" A woman shrank against the far wall and scurried faster, hiding her face.

"We need to get her down," Ardenai said quietly, and turned to where Naram stood, dumb with grief. "I am so sorry," he began, and Naram came suddenly to life.

"I am going to kill someone for this!" he screamed, and took off at a run toward the nearest shop.

"She'll keep!" Konik exclaimed. "Grab him before he gets himself into something he can't get out of!"

By the time they got into the shop Naram had a woman by the shoulders and was shaking her like a rag. "Who did this?" he kept saying. "Who did this?"

"Put her down!" Ardenai said, grabbing his arm. "She can't answer you if you break her neck."

"That's your daughter hanging out there!" Naram grated. "You gutless piece of shit! You would allow this to happen? You would let her hang there like rotting caronai?"

"Stop," Ardenai said firmly, "or I will stop you." Naram let the woman drop and she disappeared onto the floor behind the counter. Ardenai vaulted it easily, picked her up and brought her around with him. "Tell us what happened," he said. She looked through him and said nothing. "Now," he said. "Who killed Akadia?"

"Was it Telloh?" Naram demanded. "Was it her father or her brothers? Who did this to her?"

The eyes moved slowly in his direction before the head turned. "You did," the woman said.

Naram sagged against the wall beside the door and squeezed his eyes shut. "She was safe," he said through his teeth. "She was safe."

Konik stepped up to the woman and purred, "You need to tell us who did this to your daughter." He took her reluctant hand, held it against his chest, and slowly rubbed her arm with his fingertips until she looked almost asleep and leaned into him. "Who did this to your little girl?"

"She was so happy," the woman said softly. "We were happy for her. She was not being beaten. She had enough to eat at every meal. She and Naram were to be married soon. She was going to have a baby who would grow up in a beautiful place. She came to tell us these things."

"Then what happened?" Konik asked, still rubbing her arm.

"We had some food put by, and we fixed a big family meal. We all sat down together and there was laughter and joking. She said we could all go to that beautiful place, that she would make it happen for us – she and Naram. But someone had seen her come here, someone who recognized her through her disguise. And Telloh came with his brothers, and they took her."

"Did you…?" Naram began, and Ardenai shushed him.

"Akadia's father and her brothers, they said it was Telloh's right as her husband and would not fight him, and when Akadia tried to tell them she had divorced Telloh, he…cut out her tongue…and slit her throat. They come here now, every hour. They walk around her body three times and they spit on her. They said if we took her down they would kill all our children and burn our shop, and they would. Telloh has friends. Powerful friends."

"So do you," Ardenai said quietly. "When they come again, we will arrest them, and they will be put on trial for what they did to Akadia."

"And if I am not mistaken, they are here," Konik said, looking over the woman's bowed head.

Naram hit the door with both hands and barged into the street, screaming obscenities as he charged. In a moment five men had knives in their hands, and Naram had only his fists and his rage.

Konik and Ardenai were out the door behind him. *Kehailan!* Ardenai yelled in his head. *Kehailan, can you hear me?*

Yes. Are you in trouble?

Absolutely. Are the scrambleshafts working?

No! Ardenai could hear the desperation in his son's voice.

Find us when they are! Don't grab us, just find us!

Dragonhorse? Dad?

But Ardenai was into the fray and needed every bit of his concentration to keep himself and his companions alive. He used his height to gain advantage, using one long leg to kick the knife away from the smallest of the attackers, and his elbow to fend off the blade he felt slash across the top of his utility belt as he spun around. "Get him!" He yelled to Naram, jerking his chin at the small man, "He's yours!" and punched the man who'd cut him, throwing him into Konik's path.

"I want Telloh!" Naram pointed, but he applied himself to the man he'd been given, leaving Ardenai and Konik with two apiece. Telloh was the tallest, nearly Konik's height, and quick with a blade. He made a run at Naram's back and found himself kicked hard into the stone wall by the governor. He slumped, stunned, then found the extra knife and threw it.

Ardenai jerked back and it passed a hair's breadth from his chest, clattering to the floor near the door of the shop. His left fist caught one of the brothers, and he glanced over in time to see Konik snap the neck of another. The man dropped, and Konik flinched away from the blade of the third brother's knife, catching it as it sliced down across his elbow and forearm, and yanking it, owner and all in to be dispatched.

"These people and their knives!" the governor exclaimed, momentarily gripping his arm before turning back to confront the last of the brothers, who was staggering to his feet. "Stand still or I will kill you," he told the man. There was a long moment of hesitation while the man's eyes darted left to right, one brother dead on the floor, his head clear over one shoulder as if there were no bones in his neck. Another brother dead with Konik's knife in his heart. Naram pounding a third brother over and over though he was clearly unconscious. Telloh and Ardenai circling one another in a semi-crouch, each with a knife.

Konik glanced that way too, just for a moment. The man flipped his knife over, caught the blade to throw it – and dropped like a rock. "Oh,

I brought a pultronel," Konik said in a conversational tone. "Just in case." He turned and fired again, depositing Telloh at Ardenai's feet. "I know it's cheating," he said apologetically, "but we need somebody to put on trial. Naram! Leave him! He's done."

Ardenai leaned momentarily against the wall and brought a bloody hand away from his back. He looked around, then back at Konik. "Four? You got four, and I didn't even get one?"

"You threw me one of them, so technically he counts as yours."

"I could have taken Telloh," Ardenai said a little defensively.

"You were about to do just that, which is why I dropped him," Konik said, and Ardenai gave him a questioning look. Konik grinned and met the Firstlord's eyes. "I know you, remember?" he said softly. "I know how killing affects you. Besides, you got stuck early on, trying to protect Naram. You're off your game. Let's see if Kehailan has those scrambleshafts working yet, shall we?" He shook off the blood running down his left arm, then put his foot on one of the corpses, yanked his knife out, wiped it on the body and stuck it back in its sheath. "Family heirloom," he shrugged.

Ardenai snorted humorlessly and pulled the communications tab on his harness. "Dragonhorse Thirteen, can you get help to us yet? We have prisoners, we have wounded, we have dead." There was a convolution of maroon and blue. A dozen troopers appeared and began pushing back the crowd, which was when governor and Firstlord realized they had an audience, and a big one. "Thanks," Ardenai said, and leaned heavily against the wall. "Where's Kehailan?"

"Rounding up loose stock," an Equi lieutenant grinned. "Dragonhorse, you're bleeding. Let's get all of you someplace where you can get a cool drink and be tended to. Captain Kehailan is doing fine and I'm sure we will hear from him soon."

"Why would he be out rather than sending somebody?" Ardenai scowled, and the lieutenant just shook his head.

"I'm sure he'll tell you when he gets back," he said evasively. "Here, put your arm around my shoulder. You look really hot and a little woozy."

▲▲▲▲▲▲▲

Kehailan was on his third jump, checking scrambleshaft signatures at destination points, when he found himself in the huge, filthy field where he and his sire had gone hunting for shards of glastaline. He'd no sooner materialized than there was a wild whoop and a tiny boy, head down, clutching a ball, plowed full tilt into him.

The boy bounced off, landed on his back and looked up in surprise as the pack roared up behind him. "Gideon," he yelled in a voice much bigger than he was, "your brother's here!"

Kehailan just shook his head and laughed. He had Gideon, Criollo, and as a bonus he'd found Jobie as well. He squeezed one of the crys-tels around his neck and let Cutter know all three boys were safe. "And just what do you think you're doing?" he asked, setting the little Taraxian back on his feet.

"We're teaching them to play Lightning," said one of the boys, who smiled shyly and added, "Hello, Captain Kehailan. Do you remember me?"

"I do," Kehailan nodded. "You're Anmar. How is Anshra's leg by now?"

"It's better," the boy said. "Even my father says the Equi helped make Anshra better. Are you here to learn our game, too, like you promised?"

Kehailan thought about that for a moment. "Yes," he said firmly, "I am."

In twenty minutes, he was sweat-soaked and filthy. He'd been kicked, stepped on, jumped over, knocked down, punched, butted, straight-armed, probably pinched, and he was pretty sure he'd been bitten. He was beginning to think Polo wasn't such a bad deal after all when a whistle blew and there was a communal groan. "School," Anmar said.

"Was this your lunch?" Kehailan asked, trying not to sound as relieved as he felt.

"Yes," said Anmar, "but mostly we just play because mostly there isn't any food."

"Really?" Kehailan responded, squatting on his boot heels to be looking up rather than down at the child.

By that time the teacher had left the doorway and come out to the field to see what was so interesting. When he got close enough, he smiled rather tentatively and said, "Captain Kehailan, you came back. How are you? You look…ah…put upon."

"I'm fine, Master Gilim," he chuckled, grasping the man's forearms Lebonathi-fashion. "The boys have been teaching me Lightning. I did promise I'd return and learn how to play."

"You did," Gilim smiled. "And you kept your word despite our rather unkind treatment of you last time you were here."

"Friendship and trust take time," Kehailan said.

"And you have friends with you today," the man observed, taking in the three boys.

"They got dropped here by accident and made the most of the situation," Kehailan said. "The rascal with the ball is Jobie, son of the Taraxian Ambassador who is our current Seventh Galactic Alliance Observer. The dark-haired boy is my cousin Criollo, and the fair-haired boy is my brother Gideon. Boys, this is Master Gilim."

Pleasantries were exchanged and Jobie said, "This has been more fun than I've had in ages! Thanks everybody!"

"Do you want to stay out here and play some more?" the teacher asked, and despite the boys clamoring assent, Kehailan was quick to say that study was important, too. Jobie reluctantly handed over the ball, and the boys said their goodbyes to each other.

"We will do this another time soon," Kehailan said, shooing them toward the open door. When they were out of earshot Kehailan let the concern he'd been feeling cloud his face. "Anmar says they play the whole lunch hour because there is no food for them."

Gilim looked momentarily defensive, then sighed and nodded. "It's true. Good Equi food comes into the central stores every day, I know it does, but none of it ever makes it to the school. I know some of it is designated for us, and where it's really going is probably the black market." He flipped his hands outward and shrugged. "Progress is being made on other fronts, so who am I to complain?"

"You should have," Kehailan said firmly. "I will see that food is delivered directly to you here every day in time for lunch if I have to do it myself."

"I'll come with you!" Jobie exclaimed, "Yes I will. I have been looking for a Dragonhorse project and this one could be mine, yes it could."

"You're hired," Kehailan chuckled, "but not until your sire says it's all right." He nodded to the teacher, and gestured to the three boys. "They have been missing for a while. I should get them back to Dragonhorse." It seemed cruel to mention that they were probably hungry and thirsty by now, and that he was, as well. "I promise, tomorrow there will be lunch, and a way to wash up before they eat."

"Thank you," Master Gilim said with a nod and a smile, then added, "Really. Thank you, Captain."

"Expect some Dragonhorse uniforms. Jobie will probably be with them."

"We'll look forward to it," the man said, turned and walked back toward the classroom.

"I'd like to get a look inside there," Criollo muttered. "I wonder if they have books."

"I wonder if they have anything," Kehailan sighed. "Come on, let's go."

"They thought I was a rat," Jobie said. "Can you imagine that? A rat indeed." He grabbed his father's documents, flipped his luxurious tail jauntily over his back and tossed a salute in the direction of the classroom. "See you tomorrow, boys."

Ardenai realized he was looking at the white ceiling of the sanecere bay and sat bolt upright, wincing at the pain in his back. "Well, hello there," Ah'ren chuckled.

"Oh, please tell me I haven't been out for hours or days," the First-lord grimaced, swinging his legs over the side of the bed. "I have got to get to Naram."

"You've been asleep all of about twenty minutes," his wife said reprovingly. "Doctor Moonsgold says you're good to go. Sit a minute and make sure your head's not going to fall off while I find you a clean tunic."

"Thanks," Ardenai said, smiling to himself as he watched her. Precious Equus she was so beautiful, and so kind, and so good to him and for him. How must Naram be feeling right now? He'd loved Akadia his whole adult life, stepped far out of his usual role and seen to her rescue. She was carrying his baby – that normal life for both of them was right on the horizon – and now she was dead. Horribly, degradingly dead. Mother and child, both gone. Ardenai shuddered.

"The anchoress is with him," Ah'ren said, coming from the refabricator and reading his expression as she often did. She tossed him the tunic and added, "I'm sure you have time for a quick bath. It might make you feel better."

"You're telling me I stink?"

She dropped her eyes coquettishly. "It is not my place to tell the Thirteenth Dragonhorse that he is in any way less than absolute perfection," she murmured.

"Just what I need in my life," he chuckled, and promptly trotted off down the hall toward their quarters, asking questions as he went.

The governor was fine – shallow slash across his elbow and forearm. Like Ardenai's wound, a quick set of laser kedges and a little glue had been all that was needed. Pythos had then taken him off somewhere more private, probably to check his heart.

Naram was a mess in more ways than one. His hands were both broken, all but one of his fingers was broken, one thumb was dislocated. He was in shock, which was all that was keeping his blood pressure from killing him. Ensharra and Teal had him cornered. They were letting him rant.

Telloh had regained consciousness in the brig of Dragonhorse Thirteen, and so had the brother Konik dropped with the pultronel. The other three were dead. Konik had killed two, and Naram had beaten the third to death. Scrambleshafts were fixed. Everybody was accounted for.

For a man who hadn't had a single punch landed on him, Naram looked terrible. Ardenai walked in with Ah'ren beside him and settled silently into a chair. Ensharra smiled, Teal nodded. Naram just sat there, bandaged hands hanging useless between his legs as he leaned forward in his chair, staring at the floor. After a while he addressed the carpet. "I just don't understand. She was safe. Why did she go back? What was so important that it couldn't have waited until we were in a more secure position?"

"It doesn't make sense, does it," Ardenai said. "There must have been something pressing."

"We may never know," Teal said quietly. "I just…I want you to know how terribly sorry I am for two more lost loved ones."

"Women, are not like men," Ah'ren observed in a rather firm tone. "I think women feel more duty to family ties and small, beloved traditions. I think women feel more keenly that everything needs to fall into place, even the tiny pieces. I think she wanted to make things right with her family, to let them know she wasn't just running away, or a victim, but truly happy. She wanted to begin putting the smallest pieces together to form the perfect picture. For most women, that picture includes family."

Ensharra nodded. "I agree," she said. "I'm just sorry she had to die in order to find the justice that should have been hers weeks ago. Now Telloh will pay – after it no longer matters whose laws say what, and which should take precedence."

There was a brief silence during which every male in the room heard the unspoken understanding that passed between Ah'ren and Ensharra. *Men.*

"Thank you, all of you for coming," Ensharra said, "Regent Naram and I appreciate your friendship and your commiseration. For what you tried to do in weeks past and again today, we thank you. There are prayers that must be said, and we would like to be alone to do that. We care for you, but you are outsiders and this is a sacred thing with Lebonathis. If you would be kind enough to leave us, we would be grateful."

"Of course," Ardenai said, and rose immediately. "Please do stay here on Dragonhorse tonight, Regent, so the doctor can attend your wounds, and if you need anything at all, just ask." He nodded deeply, gestured his wife out in front of him, and was gone with the others.

Naram looked up and met Ensharra's sympathetic eyes. "Thank you," he said simply.

"You are most welcome," she smiled. "If what you truly desire is to be alone, I will see that you are not disturbed further." She rose as well and would have taken her leave, but Naram shook his head.

"No," he said. "Please stay." She nodded and resumed her seat. Bowing her head, she very quietly began the Lebonathi prayers for the dead.

"Let's do all of them," Naram whispered. "Lulana, Phaedra, Rakba, Brak…Akadia and the baby…." He began rocking slowly back and forth, as though he were comforting a child, his bandaged hands hiding his face.

Governor Konik enjoyed the leisurely quarter mile walk from his new offices to his apartments. The street was wide and gently cobbled in pale grey stone that reflected the light without glaring. There were no vehicles bigger than small, hand-drawn carts laden with vegetables, fruit and flowers, and it reminded him of the streets of Thura on a summer day. The fragrance of the gardens was everywhere and flowers and vines spilled over each garden wall in a riot of color and an ever-present shower of petals. Rather like living in a flickernick tale, he thought to himself, and he let it cleanse his soul of this day as he exchanged pleasantries and breathed deeply of the evening's perfume.

His cottage was on a slight setback of twenty feet or so, with the front door under a trellis of climbing rohanth and moon-vine. The rest of the space was concealed by a sophisticated configuration of crystalline lenses which afforded perfect light and absolute privacy. *Home,* he thought, and it came more easily. With the thought of home came first the thought of Addie, then of Swift, and that, too was pleasant, until he admitted that he was chief representative of a government which prized marriage, and he was living with a woman to whom he was not married, and with whom he was having sex on a regular and regularly delightful basis. While it didn't bother him personally to be doing so, he was keenly aware of how it might look to others, and what message it might be sending.

Not that the Lebonathi knew he was sleeping with Swift. Maybe they thought she was just his resident doctor, because they, especially the flamen, were so willing to extend the benefit of a doubt. He snorted with annoyance and opened the front door to the aroma of something wonderful cooking. Home, and dinner, and Swift. After a day like today? He sighed and took a deep breath, exhaling slowly through his mouth as he smiled.

He reminded himself not to take off his uniform jacket until he was alone and ready to put on something else with long sleeves, and then called, "Good evening. Something smells very good."

Swift came from the kitchen wiping her hands on a towel which she draped casually over one shoulder as she greeted him. "I was going to offer you a bath before dinner, but I see you've already bathed at work. That's good, actually. I've been holding dinner for a while, and it won't keep much longer." She turned her face up for a kiss, then pointed through the small kitchen toward the garden. "As usual, Governor, your table awaits you beside the pool. Here, help me carry some things."

He asked her about her day, and she talked about the horrors of albinizing children, and the havoc it wreaked on their hearts, and the fact that there were virtually no medical records at all except for those documenting albinization, probably because producing those records could bring a higher bride price. Konik gave that characteristic slow shake of his head and took a deep breath. "Well," he said, patting her hand across the table, "if it all gets to be too much for you and you need a sabbatical, you would be a huge hit as a chef. This is wonderfully prepared, and, oddly enough, it's my favorite meal."

"I know," she grinned. "I fixed it for you to celebrate your first day back to work."

It was the, *I know*, that stuck. "Really," he smiled, laying his eating sticks on the side of his plate. "Addie said I laughed in my sleep. Sang occasionally. Do I talk in my sleep, too?"

"No. I wanted to do something special for you, and Ah'rika shared this recipe with me as one of the things you liked best."

The smile remained plastered where he'd put it. "Why is it everybody seems to be talking to my daughters but me?"

"Now that is the question, isn't it?" came the bland reply, and Swift helped herself to more Alcibus noodles. "These make up quickly. I wonder if they'd keep if they were dried."

Konik just looked at her, and the eyebrows he got back brooked no nonsense. "I know," he purred, "I've been putting it off far too long. Nokota's note really got me thinking about how best to handle this. But right now we're both tired, and you're so beautiful I can hardly keep my hands off you long enough to eat."

"Really?" she said, putting her sticks aside. "You're going to go with the hypnotic pipes and the seductive blue eyes? Fabulous at bed time, Governor, but you can do better than that at the dinner table. Your family has reached out to you in every way they can think of, Nik. Why aren't you giving them a chance to break free from a negative fantasy that seems to be yours and not theirs?"

He stood up rather abruptly, and Swift hid a grin. "Not leaving, are you? I've been cooking for hours."

"Of course I'm not leaving," he said, still purring. "It's warm this evening, and so are the spices. I'm just taking off my…jacket." He remembered too late. Being around her did that to him. He barely knew the woman and she made him twitch inside – or tingle. Something. Maybe he knew her better than he thought he did. Maybe Pythos had put a spell on him, or given him some ancient serpent potion to scramble his brains and his breath when Swift was around. Definitely something there. He sat back down with that whuffle of annoyance Swift found rather endearing, and they eyed each other across the table.

"So, tell me about your day," Swift purred back, and pointed with one eating stick to the kedged-up gash on his arm.

"Usual stuff," he said glumly, picking up his sticks. "Regent Naram's pregnant girlfriend got murdered and hung up on a busy street corner by her former husband. Ardi and I got into a knife fight with said former husband and four of his brothers, two of whom I killed before lunch. Maybe it was after lunch. I forget. One of them gave me this little remembrance. Usual stuff. They … their institutions have been unraveled for so long, you know, and they all feel like they're on their own, with no sense of watching over one another… that poor girl was just hanging there with people walking past like she was invisible. They have no concept of coming together for protection or to affect positive outcomes, and I have not one single idea how to go about changing that for them."

There was silence broken only by the quiet clicking of Swift's eating sticks and the splash of the little waterfall into the bathing pool.

Konik brightened. "Pythos gave me a clean bill of health on my heart. Oh, the big news is, I got my office pretty well moved. Had a nice walk home after work."

"Well, I'm glad things are getting back to normal," she said. "Eat your supper while it's still hot. If you have a clean bill of health, you also have polo practice this evening, and so do I. That little remembrance of yours doesn't hurt, does it?"

He shook his head. "Not really. Stings a little. My left arm won't affect my game."

She reached across the table to squeeze his hand, and he decided to put off the discussion about living arrangements until he could present her with a solution. He was surer every minute he was with her what he wanted that solution to be, and wondered if she had maybe, possibly, thought along those same lines. Then, resisting the urge to hunch with guilt, he wondered at himself – how easily he could cast aside nearly a century of marriage in favor of a convenient self-serving arrangement like this one. Mostly, he wondered what Mountain hold and the Great House of Equus would have to say about this descendent of Kabardin and his designs on one of their own. He veiled his thoughts, picked up his eating sticks and went back to his dinner, discussing everyday things until the table was cleared, then he excused himself to change into riding boots and britches, said he'd see her at practice, and activated the little pad which would return him to the entresol.

He sat beside Ah'davan's grave without reading to her. Instead, he surveyed the countryside of Lebonath Tras from his elevated position, watching the grass ripple with ripening heads, catching the river's glimmer in the distance. "I lectured Ardenai about his failure to get on with his life after Ah'ree died, and yet here I sit, my oldest and dearest of friends. How I miss your voice – not just the wisdom – but the sound of your voice and your laugh – even that growl you put on once in a while to get my attention.

"I've never felt like I had too much trouble making decisions, and yet all of a sudden I have a whole basketful of them with no answers apparent. Who do I turn to now for advice about our girls, hm? Me, who couldn't even tell them apart until they started toddling. I never told you that, but I'm sure you realized it. Who do I turn to for advice about what is love and what is lust, what is easy and what endures, what is an extension of grief and what is the beginning of something new? I have got to get out in front of this other life I find myself leading, and I am so afraid as I do that, I will go around some bend and lose sight of you." He bowed his head and sat looking at the rich earth in which she was buried. He noticed someone had watered the rohanth bush, probably Ah'ren, or Swift.

"She…knows me, Addie. She knows what kind of monster I am inside. I don't have to hide from her. I never did. She knows the darkest parts of my soul, as you knew the deepest parts of my heart. There is such release in that."

He made a painful sound as he slept that night and Swift wondered if he'd rolled over onto his sore arm, but then he said, "Addie?" as though she was lost and he was looking for her.

“Right here,” Swift whispered. “Always. Right here. Go back to sleep my love.

CHAPTER 5

Ardenai had groomed his favorite polo pony after a brisk morning workout and was sitting on a bale of hay in the breezeway of the stable tuning up his saddle, when he heard, "Oh! Oh, oh, oh, no, nonono!" rising in pitch and intensity from around the corner where the hay was stored. A dozen running strides and he found a young woman fighting to hold several bales in place with one hand while trying to release the hooking glove she was wearing on the other. Ardenai slammed both hands into the precariously leaning wall, momentarily releasing the backward pressure on the hook and allowing her to wrench herself free. She dodged out of the way, and Ardenai let the bales topple to the floor.

"Those wearable hooks are nice to use, but they'll also get you killed," he observed. "Are you all right?"

She looked up, immediately colored, and looked back down. "Thank you, Firstlord. I'm fine," she said quietly.

Ardenai looked at her intently for a moment, then smiled. "Ah'cora, right? We met at Mountain hold."

She nodded. "I was kind of hoping you wouldn't recognize me," she said. She looked away and busied herself pushing the bales around for re-stacking.

"Why is that?"

"My stepbrother tried to kill you and take your crown, and then my stepfather tried to kill you at Mountain hold. I am so sorry for that. I really am."

Ardenai just shook his head. "My granddam, who is a very wise woman – a bit to the crotchety side – says you must never apologize for your relatives or it becomes your life's work." He eyed her and cleared his throat uncomfortably. "I am sorry for killing…for the way things turned out with your stepbrother. Were you close?"

She returned the look, and he thought she choked a little before muttering, "As in, close to killing him myself? Yes." She picked up the hay hooks and spread them like talons before bringing them together with a resounding clash.

"Here, let me do that," Ardenai chuckled. "How many bales do you need?"

"Just one. If I'd been thinking properly, I'd have climbed up and tossed one instead of trying to hook over my head." She dragged a bale aside and sat on it to unstrap the hooking glove while Ardenai tossed the rest of the hay back up in the proper configuration.

"What brings you to the Jocundome stables this fine early morning, if I may ask?" He smiled, turning to lean against the stack. "As a matter of fact, what brings you to the Lebonathi worlds?"

"I have been blessed with a job here," she said, smiling back, and it lit her face. Not a pretty woman, but striking and unusual, with large equine features and that rarest of Equi hair colors, a rich, wine red. "I… the Governor recruited me, so I assume it's all right for me to be here?"

"Stop that," Ardenai said firmly, and came to share the bale with her. "Nik does the same thing. Stop assuming that we think badly of you because your family acted badly. When I saw you at Mountain hold, tending to that crazy old man…Oh, sorry," he grimaced, "tending to your stepfather, I thought to myself what a brave woman you were to take on a task like that. Then Nik told me you had left the Eloi to care for your mother and stepfather, and I was impressed. I'm glad he recruited you, and I'm glad you could come."

"He is a very kind man. He made arrangements for my mother to be cared for by the Eloi. My stepfather I left in the keeping of his younger son, Sardure." Her tone had hardened a little, and dislike changed the shape of her green-gold eyes.

Ardenai was torn. Harrier had liked and trusted Ah'cora, had told Ardenai that in Ah'cora would lie many answers to his questions about the false Telenir, and Sarkhan, and what drove him. And here she sat, his captive. They were alone. He could ask her anything he wanted and she would answer. But here she sat. Alone. His captive. There was a pause.

"Who gets this hay?" he asked.

"Padmar," she sighed. "He's old. He's skinny and sick and useless for riding, but I couldn't just leave him with Sardure." She looked momentarily sad, and then to Ardenai's delight, she burst out into a wild chortle of a laugh. "He can have my stepfather, but not my horse. How evil is that?"

"I take it you feared abuse of one but not the other?"

"Exactly. Not a nice man."

"Not like Nik?"

"No, not like Nik."

"Please, just answer one question for me, and I promise the whole thing with the Telenir will never come up again. I'll carry your hay while you answer."

"I will try," she said. "Padmar is down this way. What is it you wish to know?"

"I have never been able to figure out how a man like Konik got involved in a plot to overthrow the government of Equus. I admit freely and up front that it's his story to tell, and that I should be satisfied with his usual eloquent shrug and suave, noncommittal grunt, but my curiosity is killing me. Taki gave me his perspective, what's yours?"

She smiled and swiveled her eyes his way, her brows arching in assessment. "Nik's involvement seems not to have diminished your trust in and fondness for him."

Ardenai didn't miss the look. "I love the man with all my heart. He is one of the most honorable men I know. How did he get involved with Sarkhan?"

"Well, you know he was raised in that faction who believed they, we, were the Telenir. His family for generations, and mine, believed it. Some believed they'd been sent to observe and make overtures of peace when the Thirteenth Dragonhorse rose, some believed they were sent to infiltrate and stage a coup when the Thirteenth Dragonhorse rose. His family, except his grandsire, believed the former, mine the latter. When my father and brother were killed and my mother married Saremanno…" she shook her head and shuddered. "That was the beginning of the end. The end, at least, of reason. Here we are. This is Padmar."

Ardenai set down the bale and reached over the stall door to stroke the neck of what had once been a beautiful gelding. He had a fine head with a wide white blaze, and his eyes were alight with intelligence. He was much too thin and his breathing was labored, but he chuckled with delight to see Ah'cora, and bobbed his head in welcome. "Wasting sickness. I've tried everything. Now it's just hospice care."

"I wish I could offer you a miracle," Ardenai said quietly.

"Me too," she sighed. "At least they let me bring him, and I'm working right here on the dome in the administrative offices so we'll see a lot of each other. He won't be alone."

But Ah'cora was. There was that ineffable sadness that strong people exude in unguarded moments, and it made Ardenai ache. Nik had been right. She desperately needed a change. "I'm glad you're here," he said simply.

"My hay has been delivered in good faith and your answer has not been forthcoming," she smiled. "So here is my take on the thing. You know Saremanno was behind all this, he and his fathers before him. Sarkhan was the eldest son, so he was the chosen seed, but he was barking mad, though he hid it well for a long time. Sardure was Sarkhan's original right hand." She stroked the horse and her eyes lost some of their focus as she thought. "Then Nik stepped in at the last minute – probably in just the last seasons before you rose to be Firstlord. He was dashing and brilliant, and a renowned senator and strategist. He wooed my stepfather and Sardure lost his place. Sardure still hates him for it. I know Nik could see what was coming. Sarkhan and Saremanno were threatening everybody – their families – their futures. I think Nik was trying to steer things somehow, so the fewest people would get hurt, or dishonored, and so that Equus would continue on her present course. And I think he accomplished that. Like you, I can think no wrong of the man."

"Taki's story exactly," Ardenai said, and looked down at Ah'cora. "Are you headed back to the administrative offices?"

"I am," she grinned. "Duty calls. You?"

"Yes, but I'm stopping off for breakfast. Would you like to join me? You can tell me over a cup of tea and something to eat what you're going to be doing here and where you're going to be living."

"Food sounds good," she grinned. She gave the horse a farewell pat, and walked toward the entrance with the Firstlord. "I'm a country girl," she said. "I need horses in my nose and loam under my fingernails, so the Papilli have been kind enough to issue me a cottage with a garden square. I think they're also going to loan me a horse to ride, though I'll have to keep him where Padmar can't see, or he'll know I'm cheating on him."

Breakfast revealed that she was also a cartographer, that her specialty was archeological mapping, and that the governor had asked her to come and begin mapping the abandoned cities and continents – working with a team to establish what had been, was now, what could and could not be restored. What was left of the cities of Lebonath Jas was mostly stone, and Ah'cora suspected that Konik was seriously considering dismantling an old city or two in order to build homes and businesses on Lebonath Tras.

It made sense. The stones were already shaped and ready to use. It would be quick and inexpensive in terms of manpower and time expended. The downside being that if they decided to try spreading the population back out more evenly, they'd be a few cities short.

It was a fascinating conversation, and Teal joined them partway through, turning the talk slightly toward expedition week which was now on top of them. Who was going and who was not, and where, exactly, were they going? Ah'ren joined the conversation and Ardenai introduced her to Ah'cora, who smiled and nodded. Ardenai thought his wife gave the woman a bit more scrutiny than he would have expected, but since Ah'cora was to be Ah'ren's assistant a good part of the time, he assumed it was for that reason and nothing more. It took him some time to realize that, while Ah'cora couldn't remember Ah'ren, Ah'ren knew Ah'cora quite well. When he remembered that fact he smiled, and his wife gave his hand a little pat of acknowledgement.

Tarpan arrived and talk turned again toward finding a replacement for Abeyan, who had resigned as head of the Equi Cavalry. Ardenai had asked him to reconsider. Teal had tried reasoning with him, reminding him more than once that he was throwing away a lifetime spent achieving that goal. Abeyan had just bowed his neck and his eyes had gone cold at the mention of the Firstlord's name. He was not going to be subservient to the man who had seduced his daughter and kept her now in a near-death state while he flaunted his new, high Equi wife. He wouldn't even make a recommendation, saying with a sneer that Teal might as well take that position, too. He seemed to hold every other office of import. Oh, except for the Military Governor's position, which had gone to that treasonous bastard, Ah'ria Konik Nokota. What a fine trio of fools. He wished them all a lingering death, just like his daughter was getting from the Thirteenth Dragonhorse. He promised none of them would ever see Jilfan again. Teal had worn himself out trying to keep a level tone and a civil tongue, but to no avail.

Tarpan had some suggestions, but Teal knew he was going to have to go to Equus, interview candidates, and hope he could choose from among men who Abeyan had always kept in the background, lest they take away from his image. It was an odd sensation, remembering that he and Ardenai and Abeyan had been close friends growing up. The three wild horses, their mothers had called them. Why was Abeyan so very angry, so full of hate? It just didn't make sense.

Teal shook his head and Ardenai gave him a questioning look. "Nothing," he grinned. "Just realizing that when we're through with our look about, I need to head for home and find a cavalry captain."

"Um hm. Sorry."

Ah'cora sat listening to the conversation, and Ardenai was pleased with the few questions she asked. A smart woman. He was just answering a question about the designation of keeps on Lebonath Tras, when the governor walked in.

"There's the man of the hour!" Ardenai said, pointing to a chair. "Three nights of practice chukkas, three nights of resounding victory. I said that when we got Nik in the saddle, we'd be unstoppable. Pardon my manners. Governor Konik, you know Ah'cora."

"I do," he smiled, and when Ardenai looked at the woman, she seemed to be lit from within. A little warning light flashed momentarily in his head, but he brushed it aside. Konik gave her a kiss on the temple and took the chair Ardenai indicated, smiling his thanks as a young man appeared with his usual breakfast. "What is the talk of the table this morning, other than polo? Did Padmar get here all right, Ah'cora?" She nodded, and he turned his attention back to the Firstlord and Master Captain.

Ardenai wondered if he was the only one who could see that Ah'cora's hands were shaking just a little. The tiniest tap of a boot against his own said he was not. It also meant not to mention it, so he didn't, at least for the moment. "We don't sing enough," he said abruptly. "I think we should form a singing polo team."

"Now there's a novel intimidation tactic," Teal laughed, noting the sudden veer in subject matter. "Are you going to write us a battle hymn to sing as we ride onto the field?"

"Splendid idea, but let us not get too attached to our present configuration," Konik chuckled. "You two big fellows are going to go back to Equus and Tarpan and I are going to be singing a duet." He set aside his tea and hailed Ensharra and Eshkar as they entered the dining room. "My morning is here," he said. "Our latest family to be reunited."

He rose and brushed right hand over left before giving the anchoress a lingering hug and a kiss on the forehead. “You look wonderful,” he murmured, then turned to Eshkar, grasping his forearms in greeting. “Have you met everyone? Not Ah’cora, of course.” Introductions were made, and Konik drained his tea cup without sitting back down. “We’re heading out to the farm ships,” he said. “Eshkar is taking the grand tour and I’m talking to Bona and company about forming a guild of Lebonathi farmers.” He tucked Ensharra’s arm through his, nodded to the table, and departed. Ah’cora’s eyes as she followed their departure, were almost haunted, and it made Ardenai uneasy.

“Eshkar’s wife is, where?” Teal asked. “Sorry, I kind of lost track in the rush.”

“On one of the farm ships, along with Ensharra’s parents and a couple dozen others,” Ah’ren replied, blowing gently on a bite of mazea cake before putting it in her mouth.

“I regret having to snatch all those people up so abruptly,” Teal sighed. “They left with nothing but the clothes on their backs. Everything they had, everything they had worked for, no matter how humble, is gone. They’ve been overpowered by an alien species, fed strange food, put up in strange lodgings. They have not a single personal possession. I do feel sorry for them.”

“And yet they live, do they not?” Ardenai responded. He was still looking at Ah’cora, who was suddenly oblivious to the conversation.

“They live,” Teal agreed, “but not on their terms. Ensharra’s older brothers both insisted on being returned to the surface, saying they’d take their chances amongst, and I quote, ‘their own kind.’”

“Her parents stayed, though,” Ah’ren said. “A bit at a time, a few at a time. Maybe that’s all we can hope for right now.” She, too, drained her cup, smiled and stood up. “Please excuse me. I have a great deal of work to do, and a finite amount of time in which to get it done. Ah’cora, I enjoyed meeting you, and I look forward to working with you.”

▲▲▲▲▲▲▲

"Even I, a humble male, could see that she's wildly in love with him," Ardenai said, still moving things around in his office. "When he took Ensharra's arm and left I thought she was going to cry."

"Well, regardless of what your impressions might be, don't encourage her to pursue him," his wife said. "It wouldn't end well for her."

"He's not ready. I know that."

"Oh, he's ready. Marriage is all he knows. That's not what I mean," Ah'ren said, and turned back to him instead of going into her own offices next door. That return, through fifty years and three wives, always signaled trouble – a deep and probably uncomfortable conversation was about to take place.

Ardenai sighed, and it made his wife chuckle. "Ah'cora is here for more than just assisting me, Ardi. She has excellent bloodlines, and she's been selected by the Great House as part of its breeding program. Whether they have told her or not I do not know, but I know that's a secondary reason for her being here, and it's why the Great House extended her the courtesy of placing her mother amongst them."

He'd known it was coming, of course. It was the most intimate and one of the most important of his duties to mate with various bloodlines, keeping them strong and viable. He'd been Dragonhorse nearly a year and aside from his unpleasant and thoroughly unfinished experience with Ah'nis, hadn't been called upon yet to set his head against a woman. He supposed he should be thankful for that. "But Sarkhan's sister? Really?"

"Oh stop. She's not Sarkhan's sister and you know it," Ah'ren laughed. "She does have ties to a neighbor of yours, and they're pretty strong, from the looks of her."

Ardenai thought about it and grinned. "She's part of Timor's herd, isn't she? One of the chestnuts."

"She is. Now don't get worked up, because it won't happen until later in the chukka, and I'm not sure if she's bending under your weight or

Teal's, but she's definitely not a good choice for our beloved governor. His daughters went to school with Ah'cora. He thinks of her as a daughter, and he'd be horrified if she tried to change that."

Ardenai winced before he could stop himself. "We know how well that works out, don't we?"

"All too well, and I'm sure you wouldn't wish the kind of conflict you're going through on a man you count on so completely."

Krush and Gideon appeared at that moment and Krush sensed the crackle in the air. "Are we interrupting?" he asked cheerfully.

"Absolutely not," Ah'ren said, hugging her father-in-law. "We were just…"

"Talking about Konik and Ah'cora," Ardenai admitted. "Do you know her?"

"Met her yesterday at the stables when her horse arrived, poor old fellow. I'm not sure how long he's going to last, even with lots of good Papilli herbs in him. What's the problem, if I may ask?"

"Ah'cora seems so fond of Konik, and we were discussing the whole idea of falling in love with a father figure."

Krush just shook his head and smiled, "Ardi, you need to admit to yourself that those things do not happen unless both parties, at least on some level, want them to. She's new here. He's her security for now, and she's translating that as infatuation. Trust me, it'll wear off as she makes new friends and her vision widens."

"I hope so," Ardenai sighed. "I do not need a conflicted, distracted governor."

Gideon saw that constant worry haunting his father's eyes and said brightly, "Teal was telling us about your newest campaign for victory on the polo field – a singing team. Do you think it would really work?"

"I just thought it would be fun," Ardenai smiled, sensing Gideon's intent. "I miss singing. We used to get together and sing almost every night after dinner. Even Teal and I, when we first set up our pavilion by the river on Lebonath Tras, we'd sing in the evening. Now we're all too busy or too scattered."

Or too stressed, Gideon thought to himself.

"Well, you've got the makings of an amazing quartet," Krush said. "I've heard you and Teal. How well Tarpan sings I don't know, but Konik is considered one of the best spinto tenors the Anguine moons ever produced. When he was still at Lycee I heard him sing the lead in the River Quartet. Amazing power and range on that man. The Anguines and the Equi both courted him for the big opera companies, but he told them all the same thing, 'I promised my grandfather I would be a soldier.'" Krush snorted and shook his head. "I'd love to hear him sing again."

"Our self-effacing governor," Ardenai chuckled. "Like peeling the leaves off a caulis. The deeper you go the sweeter it gets. How are you coming with the keeps?" He looked more at Gideon than the principles in the matter, and the boy shrugged and looked pleasantly perplexed.

"I'm learning a lot," he said. "I just have this simple-minded idea that if we blew up a map of Tras, and overlaid a grid the size we wanted, and took into consideration water rights and public lands and that kind of thing, that we could be done in a couple of hours. I'm told that's not the case."

"But it is a brilliant idea," his grandfather nodded. "'The brighter the mind the simpler the machine,' you know. Old Declivian saying. Ah'ren and I are actually working on a way to use your idea, Gideon, and we'd like you to help us with that until it's time for you to leave."

"Going where?" Ardenai asked.

"Governor Konik, Criollo, Swift and I are going to the surface to explore the old library at the Lycee – the University," Gideon said. "Would you like to come? I'd love it if you came along."

"And I'd love to go," his sire replied. "I'll see where I am on this whole glastaline code writing business by then."

"Not going well?" This from Krush, who had halted his slow saunter toward Ah'ren's chambers.

"No, it's not," Ardenai groused, plowing his fingers through his hair and tapping at the braid in the back. "Not only is it not going well on a logical path of failure, it's not making any sense on any level. The chemical compound is completely alien. I have looked at every possible combination of compounds found on the Lebonathi worlds half a dozen times. I've looked at Nargawerld compounds. I've looked at combinations of Narga and Lebonathi compounds. Nothing."

"Why don't you just fly around and poke little itty-bitty holes with a laser until you find all the domes and go from there?" Gideon joked, gave his father a jaunty wave, and disappeared into Ah'ren's map room.

Ardenai and his father looked at each other for a long moment. "Don't say it," Ardenai warned, and Krush disappeared with a chuckle, followed by Ah'ren, who paused just long enough to give the Firstlord a lingering kiss on the lips.

"Go with your boy this afternoon," she whispered. "You never know what might be in that old library. And don't forget, you're teaching first grade tomorrow on Belesprit."

That thought relaxed him a little, made him smile as he went about his work. He knew how to teach first grade – little older than he was used to, but still small, excited and cuddly. His mind went unbidden to the twin girls sleeping with their mother on Achernar. How delightful it would be to go to school with them and see their excitement as they learned of the wondrous order of things. What a blessing it would be just to have them safely birthed and their mother back in his arms. He sighed and gave himself an allover shake. No time to go out walking in his head if he wanted to go with Gideon and company this afternoon. A chime sounded, the wall lit up and he went back to his desk and a conference with Ah'krill and the council.

Two hours later there was a quiet knock which he acknowledged without turning fully around, assuming it was one of the dear souls who appeared in his life with food and drink. He wondered if he adequately expressed how grateful he was for that. His elegantly fluted ears with their external ear bones told him the person had stopped inside the door, that it was a Papilli male, and that he was not carrying anything. He turned fully around and nodded to the gentleman who stood there, waiting patiently as was their custom. "Forgive me," the Firstlord said quickly, brushing right hand over left. "Ahimsa, I wish thee peace. How may I serve you?"

"I am Pyrgus. I am a physician. May I speak to you for a few minutes?"

"Of course," Ardenai said, gesturing to the table near the window and sending for refreshment. "Please sit. I am thine."

"Before I begin, let me tell you what I do, lest you think me a meddler," he smiled. He was slight and beautiful as were most of his kind, and he reminded Ardenai of Io with his large eyes and quick, infectious grin. Ardenai nodded and he continued. "I am chief physician for that sanecere wing of the Jocundome which deals with mothers and their unborn and newly born children." Ardenai stiffened without meaning to, and Pyrgus dropped his head a little to one side in sympathy. "I know you have become used to bad news, Dragonhorse, and I am sorry for that."

"And you have brought me more?"

Pyrgus shook his head. "I have brought you hope." Again, the door opened with a tap and a young woman appeared with a tray, which she set on the table. "Cloud is one of my babies," Pyrgus said, acknowledging her smile. "And her babies, as well. I've been at this a long time." She poured the drinks and departed and Pyrgus continued. "Io's mother, Luna, was a friend of my family, so I knew her and many of her family members. There is a strange thing that runs in that family, and in many others who choose to marry outside their own species – women die the third day after childbirth."

"I think I noticed that," Ardenai muttered. "Is that what's going to happen to Io?"

"That, is a very long flight from where we are now," Pyrgus admonished. "I do think, however, that had Luna been under the care of Papilli doctors and not the serpentine dragons, she might still be alive. The dragon physicians are amazing creatures, but they created the Equi, not the Papilli. Papilli respond to stress much differently than do Equi, especially the stress of childbirth. Equi babies are heavy. They tax the delicate frame of Papilli women, pushing veins and arteries against the bone."

Ardenai could feel guilt washing over him and hoped Pyrgus couldn't see it lapping in his eyes. "Io is much taller and heavier boned than the average Papilli," he said defensively. "She is more Equi than Papilli."

"But not by much, and as you well know, Papilli blood is dominant, Equi is recessive."

"You are here to make a point," Ardenai said. "I will accept your expertise as stated. Tell me what it is you want me to do."

"I want you to save your wife's life, and the lives of your daughters."

"By?"

"Bringing her here to the Jocundome so we can care for them. The serpentine dragons are doing what they think is best, but I do not agree that it is, nor do my colleagues. We would like to take over her care, under the watchful eye of Pythos, of course," he said, nodding in acquiescence to what Ardenai was preparing to say. "You could see her every day if you so desired, and should a prenatal crisis occur, you would be here as a husband and father should be."

"And if I have to go back to Equus?"

"You would be no further from her than you are now," Pyrgus smiled. He could sense that Ardenai was battling conflicting emotions and applied himself to cider and nectar bread while the Firstlord mulled it over. Interesting people, Equi. They often thought with their eyes, moving them side to side across a surface as though they were reading something.

"Did Abeyan know about this?" Ardenai asked abruptly.

"Yes," Pyrgus nodded, picking up his glass. "He and Luna chose together to have their baby on Equus in the traditional manner, with you and Ah'ree present and Pythos attending."

"We would have been happy to go to Papillia, or anywhere that would have given Luna the best chance for survival," Ardenai said quietly, and Pyrgus could sense his sadness. "Io should have that same chance. I will ask to have her brought here. Will you arrange for her transport so she has Papilli care while she travels?"

"Of course," Pyrgus nodded. "Please do not be overly concerned,

Firstlord. It does no good, and clouds the ability to make decisions."

"No one is an older or dearer friend to me than Physician Pythos. It is his possible reaction to this that has me concerned. Please, do not as much as twitch in the direction of acting on this until I have spoken to him."

"Agreed," Pyrgus said, and gave Ardenai a deep, respectful bow.

Knowing hesitation was not in his best interest where Pythos was concerned the Firstlord wasted no time in seeking him out, finding him sprawled along a branch in the dappled shade of his favorite tree, idly contemplating the river which meandered by their encampment. Ardenai sat with his back against the tree trunk, arms around his updrawn knees, and with all the diplomacy and delicacy he could muster, explained what Pyrgus had said, and told Pythos what he'd decided to do.

For the first time in his long memory of the physician, Ardenai saw Pythos evaporate into anger. He dropped to the ground, towering over the Firstlord, hissing and spitting with rage. "Hundredss of yearss we have sspent together! Hundredss of yearss I carried *you,* and cared for *you* and educated *you*! I have devoted my life to *you,* and now that *you* have rissen to the officce which I made posssible for *you, you* cast assperssions upon my abilitiess and my decissionss? What have I done to desserve ssuch betrayal at your handss?"

"Your words are like a knife in my heart," Ardenai said quietly. "With you I began life, with you I have lived life, and with you I will spend life after this life. How can you think I would betray you? Pythos, please. I am doing what may be best for Io, that's all. If you weren't here, I wouldn't even think of moving her." Not quite the truth, but Ardenai was feeling a twinge of desperation. Being caught between Pythos and Io was something he would not be able to endure. "Please," he said, "please tell me why you are so angry."

"The decission wass mine to make, not thine," Pythos hissed, and Ardenai stopped holding his breath. Pythos was slipping back into his usual speech patterns, dropping the caustic use of 'you,' which probably, hopefully, meant his temper was cooling a little. "It wass I who brought Io into the world ...”

“And did you know that the women in her mother’s family had a propensity for dropping dead on the third day after giving birth?” His answer was an aggravated hiss and a tongue still flicking menacingly. “Did you insist that Abeyan take Luna somewhere safe to give birth? If you did, I never heard about it.”

Challenging his decisions was a mistake. Ardenai could feel the steam in the air. “Pythos, you are father, mother and friend to me. It was you who brought me into the world, too. It was you who delivered Kehailan successfully when his mother struggled to birth him. It was you who closed Luna’s eyes in death. It was you who pried my beloved Ah’ree from my arms, cold and dead. It was you who saved Io from death on Calumet. It was you who brought her back to sanity when she lost her baby. Why do you now see personal insult in my layman’s desire to save my wife and my daughters? I am not a doctor like you, or Ah’din. I must depend on others to help me discern the best path. In Pyrgus’ words I saw hope, and help. He made sense. From Achernar comes nothing but bad news. If you were there, I would feel better, but you are not. You are here. My hope for her is here. Pyrgus gives me yet more hope, because he is Papilli, and a birthing physician of many years. And in you, my old friend, lies all hope, as always.”

Ardenai just...stopped talking and dropped his head as though he had run long and hard. He felt empty, except for the anger which still boiled in the air around him. “In any case, it is done,” he said at last.

If Pythos had struck him he wouldn’t have been surprised, but he didn’t. His breathing gradually quieted, his flickering tongue grew less whip-like. “Thee makess one good point,” he said thoughtfully. In a few minutes he slid gracefully back up into the tree and assumed his previous position. There was a long silence. “Go away.”

Ardenai walked to the edge of the river and vanished in a convolution of maroon and blue.

Going to the blistering hot surface of Lebonath Jas in the middle of the afternoon was not at all what Ardenai wanted to do, but he wasn’t accomplishing much since his dust-up with Pythos, and being an overtly curious person, he allowed Gideon's smile and Criollo's passion to persuade him.

"As a rule, we wouldn't use the scrambleshafts to go anywhere but the Port of Entry," Konik said, looking at the boys and Swift, who had put aside her sanecere duties to join them for the afternoon. "We are going to make an exception today, because I don't want unfriendly eyes seeing us go into what the Lebonathi consider a derelict building. That may be all that's keeping it safe."

Criollo was nearly jumping up and down with excitement, and his excitement lifted the Firstlord's mood. "How wonderful it is to see a young man so inspired about books," he smiled.

"Beware of what might be in those books, literally," Swift cautioned. "We don't know for sure what sorts of creepy crawlies might be haunting the place. We know the snakes are extremely poisonous. Their bite kills in seconds. We know less about the spiders and other bugs, but they may be toxic as well. Hopefully there won't be any snakes."

"Or spiders," Gideon added. He wasn't fond of spiders, especially after that terrifying night on Calumet when Io had been posing as an Aranean, and Gideon had figured he and Ardenai were both dead. He still had nightmares about that, though he never mentioned it because everybody else would think it was funny. It was just Io in her costume from Macbeth. It was also the one time he knew beyond the shadow of a doubt they were going to be raped, mutilated and murdered.

"Coming my boy?" Ardenai asked, and his father's voice brought him back to the present – to being a prince of the Great House of Equus.

"Yes," the boy grinned, and leaned into his sire's shoulder as the scrambleshaft activated.

Because they were Equi, the word library conjured up an image of cleanliness, respect and order that was totally lacking in the sweltering, filthy chaos of toppled shelves and torn pages which greeted them.

"Last time I found people it was back this way," Konik said, pointing with his chin across the long room and down an uninvitingly dark corridor.

He began picking his way through the rubble with Gideon and Ardenai close behind, and it wasn't until they reached the other side and were contemplating the cobwebs in the corridor that they realized Criollo and Swift were no longer with them.

"Look at this!" came Criollo's excited voice. Their heads were already together where Swift had parked herself on a toppled book case, and they were handling an ancient tome with all the delicacy and respect they'd give Menorquin Sea Crystal.

"There are more rooms than just this one," Konik chuckled, but they didn't hear, or didn't acknowledge him. "So much for…" he began, when a jerk of Ardenai's chin caused him to turn and look to the spot where a panel in the wall was sliding back and a doorway was appearing.

"Just like in a storybook!" Gideon breathed.

His foot bumped something and as he turned and stooped to see what it was, an ancient Lebonathi stepped from the paneled doorway and said, "Soft One. You came back."

"I promised I would," Konik smiled.

"Flamen!" the old man cried. "You said you were our friend, and you brought flamen?" He was pointing a terrified finger at Gideon, who had straightened up with a set of wooden beads in his hand.

"No!" Konik exclaimed. "Gideon is Equi." But the door was already closing.

Gideon just stood there with his mouth open. "I am so sorry," he said at last. "It never occurred to me that I look flamen, but I do, don't I?"

"Momentarily and from a distance only," his father soothed. "Come on, that panel can't be too hard to figure out."

"I should stay here," Gideon said.

"No, you should not," Ardenai replied, and Gideon fell obediently into step. They spread out slightly and began running their hands over the wall to find the latch for the panel.

"Maybe it's just on the inside," Gideon said.

"Might be," Konik muttered, "but that wouldn't make sense if it's a way to escape." He raised his voice and added, "You have closed this door in the face of the Thirteenth Dragonhorse," but it availed them nothing.

"I am Ardenai Firstlord. The young man who startled you is my son, Gideon." Still nothing.

"Maybe it's just a way for them to protect the most valuable of the books." Criollo was beside them, carrying the old book he'd found. He slapped the panel impatiently and yelled, "My cousin has blond hair. He can't help it. Please, come out of there and tell me about this book! Please."

The panel crept open and the hoary face peered out. "What book?"

"This one," Criollo said, holding it out and opened to a page. "These look like chemical diagrams. Is this how you view the arrangement of atoms? What is the basis of your structure?"

"That book is nonsense," the old man said. "None of the books out there make any sense. They're props, that's all."

Criollo looked from the book to the man and back to the book with his eyebrows together and his mouth half open. Finally, after a couple of exasperated huffs he said, "Do you have any real books, then?" and put the book in his uncle's outstretched hand.

The Lebonathi thought a few moments in silence, then leaned back the way he had come. "In here," he said, and looked across the room toward Swift, who was still parked on the toppled book shelf. "The female reads?"

Konik sucked his cheeks. "The female reads, yes."

"Bring her along then," he sighed. "She's not safe out here."

Konik looked in Swift's direction. *You, female of the species. This gentleman would like you to accompany us.*

I'm flattered, came the laughing reply, and Swift quickly made her way toward them.

The old man hurried them through the panel and with a furtive glance around the outer room shut it behind them.

"I don't think anyone followed us," Konik soothed. "We didn't walk in here. We used the scrambleshaft." Responding to the look he added, "It moves people unseen from one place to another. We left the dome you see shining in the sky at night, scrambled to one of our ships in orbit, and from there into that room."

The eyebrow said it all. "Of course you did."

Ardenai resisted the pettish urge to give him a demonstration. "I am Ardenai Firstlord. This is my son Gideon, my nephew Criollo, and this is Governor Konik's friend, Swift."

"What kind of a friend?" the old man asked, and there was just the hint of a leer.

Konik cringed a little inside. He'd wondered how long it would take before people began to notice his beautiful and constant companion. He shot a glance at Swift, but if she was embarrassed by the question it didn't show. He took a breath and responded, "The kind of friend who has a great deal of knowledge about books. She and Criollo will treat them with the utmost respect, and all of us would be most grateful to see what you have saved."

Without another word the old man turned, beckoned, and hobbled at a good pace down a long stone corridor which slanted into the darkness. The low, rounded ceiling caused everyone but Swift to travel hunched over, and Gideon had more than enough time to think about spiders before another door appeared out of the gloom. It opened with a fluidity which spoke to regular use, and the five of them followed the Lebonathi into a dim and seemingly endless expanse of undusted bookshelves and the musty smell of old paper. He gestured vaguely, rolled his eyes to indicate his assessment of their mission, and vanished while they were focused on the books.

Criollo and Swift went immediately to the shelves, Ardenai parked a slim hip on the corner of a table and began studying the book Criollo had handed him earlier, and Konik leaned against the wall, allowing his eyes to move slowly around the space.

"What are you thinking?" Gideon asked, hardly above a whisper.

"That this is an excellent place for an ambush," Konik whispered back. "Follow that wall, but don't stoop to look at anything. Keep your head above the shelves. I'll follow this wall and meet you at the other end."

This room, unlike the one they'd entered originally, was long and narrow with stone walls and a barrel-vault ceiling of the same material. It was lower in height and better ordered, but equally devoid of personality or any sign of caring. By the time they met at the far end of the space both Konik and Gideon were pretty sure they'd been duped. Furthermore, they'd come in through the only door, and it was locked.

"So, who did he call when he vanished?" Gideon muttered. "Who's going to come rampaging in here?"

"Probably nobody," said the Firstlord, glancing up from his book. "He's curious. He wants to know if we can really appear and vanish at will." He closed his eyes a moment, and tipped his head slightly toward his dominant left hand. *Kehailan, are you there?*

I am here, came the prompt reply.

If we should want to leave suddenly?

It will be so. Are you in trouble, Sire?

No. I don't think so. We're currently locked in, but the book-mites are having a good time. Do keep an eye on us just in case.

"Talking to my brother?" Gideon grinned. His father's smiling nod and casual attitude toward the place and their circumstances was comforting, and he relaxed enough to help himself to a book. Names, numbers, dates. He chose another. Names, numbers, dates. He walked to another shelf where the covers were a different color and tried again. Names, numbers, dates. "This is the definition of a real book?" he grimaced.

"Absolutely," Swift breathed. "And we were definitely not duped. These are records. They're priceless. Undecipherable at this point, but priceless."

"And the books out in the main part of the library are hardly props, if this is any example," Ardenai said, closing the tome and using one finger to hold his place. "This is exactly what Criollo thought it was, a chemistry book."

"Why would they say it was just a prop, then?" Criollo asked, scowling up from his seat on the stone floor. "Why would they leave valuable books in such disarray?"

"Maybe the same reason the Thirteenth Dragonhorse hid under brown curly hair and a beard," Gideon mused. "To escape detection? It's beyond them to carry the books to safety without being noticed. The next best thing would be to hide them in plain sight under a veil of disregard. Either that, or they're so intellectually stunted that they honestly don't know what a real book is, anymore. I doubt it, though. Did you notice how that old man scanned the room before he closed the door? It was as though he expected someone to walk in."

"Or he feared observation of another kind," the governor said.

"Wonderful," Criollo sighed. "My idea of wanting to clean up the library would be about the worst thing I could do. I feel very foolish and short sighted."

"Not so," Konik soothed. "We are here, and see what we have found already? In that alone is triumph, Criollo. Don't doubt yourself. I'm going to scramble back where we started and have a bit of a looksee."

Two hours of crawling and climbing in a floor to ceiling search turned up two devices of unknown capability, which Konik noted and passed over without reacting. He was sitting on one of the toppled bookshelves mopping the sweat off his face and wishing for ice skates and snowball fights with his grandchildren when a thought struck him and he squeezed one of the crys-tels on the chain around his neck to get Cutter's attention.

Commander Cutter, can you hear me? This is Governor Konik. No words, please.

There was a pause of a few seconds. *Yes, Governor. How may Dragonhorse Equus be of service to you?*

Please scan the room I'm in and tell me if there are any listening or viewing devices present. Use every tool you have and be as thorough as you can. Please relay and ask Belesprit and Captain Eletsky to do the same thing.

Of course, Governor. Right away.

Even telepathically Konik could hear the puzzlement in Cutter's voice. *Thank you,* he said, and gave no more information. He slid off the dirty bookcase, realizing with a grimace of distaste that he'd left a perfect imprint of his butt and thighs in sweat and wondering how much of that ancient dirt and whatever was crawling around in it had soaked through and was now adhered to the most personal parts of his anatomy. He prowled through the jumble of books – thousands of books, upside down, inside out – torn and bleeding remnants of civility and hope. He knew he was being watched; he could feel it on the back of his neck, that other prickle that was not sweat running down his backbone, and he was careful to maintain a posture of disinterest and disdain. A book on art and artists. An encyclopedia of animals. A child's book about the rivers of the world. Onto each of those and others he flicked sweat with his fingertips in passing, leaving a DNA signature for the scrambleshaft.

When Cutter sent the completed scans to him that evening, he studied them awhile then said, "I kind of guessed that's what they'd find."

Swift looked up from where she was stretched out on the hearth rug, studying one of the old books Konik had purloined. "What did he find?"

"Nothing," Konik said. "Absolutely nothing." His eyes narrowed and he sat staring off into space, rubbing absently at the scar Sarkhan had left on his breastbone.

"What are you thinking?"

His answer was a long time in coming. "The same thing I've thought since the day I got here. Things are not what they seem on this world."

"And what does that mean?"

There was another pause. "I don't know yet, but I may be a step closer to finding out."

CHAPTER 6

Ardenai took a deep breath, momentarily touched the spot where his wife had kissed his cheek, and let himself into the primary classroom on Deck Two of the good ship Belesprit. He was concerned that he'd not prepared a lesson, but this was his first day and he wanted to meet the children. He wondered how many of them would be the same ones he'd met as he was returning from Calumet, the day he'd returned to Equus to be instated as the Thirteenth Dragonhorse and take up the reins of the AEW. The day he'd been exposed to the children's disease which had nearly killed him, and which had ultimately taken what was left of his baby daughter from him. He shook himself mentally and grinned as the class stood up. A lifetime of teaching filled his senses, and his whole body relaxed.

"We weckome you, Dwagonhothe," said a little boy whom he recognized as Amir Cohen's son. "We aw happy that you aw going to be our teacho thumtimeth and we would wike to know what to caw you." He responded to a hiss and added, "I am Yuthef Cohen. I was toposed to say that at firsth but you aweady knew me from befoe and I haven't changed my name, tho …." He shrugged, then turned and cast a disparaging eye in the direction of the hisser. "Weynawda ith thuch a thsticklo for pwotocaw."

"I do remember you," Ardenai smiled, "and I remember you, too, Reynalda. I remember most of you, as a matter of fact." He looked up and smiled at the teacher, who was standing well to the back of the room. "Orlov teacher, thank you for letting me come and learn with you today."

Orlov nodded and smiled. "You are welcome. For those of you who do not remember, the Dragonhorse was my teacher when I was your age or a little younger."

Reynalda turned to the speaker. "So, what did you call him back in the olden days?"

"Ardenai teacher, as was proper," Orlov grinned, then raised an eyebrow.

Ardenai nodded. "And that is what you may call me, as well," he chuckled, "though Dragonhorse is fine, too." He seated himself to be at eye level, folded his legs in front of him and beckoned the children to sit around him. "Is there anything you would like to know before we begin this morning?"

Yussef raised his hand and got the nod to speak. "What did you do with the faiwy-wady you thaid wath your wife? Did that one die, too?"

Not at all the question he was expecting, and it registered on Ardenai's face. He thought a moment. "You're talking about Ah'riodin. No, she didn't die like my first wife. She's going to have a baby, and she's staying someplace safe right now so the doctors can take good care of her."

Another hand shot up. Ardenai nodded. "The really, really, REALLY tall beautiful lady? I just saw her yesterday and she did NOT look settled. My mum is settled, and her belly is WAY out here." A gesture accompanied the observation and the young man speaking fixed Ardenai with a penetrating gaze. He knew about such things. "My name is Casey."

Ardenai began to get a sinking feeling. "The very tall beautiful lady is Ah'ren, and you're right. She is not settled."

"But she is your wife?"

"Yes."

"You have TWO wives?" This from Reynalda, who was obviously aghast. There was a ripple of consternation and Ardenai felt his face getting hot. He shot a glance at Orlov, who had his hand over his mouth, shoulders shaking with what was most likely panic-induced laughter. He wasn't going to be any help. Ardenai made a quick decision, exhaled a good deal of air that was tinged with his own panic and said, "I do have two wives. Ah'riodin is small and has hair the color of a fresh, ripe peach. Ah'ren is tall, with hair the color of a raven's wing. Io and Wren, my butterfly and my bird, and I love them both very much."

"Why would you do that?" Casey asked, his face twisted with the puzzlement of it all.

"The ancient laws of Equus and Mountain hold tell me what I must and must not do, and one of the things I must do as Dragonhorse, is have three wives."

"Well, that's just mean," Casey responded, and followed up with an enigmatic sigh.

"Not really," Ardenai said. "The longer I am Dragonhorse, the more I can see the wisdom in it, though it was very hard for me at first. I need a lot of help with my job, and I need to be in a lot of different places, sometimes at the same time. My wives are part of me, and they can represent me, and help me make wise decisions."

There was a momentary silence while this was digested. Yussef's hand went up. Ardenai nodded. "I justht have to asthk," he said apologetically. "Ith it weally weiod having two wifeths?"

Ardenai nodded and grinned. "It really is, but I'm trying to get used to it."

"You're supposed to have THREE wives," Reynalda observed. "Where's number three? Aren't you breaking with tradition by having only two?"

Ardenai gave her an exaggerated gasp and said, "Patience if you please, Mistress! Finding just the right partner is time-consuming. You seem very smart. Maybe I'll just wait another forty years or so for you to grow up."

"You can't have me," she sniffed. "I'm going to marry Yussef. That is if he ever gets his teeth back. I don't want the responsibility of feeding a man with no teeth."

Yussef just rolled his eyes and shook his head. "I don't know how you do it," the child muttered. "I weally don't."

A girl with elongated Menorquin limbs and gorgeous lavender eyes said, "I am Coral. Are Lebonathi children like us?"

Ardenai sighed with relief and smiled at her. "That's a very good question, Coral. Can you tell me a bit more about what you want to know?"

"Well," she contemplated her response. "Do they look like us, do they act like us? Do they play games like us?"

"We ought to go thee them and thay hewwo," Yussef observed. "Or they could come and thee uth."

"Let's talk about how we could do that," Ardenai said, and it felt like mere seconds before a smiling Ah'ren was opening the classroom door, indicating that it was time to go. He said his goodbyes to the children, promised to return the following week and stepped into the hallway. The door shut behind him and he sagged into her and burst into peals of the merriest, most contagious laughter she'd ever heard come out of him.

"It was awful!" he managed, nearly choking as he leaned into her. "It was absolutely horrific! All my nightmares about appearing in the classroom naked, drooling and painted blue were realized and eclipsed in that hour."

She patted his back and laughed with him until he reached the snorting, snickering stage. "Are you going back?"

"Of course I am," he grinned, spun her around, kissed her thoroughly, and walked her down the corridor in the direction of the scrambleshafts. "The children brought up some good points, and I realize I don't know enough about Lebonathi children. They really are the hope in all this, you know."

"What did they want to know?"

"What children always want to know," Ardenai mused. "Are they like us, and in what ways?" He walked a bit in silence and then smiled. "Children are such wise and beautiful creatures. They don't ask, 'How are they different from us?' They always ask, 'How are they like us?' We could learn so much from the little ones."

It was a segue for Ah'ren to bring up Io's transfer from Achernar to the Jocundome, and perhaps to ask her husband about the deep and painful rift which had opened up between him and Pythos, but she got as far as, "Speaking of children," and thought better of it. He was so happy at this moment, it seemed a shame to take it from him. She had his attention, and an inky eyebrow told her he was waiting. "Sorry, I distracted myself," she smiled, hoping she could dazzle him long enough to think of something. "You…may have a couple of insiders in this. Kehailan is going down to play a game called Lightning with the Lebonathi boys, and Jobie – Dahman's boy – is going down every day with lunch for the school that's next to that big dirty field. The one that had the glastaline dome in it."

Ardenai winced a bit at the memory of that dome and the pain it held. "I know Jobie. He's the same age as Gideon. They, along with Criollo, make quite the threesome. I'm a little surprised that Dahman lets him go to the surface."

"He does look slightly like a big spinklemaus," Ah'ren agreed, "but he's got Dragonhorse personnel with him, and quite often that includes Kee, so I think he's safe."

"Good. Because, 'slightly like a big spinklemaus,' is an epic understatement," Ardenai said, and grinned as Marion Eletsky hailed them, inviting lunch and a confab before they left the ship.

Jobie considered himself safe as well, trotting along next to Kehailan and rather enjoying the attention being in the company of the big, handsome captain brought him. Everyone it seemed knew who Kehailan was. Son of the Thirteenth Dragonhorse. Romantically linked to the beautiful Lebonathi Princess Eridi. There was rumor that it was he who would take the throne of Lebonath Jas, with Eridi at his side.

Just now they were on a mission together. Master Gilim had told them of another school which existed in the dim maze of subterranean streets and buildings, and Kehailan had decided they should try to find it and see how they were doing. Were their lunches being stolen, as well? The very thought of it annoyed the captain. He'd asked Master Gilim for a guide, and now a rather reluctant Anmar trotted just half a step in front of them, head down, pretty much ignoring passersby, but keenly aware of the notice being with the powerful Equi garnered. In his case, it was not welcome. It flustered him and divided his attention. He turned them left into a long, sloping corridor that grew darker and darker and more and more twisted and empty until he finally stopped and admitted that he'd gotten them lost.

Kehailan smiled and said they weren't lost, they just weren't in the right spot, and turned them around to head back up. It was then that Kehailan and Jobie both heard the sound – a faint mewing – but the Lebonathi had no lithopeds, no real pets of any kind, only mechanical ones. No adult voice accompanied the whimper. "That sounds just like my new baby sister," Jobie whispered.

They looked at each other and began to follow the sound down a side corridor, though Anmar's eyes were wide with fear and he begged them not to go. "We'll be fine," Kehailan said, patting the tab on his harness to reassure the boy.

"That won't help if it's diseased or deformed," Anmar insisted. "Just leave it alone. It's the law."

Now Kehailan was alarmed. The Lebonathi abandoned babies to die and everybody knew and accepted it? He heard Jobie chitter with dismay and knew he'd heard the same thing. They pressed on but not too fast, moving as quietly as they could. Jobie's sensitive nose was twitching, his eyes darting from side to side along the ancient stone corridor.

"There's dead stuff in here," he whispered, and was comforted when Kehailan's hand came to rest on his shoulder. "Maybe…here?" he said, pointing to a small hole at the base of the crumbling stonework. He dropped to his belly and wiggled in, barely clearing the opening. As his feet flattened out behind him, he felt Kehailan's strong grip close around one ankle.

"No further than that," the captain said.

Jobie stuck his arms out in front of him and found fabric. It was slightly warm and damp. He pulled it toward him and grunted at Kehailan to pull him out. They squatted together in the comparative light of the corridor and unwrapped the bundle of rags. It was a newborn. Kehailan's finger told him the little heart was still beating, that the child still drew breath. "Take it, quickly!" he exclaimed, handing the bundle to Jobie. "Jocundome, Sanecere!" he said and pulled the strap on Jobie's harness, setting the relay in motion. Jobie and the baby disappeared.

"If anybody finds out you did this. That I was with you," Anmar moaned. "Oh Gods!"

"Nobody is going to find out unless you tell them," Kehailan muttered, "Let's get out of here and go find that school before anyone sees us. You can explain this to me later."

Jobie sprang off the scrambleshaft platform and streaked down the main hallway of the sanecere, yelling, "Help! Help! Somebody help me, please!"

Swift dropped what she was doing and ran to intercept him in his flight. "What's wrong?" she asked, scooping him to a halt. "Jobie, what's the matter? What have you got there?"

"Oh, I'm so glad it's you! We found this baby! Help this baby!" he exclaimed, holding out the little bundle.

Swift took it quickly into an examination room, Jobie beside her. She got one look at it and despaired. It was not a day old, not more than three or four pounds and still covered with blood. The umbilicus had been neither clamped nor tied and it was a miracle the child had not died immediately. It squirmed and made sucking sounds, mewing piteously. Swift glanced down at Jobie. "Where did you find her?"

"Shoved in a wall," he whispered. "They shoved her in a wall. Why would anybody shove a baby in a wall and leave it?" He blinked and two big tears ran down his cheeks. "Why would anybody shove a baby in the wall?"

"That's a very good question," Swift muttered, and paused to give him a kiss on the top of his fuzzy head. "You did exactly the right thing." She put the infant under a heat lamp, called Pyrgus, and began to sponge it with warm water.

"It's hungry," Jobie said. "My mother could feed it. She has milk."

"That's a wonderful idea on so many levels," Swift said, "but we don't know if Taraxian milk will help her, or kill her. Help me think. What else could we do?"

"We could call Ensharra. She must know somebody with milk."

"And even if that person isn't willing to nurse the baby, she might let us have enough milk to analyze," Swift smiled. "You're hired, my fine Taraxian. Go find Ensharra and tell her what we need."

"Absolutely," he said with a jaunty salute. "Uh…how do I do that, exactly?"

"Get the governor to help you," she said absently, and bent her attentions to the baby.

Ordinarily he'd have enjoyed the trot down the gracefully curved cobblestone streets to the Administrative Offices, but today he said, "Governor," pulled the strap on his harness, and found himself standing precariously on the edge of Governor Konik's desk.

Konik looked up from the data he had spread out in front of him and grinned. "Hello Jobie. Learning the ins and outs of the scrambleshaft patterns, are we?"

"I guess we are," Jobie said, jumping backward off the desk to land beside it. "I'm sorry. Swift told me to find you in a hurry."

Konik's eyes widened a little. "Is there a problem?"

"I need to find Anchoress Ensharra," the boy said. "Right now. A baby is dying and we need Lebonathi mother's milk, and Ensharra might know somebody."

Konik asked no questions. He trotted with Jobie to the scrambleshaft pad, spoke a code which activated a relay, and two minutes later they were standing beside the lake at Stone Spring, with Ah'din and Ensharra hurrying to meet them.

"Tell all of us," Konik said. Jobie gave them the shortened version, emphasizing the need for milk, and Ensharra immediately turned and went back to the pavilions, calling for Larsa.

"This is beautiful," Jobie said, looking around. "This is Lebonath Tras?" Konik nodded, but there was no time for exploration. Ensharra and Larsa were back at a run, Umma bouncing on Larsa's hip. Ah'din and Ensharra waved them off, and they were back on the Jocundome, this time in the sanecere. The whole trip had been less than ten minutes.

Jobie was a little in awe as he looked up at the governor. "How did you know where to find Ensharra so fast?"

"I didn't," Konik replied. "I knew where to start looking for Larsa."

They sat for a while together and played with Umma while Larsa went with Swift and Pyrgus, and Jobie told Konik the whole story, starting with Kehailan and him looking for the school, and the part about getting lost, and how worried Anmar had been that they were breaking the law by looking for the baby. Konik just nodded, holding Umma on his forearms and gently bouncing one knee and then the other as she drifted off to sleep.

"I know you're busy," Jobie said. "I can hold her if you need to get back to work."

"Much as I hate to give her up, you're right," Konik sighed. "Can you handle this?"

"I can," he grinned, and took the baby as Konik stood up.

"You did good work today," Konik smiled. "I'm glad you and your family are here."

He took the time to walk to his office, because he wanted to think. He could smell the lingering, milky fragrance of Umma, and wondered what kind of mentality it would take to stuff a baby in a wall and leave it to die. What kind of fear, or disregard for life? He just shook his head. He'd handled his daughters like they were Menorquin Sea Crystal, one cradled in each arm, and he'd looked at them and marveled. If they so much as squeaked he was there, or Ah'davan was there, or they were both there. When his grandchildren had been born – his babies having babies – doubly precious. Why, how, could anybody stuff a baby in a wall and leave it to starve to death?

He'd nearly passed his building when he remembered to veer off and go inside. He nodded to Ah'ren and Ardenai, but didn't stop to chat. Instead, he went into his office, closed the door, cleared his desk and activated his communications system. The request to talk was answered by a young woman who was sitting near the fireplace, a child asleep on the rug at her feet. A man was reading close by. She gasped when she saw his face, and then smiled, setting her needlepoint aside. She looked just like her mother. "You're beautiful," Konik breathed. "Hello, Ah'rika. I've missed you so much."

Swift was not there when he got home. He wondered if the baby's arrival had put her behind in her work. He thought about going to one of the dining rooms for dinner, decided Swift might be too tired, and set about preparing a simple meal of the kind the Equi most enjoyed: a hearty soup, crusty bread, crisp vegetables, a fresh pot of tea and a little something sweet. He was just finishing up when the door opened and Swift appeared.

"And he cooks," she smiled, but only momentarily. He could tell it was an effort.

"Lose the baby?" he asked gently.

She nodded. "We did everything we could. She will be valued in death. Her body will provide us with many answers to Lebonathi physiology, and we now have a chemical breakdown of mother's milk. I just…" She shook her head and walked wearily into Konik's arms. He held her for a bit, rocking her gently from side to side and kissing the top of her head. "Jobie was broken-hearted when I told him," she said at last, "and Kehailan was furious. He's ready to use Dragonhorse Thirteen to take the place apart stone by stone and see how many other babies are stuffed in there."

Konik did not mention that he was more than ready to help him. "I talked to both my girls this afternoon," he said, and Swift began to sob softly against his shoulder.

"You, are worn out. You need food," Konik said. "And a warm bath and a good massage."

"But first, I need a good cry," she sniffed, and she could feel him nod.

"You may have that, as well," he murmured. "I may join you."

^ ^ ^ ^ ^ ^ ^

Ardenai's description of his encounter with the children made his mother laugh until the tears ran down her cheeks and she stamped her feet and gasped for air, and the family laughed to see her laughing so hard. That's when Kehailan showed up. He came stalking across the grass from the point where he'd materialized and dropped with a thud into his place at the dinner table. All eyes turned his direction. He sat staring at his hands and then said, "Those miserable, stinking..." There was a pause. "They bury their children alive. They shove them into holes in the walls and leave them to starve. Their babies. Their newborns!" He felt his father turn to ice beside him. "Jobie and I found one of them today. Swift did all she could to save it, but it died – this beautiful little girl – brand new. I swear to the gods of the universe, I just want to open fire on those people. I just want to cleanse this planet of their filth and start over again." He exhaled sharply, wiped angrily at his eyes, and sat a moment to compose himself. When he finally caught his breath and looked around, he realized there was a guest at the dinner table. "I am so sorry!" he exclaimed, giving her a wry smile. "Please forgive my outburst. I'm Kehailan. Kehailan the Uncouth, by title."

"I'm Ah'cora," she replied. "Please don't apologize to me for being angry about a dead baby. That's horrible."

"Then I apologize to all of you," he said. "I could have been more civil in my explanation."

"And now that you've blown off the worst of the pressure, do tell us the story," Ardenai drawled, and his eyes were not at all pleasant.

While they ate, Kehailan told the story from beginning to end, answered their questions, mentioned Jobie's comment about smelling dead things, and ended on a lighter note by telling them he and Anmar had found the school they sought, and that there were both boys and girls in attendance in their separate venues. They hadn't received any of the promised foodstuffs, either.

"It sounds like you need someone to take on the schools as a Dragonhorse Project," Krush observed, passing around dessert. "Someone to go and sniff them out one by one, each school pointing to the next like the first school pointed to the second. Inside information is what you need. Working from the outside looks good and garners praise, but working from the inside a bit at a time is what will get the results you seek."

"I agree," Ardenai nodded, and his dimples asserted themselves as he glanced sideways at his sire. "I so wish I knew someone wise enough to take on such a task. You know, someone who could find the schools, assess their needs, and assign a team to bring them provender each day. That would take a very special kind of person."

"What *is* that smell?" Krush replied, and the table was once again laughing.

Ah'ren and Ah'cora insisted that they could handle the mapping of the keeps, and Ah'rane said she had access to some excellent if ancient city maps that could be used. Gideon said he'd been wanting to explore the city and meet the people, and that whomever decided to do this thing would have his company. Providing of course it was someone he liked a great deal.

"Not that anybody's twisting your arm," Teal chuckled. He looked tired, and admitted he'd been hobbled to his desk, sifting through personnel records in search of a new Master of Cavalry. "I'm looking forward to beginning our exploration of the abandoned continents tomorrow," he said, setting aside his tea cup. "As a matter of fact, I think I'll take a swim and turn in early."

"I know you probably didn't have a chance to look at Padmar," Ah'cora said shyly. "Maybe when you get back?"

"I did look at Padmar," Teal smiled. "I think it would do him a world of good to come down here and be turned out to graze on some of this excellent grass, and enjoy the fresh air and sunshine."

"That would be wonderful," Ah'cora replied, "but…I want to spend as much time with him as I can."

"This is a two-minute relay from the Jocundome," Ardenai chuckled, "so that's hardly a concern."

"And it's your private space as a family," Ah'cora reminded him.

"You're not going to want me under foot all the time."

"You are working very closely with my wife. I'm sure in a few days you'll blend right in with the rest of us," the Firstlord smiled.

Ah'cora returned the smile and dropped her eyes. "Thank you," she said. "I'd like that."

"It's settled then," Teal said, rising from the table. "We'll work out the details when we get back from our jaunt." He held out his hand to Ah'din and they wandered off in the direction of their favorite swimming hole.

"I should go, too," Ah'cora said. "I'm on a pretty steep learning curve right now and I need my sleep."

"I'll go with you," Kehailan said. "I can apologize again for acting the ass."

"And I can tell you how I really feel about people who murder their children," she muttered. "I suppose I should also mention in advance that I have a temper and the vocabulary that goes with it."

They both took their leave, Krush and Ah'rane excused themselves to retire, and the two boys were rising to head downriver to their own pavilion when Ardenai gave Criollo a look that went right through him. The boy sighed and sat back down.

"Something you fear will be an unwelcome comment has been festering all evening," his uncle said gently. "What's on your mind?"

"I just think hating the Lebonathi is not the way to win them," he said, and there was a hint of defensiveness in his tone.

"Anger is not hatred," Ardenai admonished. "Kehailan is your kindred spirit. He loves Eridi as you love Jasreth. You know this. Something bigger is on your mind. Speak."

Criollo gave his thoughts due consideration, then said, "I know from examining Lebonathi law – pardon – Flamen law with Kehailan, that babies who are disfigured are to be abandoned; in their terms, 'Sacrificed to the gods, that they may be healed and made queens and goddesses.'"

Gideon was leaning against a tree just outside the circle of lamplight, idly stroking Lionel and listening to the conversation. Now he spoke.

"Jobie told me there wasn't a single thing wrong with that baby girl. She was perfect."

"My point exactly," Criollo said, and met his uncle's gaze. "These people know we can kill them on a moment's notice, wipe their minds, and destroy their culture. We tell them they are grossly overpopulated for the space they are occupying, that two children must be the rule. What if this was a third child, or a fourth or fifth? What if we caused this? What if we killed that innocent little soul with our rhetoric? My grandsire is right. We need to be working in small ways, from the inside out." He dropped his head and examined his fingernails. "These are good people, Dragonhorse. Good people with bad people controlling them. I don't want us to be just another form of bad. We can't be right simply because we think we are."

There was silence while Ardenai sat, nodding slowly and staring off into the darkened woods. "I appreciate your words, Nephew. You and the governor think much alike. Stay with him and he will show you better than any man alive how to act with reason and integrity upon your principles." Ardenai shifted in his chair and smiled to break the mood. "Do you gentlemen have all your equipment ready for tomorrow morning?"

"No. Well, yes. Maybe," they said, more or less in tandem, and Ardenai waved them off in the direction of their sleeping quarters. "And I need to get Lionel packed for his sleepover with Jobie," Gideon added. He kissed his father goodnight, gave Ah'ren a brief hug, and followed Criollo.

"Well, there go the last of them, and we're stuck with each other," Ah'ren sighed.

"Horrors," Ardenai murmured, catching her around the waist as she walked by and pulling her down across his lap. "Have I told you how much I appreciated your advice to get back into teaching? That was so kind of you, and so astute. Despite the gist of the conversation today, I had a wonderful time."

"Your laughter told me you did," she said, tracing his aquiline profile in the dim light. "You seemed genuinely happy."

"I was, and I am. Every day despite it all. Mostly because of you,

Wren."

"And yet you keep things from me," she murmured, stroking his hair back into its braid. "You and my father, Pythos, are both so very sad, but neither of you will tell me what has transpired." Her answer was a sharp exhalation and eyes that moved off her gaze. "Swift tells me the sanecere is preparing to receive Ah'riodin, because Pyrgus persuaded you to transfer her here from Achernar."

"Oh, all right," Ardenai muttered, and looked at her again. "Yes, he did. He seems to think they can give her better care here, her personal physician is here, and her husband is here. I just...I want to see her. I need to see her breathing. I need to see her belly swell and know those babes are real. I can't leave here for seasons yet, Wren. I'm committed to at least two years of active campaigning. I may make it home a time or two for a few days. If she's here I can be with her. We can be with her."

"So why is our father Pythos so angry and so hurt?"

"Aw, precious Equus, I don't know! I tried to explain my motives as best I could. He told me to go away, and I did. I haven't seen him since. Apparently, you have."

"I have. Now I can honestly say I've met the Jade Python of legend. Stony and cold."

"It comforts me to know he's close, though, and that he's safe." Ardenai said, scooting Ah'ren off his lap and getting to his feet.

"He would never be far away from you, his precious hatchling," she said, and slid her arms around his neck. His lips found the side of her neck and his hands slid inside her tunic, his thumbs caressing her nipples as she sighed with pleasure. "If anybody comes back for a snack, we'll be in the way here," she whispered, "though that table does look inviting."

"Mmmmm," he responded, but he dropped his hands and walked her toward their pavilion, where he spun her gently around and with practiced hands removed her tunic and underbodice. His hands were shaking as he stroked her, and she wondered if he was building toward another heat cycle. This is the one that would tell the tale – had they been successful in quelling the Imperial Dragonhorse? And if Ardenai was building heat, was Ah'din escalating as well, and Ah'rane? What if Teal took off for Equus and Ah'din went into heat while he was gone? What a situation that would be. And where was Kehailan in all of this? He'd changed so much of late.

"You have no idea what I'm doing, do you?" Ardenai chuckled.

She responded by sliding down the front of him and releasing him from his trousers. She ran her tongue languidly up the length of his extended phallus and flicked the head gently a few times, as though she were licking off icing, before applying lips and tongue. She felt his hands on the sides of her head and increased the motion, allowing his phallus farther down her throat. He made a sound that was almost pain, then gasped with relief. The trembling subsided. He pulled her back to her feet and kissed her, long and deep, then tossed his tunic aside, removed the rest of his clothes, and impatiently helped her out of the remainder of her garments.

He pointed toward the priapic bench, a gesture barely visible in the dimness of the tent. "If you don't mind," he said. She crouched, positioned forearms and knees and presented up to him in the traditional manner. He was quick to cover her, quick to release, resting only momentarily before beginning to pump again. This was mating, not recreational lovemaking, and she made note of it.

After a while he withdrew and moved them to the low platform of their fleecy bed, asking what would please her. She put him on top so their sweat mingled and her breasts felt the movement of his body as he pushed into her. As she often did in lovemaking, she reached up to caress his face, and as her hand paused, she felt the chuckle start in his belly. "No," he said, "My temperature is not up. I'm not in season, or anywhere close. I'm just in love. And, I must admit, I'm working off a little stress that my morning run doesn't seem to assuage."

"Still, it's part of my job," she whispered, and pulled him down to kiss him. Though she saw no more signs of heat in him, she reminded herself to keep a closer eye on the Dragonhorse blood in the family, and decided she should probably let Kestrel and the others know they were getting close.

Probably time to have an uncomfortable conversation with Teal and Krush, as well.

CHAPTER 7

Considerably less than half of Lebonath Jas was water, and almost none of that was fresh. There were four huge continents, and only the northernmost one was occupied. The Lebonathi had abandoned all the rest, packing themselves together as though they feared space and privacy, even as they bred themselves toward extinction.

The continent which straddled the equator was the largest, longer than wide, and uninhabitable because of the intense heat. According to the Child's Book of Rivers, it was called Anurash, and from all indicators, it had not been occupied past a few long-extinct nomads and some largely unpalatable brush for over a thousand years. There were two cities located on the far, southwestern tip of the continent that were made from the same stone as the foundations they had found at Stone Spring, smaller, lighter in color and weight than the later stonework which had built the cities to the north.

It was those southern cities, and those lighter stones the governor considered when he thought of building materials for Lebonath Tras. The archeology must be done first, of course, and any research, and he was pushing hard for that to get finished. He was disappointed that they weren't starting there, but acquiesced with his usual grace.

The smallest continent – the one probably called Enki-Dara – was still huge and ran northwest to southeast nearly from one pole to the other. It had tall, rugged mountains and dry lake beds of great depth, with towns and small cities tucked neatly into the valleys and spread along the seashore. It had once been heavily forested, and to the Equi it seemed the most likely one to have retained its population, but it, too, stood empty. The sensors on Belesprit indicated there was water below the surface, and Ardenai held out hope that it could be recolonized rather quickly.

Only one of the continents seemed to have a name the Lebonathi recognized – the Old Man's Face. It was spoken of in legend and was supposedly the beginning of all things. According to the book it was called Shala-Anshar, and at its northernmost point it came close to touching the southeast corner of the occupied continent the Equi had been calling Carillia, after the Planetary Capital, and which was – again, with no certainty –probably called Namen. On the old man's face were the scars of civilization – cities, towns, what must have been huge orchards, farms and factories, and there was conjecture that it had probably been the agricultural hub of the planet. It was here that they had decided to begin their explorations.

This was a concerted effort to find out all they could about why the Lebonathi had abandoned most of their world and their way of life. Pathetically few anecdotal records remained, as though someone had systematically destroyed the Lebonathi past. Where had the animals gone? What had happened to their agriculture, their educational system, their government? Who had allowed the last tree to be cut, the last well to be drained? These people were stalled, and had been. They'd not made any progress for probably hundreds of years. Their intelligence was slipping backward, their morality was polarized between religion and violence. Had someone interfered? If you asked Governor Konik, he'd have said yes immediately. Teal would have shrugged, but nodded. Ardenai's mind was still going in a hundred different directions with no one thought on the matter taking precedence. Hopefully, a few days from now, they'd have enough information to make at least some informed assumptions.

So they gathered, a thousand strong – twenty teams of fifty – and listened to Ardenai's instructions.

"Find anything you can: artifacts, machinery, plant life, books, skeletons, tools. Anything that will answer the questions about who they were before and why they left to become what they currently are."

Even as he spoke, he realized how blessed he was that the Equi and most of the Affined Equi Worlds required twenty-one years of compulsory education before Lycee, which could take another five to ten years. Most of these people were experts, and all of them could take complex instructions and act on them.

Amberians were the knowledgeable ones on warfare and machinery. Menorquins would be able to figure out what had happened to the water. Papilli would study remnants of plant life and how the sun and manmade chemicals had affected it. The Taraxians fit anywhere, and their sharp eyes and twitching noses missed very little. Phyllans could recognize animal life where no one else could. Terrenes and Demetrians knew a great deal about how societies functioned, Anguines how governments worked. Calumets and Equi knew agriculture. The Corvi were meticulous recorders. With the exception of Taraxia, all were AEW. All were here because they had volunteered. In every group of fifty were half a dozen or more from each Affined World, and a sprinkling of Taraxians and Declivians from the Seventh Galactic Alliance.

Ardenai, with Teal and Konik beside him, nodded and dismissed the assemblage to the three big horse transports refitted for the purpose – two and a half ships for people, half a ship for initial lab analysis and medical triage if needed. Every person was recording every minute of exploration, and those recordings and their keeping were the special province of Marion Eletsky and Timothy McGill on Belesprit, and Cadence Holofernes and her wife Merrilina on Dragonhorse Five. The relay ships remained in place, and the time from surface to any ship in orbit and thence to the Jocundome was a matter of minutes. Still, Ardenai took Dominus along, just in case. Several people had teased that he just wanted a way to go home early, and he had laughed and agreed, but knowing he had that firepower right in his hands, and that speed and technology, made him feel better. This felt more like exploring another planet than another continent. Lebonath Tras wasn't nearly as alien as the ancient cities broiling below them under the angry orange sky.

Ardenai had wanted to bring Naram along, and the Regent had agreed to come, but his hands were still painful and largely useless, so Ardenai had put him off a day or two, just until they knew what they were getting into. Ah'din and Ensharra were in the middle of something they didn't care to leave. Ah'ren had wanted one more day with Ah'cora, though Krush had said he'd keep her company and save his school project until everybody got back. Swift had said she still had sad duties to perform with the baby girl and had begged off going for the day. Both Wren and Swift promised they'd steal a ship and be along on the morrow. Today it was just the menfolk – Ardenai, Teal and Konik, Gideon, Criollo and Jobie, who had pleaded his case for going so eloquently that Dahman and Ardenai had finally agreed, and Lionel had found himself in the tender care of Krush and company. Ah'cora had proven herself an instant pushover, and the tiny terrier had been settled contently belly-up beside her on the map table as Gideon left.

They'd timed their departure so they could drop the teams before sunrise. It was still hot, but the sun was not beating down with full ferocity. Ten teams in the first city, ten more broken down in the surrounding towns and countryside. The huge ships hovered, scrambling personnel to various positions, then landed close by and rolled out the small craft so they'd be ready to go in case of emergency. A lot could happen, and all three adults warned the boys about poisonous snakes, falling stones, empty wells…

Criollo finally smiled and said, "Thank you so much for your concern. We know we will be in danger every minute, but remember, we will be with you. Gideon with his sire, Jobie with mine, and I will be with our good governor. We know you will keep us safe."

"But we thought you were going to keep us safe," Teal grinned. "Let's get going before it gets too hot."

Ardenai and Gideon chose what may have been a factory farm, Teal and Jobie decided to scout around a hamlet on the banks of a dry lake bed, and Konik and Criollo returned with Dominus to the city to see if they could find government buildings or a library. They probed for a while with the sensors, then landed in an open space and made their way on foot down a street perfectly ready to accept traffic. The hot, dry air had preserved everything. Except for a thick layer of sand covering the roadway and drifting against the sides of buildings, it could have been a city asleep, awaiting the first rays of the sun. They half expected to see baker's stalls opening to welcome customers, and when two Amberians came around the corner of a building, both Konik and Criollo jumped.

"The mighty explorers," Konik laughed, giving Criollo a gentle slap on the shoulder.

A Terren officer called across the street, "Governor, you need to see this," and beckoned them through a doorway into a room that, aside from the drifted sand, might have been used the day before. It was an office of some kind, with maps and posters on the wall, desks in place, equipment accounted for. Books on the shelves, papers in the drawers. Konik stood for a long time and stared at it. "Did these people move, or were they removed?" he asked. "Is this real, or is it staged for our benefit?"

Criollo said nothing. He just stood with his mouth slightly ajar, eyes working their way around the room.

"Put everything else on hold," Konik said to the woman who'd beckoned them over. "Bend every team to finding a school, or a library."

"Why?" the boy asked.

"They'd be the hardest things to fake. Come on, let's keep going."

"Why would they, whomever they may be, fake something like this?"

"To divert our attention? To make us think we've found something so we'll spend our time here and not look further? To plant information, or misinformation, they want found in case any Lebonathis get adventurous and come exploring on their own? Choose one."

Criollo nodded. "What seems easy rarely is, I guess," he sighed, and walked with Konik out into the sweltering heat and the path they'd first been following.

Gideon and Ardenai were not at all confused by what they'd found, though they were dismayed. They stood contemplating the interior of the slaughterhouse on the factory farm they'd chosen to explore. The place still stank of death and the floors were stained black with blood. Somehow a few rats lived here and found things to eat, perhaps each other, perhaps something else. The thought made Gideon shudder. Based on the size of the equipment, they'd decided it was a place for processing small animals, probably poultry. He could see the assembly line where animals had been hung alive, had their throats cut, and been scalded in vats while still struggling.

"Can we get out of here, please?" he asked, and Ardenai nodded.

"Let me get a couple samples of things and I'll meet you outside."

"Do you…need help?"

"I do not," Ardenai chuckled. "I take it you're no longer the meat eater I met all those seasons back."

"Ugh," the boy grimaced, "I may never eat anything again. Ever." He turned, gave the Firstlord a weak wave and trotted toward the huge open door, shaking his head to remove the images he'd conjured.

He stood in the shade until Ardenai joined him, then said, "It seems odd to me that they continued to slaughter big animals, but not smaller ones. For all we know the poultry that was here is now extinct."

His sire nodded and took a drink from his hip canteen. "It is a little odd," he said, offering the canteen to Gideon. "But processing small animals, where one animal wouldn't feed a family for more than one meal, might not have been as efficient as processing large animals, where one animal could feed a family for months."

"Large animals eat a lot more than small animals," Gideon countered, refusing the canteen with one upraised hand.

"Maybe it's what they ate, not how much," Ardenai said, and jerked his chin in the direction of a long, low building that looked a lot like their sheep dairy buildings back on Viridia. For a moment that realization made him intensely homesick. "Maybe as food production fell, the Caronai found ways to survive on what was left. Marion still swears they're closer to giant swine than anything else, and he may well be right. They did eat some pretty amazing and, I might add, disgusting things – date palm leaves, pressed bars of mushrooms and human waste…"

"Dad, stop." Gideon said. "So, everybody subsisted on mushrooms and dates, or did until you came?

"Actually, mushrooms are an amazing food source. They're high in nutrition, many varieties are medicinal, several varieties will actually eat waste, including petrochemical residue. Dates are high in carbohydrates and essential nutrients, and they're growing outside in absolutely blistering conditions. But as one's primary foods, along with those long white tubers and half-rotted Caronai flesh, not so good. Not enough color in the diet."

A few more steps took them to the doorway of the long shed and they paused a moment for their eyes to adjust before stepping inside.

"Oh…" Ardenai ended with a groan, and Gideon gagged and turned away. The shed was heaped with thousands of birds, left to die, and perfectly mummified by the desert heat.

"I hate these people," Gideon whispered. "I'm sorry, but I do. I'm going back to Canyon keep with my grandsire and raise horses and never step foot on this benighted planet again as long as I live."

"So much for understanding another culture," Ardenai replied, snapping on a pair of gloves. "Aren't you even a little curious as to why they would do such a thing as this? What happened to cause a farmer to do this to his animals? And what are these things, exactly? I'm going to go get one. I don't have a specimen bag large enough, so I'm just going to carry it along with me. I hope that doesn't bother you."

Gideon hung his head and sighed. He was the son of the Thirteenth Dragonhorse. He had attitudes he couldn't afford. A thought struck him. "So, why didn't the rats eat these birds?"

Ardenai just shook his head and laughed. "I love you," he said. "I'll be right back."

They went next to a low stone farmhouse, octagonal in shape with two elongated sides, set into a rise above the barns. A small building close by contained equipment which said it was a pump house, and a straggle of sticks and fallen trees spoke to shade and ornament around the dwelling. Ardenai set the bird aside and they went cautiously, testing each of the three steps leading up to the front door. Again, the dryness had preserved the wood, and they crossed the porch and entered the house with only a few squeaks and groans from the long unused boards.

"This house could be on Declivis or Demeter and not look much different," Gideon observed as they stepped into the living space.

"Or Terren, or Equus," Ardenai murmured, but his sharp, draconic eyes were busy with the details and any signs of potential danger. There was a rug covering the wood on the floor, pillows piled on low platforms used for seating – small things which spoke to comfort. There were shelves containing well-thumbed books of various kinds, which indicated an educated family, fond of reading. In the corner was a neatly stowed box of toys.

A few steps took them into the kitchen, and while much of the equipment was unfamiliar, there were pots and pans which spoke to a variety of foods being prepared. A side door opened onto a patio which had once had vines thick above it on an arbor, and here, too, was a place to cook, probably in hot weather, and a table with benches.

"They didn't take anything with them," Gideon observed. "They could walk right back in here, clear away the dust, and go back to their daily lives."

"So where did they go and why?" Ardenai muttered. He was beginning to get a bad feeling, which solidified itself as they stepped into the sleeping area. He put his fist over his mouth and just…stared. The family hadn't gone anywhere.

"El'Shadai," Gideon breathed, leaning against his father's shoulder. "What do you suppose happened? Did they die of disease?"

"I don't think so," Ardenai said, swallowing hard to steady his voice. "If they'd died of disease they'd be in the bed, not on the bed, they're all dressed, and they're all here, the whole family." He stepped forward and got a better look at the mummies – parents and children. "Stay!" he said sharply, and Gideon stepped back. They'd been gutted – cleanly, surgically – right through their clothing. In death their rib cages had spread just enough to reveal that fact. Ardenai turned away and pointed back into the other room.

"There's another door here," Gideon said, and opened it into what had been the children's room. There was a raised baby box in the corner, but there hadn't been a baby on the bed with the others. "Maybe it's empty," Gideon said hopefully, though he knew, just as Ardenai did, that baby boxes were stored to save room unless they were being used for an infant.

"Better let me look," his father advised, but Gideon shook his head.

"No," he said quietly. "I said I hated these people. I owe them at least my shock."

Ardenai nodded and they crossed the room together and looked in the box. They stood there a long moment before Gideon said, "Were the others cut open like she is?"

Ardenai nodded again. "Why has this taken us so long?" he said abruptly. "We've been on this planet for how long? And we're just now doing what we should have done weeks and seasons ago? Why did I not see this coming, Gideon? Eladeus, how could I have been so…" his fists went skyward. "The word which would describe the depth of this blunder escapes me!" He turned on his heel and stalked back through the house and out onto the porch, banging the stone walls with his fist as he went. He parked himself on the stone railing and sat staring across the abandoned farm. "How could I NOT have realized that these people were acting contrary to nature?"

"Because maybe they're not," Gideon said reasonably. "This packing together may be contrary to Equi nature, but you are the Lord of many worlds, not just Equus. Because you were cautious does not mean you were wrong."

"Don't simper to console me," Ardenai snapped.

"Don't doubt my father!" Gideon snapped back. "You took care of immediate needs first. You stabilized the government and got food to the people. They've stopped running and hiding, schools are opening, street corner saneceres are caring for the sick, vehicles that use petrochemicals are being quickly phased out – the air is already measurably cleaner! What the kraa do you want, Dad, some magic horsehide that drifts down and covers every aspect of civilization, and when you lift it, all is perfection? Even a mind like yours isn't capable of that. Even the AEW isn't capable of that. Humanitarian aid comes before archeology, so just forgive yourself and move on. Figure out who killed these people and why. Who moved these people and why? Who convinced these people they had to knot up like bees in a hive, and who does it serve? I saw stairs to a cellar, and I'm going to go see what I can find. You can come, or you can sit there and beat yourself over the head. Just don't fall off the porch if you knock yourself out."

The boy kissed his father lingeringly on the temple, strode back into the house, and Ardenai heard him go out the side door. He sat there a minute more, huffed with frustration and then began to chuckle quietly to himself. *There are a few things you got right, Ah'krill Ardenai Morning Star, and that boy is one of them. Creator Spirit, thank you for that boy. And bless the poor souls who have laid here so long, waiting for someone who cared.* He stood up and went back into the house. He lifted the baby from the box and put it gently on its mother's outstretched arm, then called for a team of forensic recording technicians, informed them of the situation, and went to find Gideon.

In some miraculous fashion, or by some fabulous luck, the heavy cellar door, like the doors to the house, had held against the incursion of rats and dust, and within was a treasure trove. There were sealed containers of food which appeared to be commercially produced, jars of home canned fruit and vegetables, sacks and bags of dried food and supplies. How old were they? Gideon wondered. How quickly had the planet become too warm to grow the things displayed in this cellar? How far had this food traveled, or had there been a garden, an orchard, a berry patch like there was at Canyon keep?

He sat on the bottom step and contemplated it all, wondering at the same time how Tolbeth was doing in her gestation, feeling her soft muzzle against the side of his neck. How were things at school? How was Ah'brianne, who by some miracle of its own, seemed to care for him despite his disability…his inability? His father was here, and home was there. Father, home. To his relief, and his sadness, he knew which one he'd choose. Much as he needed his father, his grandparents needed him more. Much as he loved his sire, he needed his education, and he wanted to get it in the classroom with his friends, wanted to continue the polo lessons he was taking to surprise Ardenai. He wanted to go home. To the Great House. To Canyon keep.

He turned at the sound of boots on the stairs, and rose as the Firstlord straightened warily to full height beside him. "Yes, watch those beams," he advised, "and feast your eyes on this."

They spent half an hour or so looking, marveling, and asking each other questions before they heard footsteps above them and reluctantly went back upstairs, sealing the door behind them. They'd return later with a team to catalog and remove the food for further study.

The little town by the dry lake was abandoned, as though the population had just walked away one morning and not come back. The houses were fully furnished, there was food in the cupboards, pots on the stoves. They'd been down in cellars and up in attics, into homes and businesses. Jobie, as it turned out, was a real asset. He and Teal figured out early on in their exploration that if Jobie stood on the palms of Teal's upstretched hands, they were over twelve feet tall. It gave them the opportunity to peer into some pretty dicey places without committing to a climb or a crawl. So far, it had availed little in the way of enlightenment.

They'd found what they decided was a school, and just now they were exploring a house of worship, or so Teal surmised from the carillon inside – that instrument which so fascinated his brother-in-law – that music to which the witches danced while sinners burned, or so the flamen would have one believe.

It was Ardenai's wish that the big carillon in the planetary capital be fixed, and Teal was prowling around trying to find anything, any book or scrap of paper, that might tell them how to do that. There was plenty of sheet music, which told them how it was played, but nothing to tell them how to get it working. The Firstlord wanted it fixed by a Lebonathi, but Teal reasoned that if he could find instructions a Lebonathi could read, say, Isin or Elam, it would be both expedient and within the parameters Ardenai had set. He made note of the coordinates and decided he'd come back with Ardi.

Jobie had been all over the interior of this place and now he was twitching to get on to the next building, the next block. "Or maybe down by the lake," he said. "There are boats still tied to the dock. I can see them from here. When I was little…" he caught Teal's quick sobriety and amended, "young. When I was younger, we used to go to the lake near our house. The water would recede with the tide and I'd find all sorts of interesting things on the lake bottom. Of course my parents didn't let me keep most of them, being adults and all and not seeing their value."

"Lead on," Teal grinned, and they left the church, crossed the road and walked past boat houses and what had possibly been a fish processing facility before reaching the marina. Ancient marks on the pilings indicated high and low water, and at one time the docks had floated accordingly. Now they were collapsed, still keeping a firm tether on the boats which had collapsed with them into a jumble of wreckage: rusted chains, splintered wood and shattered glass.

"I wonder how long it's been since there was any water in here," Jobie mused, carefully picking his way around the boats.

"I think, a very long time," Teal replied. "Everything we're seeing here is a hundred and fifty to two hundred years behind where the Lebonathi are now, and they've been stagnant for at least that long again."

"Really? Three or four hundred years?" Jobie shook his head in wonder. "This climate may be a killer, but it's also an amazing preservation tool."

They poked around without any real hope of finding anything, and the increasing heat told them that they'd have to hurry if they wanted to stay outside. Teal was examining the pilings for signs of fossilized life, Jobie kicking through the dust of the lake bottom when the boy called, "Look what I found, Master Captain! It's a bracelet. I think it's kind of stuck to…uh…" his voice went up an octave. "Teal, is this…? Oh, help!"

By that time the Master Captain was beside him and Jobie was holding up the bracelet, still attached to the skeletonized wrist of its owner. Teal realized the boy was frozen, and gently took the bracelet, and the arm, and set them back down. "Are you all right, my friend? Where did you find this?"

Jobie pointed with a not quite steady finger. "Right where you're standing."

Teal touched his communications tab. "Belesprit, this is Teal. Do you have eyes on us?"

"This is Marion. I can see you just fine."

"What am I wearing?"

Marion chuckled. "You're in a white tunic with long, bloused sleeves and grey trousers. Standard expedition issue, but you wear it well. Standard cavalry clip in your hair. It's undone, by the way. Jobie is wearing the same thing."

"So, you're looking right at us with plenty of detail. Good. I needed to make sure," Teal said, reaching back to refasten the clip.

"How can I be of help, or did you just need to know if you look good in your clothes this morning?"

"Funny. Give this lake bed a quick sensor sweep and tell me what you find."

There was a pause of half a minute before Captain Eletsky said, "Absolutely nothing. It's just a huge, dry lake bed. Why, what do you think is there?"

"I'm sending Jobie up to you with what he's discovered," Teal said, turning to the boy.

Jobie nodded, gingerly picked up the arm by the bracelet, said, "Belesprit," pulled his harness tab and vanished.

"Are you still there, Marion?"

"I am. What's up?"

"I'm not sure, but I have an awful feeling. Jobie is bringing you an arm bone. Please test it for any sort of chemical residue, will you? And I need you to fire one of the pulse cannons, just enough to break up the crust on this part of the lake bed and create some heave."

"I can do that. Get on up the bank and sit down so I don't knock you down."

Teal did as he was instructed, tucking his face against his thighs and covering his ears. There was a thud like mortar fire, then a heave which tipped him slightly to one side, a small after-shock, and silence. He got up and walked back out onto the lake bed. "Now what do the sensors tell you?" he asked.

"Still clean," Eletsky responded.

"Now use your eyes."

"Oh my Dear God!" Marion exclaimed.

There were thousands of bones, whole skeletons, rotten shreds of cloth, and the occasional gleam of jewelry. And yet, none of it registered on the sensors. The mystery of the glastaline domes was becoming a little clearer, and the mystery of the townsfolk had been solved.

"Coming your way," Teal said, and pulled his harness tab.

He checked on Jobie, who insisted that he was fine and that he wanted to come along, and together they went into Belesprit's lab where Winslow Moonsgold was passing the skeletonized arm back and forth through the bone-scan.

"Look at this, Teal." He passed his own arm slowly through the machine – bones outlined with the fainter image of the flesh surrounding them – then passed the skeleton arm through. Nothing. No image at all. "What do you make of that?"

"More than my poor brain can handle," Teal replied. "Let me try something Winnie."

Moonsgold stepped aside and Teal passed his hand, palm down, through the machine, getting what, for him, was a normal image. He then passed his hand through palm up, very slowly, and there were only fragments of an image from the wrist down.

"How are you doing that?" the doctor breathed.

"I picked up the arm, like this," he made a closed-hand motion, "and I had discarded my gloves because they were torn. If you weren't wearing gloves to handle that bone, I'll bet your image would look just like mine. My question is, how soon is this going to eat my hand off?"

"Maybe it'll melt off," Jobie offered.

"Just remember you touched it, too," Teal reminded him, and Jobie laughed, too young to be worried.

"Wash your hands and see what happens," Moonsgold suggested.

"I'm betting – nothing," Teal said, but he complied, giving his hands a good scrub just with water and passing his right hand through again. There was no change. He scrubbed with soap. No change. He rinsed with surgical cleaner. No change.

"Well, I can't say I'm surprised," Teal said. "Whatever this is, it was meant to last a long, long time, and probably through all kinds of weather. I do wonder why it stuck to Jobie and me so fast and so thoroughly, and if it's going to wear off."

They allowed Jobie to entertain himself for a few minutes, looking at his partial bone-scan while Teal worked on what he was going to tell Dahman and Kerala. Jobie had already admitted to having a penchant for picking things up on the lake bottom, hopefully this would be an understandable transgression. Still, as fathers will do, Teal was worried. Bad enough this could be burning a hole in his tough hide, but Jobie was a teenager, and a tiny one.

"Stop," Jobie grinned, and Teal looked startled. "You're fretting so hard I can smell it. I'm fine. Let's go see what Criollo and the governor are up to, or the Dragonhorse and Gideon."

"No going back to the lakebed?" Teal queried. He still had a lot of questions, and returning with a team had been in his plans, but an emphatic shake of Jobie's head, said he'd had enough of that for the day. Teal smiled at him and tipped his head just slightly toward his dominant hand, touching the crys-tel around his neck. *Ardi?*

I'm here, Brother Mine.

Are you doing anything interesting?

Staring at a family of mummies, gutted on a bed.

There was a pause. *Say that again.*

I'll tell you later. Have you found anything?

Skeletons. Invisible skeletons. I'll tell you later, too. Jobie wants us to come your way. Sounds like a bad idea.

Absolutely! One traumatized child is enough. I'll meet you later.

Teal paused and smiled at Jobie, who was not deceived. "The First-lord found dead people too, didn't he?"

"I'm not sure what he said," Teal hedged. He took a deep breath and tipped his head, again fingering the crys-tel. *Nik?*

I am here.

Have you found anything that isn't dead?

That sounds ominous. Nothing dead here, except ends. We've found books, though whether or not they're, for the lack of a better word, real, remains to be seen. The whole city is a showplace.

Fascinating. Jobie and I are coming your way.

They discovered Konik and Criollo sitting in the deepest shade they could find, a set of gracefully curving steps the width of a street, behind some particularly tall buildings. Criollo looked half cooked, and the governor was shaking sweat out of one of his field boots. "This place is an opera set," he said peevishly. "This entire city has been staged for the curious. It is full of fascinating venues, including the library in which we have just spent the last two hours."

"This is making my head hurt," Teal muttered, dropping down beside him. "You didn't find any bodies? Skeletons?"

"No." Konik gave the Master Captain his full attention. "Did you?"

"Oh yes."

"My hand doesn't show up on a bone scan anymore!" Jobie exclaimed, unable to keep it quiet any longer. "Teal's doesn't, either. That's because we touched one of the invisible skeletons in the dry lake bed."

A silvering eyebrow hiked. "Really? Invisible skeletons?"

Teal nodded. "I'll tell you later. What have you got there, you two? Did you check those materials out through proper channels?"

"The librarian was out to lunch," Criollo chuckled. "We found some fascinating books! So much information that we've been wanting to know, just waiting for us to find it."

"Like what?" Jobie demanded, craning his neck to look.

Criollo lifted the books one at a time. "A book on animals of the different continents, so we can learn about the animals *and* confirm the names of the continents. A book on farming practices. A book on religion, or so we think. A book on the care and repair of Carillons – the governor found that one for my uncle. A book on ancient cultures." He set them gently aside. "They're pretty fragile, but in remarkable condition."

"It's all there," Konik sighed. "All the information we've been wanting about the Lebonathi people and their culture. I just wonder why. Why was this so easy, and is any of it genuine?" He pulled his boot back on over his soggy sock and stood up, stomping his heel into place. "Master Captain, would you be kind enough to take me to your village beside the lake? And I think we should visit the Dragonhorse, as well."

"I will take you and gladly," Teal said, "but I think these two should go back to Dominus with the books and see what they can figure out. It will save us a lot of time if they read and report back."

"Good idea," Konik nodded.

Criollo opened his mouth, thought, and shut it again. Both his father and the governor were twitching to get on with their evaluations, and he and Jobie had suddenly reverted to what they were – children. Children needed to be somewhere safe and guarded. He guessed he should be more grateful for that than he actually felt at the moment.

"Could I at least see the library first?" Jobie asked, trying not to sound plaintive.

"Aww..." Criollo began, and again forced himself to shut his mouth.

"I think that's a reasonable request," Teal said, turning to the governor, "Don't you?"

"Yes. And I know just the person to keep you company and see that you stay out of trouble."

"Back to the library?" Criollo grimaced. "Marginally better than back to the clipper, but I really do want to go with you. You know this of course."

"I do," Teal said gently.

Within seconds there was a shimmer of maroon and blue and Kehailan appeared in the white tunic and trim grey pants of the expedition. He had two ice cold water packs in each hand and one on his own back, its drinking tube just visible at the edge of his banded collar. "Did somebody mention a library?" he said excitedly, handing out the packs, and Criollo was instantly on his feet, his disappointment forgotten.

"Right this way! Who called you anyway?" he asked, pulling off his tunic and shedding the used water pack before strapping on the fresh one. "You must have been contacted or you wouldn't be in expedition gear. Here, Jobie, this little pack is yours. Sire, can we scramble these books directly to Dominus? I hate to carry them around and risk their bindings." Teal nodded, and a second later the books vanished, along with the empty water packs. "The governor and I spoke earlier," Kehailan laughed. "He knows my fondness for hoary tomes. Well, come on. It's not getting any cooler out here." He winked at the two men and followed Criollo and Jobie through a graceful arch at the foot of the steps where they'd been sitting. "I'll see they get lunch," he called. "And Governor, I would speak with thee this evening at dinner if that is convenient."

"And now that they're gone," Teal said, pulling his tunic back on and reveling in the brief coolness the fresh water pack brought, "do you want to see the village itself, or the thousands of Lebonathi bones in the lake bed?"

"I wonder what the captain wants," Konik mused, still looking after them. "I want to see the village. Take me to the most interesting thing you found there."

Teal nodded, and they materialized moments later in the house with the carillon. "This feels so familiar. Almost like a picture in a book, or a picture book for children. I can't quite put my finger on it."

"Missionaries?" Konik suggested, and the Master Captain looked skeptical. "Teal, at this point it's not any more far-fetched than anything else I've seen today."

Teal went back to his own explorations and the governor applied himself to the room, examining the carillon, the shape of the windows, the seating, and the books. The carillon looked surprisingly like the harp key he played at home. On a hunch he checked the bench at the carillon and found that it opened, just like his own music bench. Inside was sheet music, and Konik took it carefully in his hands, trying not to get it wet with sweat as he walked to one of the windows and stood looking through the dust and the pitting over what had been a view of the lake. He studied the music, and began first to tap his fingers, then hum, and then sing.

In the house next door Teal looked up and smiled, wondering how long it had been since anyone had raised a voice in song in this place. He was struck first by the beauty of the voice itself, then by the familiarity of the tune. Was Konik singing a blessing on the village? If so, Teal wanted to join him, to help shake off the terrible sense of loss – of people not knowing what was happening or why, spending their last minutes, or hours, or days in abject terror.

What Teal found, was Konik, standing by the window, singing the sheet music he'd found in the bench. He stopped abruptly and waved the music in Teal's direction. "Look at this!" he exclaimed, and Teal hurried to join him. "Tell me what you see!"

The master captain took the sheet music and studied it minutely for some time. "This is standard SGA musical notation," he breathed. "Why didn't I notice this earlier when I was here? Variation on a tetrachord scale. Harmonic minor. Standard lines and spaces." He looked at Konik, his mouth half open with an unasked question. "Say, 'missionaries' again and this time I won't roll my eyes."

"Sing with me," Konik demanded, and their voices filled the church and stirred the silence. Some of the harmonies were at odd intervals, and they ribbed each other about their ability to properly read music as they swapped off baritone and tenor, but they heard tunes that were eerily familiar, and words that said nothing of devils dancing to the music of carillons, or the fires of kraa consuming those who listened, or who trespassed upon abandoned continents.

They spent half an hour working their way through the sheet music in the governor's hand before realizing it was hard work, and that they were getting dangerously overheated. They sat on the floor with their backs against the wall and drank half the contents of their water packs before Konik announced that he was going to skulk about a bit. He put the sheet music in his hardpack, invited Teal to come along, and began a minute door to door study throughout the village. Teal realized it was literal. Konik was examining the doors, both inside and out.

Over lunch Konik explained. "These were good people. They did not mistrust one another nor did they fear for their possessions."

"You know this because?" Ardenai queried, holding his tea glass against his chest and trying to remember what it was like not to be sweating. He'd just had a cool bath, and despite the moderated temperature inside the clipper, bare feet and an unheated floor, he felt like he was at a slow simmer on the back of the big stove at Canyon keep.

"There are no locks on the doors. They're not even built to accept one – no bars, no bolts. Whatever came at them came from outside."

"Another part of the country? Another continent?" the Firstlord asked.

"That, I do not know," Konik mused, "but I think not. I think it rained death from the sky."

"I would agree," Teal nodded. "The whole thing with the invisible bones is technology they just didn't have, not from every indication of where they were when this happened."

"Since Gideon has opted to spend the afternoon with Kee and company, I would like to see these invisible bones of yours," Ardenai said to Teal.

"And I want to see the house you found, and the people, and that cellar – before the technicians move everything around," Konik added, downing the last of his tea and preparing to rise.

"Not so fast, Governor," Ardenai warned. "I promised Swift I'd keep you at a slow jog today. I think we all need to stretch out for an hour or two and let the sun drop a little. Nobody's going to move anything anywhere yet."

Konik gave him a deprecating snort. "How is she going to know how fast I do or do not go, Ardi? Unless you're planning to tell tales."

"I won't have to," he replied. "She will know. They always do."

"They can smell it, like horses smell water," Teal intoned.

"Well, I'm glad I'm single and have no need to answer to a wife… or two," Konik responded.

Both Teal and Ardenai looked at him and laughed. "What you are, is delusional," Teal said. "You may not have said the words, but the way you look at Swift? The way she looks at you? Nik, you're a goner, just as surely as we are."

"And this has finally come up," Konik sighed, settling back into his chair and looking slightly irritated.

"We're teasing you," Ardenai said quickly. "I know you adored your wife. I'm sorry if we've caused offense."

"No, not at all," Konik replied. "Ah'davan is gone, and that's a fact. I do care for Swift, and that's another. She fits into my life like she was made for me, and she's spent her whole adult life assigned to me as my hetaera. That fact makes me ask myself how much more of her life she wants to spend with me."

"She doesn't seem to be suffering," Teal observed.

"I'm trying to get to a point here," Konik groused, and told them what had been bothering him, ending with, "So here I am, the face of Equus before the Lebonathi people, who are now supposedly adapting to and adopting our ways, and I'm living with a woman to whom I am not married. Doesn't bother me – except for the fact that Ah'davan is hardly cold in her grave. Doesn't seem to bother Swift in the least, but…the concept bothers me."

"I can see where it would," Ardenai nodded. "Have you talked to Swift about this?"

Konik snorted. "Don't be silly. I have practiced it in my head a few times, does that count?"

"What would be the ideal outcome?" Teal asked.

"I would be happy being married to Swift. Someday. I suppose. The question is, how happy would she be, being married to me, and would Mountain hold even allow her to marry me? Hetaeras marry like anyone else, of course. But I already went against custom and married my sexual trainer. I'm not sure I can push my luck a second time."

"Number one, your sexual trainer and your hetaera are vastly different entities," Ardenai observed. "Men marry their hetaeras all the time. Number two, you were extremely young – two years out of childhood – when you married Ah'davan and she was over fifty years your senior. I think both those things factored in more than the fact that she was your sexual trainer. You should talk to Swift. If she agrees to a marriage, then speak together to them."

"Ah yes, the great ethereal *Them*. I'm not even sure where to start, given that they just galloped onto the scene when you rose to be Dragonhorse."

"Swift will know," Teal said reasonably. "They sent her to you."

"Yes, they did," Konik responded thoughtfully, and lapsed into silence.

Ardenai realized he hadn't asked Wren all the questions he needed regarding Swift, and that they'd pushed the governor about as far as he was going to go before he lost his humor. He changed the subject to the reports coming in from all the teams – things they'd found, things they'd not found. It was more perplexing than illuminating, and they spent an hour stretched out on the cool floor watching the crys-tel records from the morning's activities. About one hundred of the people who had gone out that morning, would not be going out that afternoon – heat sensitivity. They were assigned to examine, evaluate and record. The books and journals alone from libraries, schools and homes could keep them busy for seasons.

Finally, Konik could be stalled no longer. He donned a fresh water pack, and with a courteous nod to his companions, vanished. He examined the house first outside, then inside, most especially the kitchen, then stood a while contemplating the family on the bed before heading down to the cellar. He struck the light he'd brought, painstakingly studied the different items one by one, then sat on the steps, put his elbows on his knees, his chin in his hands, and tried to make sense of it all.

On impulse he asked Dragonhorse Thirteen to locate Bona on the farm ship where he worked. When he was located, Konik went to see him, luxuriating momentarily in the smell of ammon blossoms and the hum of bees, before crouching down beside Bona where he was building a new hive.

"Soft One!" Bona swiveled on his haunches and smiled, "It is good to see you."

"And you, my friend. I know you are busy, but there is something I need you to see, to help me figure out. Can I take you from your work to accompany me?"

"Of course," the man nodded, and immediately set aside what he was doing.

"As you know we are exploring the other continents. The records will be streaming soon for everyone to see, but what I want you to look at with me is not pretty. It is sad."

"Of that, I have seen plenty. I will go with you, prepared to be saddened." He paused. "It's not…my children, is it?"

"No," Konik said quickly. "Nothing like that."

"Then I am prepared," Bona said.

Konik outfitted him, changed his own water pack, and took him back to the little house. The sun was sliding behind the hills, and there was some relief in the long shadows. "This is an old tragedy – hundreds of years," Konik warned, "but it has a great deal of impact yet."

Bona nodded and they went inside, through the main hearth and the kitchen to the bedroom, where the family was laid out on the bed. The man winced, but did not look away. He studied the bodies for a long time, then said, "What were they looking for I wonder?"

The comment rocked Konik back and he stared at Bona. "Looking for," he breathed. "Very good question." He rubbed his forehead as he stared at the family, trying to tell himself a different story than the one he'd already formulated. What were they *LOOKING* for? He looked at the baby girl lying on her mother's arm, then thought about the baby girl Kee and Jobie had found and wondered if Swift would be able to discern what one had that the other did not. He shook off the impact and took a deep breath.

"This is a nice house," Bona said, a hint of wistfulness in his voice. "Look how well it has stood the years. Someone built it with pride, and to last a long time."

"Yes," Konik nodded. "Come look at the kitchen with me. Tell me if any of these implements are familiar to you, and if so, how are they used?"

That took until dark, and Konik asked for more lights to be sent down. Some of the kitchen tools Bona recognized from his grandmother's small village kitchen, and between the two of them they surmised a purpose for most. "Perhaps if we look at the foodstuffs, we can better figure out their function," the governor said, and took Bona to the cellar, walking close behind, ready to grab his belt should he stumble on his mutilated feet. He had time to wonder when Pythos was going to come up with the promised prostheses. He'd gone silent the last few days. Silent, and absent. Konik hoped he was nearby; these expeditions could be dangerous, and accidents were bound to happen, even to the Thirteenth Dragonhorse.

They studied the food stores together, the supplies, and Bona found seeds carefully labeled for planting in the growing season. "These will be priceless!" Konik exclaimed, wondering how he'd missed them in two careful passes over the cellar. He wanted to take the grain immediately to Ah'davan's graveside, where ancient cultivars sprang from niches in the rocks. Were they the same? Had these people been to Lebonath Tras? He reminded himself it was all going to get figured out, and that he needed to keep himself to that slow jog. Again, he sat on the steps, Bona beside him.

"This is your heritage," he said quietly. "There were people everywhere, and plenty of food, and times of peace. There was music. We found some today and Teal and I sang it together. There were books. Things and places had names, and people were not so crowded. Times were good, and people did not fear one another."

"With the truth, times will be good again," Bona said. "When the flamen are gone away."

Konik felt his ears prick up. "When the flamen are gone? Not dead?"

"Legend says they came in the burning time. Maybe in the time of peace they will go," the man said. "They tell us the Gods sent them to save us from the burning time, to save our souls, but I do not believe them. Few of us who have felt their merciless wrath believe them." His stomach rumbled in the silence and Konik felt a twinge of guilt.

"It is long past your suppertime. I should get you home."

"I am home," Bona said quietly, and he sat a few more minutes before rising and making his way upstairs. "Thank you for including me. Please let me see more of what you find."

Konik assured him that he would. Together they extinguished the lights and left the surface, Bona for his old terraformer-turned-farm-ship, and Konik for Dragonhorse Thirteen and dinner with Kehailan and his expedition companions. Truth was, he'd have preferred to go with Bona, back to the farm ships to dine with the Lebonathi and see their reaction to the day's recordings. But, Kehailan had asked him to come, and he was a creature of duty. He took a hurried bath, grateful that he still had quarters on board, put on fresh clothes, and joined the others in the dining room.

The boys were full of news about their trip to the library. Gideon was clutching a book on trains, Criollo one on women in government. Jobie had one on cheese making, which made Konik laugh, and laughter lightened his mood. The records of the day were playing on different backdrops all around the room, and the atmosphere was charged with excitement. At last – maybe –they were getting somewhere. Just before dinner was served the women arrived, Ah'din and Ensharra, Swift with Ah'cora and Ah'ren. Swift gave Konik's thigh a gentle pat as she sat beside him, and he relaxed at her touch. Last to come was Naram, who nodded, unsmiling, and took the chair beside Ensharra.

She seems attentive to our Regent, Ardenai observed, reluctantly closing his book on the repairing of carillons and setting it aside.

And he to the lady, Teal responded, smiling and nodding in Ensharra's direction.

Perhaps you two should open a matchmaking enterprise. You've been at it all day, the governor remarked, and the topic was dropped.

"You know it's obvious when you're having one of your mental conversations," Ensharra grinned. "You look at whomever is speaking. You nod. You wiggle your eyebrows."

"That's only when we want you to know we're conversing," Ardenai chuckled. "Regent Naram, you seem improved. Will you be joining us soon? Fascinating stuff out there."

"So I hear," Naram nodded. "You know the flamen are already saying it's a ruse. A deception to knock the people off guard and open them to the wiles of the demons."

The record of Teal and Konik singing the sheet music they'd found looped in at that moment, and the dining room was suddenly quieter as people watched. The music was beautiful, the banter was funny, and as the segment ended, they got a round of applause. They stood up, took a flourishing bow, and sat back down, laughing.

"That, being a prime example," Naram said, pointing toward the wall. "No Lebonathi is going to believe you didn't stage that singing. They don't hear music, they don't see music, and they're going to be easily swayed into believing it isn't theirs at all."

"If we'd staged it, we'd have figured out who was the tenor line and who was baritone to begin with," Teal snorted.

"Still, he makes a good point," Konik sighed. "Trust is sometimes hard-won, and the truth dazzles but slowly. Ensharra, how is your family adapting to their new life?"

"Good," she nodded. "Right now, they're on the farm ships where it's safest. Eshkar's already been accepted into SGA service as an apprentice. He's been assigned to a slot aboard Belesprit and going to school at night, but he's being allowed to travel back and forth. His wife is with rescued cousins, and my parents are there, so she has company when he's gone."

"Excellent," Kehailan said. "We're slowly filling the gaps in personnel, but we are still short. Which reminds me, Governor, do you know a man named Ah'lauren Eriskay Tersk?"

Konik started slightly. "He's my son-in-law. Why?"

"Because, pending your approval, he's the new communications officer aboard Dragonhorse Thirteen. Cutter reminded me some time back that he'd come short-term, and that his heart was within the Great House itself. He wanted to go home, and Eriskay wanted the position. I was impressed with him. I wanted to make sure you were, as well."

"He has a warm heart and a cool head," Konik replied. "What he does, he does well. I approve." He paused a moment and tried for a casual tone. "Is he bringing his wife and son?"

"Again, pending your approval."

There was no hesitation. "Of course. No man should be without his family."

CHAPTER 8

Swift stood shaking her head slowly from side to side and staring at the family which still lay together on the bed. "Maybe with some really sophisticated equipment I could figure it out, but I doubt it," she said, and saw disappointment register on the faces around her. "But you know, I'll try it anyway. Ensharra has been such a good sport about letting us stare at her, and we know where there's a nursing mother. I'm sure Eshkar or Bona or one of the Stone Spring scientists would let me use them as a comparison for the man. Nothing for the boys. Maybe if we asked very carefully, we could examine Umma." Again, she shook her head, "This babe is so young, and so undeveloped, and she's been dead so long. I doubt very much I can figure out what might be missing."

"It looks like there's a lot missing on all of them," Teal winced.

"True too. Do you know for sure this is not the cause of death?" She looked to Ardenai, who was standing at the foot of the bed, mouth turned down in appraisal.

"Scans indicate they were suffocated in some manner, which tells me whomever did this wanted the bodies untrammeled. Except, of course, for being dead."

"I truly think Bona hit the ball dead center when he asked what they were looking for," Konik muttered. "If we can figure that out, all of this – every bit of it – will fall into place."

"Do you think, once the technicians are through documenting the scene, that the bodies could be moved to a facility on the Jocundome?" Swift asked. "The science labs on Belesprit are already inundated, and the makeshift lab on the expedition transport just isn't sophisticated enough to be of much help."

Ardenai nodded. "I will put in a request. Let's leave this poor family to the techs and get back to the city."

"Strange, isn't it?" Wren said, looking back a last time at the little farm house. "Out here in the countryside, in the small towns and hamlets, you have uncovered so much death, and the city is a showplace. No signs of death or disruption of any kind beyond centuries of dust and drifting sand. It's an archeological treasure trove, and so far all of it seems genuine."

"I'm sticking with my theory that it's a stage," Konik said. "So complete and so very fascinating that any adventurous Lebonathi who came ashore would explore it forever and not look any deeper, or any further."

"Not that they'd wander even this far," Teal said. "They're too terrified of witches and devils and their own unmerciful gods, and what those gods will do to them if they leave the pavement, much less the continent. Their religion is very effectively holding them captive." They stood in a group, engaged the scrambleshaft, and found themselves in front of the ornate arch of a huge, gently sloping tunnel, much like the one connecting the Great House of Equus to the Great Stables, though not so large. "Where's the rest of our party?" Ardenai asked, and in answer Kehailan and the three boys appeared in a convolution of maroon and blue. "Right on time," the Firstlord smiled. "We have expeditionary forces ahead of us, so I don't expect any surprises, but do look sharp, just in case."

The first hour felt much like the subterranean rambles they'd been on in the ancient planetary capital, except that this was cleaner, smelled better and might have been slightly less torrid. It was also completely devoid of anything interesting. It was simply an endless labyrinth of beautifully constructed tunnels which had, from the marks on the walls, once supplied water to the city.

"Which means there's most likely another set of tunnels under this one," Ardenai said, sliding down onto his haunches and resting his back against the wall. "Nearly all ancient cities ran the water above and the sewers below. All we have to do is find the portal to the lower tunnels and we'll find another way out of the city."

"Why don't we see this in the capital?" Gideon asked, pushing away stray bits of gravel and preparing himself to sit.

"We do. It's just not recognizable because they're living in both the old aqueducts and in the sewers," Ardenai responded, sipping at the water in his pack.

"Sewers being the most desirable housing, since it would be the coolest," Konik said with a chuckle.

"Governor, sit," Swift invited, patting the floor beside her.

At that moment Gideon's foot rolled on a pebble and Konik reached to steady his sudden descent. The back of Gideon's head thumped against the wall, hit an unseen switch, the lower section of wall against which the boys were leaning dropped away, and the boys went with it, shrieking with startlement and fear. Two seconds later it was rising again. Konik dove over it into the darkness and disappeared as the wall rumbled back into place.

There was a moment of shocked silence, then a scramble as five people tried without success to find the brick that held the switch.

"I think this is it," Ardenai said after a minute or so, "but it's not responding. It's probably part of the automated drainage system." He sat abruptly and stared at the wall. "The water got that high, the pressure triggered the switch, and it released water in five second increments into the discharge system below, cleaning the sewers down there and preventing flooding up here. Ingenious, really."

"Thank you so much for that exhaustively complete evaluation," Swift snapped. "Can you tell me why the governor…" she paused and sank down beside Ardenai. "Never mind. I know exactly why."

"So the boys wouldn't be alone," Teal said quietly. "I just hope they didn't fall too far."

"Dragonhorse Thirteen can't locate them," Kehailan said. "They can barely locate us. We'll just have to find the master mechanism, wait until that wall decides to open…"

"Which it's not going to do a second time, because there's no water pressure," Ardenai said.

"…or, we can backtrack and try to find another entrance."

"Let's do all three," Ah'ren suggested. "Two go down, two go up. One stay here, just in case."

"Good idea," Ardenai said. "Wren, you and Kee go back up. Teal, you and I will go down. Swift, I'm assuming you want to stay here and see if it opens again?"

"And if it does, what good will it do me? How am I supposed to block it?" She retorted, short with worry.

"I'll get you some help," Kehailan said quickly. "Don't worry. Sewer tunnels are smaller than water tunnels, they can't have fallen far."

They hadn't. It had been a drop of eight feet or so onto a rolling, rattling surface that didn't do much more than knock the wind out of them and inflict a few scratches. "Good job finding the sewer access," Konik groaned, trying to sit up on the unstable surface. "Is everybody unhurt? Ouch."

"What in kraa are we on, anyway?" Criollo groused.

"It feels like…oh…shit!" Gideon quavered. "Oh hell oh shit! Is this fabric?"

"It's bodies!" Jobie squeaked, panic rising in his throat. "It's skeletons!" He began to scream and scramble and found his tail firmly grasped by someone in the darkness.

"You're all over me, and you're going to break your neck!" Gideon yelled.

"Let go of my tail!"

"I don't have your tail!"

"I do," came the governor's soothing voice. "Jobie, stop scrambling and I'll let go, but Gideon's right, you're going to hurt yourself, or cause this pile of bones to topple, and we're going to be buried alive." The struggles stopped abruptly and Jobie subsided, shaking and sobbing quietly. "I'm going to turn on a light. It won't make us feel any better about where we are, but it will help us assess our situation. Are you ready?"

There was a communal groan, then affirmation, and Konik pointed his small, powerful expedition lantern toward the ceiling and activated it. "Eladeus," he whispered, and fought the urge to vomit. Criollo did vomit, and Jobie buried his face against his thighs and screamed. There were heaps of bones, some higher than others, many higher than the one they found themselves on – all along the tunnel for as far as they could see in either direction. Anywhere there was an access port, the citizens of the city had been dumped. Konik put his hand down to get something that felt like a rib out of the small of his back, and realized he was pushing down on a baby's skull.

"Where was Mighty Equus when this was happening to you?" he snarled, fighting anger so intense it felt like he was going to pass out if he couldn't hit something – throw something – tear something to pieces. He ground his teeth and forced himself to breathe.

"Mighty Equus was between Dragonhorses," Gideon managed. "Nik, how are we going to get out of here? I want to get out of here, or at least try. I can't sit here on these people. I just can't. Please!"

Even Gideon's voice was going up in pitch, and Konik realized he was going to lose all three boys to panic if he didn't get them moving. Knowing five powerful telepaths were just outside, he tried telepathy and got nothing, which was odd. His communications crys-tel availed them more of the same. He flashed the light down the tunnel one way, then the other. Maybe, if they could get down without bringing the bones down on top of themselves, they could hug the wall and make progress. He looked at his compass, ascertained which way they had come, and jerked his chin in that direction. "The water and sewage flowed slightly downhill. We saw that as we walked. There has to be access somewhere."

"What if we move and they can't find us?" Jobie quavered, trying to control his voice. "What if we end up in the wrong tunnel? Why haven't they opened that back up again? We're right here!" He raised his voice and screamed at the top of his lungs. "We're right here!" Gideon put his arms around the smaller boy, and Jobie once again subsided. "Sorry," he said after a minute. "I'm not really a rat, you know. I don't like dark places full of bodies."

"That's a comfort," Criollo said with a weak laugh. "Governor, what do we do?"

"Logically, if they could open the portal, they'd have done so by now. Let's mark the direction we're going to travel, and if they do get it open, they'll know which way to go to find us. We have air. We have water, we have food, and we have light. What we most need to do is keep ourselves from getting hurt."

"I think we should rope ourselves together and try running down the gentlest slope, one at a time," Jobie said. "That way if one of us gets buried the others can pull him out."

"Good idea," Konik praised, and the boy looked more hopeful. "Jobie, how far do you think it is to bare floor?"

"Sixty hands? Fifteen or twenty feet, maybe?"

"I think so, too. Criollo? Gideon?"

They agreed. The four of them roped themselves loosely together, leaving about that length of high-tensile cord between each of them. Steadied by Gideon above him, Criollo went first, slipping and sliding. He fell only once, but got up and made it to a bare spot, pulling the line taut at the bottom for the next person to descend. Gideon went, then Jobie. Konik, having marked their route with bright white directional dust, came last. They walked about a sixth of a furlong, Criollo estimated about one hundred feet, before encountering the next pile of remains. They tightened the cord until they were close together, faced the wall, and inched their way past.

"How many people are in each of these piles, I wonder?" Gideon said almost to himself. "Did they all die at once?"

"Good questions both," Konik said. "And something the technical crews will be able to tell us."

"Unless we become part of the statistic," Jobie whispered. It became apparent when they reached open floor again that he was beginning to limp, and Konik halted them to ask why. "I think I did it when I fell initially," he said. "I can walk on it. Can we please just get going?" Konik nodded, but he kept an eye on Jobie's progress, and it was not improving with the passage of time.

When they paused for a few minutes to drink and nibble on fruit and nut bars, trying not to think about where they were, Gideon mused, "The first time I ever rode a horse was in the middle of the night. Squire Fidel had gone to get the bounty hunters, Ardenai was concussed and bleeding from a head wound and a knife wound, and we had to move fast. How I stayed on that horse's back I will never know, but I did. And we got to the Port of Entry and onto dear Josephus's grain freighter. Little did I know how much my life had changed in that one night. I gained a father, and a future, and a proud and ancient heritage. Sometimes, I still can't fathom it."

"You and your sire did very brave things together," Konik said quietly.

"We all did brave things together," Gideon corrected. "I'm glad you survived that crossbow bolt, Governor. We'd be lost right now without you."

"Thank you," Konik smiled, "but the three of you are resourceful. You'd have overcome your initial panic and figured this out. You'd have been fine without me."

"And yet here you are," Criollo observed. "Why is that?"

"Instinct," Konik shrugged. "You'll all have it when you have children of your own."

Gideon remained quiet. *I will never have children. Right now, that makes me sad. What will I miss? What instincts will never be stirred in me, I wonder? Ah'brianne says we will find joy in raising the children of others. I wonder if that's true. I wonder if she knows I truly mean it when I say I can never make love to her. I'm really hungry. How can I be hungry? Look at where I am. I'm starving. I wish I had one of my aunt's flatwraps. I'm weak, that's what I am. I wish I had two of Ah'din's flatwraps, with chopped nuts and fresh honey, maybe some azure berries.*

Will you please shut up! Criollo groused. *I'm starved, too. We're weak, that's what we are. You're right. We're sniveling, privileged princelings. Nik will think we're weak.*

Nik will think no such thing, came the amused response. "We'd better keep moving," the governor said aloud, but when Jobie got up, he couldn't put weight on his foot.

"I should never have sat down," he said disgustedly, trying not to let them know how much it hurt.

"I'll put you on my shoulders," Criollo said. "You can bang on the wall as we go along and let people know where we are."

"Which would work if you were as tall as your sire and I was standing on your hands," Jobie replied. "I can walk."

"You cannot," Konik said firmly. "We'll switch off carrying you."

Jobie didn't argue. To do so would have been fruitless in any case, and his ankle was hurting all the way to his knee by that point. He wondered if taping it would help, but realized once his boot was off it would have to stay off, and he would be barefooted on the bodies. Apparently, the governor had realized that as well, because he didn't mention removing the boot, though he did give Jobie something to nibble from his med kit, and the pain subsided a little.

They trudged slightly uphill in what they hoped was the right direction, picking their way around the huge piles of bones, over the remains scattered by water or rodents, being careful not to get tangled in the rotted shreds of clothing. Once they even found a toy, apparently it had been clutched so tightly it had been cast, child and all, into the sewer. "There was still some water in here when this happened," Criollo observed. "That fleecy-toy had been soaked, from the look of it."

"Bodies lose urine as they relax," Gideon said. "If enough of these people were thrown down here at once, that could have done it." There was a long silence.

"I've never been on a horse myself," Jobie said thoughtfully. "I would like to though. I would like to play polo, but I would need a very short horse or a very long mallet."

"You might be a real success," Konik laughed. "You could gallop around under the other horse's bellies and have your way with the ball."

Again there was silence. The heat was weighing heavily on them, and the air was increasingly fetid despite the age of the corpses. They were tiring, and they could feel all the spots they'd landed on, and all the places they'd hit stumbling over bones on their endless journey toward endless darkness.

Criollo lost himself in thoughts of Jasreth and what kind of home they'd build on Lebonath Tras. How big would it be? What would it look like? Would it be one of the thousand-square-foot octagons like the one in which they'd found that first family? That would be very small for the Equi physique, especially if he were to grow into his father's stature. He pulled up a vision of Lebonath Tras, and began looking for a suitable home site – maybe overlooking the river and their original pavilions. No… further back, on one of the verdant hillsides, overlooking a stream, or a pond. A pond with frogs. They would plant frogs.

Gideon thought of Canyon keep and the snow, and his mare's soft breath and Ah'brianne's crazy laugh, and putting together his train with his grandsire. He thought about the wonderful adventure of riding into the wilderness with friends, and looking up at the stars in the clear night sky, and how good it was going to feel to be held in his sire's arms when this was over.

Jobie thought about big plates of food, and holding his new baby sister on his lap and tickling her until she giggled, and playing Lightning with the boys at lunchtime. He saw to it they were getting lunch every day. That made him feel good. He let his thoughts meander through all the kinds of food they were bringing – the colors, the textures and the tastes.

Between trying to communicate with the outside every few minutes, Konik thought about all the ways he could hunt down and kill those who had done this horrible thing to the people of Lebonath Jas. He was an inventive and efficient killer, and there were times it didn't really bother him much. Right now, the thought was downright pleasurable.

He wandered around in his days as a test pilot. That day when all systems had failed on the prototype fighter, about hitting the ground before the chutes fully deployed. About realizing it was blindness or blue eyes instead of green. How could they not have had a good supply of green eyes? All high Equi had green eyes – all but him. Ah'davan had told him they were beautiful. Him, with his blue eyes and his too-soon silvered hair. She was gone now. Dead, like the people around him as he walked, stumbling occasionally, once whacking his still-tender elbow against the tunnel wall, resisting the urge to apologize aloud as he stepped on parts of folks. Maybe he should have his eyes dyed their original color, that ubiquitous green-gold of the Equi princes. Maybe if Mountain hold fixed his hypersexuality, his hair would turn black again. Trying to shock it out of him had turned it grey. Shit, how that had hurt! What had they been thinking? What were they thinking now? Who would he hug first, Ah'rika or Nokota? Was the air getting heavier, or just hotter? They'd come much farther than the original mile they'd walked in the tunnel. Maybe they were getting closer to the surface – maybe an entrance outside the city. This had to come out somewhere. It had to.

"Time out," Criollo groaned. He was again carrying Jobie, who had gone to sleep and become dead weight. "How long do you suppose we've been down here?" he said, tipping the Taraxian over his head and lowering him to the floor before dropping down beside him.

"Days," Gideon muttered.

"Most of one day," Konik amended, sinking to the floor and sipping carefully at his water supply. He was dehydrated and he knew it, but rescue seemed no closer than it had six or eight hours ago, and the miles they'd walked seemed to be getting them nowhere. If they ran out of water, they would die quickly, or horribly. In either case they would be dead. "It's my turn to carry Jobie awhile, but I think we should take a good rest, maybe nap a little before we go on."

"Nap, down here? How could we possibly sleep down here?" Criollo said, and seconds later, he was asleep with Gideon's head on his shoulder and Jobie sprawled beside him.

Konik let his head drop back against the wall and pulled his tunic away from his chest to move the air. It was at that point he realized – his shirt was dry. His trousers were dry. He'd stopped sweating, and he was panting for air. How had he not noticed that? Part of him wondered idly about it while he considered a cool bath, and part of him staggered to his feet and shook the boys none too gently awake. "Use your oxygen," he said harshly. "Not all of it, just some. Now! Move!"

They just looked at him, and he straddled Criollo, yanking him to his feet and grabbing his oxygen from his utility belt. He turned it on and held it to the boy's face until he gasped and his eyes came fully open. "What's happening?" he said through the mask.

"The air's bad. Get Jobie up and into his oxygen." He jerked Gideon to his feet and repeated the process, then sagged against the wall and opened his own rebreather. The units were designed to last two hours with constant use, four with intermittent. If they didn't get somewhere in four hours, and if they hadn't already died of dehydration, they'd die from the putrid air.

Ardenai, Ardenai, Ardenai, it became a litany as they pushed forward, Jobie hobbling between them, refusing to be carried any longer. What had the Firstlord said to Konik all those seasons ago? *Put your head against mine and think only of Ah'davan.* "Stop," he said. "We're all going to put our heads together and think only of Ardenai, as hard as we can, for half a minute. We're going to do that every ten minutes from now until they find us."

If it didn't bring success at least it brought hope, and they did it twice more in the open spaces between piles of bones. They had just inched their way past a pile that seemed even bigger than the rest, when there was an ear-piercing metallic shriek, the walls shook and rained dust and stone particles, and every one hundred feet the walls dropped down and light poured in, followed by the head and shoulders of an expedition member. "Dear Ahura!" exclaimed the big Amberian closest to them. "Oh, dear Ahura! Here are the poor souls of the city."

"And here we are as well," Konik said loudly. "Can you get us out of here?"

The head disappeared. "All praise! I have them!" he called, and they could hear the message being passed. The head reappeared with a light and the man swung himself over the edge, hugging the wall and dropping down beside the pile of skeletal remains. A second head appeared in the opening, also Amberian.

"I'm Joss," said the man on the floor. "I'm going to hand you up to Aurus. Are you strong enough to stand on my shoulders?"

"We are," Konik said. "Thank you. Let's get the boys out of here first."

They put Jobie on Gideon's shoulders, then Joss stooped nearly to the floor so Gideon could step onto his shoulders. "Going up," the Amberian said. He grasped Gideon's knees and lifted both boys easily to stand, and then at arm's length by the ankles, to be plucked one at a time over the edge. Gideon's head immediately reappeared beside Aurus as Criollo was lifted and pulled over the edge to collapse in a shaking heap on the floor beside Jobie. At that point Gideon, too, gave in to his trembling knees and folded, trusting that Nik was safe and instructing himself firmly not to cry. A third person was there with water, which was promptly poured in and on them, and they were given juice to drink.

"Ready Governor?" Joss grinned, and Konik answered with a single nod. "You're a fabulous polo player so your balance is good. Just step onto my palms and I'll take you up in one motion."

"You assume much," Konik muttered, fighting the black spots in front of his eyes, but he did as he was told, and found himself beside the boys on the floor of the aqueduct. He was given a drink, sloshed with water, and a cold, wet towel was draped around his neck and shoulders.

"You were all very nearly dead, you know," Aurus observed in a matter-of-fact tone that made Konik want to chuckle. "Captain Kehailan was nearly dead himself, trying to find the mechanism that would open these portals."

"He must have found it, though," Konik said, downing another few ounces of heavily diluted juice.

"No. He finally realized that when it came to water, the Menorquins were who he needed, so he called upon his friend Gallios, and Gallios found the equipment. Together they got it to work. Luckily you have powerful and determined friends."

"Luckily," Konik echoed, but he was suddenly exhausted, his head too heavy for his neck, and he was shaking like a leaf in the wind. He let himself lean back, and when his head touched the bricks there was a shock of premonition, as though he was about to go through this day again, as though they'd not been found, as though the air was bad and he was hallucinating! His head snapped forward, his eyes came wide open and he gasped and looked around.

Aurus looked concerned. "Governor, are you all right?"

Konik nodded as Aurus found the pulse in his neck. "Not a heart attack," the governor said, and Aurus withdrew his hand.

"Do you know where you are?"

"All too well," Konik grinned, giving Aurus's thigh a slap. "This is a most disturbing place. The things that should work, do not. The things we think we know, we do not." He turned and gave the boys his attention. "Criollo, are you all right?"

"Yes," he replied, forcing a smile he didn't feel. "Glad this day is over. I suppose this means we won't be shuffled away from the corpses anymore."

"I've seen enough dead people, or what's left of dead people, to last me a lifetime," Jobie said emphatically. "I'm going back to my job with the school!"

"I'm with you on the matter of corpses," Gideon said, "though I'm sure this is far from over."

"Well, it won't last long if Governik…that's not right. If… Gover… nik…anyway, the governor…gets his wish," Criollo stammered, obviously fighting sleep.

Konik had to chuckle, realizing that the boys' thoughts weren't the only ones that had been open, and hoping he hadn't shocked anyone too badly. "What crossed our minds in the sewer should probably stay in the sewer, for the sake of everyone," he said, and looked up at the nearly inaudible purr of an AEW glider carrying three sets of worried parents.

He watched them embrace their children – Kerala and Dahman in a group hug with Jobie. Criollo leaning into his father while Ah'din stroked his hair. Gideon, with his face buried against his father's neck, Ardenai's hand holding his head in place as though he were an infant, Wren rubbing his back and laughing softly. *How lucky they are,* he thought, feeling the small skull under his hand, seeing the forlorn fleecy-toy, and feeling emotions pounding up the center of his chest that were threatening to come out as tears, angry ones, and there would be cursing – probably throwing things or punching a wall. He once again gave himself the firm command to stop, and stood up as the Dragonhorse came to embrace him. He accepted the thanks and praised the boys for their bravery and ingenuity, but his thoughts were divided, some by exhaustion, some by concern. Where was Swift? Was Swift all right?

"She stayed right in the spot where all of you disappeared," Ardenai said, sensing the question. "Kee went to get her with a glider. They'll be here, we'll get all of you checked out, and get all of us fed and into bed. It has been a very, very long day."

Bed, it seemed, was easier than sleep. Kehailan stood in front of a whole wall of levers, knowing they had to be pulled in a certain order, and as he figured them out, they re-arranged themselves, and they were red hot and razor sharp but he had to touch them or people would die. He finally crawled out of bed, drank half a bottle of his uncle's good wine, and crawled back in bed, wondering what Tim was up to and if he'd be interested in a sleep-over, or what was left of one.

Gideon galloped endlessly through the darkness following a man he hardly knew, whose deep red cloak flowed out behind him like Declivian blood, and whose face, when he looked back at Gideon, was a death's head with spiders in its eyes. He sat up with a muted scream and the death's head became his father's well-fleshed face. "Everything's fine," Ardenai whispered. "You're dreaming."

Criollo wandered through houses and schools and streets made of bones and rags, holding out the fleecy-toy and asking, "Is this yours? Do you know who this belongs to? Is this yours?"

Jobie slept between his parents that night for the first time in years, his bandaged ankle elevated on a pillow, his baby sister in the crook of his arm. When she cried, he was comforted, because she was alive, and she squirmed and popped her lips and kept him awake, but he didn't mind, because it reminded him that he, too, was alive and in a safe place.

Konik sunk into an exhausted slumber, only to realize with a growing sense of panic that they'd not been rescued at all. The walls had not opened. The screech was the sound of the knife on his utility belt digging into the wall as he slid toward the floor. "I have to get up!" he cried, struggling to rise. "I have to wake them up or they'll die!"

"Nik, wake up," Swift grumbled, sitting up to shake his shoulder, and staying out of his way in case he exploded up out of bed again. This had been going on for some time, and Swift was as tired as he was. This time she'd been dreaming about hundreds of baby girls all in a row, and she'd said, "My goodness, aren't all of you beautiful, and dead, too. All nicely gutted. That's convenient. I'll just have you for dinner."

Konik didn't come bolt upright this time. He lay gasping and grinding his teeth in frustration. "I am so sorry," he said. "I'll go sleep by the hearth."

"No, you won't, because you won't sleep and neither will I. Come on, we're going to have a bite of breakfast and a cup of something hot, and then we're going to go play a little one on one polo."

"At three-thirty in the morning?"

"There are lights," she said firmly, "Get up."

He did. Pulled on britches and riding boots, wandered to the table, downed what she put in front of him and followed her obediently to the scrambleshaft platform and thence to the polo field. Somewhere in the back of his mind he kept hoping it was a joke. A ruse. A dream, but it was not.

He brushed his favorite mare and was getting ready to saddle her when Swift appeared, leading her own pony. "You're riding mine; I'm riding yours," she said. "I want you to see why she's keeping her nose so high in the tight inside turns."

"Fine," Konik muttered. "Here you go. This is Tinker. You will love her. You may not keep her."

"This is Isabelle. You'll hate her. She's moody and given to pitch. Watch her. She bites."

"Better and better," he said, reaching for his saddle with one hand and keeping the mare at bay with the other. He snubbed her up short to saddle her, grabbed his helmet and mallet and trotted out into the darkness. "Isabelle, I need you to listen to me," he said quietly. "You try to throw me, and I will lay this mallet right between your pretty little ears. Do you understand?" The right ear swiveled his direction and she snorted. Amusement or contempt. He couldn't tell for sure.

There was a sudden flash as night became day, and as his pupils recovered, he spotted Swift, jogging toward him on Tinker. "Since you challenged me, did you bring a ball?" he called.

"Yes! Screw your ass to that saddle and let's play!" she responded, threw a willow bark ball out between them and leaned over Tinker's neck yelling, "Pulu!"

In a split second they were at a dead gallop and Konik knew he'd either wake up or die, and that's when he began to laugh. He spun Isabelle on her haunches, his mallet whistled in the crisp, pre-dawn air, and he applied himself fully to the game.

Teal had gone over every inch of Padmar. Examined his eyes, sniffed his nostrils, checked the inside of his mouth, the inside of his rectum, the inside of his ears. He sat now on the straw of the stall and stroked the still figure lying there. "You found him like this?"

Konik nodded, squatting on his boot heels slightly to one side. "Pretty much. We'd been out playing polo and we were just putting our ponies away when we happened to walk by and saw him struggling, but he was already down. That's when I hollered for you. What happened? Do you have any idea?"

Teal shook his head and looked flummoxed. "He was fine when I examined him. I mean, he was aging and failing, but he wasn't sick. He sure wasn't dying."

"Well, he's surely dead now," Ardenai sighed. "Poor Ah'cora is going to be devastated."

"Someone should probably go tell her before she comes to feed him," Teal said, looking at Konik, but it was Ardenai, noting Konik's exhaustion, who said he'd go. Ah'cora was his wife's working associate. She seemed fond of the rest of the family, especially the womenfolk. Perhaps between all of them they could bring her some comfort. Konik nodded absently and gestured him off.

Ardenai chose not to scramble, instead walking the route he hoped she would take, partly to intercept her, partly to rehearse what he would say, and work through a few scenarios. He did fine with hysterical five-year-olds, not so much with grown women he didn't know very well. What, exactly, was he going to say? What if she opened the door *en deshabille* and collapsed at the news? He realized with a self-deprecating snort that he was more worried about what she might do, than how she might feel – this young woman without home or family to turn to. It was at that point that he realized he was the wrong one for the job. It should be Wren, or Ah'din, or his mother, someone with whom she had laughed and bonded, but his long strides had carried him too quickly and he was in front of her cluster-cot still unprepared. A moment later, she opened the door.

She flashed him a charming if guarded smile which faded almost immediately. "What's wrong?" she asked, coming down the walk to meet him. "It's not time already, is it?"

"I'm…not sure what that means," he frowned, "I came to tell you that Padmar has died. I am so sorry."

She didn't flinch, but her eyes changed shape. "You are Firstlord of the Affined Equi Worlds. How came you to be messenger?"

Not at all the response he was expecting. "I…was out running with Teal when Konik summoned him to the stable. I came along, partly because I thought Padmar was quite the horse, and partly because I thought I might be of help to him…Padmar, that is, or to you. Teal was busy, of course, and Nik was…." He realized his explanation was becoming much longer than it needed to be. Then, it hit him. "Why do you ask? Are you suspicious of me or my motives?"

She smiled without warmth and said, "Should I be?"

By now Ardenai was thoroughly confused and slightly offended. "You should not, but I see that you are. Padmar is still in his stall if you want to say goodbye. Teal will want to do an autopsy to make sure the animal did not meet with foul play."

"And he will need my permission?"

"No. But he will ask as a courtesy."

"So, the highest-ranking officer in the Equi military responds to help a dying and worthless horse, and the Firstlord of Equus delivers the message to his owner? Which one of you, exactly, is the one into whose arms I am supposed to swoon and wake up pregnant?"

"Uh…?"

Her bottom lip trembled, then stopped. "They could have told me before I came that it wasn't my expertise that was important, but my fertility," she said quietly. "I was so happy to have this job. For the first time since I left the Eloi, I really felt I was going to contribute something and be valued, and now…" She made an angry, hopeless gesture.

"And now what, exactly?" Ardenai retorted, having recovered his wits and the gist of the dialog. "Yes, my wife told me you were here for more than one purpose. Cartography being the more important, by the way, not the breeding schedule of the Great House. Yes, we were reasonably sure you hadn't been told yet. I didn't know you'd found out, but whoever told you must have given you some really wrong impressions. If I'm told to set my head against you, I will. If Teal is told to set his head against you, he will, because that's part of our job. But if you don't want me to touch you, or Teal to touch you, we most assuredly will not, Ah'cora. That choice remains yours alone.

"If your next question is, did we kill your horse to flood your system with adrenalin and push you into heat, the answer is no. Teal responded because he is the kindest, gentlest, most caring man I have ever known. I came to tell you because I like you and admire you, and my family likes you as well. I'm sorry if my presence takes away from your necessity to grieve for your old friend. Good day, Mistress." With that he turned on his heel and strode away, leaving the girl standing under an arbor of climbing rohanth, their yellow petals drifting lazily into her hair. She bit her bottom lip until he was out of earshot before sinking onto the pavement and sobbing.

"Remind me never, ever to volunteer to do something like that again," Ardenai grumped, scowling under his brows at Ah'ren. "And who told her she was to be part of the breeding program? I thought that was somewhere in the future, not the current chukka. She half expected me to inflict myself on her right then and there. She was scared. So was I."

"I have no idea who told her," Ah'ren said, stirring her tea and looking at the four people at table with her. "But I will find out. From her reaction it was handled very badly, and now we'll have to do damage control before we can make progress."

"She told me she had received a letter," Konik said, and he did not look happy.

"When did she tell you that?"

"Just a bit ago, when she got to the stable. She'd been crying, by the way." He shot Ardenai a mildly disapproving look, though a comment did not follow.

"She's still with Padmar?" Swift asked.

Teal nodded. "She asked for a little time alone with him."

"Well, that's probably been rethought by now," Swift murmured. "I should go and sit with her until we're ready to head off."

"I'll come along," Ah'ren said.

"I'll meet you at the administrative offices," Konik said, giving Swift's hand a quick pat. "I have an appointment for a haircut, but I won't be long, no pun intended."

"You should be long," Swift smiled. "That's such a rare hair color on a young man. That gorgeous silver stuff should be sweeping your shoulder blades."

Konik stiffened, but Ardenai, still a little rattled from his encounter with Ah'cora, didn't catch it. "I second that," he joked. "You worry about being a proper Equi, but you have no proper Equi overbraid. Why is that?"

"I promised my grandsire I'd keep it short," Konik purred. Again, the warning was missed.

"That seems a little...pardon the term...over-reactive," Swift responded. "The man has been dead for years. If you want long hair, you should feel free to have long hair."

Konik's cup hit the table hard. "So now we're dictating hairstyles?" he said sharply. "That seems a little...pardon the term... overweening. Do you badger everyone who has short hair? Krush has short hair, do you annoy him like this?"

"Nik, I do apologize!" Ardenai exclaimed. "I should keep all my brain in one place. Again I've hit a nerve with you. I am so sorry."

"We both are," Swift said, giving his hand a squeeze. "Not for anything would I offend you, my friend. You have every right to keep your decisions private. You go right ahead and get your hair cut."

Konik retrieved his cider with both hands and hunched over it, sensing the uncomfortable silence and the eyes, full of concern. It made him feel like a spoiled and petulant child – something he had never been. He blew across the cup while he thought, then said abruptly, "One afternoon when I was almost nineteen years old my grandsire and I were working with some new horses, and I foolishly tried to let him know that I thought most things responded better to love than fear.

"He grabbed me with his fingers through my braid, forced me to my knees, slammed my forehead into the dirt, and told me I was a freak of nature. I wanted to sing instead of fight, probably wanted to be an Equi and not a Telenir – I would never be a real man in personality or stature and certainly never a Wind Warrior. Then he took out his knife, jerked my head back, and starting at the crown of my head, he shaved that braid off. He said freaks should be branded as such, and he told me that if I ever grew my hair back, he'd geld me. That night he threw my hair in the fire as a reminder." Konik took a deep breath and quieted his insides. "Even after a hundred years, the feel of an overbraid is a memory I do not want. Now, I'm going to go get a haircut. We're going to be moving continents today, so to speak, and I want to be as cool as possible." He put the cup down quietly, rose with a courtly bow and left the table.

Ardenai put his elbows on the table, his forehead in his palms and sighed, "I am such an ass. I know how tired I am from yesterday, how tired all of you must be. He's the one who actually went through it. The boys are still in bed, probably will be all day, and I'm guessing Nik didn't sleep at all."

"About fifteen minutes – five minutes three times," Swift said, seemingly unconcerned. "But even dead tired he plays a mean game of polo. Be comforted," she added, "Nik bottles things up inside, and it's not good for him. Not good for his heart. It speaks to his friendship with us, and his trust in us, that he would tell us something that painful." She stood up, Ah'ren got up with her, and they headed off for the stables.

"I still feel like an insensitive ass," Ardenai muttered. "When did I get to be such an ass? Is it part of this whole emergent Dragonhorse personality?"

"Not at all," Teal said soothingly. "You've always been an ass." Then he laughed. "I'm going to follow the girls. I want to make sure Padmar is stored somewhere safe until I can do a thorough examination."

"You think someone killed him, don't you?"

"I do," Teal nodded. "I think the horse was poisoned."

"How?" Ardenai grimaced. "Why? I can see if it was your horse, or my horse, or Nik's, but Ah'cora? She just got here. Nobody even knows her."

"Somebody does," Teal responded. "And it's somebody who has full access to the dome."

CHAPTER 9

At planet-rise they were once again on the pock-marked surface of the Old Man's Face. According to the Lebonathi history books it was indeed called Shala-Anshar, same as the beautiful city with the sewers full of bodies. They left half the teams to work there and moved counter-clockwise around the planet to investigate the smallest continent, Enki-Dara.

Long, mountainous, and rugged, it was higher in elevation than Shala-Anshar, and slightly more bearable temperature-wise. They'd chosen a pretty little city on the southeast side of the continent to begin their explorations. It was set on a wide bay, and the sea had once lapped close to its walls, which were fortified against its possible incursion. Ruins of boats dotted the sand and old pilings spoke of many ships and prosperous trade.

They approached the city with trepidation, wondering from which opened door the first bodies would fall. By now they'd figured out that whomever, or whatever had destroyed the population had done so systematically, and then sprayed the evidence with whatever substance it was that kept the AEW, or anybody else for that matter, from seeing what they'd done. It looked to the casual observer like a planet on the road to self-annihilation, nothing more. Certainly it did not look like a planet being deliberately driven to destruction, but that was the conclusion they were coming to.

Gideon may have hit it square when he'd mentioned that this had happened when Equus and the AEW were, "between Dragonhorses." Konik had brought it up, and both Teal and Ardenai had seriously considered it. A male rose to govern only every seven hundred years, and he governed about a hundred and fifty years, from the age of one hundred when he reached full maturity, to about two hundred and fifty, when he died or became too frail to rule. That left several centuries for something like this to happen on the outskirts of the AEW without anybody noticing. The priestesses and the Great Council who ruled between Dragonhorses rarely sallied forth to conquer or correct. That, was the job of the Dragonhorse. Always had been and everybody in the various galactic alliances knew it. But why would anybody do this? What they'd done was now horrifyingly clear. Why, remained as elusive as ever.

In this city they looked immediately for the ancient symbol of the icosahedron, the twenty equilateral triangular faces which, according to Gallios and Kehailan, would represent clean drinking water. It was found in roughly the same place as it had been in Shala-Anshar, with roughly the same equipment surrounding it. Smaller city, smaller system. Ardenai braced himself and nodded for one of the expedition hydrologists to activate the water doors. These slid open more easily. No bodies. They all breathed a sigh of relief.

"There's been water through here," the hydrologist said, almost as an apology. "The bodies could be downstream. If they've been sprayed, we'll have to find them on foot, or with the gliders."

But two hours of searching up and down the watercourse turned up nothing. The people were simply gone. They did find living scrub-brush, and even signs that, on occasion, it rained here. There were many places around the city where gardens had been planted, fountains had splashed, and it gave Ardenai more hope than he'd felt for a while.

He and Teal were sitting on a low stone planter in the shade of a gracefully curving wall when they heard laughter and Gideon and Criollo came around the corner, looking fit and ready for adventure. When they asked if they could join up, both fathers nodded their approval. "We're getting ready to head up into the mountains," Teal said. "Why don't you two come with us? There are some big caves we'd like to explore, and some outlying farms, as well."

They took a small glider, Dominus being too unwieldy for the mountains, and gave a wiggle of stubby wings to the governor and Swift, who were below them on a rocky outcrop, exploring what might have been a guard tower or small monastery.

"Headed for the caves, I suppose," Swift said, running her sleeve across her sweating forehead. "I wonder if they're any cooler than this is."

"Perhaps," Konik chuckled, "using a scale of hot, hotter, hottest. I think until we can get water flowing here again, and get some shade trees planted, true cool in the sense we Equi know it won't exist."

Swift looked at him and smiled. This place excited him, and when he was excited, his eyes sparkled like a boy's and he bounded gracefully from place to place, rock to rock, willing things to be alive and productive again. Who could Ardenai have chosen, had he been given a thousand lifetimes, who would bring such caring to this planet and these people as Konik? Sometimes she loved him until she ached inside, and hoped he couldn't see it. His life was complicated enough as it was.

She climbed more carefully up to stand beside him and look over the countryside stretched out far below. "What a shame," she said quietly. "They took it all. Either the Lebonathi, or those who came to conquer. Trees, grass, water, anything to give rest to the soul, is gone. Even alone out here I can feel the stress. How much more must they feel it in those crowded cities?"

Konik's head turned slowly in her direction, expressive brows working. "Swift, say that again," he demanded. He sat on a boulder, legs dangling, and looked intrigued.

She chose a rock slightly below and across from him, and seated herself, pulling her hip canteen and taking a drink of juice while she thought. "I said, truncated version, that there isn't anything anywhere to relieve stress or…oops!" The slick metal canteen slipped from her hand and dropped to the base of the rock. She leaned forward and reached slightly under to retrieve it, and in that instant Konik saw a blur of motion in and out, and Swift was bitten.

In the second it took him to get to her, she'd already collapsed. He gathered her in his arms and just for a moment her hand touched his chest. "Don't be afraid," she whispered, and she was gone. No breath, no heartbeat. Konik made a sound too shocked to be a sob, and clutched her to him, rocking back and forth and trying to get himself to breathe without realizing he was doing it.

She was gone. She was gone. The two women he had allowed himself to love, both gone in a space of days. He moved away from the rock with her, realizing on some level that he, too, could be bitten by whatever monster was under there, and slid down the face of a smooth stone to sit with her in his lap. He needed to do something, to call somebody. Like Ah'davan, she was just…gone. Talking one second, dead the next. His brain just wouldn't let it penetrate enough to cry or scream, move or make sense of what was happening – had happened. She was gone. He just sat there and looked at her sweet face, brushing an errant, honey-brown wisp back with his fingertips into her thick mane of hair while some wildly rational being deep inside kept demanding that he do something, call someone.

He decided that could wait a bit. When they came, they'd take her, and she was still warm and soft in his arms, almost seeming to sleep but for the lack of breathing…and the lack of snoring. She snored sometimes. Very quietly, almost a purr. He closed his eyes and let his forehead drop against hers one last time.

Suddenly, her whole body jerked in a single motion, startling Konik nearly to death. Both her elbows bent in tandem and her eyes snapped open – closed – opened, in what could only be described as a mechanical reset. Konik recognized it immediately. Androtechnology. Swift...had android eyes. She drew a long, shuddering breath and whispered, "Pythos. Only Pythos. Please Nik."

He managed to nod, fumbled with the strap on his harness to initiate a scramble relay, said, “Medical emergency. Dome Sanecere, alert Physician Pythos.” In two seconds they were both gone. Only Swift’s canteen and the glider remained behind.

“These are huge,” Gideon breathed, holding up a light and looking around. “It looks like people may have stabled animals in here at some time, too.”

“We probably shouldn’t go any deeper until our sires get here,” Criollo cautioned. He really wasn’t much for dark places after yesterday, but he didn’t want to say that to his intrepid cousin. Criollo had to admit it, Gideon had been through far more than he ever had, and probably been braver about it to boot. He’d surely had more experience with death. As for himself, Criollo could still smell, however faintly, the rotten cloth and long dead bodies, as though it was stuck in his nose. He wondered if it would ever come out, if the images would ever fade. “I’ll just go back to the mouth of the cave and see if they’re through down at the farm yet.”

“Good idea,” Gideon said absently, eyes busy studying the cave walls, the ceiling, the floor – perfect place to keep animals. Not a bad place to keep a family, for that matter. Dry, relatively cool. He wondered if it had always been so, or if in ages past it had been damp inside. He wondered if there was water beneath his feet in some hidden grotto. The sensors on Belesprit had said there was water under the surface. How exciting would that be? Gideon could picture it bubbling up to fill the small lake bed they’d found in a notch above the farm house. That little lake had watered the old orchard which tottered crazily east of the house, and there were signs that there had been a big garden, as well. They must have raised animals, Gideon thought. The country was too rugged to farm beyond the immediate needs of the family.

To their communal relief there hadn’t been any bodies in the house.

No dead animals in the shed or the barn. Again, everything and everybody had just vanished. More comforting than the findings on Shala-Anshar, but no more enlightening. Gideon allowed himself the question which most burned in his mind – where were the animals? Why were there no signs of animals? He could look around outside and picture grass and trees and water, goats or sheep on the hillside, maybe caronai or horses, maybe even a dog barking in the doorway, a tabby ped like his aunt's ped, Mikilosh, stretching in the sunshine – a scurrying spinklemaus, a gracefully soaring raptor. What was civilization without animals?

As if in answer to his question he heard a rustling in the cave ahead of him. A pair of eyes glowed momentarily eighteen inches or so off the floor and then disappeared as whatever it was turned and ran back into the cavern. Without a second thought, Gideon pursued it into the darkness. An hour later his worried sire found the light where Gideon had dropped it.

Gideon wasn't hurt, but he, too, was a little worried. He was sitting on a stone bench against the wall of a large well-lit room that seemed to be part of the cave system. He wasn't sure. They'd whacked him over the head with something and he'd been out for a while, probably not very long. They, whoever they were, aside from obviously darker-skinned Lebonathi, sat across the room from him. Four men, a teenaged boy about his age, two women, one with a baby, and two small children, probably girls, all contemplated him in silence. At the feet of the boy were the two eyes that had glowed in the dark. A long-legged dog, with a smooth coat and small, upright ears. In spite of his fear, Gideon smiled.

"You have animals!" he said happily, and the people jumped at his voice. "Sorry." He pointed to the dog. "We have wondered if there were any animals left at all on your planet."

"You are flamen," one of the men said. "You are one of them."

"That again," Gideon responded, shaking his head. "I am not flamen, I am simply fair of skin and hair. I am Equi. My sire…my papa, is the Thirteenth Dragonhorse." Probably not the best term to use in conjuring up a soothing image. "My father is the leader of our planet. He came here with our people to rid your world of flamen. To bring your water back, and your crops. Who are you?"

They just looked at him. "You are flamen," the man said again. "How did you find us?"

"I am not flamen. My name is Gideon, and my father is…" He sighed and shook his head. "Never mind. I followed the dog. I saw his eyes glowing in the dark and I was excited because we haven't seen any other animals so far in our explorations of your planet. Well, caronai, some birds, and supposedly there are snakes." He caught the communal glare and subsided. They weren't hearing him.

"That was foolish," the man observed. "You could have been following anything."

"And that, is precisely what my sire is going to say, just before he tells me I can't explore anymore because I have no impulse control." He shifted on the hard seat and reached back to rub at the bump on his head. His hands were not bound, though he was loosely tied by one leg to a stake in the floor of the room, mostly to let him know he was a prisoner. He put his mouth to his drinking tube and took a few swallows of water to calm a growing sense of unease. If they thought he was flamen, they were going to kill him. No, maybe they'd hold him for ransom. No, they hated the flamen. They wouldn't want the flamen to know, would they? "Do the flamen even know you exist? We didn't. Our sensors can't see anything living on this continent, or any of the others, for that matter. How do you live? What do you eat? Do you have animals other than the dog there?"

"You flamen make mock of us," the man said. "And yet, we have survived your occupation of our world all these many years."

"Occupation? Like from another planet occupation?" Gideon wracked his brain. "Are you saying the flamen...are aliens? The people who are white all over are the ones who invaded you?"

How was that possible? Eridi was white all over. Halaf had been white all over. Suddenly Gideon had a headache. He was half afraid he was going to die, and he really wanted to pet that dog.

"Best you be silent," the man said. He dismissed the others to go, "Summon Muru and the council," and settled back to stare at Gideon.

The boy let his head lounge back against the relative cool of the wall and concentrated with every ounce of clarity he could muster. *Dad! Dad! Dad!* Over and over, just like yesterday. What if, like yesterday, his thoughts couldn't escape these walls? What if he was totally alone in this situation? If he got out of this, he was staying home tomorrow and going for a nice long horseback ride with Lionel. Maybe if Jobie's foot was better, he'd start teaching him to ride. The fantasy allowed him to relax a bit and he jumped when his father's voice penetrated his mind.

Gideon! Precious Eladeus! Where are you, Son?

I have no idea. But there are people here, and a dog! They think I'm flamen. They've summoned the council, whatever that means.

Just keep your mind open and your thoughts flowing our way. Your brother is trying to find you.

But, try as he might, curse though he did, Kehailan couldn't find Gideon in the maze of caves, or anywhere in the surrounding countryside. The fact that anything could have been made invisible to the sensors, or that they might be under a glastaline dome, made it all the more confusing. Ardenai was growing frantic, Gideon was growing tired, minutes were turning to hours and for the second day in a row they had a crisis on their hands that involved the same people.

Kehailan just shook his head, waved away the food he was being offered, and focused on his sensors, knowing four other Dragonhorse Cruisers – he corrected himself – there were five others now that Pen Darus had arrived with Dragonhorse Demeter – six cruisers and Belesprit were doing the same thing. But how had they gotten Ardenai and Nik out of that glastaline dome? Not with technology, but with telepathy. What if they couldn't find Gideon? Kehailan knew his father was a gentle, rational man. He also knew that if Gideon screamed loud enough, six Dragonhorse Cruisers would start taking that whole mountain apart and people would die. People who had a dog. Kehailan loved dogs.

At that moment, a big, blue-clawed hand closed over his shoulder and Bonfire Dannis kissed his cheek, saying, "Don't you worry, my friend. My sniffer and I are going down here in just a bit." She tapped the side of her nose and smiled, revealing her fangs. "I'm taking a couple of friends along, so you can stay right here and help us if we need it." Dannis-speak for: *I'm not taking you because you're too slow and you'd only get in the way.* Kehailan nodded and let Ardenai know Bonfire and company would shortly be on the hunt. Surprisingly, Ardenai told them to hold off and stand by – just for now.

The cavern began to fill with people. A dozen or so men and women came to sit close to where Gideon was tied, and a man whose smile was warm and genuine sat in the center. Gideon rose, bowed to them in respect, and sat back down, passing right hand over left. "Ahimsa. I wish thee peace. I am Gideon," he said. "Ardenai Gideon Morning Star. I am Equi. We are exploring your world in hopes of freeing you from the flamen. We are sorry it has taken us so long to get here. We only just realized you were in trouble."

"Interesting," said the pleasant man. "You are not flamen?"

"No. I am Equi."

"The Equi are darker people, Gideon. They have ears like cut seashells, like the curving horns of mountain rams. You are not swarthy, nor are your ears like theirs."

Mountain rams? You have mountain rams? He bit back his excitement. "No. Though not all of us are olive skinned. I am adopted. Chosen, which accounts for the ears. I was taken in by the Equi and am being raised as such. I am a mix of races. Equi, Declivian, Coronian and Terren. My eyes are golden like Declivians, my skin is fair like theirs, and Coronians as well. Terrenes are all sorts of colors, but mostly brown and black, and their ears look pretty much like mine."

"And what part of you is Equi?"

"My heart," the boy replied.

"I am Muru. Tell us why you are here."

"He will only tell us lies!" someone exclaimed. "Why are we listening to him? He is flamen!"

"And we are not," Muru said reasonably. "The flamen have destroyed our world with their rhetoric, let us not destroy our civility with ours."

Gideon nodded, admiration flooding his eyes despite his fear. This man sounded like his sire. Starting at the beginning and using as many interesting details as he could, he told the council and those with them how the Equi had come to be amongst them and why. He even told them about the city they had found on Shala-Anshar, and the bodies in the sewers, and how he had been trapped for a day in the darkness with his companions.

They listened in a respectful silence, though Gideon doubted very much if they believed him. He'd been through it and wouldn't have believed it from the mouth of another. He sighed, and fell silent a moment, then said, "I would like very much to find out more about you! How have you survived? Do you have animals? You said mountain rams. Do you have mountain rams?"

Muru just smiled. "Perhaps later," he said, and addressed the others. "For all his size, this is a boy no older than mine. I have every reason to think he's telling us the truth, but…" Gideon's heart stopped momentarily, "…if he is who he says he is, he can summon a man who it is said entered the tunnels with the slaves of Namen, and freed them with his own hands, and bathed them and tended their wounds." He turned back to Gideon. "I know him only as the Soft One."

Gideon nodded and smiled. "Ah'ria Konik Nokota. Equi governor of the Lebonathi worlds. What you have heard of him is the truth. My father not only admires him, but loves him like a brother. Would you like to speak with him?"

"How will we know it is he?"

Gideon thought about that. "Who do you know that he knows, or who would recognize him?"

Muru shrugged.

"Perhaps someone who was enslaved in the tunnels? Who bears the scars? Would that help?"

"Perhaps," Muru nodded. "Can you summon him?"

"I can try," Gideon said. "Like my father I am a telepath. I suppose that's another part of me that's Equi. I'm not nearly as good as he is. If I can get the message to him up there near the surface…if we're down lower. Anyway, let me see what I can do. But even if I can get the governor to come, which shouldn't be a problem, I can't tell him where to come, because I don't know where I am."

"We will worry about that later," Muru smiled.

Gideon squeezed his eyes shut and forced his thoughts to be clear and precise. *Ardenai? Dad?*

Right here. Making any headway?

They want to talk to Nik. Apparently, he's the one they trust, but they want someone with him who was in the tunnels. Would Bona come? And there is a woman here who is bald like Ensharra. Or like Ensharra used to be. Maybe the anchoress would come as well?

Are they going to let you go?

I haven't asked. Besides, they still haven't told me if they have more animals than just the dog.

Gideon could hear his father's exasperated sigh. *Tell them I'm going back down the mountain to get the governor. I will send Teal to get Bona. Tell them if they hurt you ... never mind. I love you. Hold on tight.*

It took Ardenai fifteen minutes at a hard run, Teal beside him, to get back out to the mouth of the cave, another two minutes to where they'd left the glider. They dropped panting into the seats and went flashing down the mountain to land next to Konik's craft. They called aloud, they called telepathically. They found Swift's canteen. No Konik, no Swift. "Now they have them, too?" Ardenai cried, nearly tearing his hair in frustration. "How can they want him and have him at the same time?"

"Just stand still," Teal responded. "Ardi, stand still, you're erasing any signs of what went on here." Teal spent interminable minutes looking at the ground, then tapped his communications crys-tel and said, "Kehailan, have there been any emergency medical transfers today?"

There was a pause. "Yes, from right where you're standing." Another pause. "Oh…shit. Swift was bitten by a snake," he groaned. "They took her to the dome."

"Thanks," Teal said, and took a deep breath before grabbing Ardenai, who was leaning against a rock, looking stricken. "Get away from the boulders!" He activated his crys-tel. "Criollo?"

"Yes Sire. Have you found Gideon?"

"Sort of. Are you with your grandsire?"

"Right where you told me to be, yes Sir. I can reach out and touch him, just like you told me. What do you mean, sort of? Is he hurt?"

"No. I have a very difficult job for you and you need to do it quickly," Teal said, and explained what had happened.

A few minutes later Criollo stepped quietly into the room where Konik was sitting beside Swift. There were tubes running in and out of her at various places, and she was pale as death. Her left hand and arm were grotesquely swollen and nearly black beneath the pressure wrappings. There were machines beeping and huffing, and the room was very dim. Criollo took one look at Konik's face and wondered if he could even ask, much less get the man to go with him. He moved a little further into the room and cleared his throat. Konik turned his head.

"I am so sorry about Swift," Criollo said, "Is she…going to be all right?"

Konik shrugged just a little. "I have no idea. What brings you?"

"I am sorry to have to ask, but the Dragonhorse needs you desperately. There are people on Enki-Dara, they have Gideon, and they want you."

"Then they shall have me," Konik said. He stood up, contemplated Swift for a moment, then bent and kissed her forehead and followed Criollo out of the room.

They arrived within two minutes of each other – Konik from the Jocundome, Teal with Bona, and Ardenai with Ensharra. "Well, here we are, for all the good it may do us," Ardenai said, and reached to grasp Konik by the shoulder. "I am so sorry to hear about Swift, my friend."

Konik raised one hand. "Another time," he said. "Right now we need to get your son back. What's the plan?"

"I have no idea," Ardenai muttered.

He turned to re-establish communications with Gideon and Bona turned to Konik, concern filling his features as he grasped his forearms. "What happened to your lady, Soft One?"

"She was bitten by a snake," Konik said quietly. "Our newfound books tell us it is called a Rock Adder. I…Pythos…says she will recover." Even as he said it, he felt woozy from sheer shock and confusion. She was going to recover…because she was not a living being. And yet, she was. A loving, laughing, wise and caring person who played polo, contacted estranged children, emboldened weak hearts, and made love, gave love – to him. Her only assignment, she'd said, and silly him, he'd thought it was just a turn of phrase, or a job description. What magnificent programming! And he would have lived with it and happily, none the wiser for the rest of his days. He wanted to throw himself on the ground and scream until he passed out.

"Nik?" Ensharra was looking up at him.

"I'm fine," he smiled, stepping gratefully into the offered hug and kissing her forehead. There was that tingle of response he always felt with her, and he pushed it firmly aside. "Ah…how goes the exploration of medicinal herbs on Tras?"

"Good," she nodded. "Ah'din is brilliant. I'm learning a great deal, but I'm excited to be here, too. This place is beautiful, and for some reason it rather makes me feel like I'm home."

Ardenai turned back. "Gideon says to step inside the cave and start walking. Just you and Bona. They'll talk to the rest of us later if they like your story."

Konik gave Ardenai's arm a gentle rub and soothed, "If they were going to hurt him, they'd have done so by now. Rejoice, Ardi! There are people here, and they're alive!" With that he gestured Bona ahead of him into the cave.

They walked until it was too dark to see the floor and then snapped on a light. "That won't be necessary," a man's voice said, and a section of the cave wall slid aside to reveal an adequately illuminated tunnel going down. "This way," he said.

They're showing us how to get in, so you can bet your son did an excellent job of convincing these folks we mean them no harm. "Bona, are you able to walk on this downslope?"

"I know that if I start to fall you will catch me," the man replied, so Konik didn't know whether he was all right or not, only that he was brave.

"I will do my best," Konik chuckled. "How are your bees?"

"They are so beautiful, and so busy!" Bona replied, immediately enthused. "I have put a new colony in the box I was making. Gallios says he thinks we should put bees on Lebonath Tras."

"An interesting animal to introduce," Konik said. "Bees can tell us so much about the health of other species."

They chatted back and forth to pass the time as they walked, but the man whom they followed said nothing. He did slow his pace when Konik asked him to, and Bona apologized for his slow feet. "Has Pythos said anything to you about when you'll get your prostheses?" Konik asked.

"Yes," Bona nodded and was starting to explain when the lights went out, they were both seized firmly and steered through a sudden maze of twists and turns which left them thoroughly lost. They stepped into something with a wooden floor that was hollow beneath, and felt themselves going rapidly downward. When the lights came back on it was only a few steps to the room in which Gideon waited.

"Governor!" Gideon laughed, and there was real relief in his voice. Konik strode the length of the room and gave Gideon a reassuring hug, then sat down and patted his hands on either side for Gideon and Bona to join him. "Are they going to let us go, do you think?" Gideon asked.

"Of course they are," Konik soothed. "They're being cautious, that's all. You would be too if you'd managed to remain hidden for centuries and someone suddenly popped up on your doorstep."

"You're right," Gideon nodded, and looked across Konik to where Bona was sitting, rubbing his knees. "Thank you for coming," he said, and in that moment he realized fully that both these men were risking their lives for him. The thought made him want to cry with a pride he couldn't quite put his finger on. Konik reached across the boy, untied the rope which bound him to the stake, coiled it carefully, and placed it at his own feet.

By this time the room had once again filled with people who seated themselves in cushioned rows on the hard packed floor. Konik rose, nodded respectfully and made the ancient gesture of greeting, right hand over left. "Ahimsa, I wish thee peace. I am Ah'ria Konik Nokota, Equi governor of the Lebonathi worlds. The man to my right is my friend Bona, of the Guild of Lebonathi Farmers. We understand you wanted to meet with us."

"I am Muru," said the pleasant man, rising to grasp his forearms. "We have heard you care for the Lebonathi people, and that they call you the Soft One. Is that true?"

"Both statements are true," Konik said. "But before we begin, I must ask a favor. The boy's father is deeply distressed. This is the second time in two days Gideon's gone missing, and a father can take just so much. If you will release him to his father's arms I will spend as much time with you as you desire and tell you anything you want to know."

Gideon looked both relieved and unhappy. "But they have a dog!" he whispered. "I was hoping they had other animals as well."

Konik looked at him and chuckled softly. "You are so much like your father. Gideon, this is the beginning, not the end of our conversations with these people. Our friendship will last many years and together we will rebuild this continent – unless your father finally loses control and opens this mountain with a pulse cannon." The boy did not look convinced. "You are a prince of the Great House and the son of the Thirteenth Dragonhorse," Konik said firmly. "It is your duty to protect these people, not put them in jeopardy. If they say you may go, then that is what you must do."

Gideon bowed his head and nodded, and Muru gestured toward the back of the room. "Garash will take you to the surface," he said. The boy stepped forward and with him, the canine. Gideon rose, bowed to the council, then to Konik and Bona, and allowed himself to be shown out, stopping outside the circle to introduce himself to Garash and ask if he could pet the dog.

Konik just smiled. "He does love animals," he said. "Thank you for letting him go."

"He was never really a prisoner," Muru replied. "We do not imprison children. Speaking of which, we had asked that you bring a prisoner of the tunnels with you, Governor."

"I am that," Bona said. "When I first saw this man and his companions, I was chained naked to a mushroom cart, sleeping in the dirt and drinking my own urine to stay alive. The governor chose me from amongst the prisoners because he said I was a runner."

"And were you?"

"Yes. I wanted to go home and find my children. The flamen had come to our house. They took my daughter and when my wife resisted, they killed her. They took me prisoner. My boy was left hiding alone. Still the Equi seek him and my daughter everywhere in hopes of returning them to me."

"You look good for a man who has been chained to a mushroom cart," one of the elders said, and there was a hint of disbelief in her voice.

Bona said nothing. He stood, turned around and lifted his tunic so they could see the scars on his back and his still prominent ribs. Then he sat, pulling off his boots and socks to reveal his mutilated feet. "They chopped my toes off so I couldn't run," he said simply. "All of us were starved nearly to death. Sneaking bites of the mushrooms was punishable with whipping, or mutilation, or even death. Then the Equi came. This one, with the soft voice and the gentle hands, he knelt in the filth and unchained us, and gave us our names back, and bathed us and clothed us and took us to a safe place where there was food and shelter, medical care and companionship – up on huge ships which light the sky at night like giant stars.

"They are farm ships, brought in to feed the people, and to teach us how to feed ourselves. I would love to take you there and show you my bees! I left my bees to come talk to you. The governor left the bedside of a very sick lady whom he loves. The Anchoress of the Ancient City, who helped us in the tunnels, has come as well. We mean you no harm. What I can say to make you trust us I do not know, but I have said what I can so that you will not fear us." With that he bent once again, put his socks and boots back on, and straightened up.

"We are here to serve you. Ask us anything," Konik said, and the questions poured in.

"Thank you, Garash," said Gideon, blinking against the brightness coming from the mouth of the cave, "and you, too, Alfah. You're a good boy." Gideon hesitated and then gestured toward the opening. "I have met your father. I would like it if you met mine."

Garash was thoughtful. "We don't usually come up here, and almost never do we go outside. But still, many have taken risks today," he said at last. "I suppose I should, as well."

They walked slowly toward the mouth of the cave, and just inside the entrance a man stood up – the biggest man Garash had ever seen in his life – and beside him another, bigger yet, followed by a Lebonathi woman, tiny in comparison. Garash shrank back, but Gideon smiled and said, "Garash, this is my sire…my papa, Ardenai. This is my Uncle Teal, and this is Ensharra, Anchoress of the Ancient City. Everyone, this is Garash, son of Muru, and this is Alfah!"

"A Darian Chase Hound!" Ensharra exclaimed. "I've only seen them in books! All praise to the Gods, all is not lost after all. Garash, we are overjoyed to meet you!" She caught her breath and two tears ran unheeded down her cheeks.

"On this day much, it seems, is found," Ardenai smiled, resisting the urge to clutch Gideon to his breast and then give him a tongue lashing. "Gideon, I assume you are unscathed?"

"Unscathed but starving," he admitted, hugging his father. Then, lest Garash think he found them inhospitable he added, "We Equi eat at all hours. It's one of our planetary pass-times."

"May we offer you something?" Teal said, and his voice was gentle despite his size. Alfah had not growled at either of them, and now he went eagerly from the anchoress to Teal, licking and wagging his tail against the wall. Gideon realized that's what he'd heard just before he saw the eyes.

"Thank you, but I should get back," Garash said. "I would be honored if…" he looked first at Gideon, then from one face to another. "Would you like to come with me and meet my Papa?"

There was no hesitation. "I would love to!" Ensharra said.

"Yes," Ardenai said, putting an arm around Gideon and smiling at Garash. "The moment your father invites us. We look forward to it."

Ensharra frowned up at him. "I can go? I can't go?"

"Of course you can," Ardenai chuckled. "You are not six and a half feet tall and a Lebonathi and a half in weight. I just…much as I would like to go, I have not been formally invited – though a child's invitation is always best…" he paused and thought a moment. "I would be honored to come," he said.

"I will come back with you, as well," Gideon grinned, "But I do need just a bite of something first."

Teal respectfully declined, saying he must be about other business and letting Ardenai know that he would be close by – very close – if needed. If he thought it was a bad idea he didn't say so, and Ardenai appreciated that. He also appreciated the promise of a close eye.

While Gideon grabbed something to eat, feeding Garash and Alfa in the process, Ardenai asked Kehailan to scramble a gifting box of cinnamon orange tea. When it appeared out of thin air Garash gasped, but Ensharra leaned into him and whispered, "You'll get used to the way they move things and people, as well. They really are a very kind folk, despite their size, and they have marvelous animals."

Her words made Ardenai wonder if they were being indiscreet. These people had managed to remain hidden for centuries and suddenly there was a whole convergence at the mouth of this cave system. Certainly there was evidence of alien incursion, of alien technology. Were there still aliens about, as well? He opened the thought and Gideon gave him a slight, single nod. *And you're not going to believe who they are.*

They returned unescorted. There were no guards in the passageway and less than an hour's travel found them at the back of the large gathering chamber without anyone noticing. They were all focused on Konik and Bona, and they could hear Konik's rolling laughter before they could see him. Ardenai touched his thoughts momentarily, just to let him know they were there, and then sat cross legged on the floor with Gideon and Ensharra beside him to listen.

Nik is putting every ounce of strength he has left into this, Ardenai thought. His long association with the governor told him the man was nearly exhausted, sitting forward with his hands folded casually between his legs to hide their slight trembling. There was also a look – subtle, almost unnoticeable – but the same look he'd been wearing the day Ah'davan had died in his arms. Getting on with life at the expense of his soul. Hopefully not at the expense of that new heart. Androtech or not, they were a long way from help.

The thought had no more than passed through his mind when Muru stood up and came to sit beside the governor and Bona on the stone bench. "We have questioned you nearly to death," he smiled, laying a hand on Konik's forearm. "Let us offer you some refreshment and your voices a rest."

"Thank you," Konik nodded, and cleared his throat. Muru was right; he was hoarse. Bona was only slightly better off.

"Garash is back, as well, and he has brought guests," Muru said, though neither Ardenai nor Konik had seen him glance that direction. "Please, Son. Bring those whom you invited." He made a beckoning gesture and then grinned. "I see our friend Gideon has returned, which speaks to his bravery and his indefatigable curiosity, or I miss my guess."

Ardenai laughed and nodded as he stood up and walked forward, staying close to the wall so as not to be compared in height to the others in the room. Konik was substantially taller than most, Ardenai six inches over Konik, and for some reason he found it disquieting. He bowed deeply, turned and waited for Garash to make introductions. Intriguing. Muru not only knew they were there, he knew Garash had invited them. "Papa, this is Ardenai…" the rest of the title escaped him and he stammered an apology.

"I'm Gideon's father," the Firstlord said, and grasped Muru's forearms in friendship. "Ahimsa, Muru. I wish thee peace."

"This is Anchoress Ensharra," the boy said with more confidence. "She is of the Ancient City. She helped Governor Konik in the mushroom tunnels."

Muru bowed deeply over Ensharra's hand and returned the smiles as he studied the faces. Ardenai, Firstlord of Equus and her affined worlds. Purportedly the most powerful single entity in the known galaxy – here in the flesh. No fanfare, no entourage, no crown, no adornment at all except for the armbands, which appeared, from the scarring, to have been burned into place. Every inch a prince in carriage and demeanor. Obviously adored his son. Tired right now, and concerned about coming uninvited, and yet he had come, because a boy had asked him to.

So, this was the magnificent Dragonhorse. Word had come concerning him and those whom he had brought, those whom he had found, those whom he had killed. He had not marched in wearing hobnailed boots, but flown on wings of mercy, bringing succor to those who most desperately needed it, or so the stories went. Just now he was openly and sincerely allowing himself to be studied and evaluated by someone he could easily have considered an inferior.

The woman with him was a beauty. Not young, but with a face full of character and strength. Dressed all in black, but dressed for movement, without the flowing robes and bald head which had marked the anchoresses the last three hundred years or so. This one was letting her hair grow back, ready for change and willing to sacrifice to make it happen. From the look of her she trusted both Firstlord and governor with all her heart and courageous soul. Even as he felt a slight and very pleasant tingle which had been too long absent in his life, Muru heard himself breathe a sigh of relief. Was he really going to live to see the end of the flamen? To go outside into the world and reclaim the land of his fathers? He remembered his guests, standing patiently and apologized.

"No need," Ardenai chuckled. "I've been studying you, too. I brought you this. It is cinnamon orange tea, the gift we traditionally give upon a first meeting. When we know your needs and desires, we will help with them as well, insofar as we are able."

His voice flowed rich and carried easily, with a resonance which said he sang. Slightly deeper than the governor's, without the strikingly unusual timbre.

"We must sing together sometime," Muru said, and laughed self-consciously at the random intimacy of his statement. "Thank you for the tea. Please come with us. We have set a meal for you. Of course we will ply you with questions, but in that you can offer your kind friend the governor some relief. He and…" he looked around then, and saw Bona leaving with two men, deep in conversation. "Bona. He's been stolen by the mycology council. There's an odd blush on the mushrooms this year and they're probably wondering if he recognizes it. Please, come and join us," he said, and offered his arm to Ensharra, who smiled and slipped her arm through his as they walked.

Ardenai dropped a step behind and glanced over at the governor. *Nik, please tell me what happened to Swift, and if she is going to be all right.*

Later. Even as a thought it was a warning growl.

Ardenai brought up a quieting hand. *You said that hours ago. It is later. You look hard-ridden, my friend, and you need to rest. I know Muru and the others will understand if you want to leave to be with her.*

No need. Pythos says he will keep her asleep a few days – through the worst of the pain. He made a humorless sound, wishing Pythos would do the same for him. Spare him the worst of the pain.

Tell me what happened and I'll leave it be.

Precious Equus, you are nothing if not persistent. All right, but do bear in mind that no matter what I tell you, I haven't the slightest idea what actually happened.

Fair enough.

Swift had just said the most intriguing thing, and I was sitting there realizing how much I valued her words and her wisdom, when she dropped her canteen...such a simple thing...and she was bitten when she reached to retrieve it. Ardi, she was... the thought stopped abruptly in confusion so palpable it made Ardenai wince and Konik steady himself momentarily against the wall.

Nik...

You have got to let me work through this.

There was a slight shake of Ardenai's head. *She was what, Governor?*

There was a long pause and an audible whuffle, which Muru was too occupied to notice. *Dead. And then she wasn't. Now will you please, please...leave me alone?* Just for a moment he looked like he was going to pass out, and Ardenai resisted the urge to reach for him.

For now, Ardenai replied, wishing he'd had that conversation with Wren one of the times it had occurred to him. Not that she was ever there when it did. In another of what he'd come to call, 'Dragonhorse Moments', he realized that even those conversations which seemed insignificant in the broader scheme of things, needed to be had. He could only imagine Nik's sense of grief and betrayal, which, given his own experience, was more than enough to make his head pound. Speaking before he knew for sure what he was talking about, would be even greater folly than the painful silence which had fallen between them. One thing was becoming obvious; Swift was one of Mountain hold's beautifully sophisticated Androtech beings – all praise to the Creator. If she wasn't, she'd be dead right now.

"We tend to eat as communities or extended families, but always a personal choice," Muru was saying, gesturing them onto comfortable cushions at one of several long, low tables which seemed to be lit by sunlight, though the light was cooler, and slightly greener. "Everybody brings whatever they've fixed and we sit together and discuss the day. Tonight, will be exceptional. Word has gone out of your arrival. Word which says you are not legend or wishful fantasy, but flesh and blood and as real as we are. As people can leave their crops and their chores over the days, they will come to meet you and your representatives. We are spread out through the valley, using flamen technology against their own sensors, and since they consider Enki-Dara an empty continent, they haven't been watching too closely, or so we think and hope. They seem to have focused all their attention on Namen. That's where they jammed up the survivors."

Ardenai had been looking up, studying the light which filtered in. "Glastaline!" he exclaimed. "You've gotten your hands on technology that has baffled us for seasons!" He looked at Muru with unveiled admiration. "I'm assuming this is their technology, not yours."

"You assume correctly," Muru nodded. Pitchers were passed down the table and Muru poured everyone a drink before filling his own glass and intercepting a tray of breads and cheeses. "In the short run we saved ourselves by getting our hands not only on what you call glastaline, but the spray solution which renders things invisible to sensors. Not just yours, but theirs as well. Odd, and rather amusing, really, that they would invent such a thing and then use it without having first developed the technology to detect it, but that oversight on their part has allowed us to survive for hundreds of years."

"What do you mean, 'That's where they jammed up the survivors'?" Konik asked, sipping his drink and nodding his approval.

"Herded them, corralled them – everybody on one continent – mostly in that one, massive, beleaguered city. Cowing them into being afraid to go out in the world."

"Why?" Konik scowled.

"We wish we knew," Muru sighed. "We only know they are here to destroy us."

"The people in the city are alive," Ensharra said.

"If you can call that living," Muru replied. "Look around you, Anchoress. Four hundred years ago we were a verdant and fruitful world.

Happy. Making progress. Now look at us. All this destruction, death and intellectual backsliding in a scant four centuries? Except for what we've managed to save, everything has been destroyed. Our beautiful forests are nearly gone, our lakes and rivers, most of the animals which so intrigue Gideon. Everything but the air, and without the forests that will be gone soon. Our world will cease to breathe."

"What...are they...after?" Konik muttered, holding his glass up to the light like a crystal ball. "What are they taking? Obviously they're still taking it, or they wouldn't still be here."

"Water? Timber?" Muru offered. "We can't tell. We have no idea what might yet exist elsewhere. They ravaged us, rounded up the ones of us who hadn't fled the city and the surrounding countryside, and left. If we'd not been forewarned by what was happening on the other continents and made a plan for escape, they'd have gotten us all. We know they are heartless monsters, and I'm sure if they knew we were here, we'd be dead or gone. Please keep that in mind as you come and go."

"Of course," Ardenai nodded. "We will be discreet, and you will be discreetly protected, as well. Tell me something," he said, leaning back on the cushions to rest one elbow, "How do you know so much about what happened here, when the people in the cities of Namen have no idea how they got where they are?"

Muru looked a little surprised, and then sad. "We have written records from that time and forward. What people planned, what they tried, how we got the alien technology, how we saved some of the animals and vegetation on our continent. We also have teaching songs that we sing in school. There's one I'll have the children sing for you. It tells the story of the brave Enki-Daran who captured a glastaline web weaving ship and laid the web which keeps us safe. He forced them to crash the ship into the sea to the north, losing his life to save us all, and keeping the secret of our valley for all time." The man shrugged and then chuckled to shake off the somber mood. "Because our records were kept in simple form, they have endured, and we have treasured them."

“If they wanted only the natural resources, then why keep alive those who consume them?” Konik said. “No. They kept many of the people alive, barely, and not for any kind of obvious slave labor. The people who live are slaves only to themselves, or so it would seem. What are we not seeing?”

His musings were interrupted when a young woman, sleekly dressed but with the shaved head of an anchoress came with a respectful nod and sat across the table from Ensharra. “I am Lillahn,” she smiled. “Your name is spoken amongst us, and we would be honored if you would join us for a discussion.”

Ensharra was immediately enthused and rose, excusing herself and taking her glass. “Please don’t take her out of sight,” Muru said, “lest Ardenai grow concerned that Bona has gone one way, Gideon another, and now Ensharra a third. It feels like we are deliberately trying to separate them.” He caught Ardenai’s sidelong glance and the hint of a grin. “Or so it would seem to me if I were in his position.”

The girl nodded again and smiled. “Yes, Papa. We’ll be right over there.” She extended her hand to Ensharra and they hurried away, giggling like children.

Muru gestured in the general direction of the anchoresses and sighed. “The delightful unease of having adventurous children. It is those brave women and a few men who bring us such information as we have. They travel thousands of miles and risk much, and sometimes they do not return. My precious wife was one of them who did not come back. She and her father died on the same trip. Nearly three years gone now.”

“Not a very pleasant thing for us to have in common, and yet we do,” Ardenai observed. “You, Konik, Bona, me. All of us have lost a beloved wife. Bona his children, as well.”

“And yet life continues,” Muru said. There was a slight pause. “Is Ensharra alone, too?”

“By choice,” Konik drawled, sensing the intent of the question and resisting both the urge to snicker and the urge to bristle. “Still looking for the right man. He’s going to have to be something to deserve that one.”

Muru nodded thoughtfully and watched the conversation going on at the far table.

"Gideon says you think the flamen are off-worlders," Ardenai said, disturbing his reverie. "This is the part where I become confused. Our doctors tell us the flamen are just albinized Lebonathi – the sons of the rich, not aliens of any kind. And, if this is an occupied world on some level or another, why are there rich people?"

"The same reason there are albinized people, I would suppose," Muru shrugged.

There was an electrified silence, then Konik brought both his fists down on the table and laughed. "Camouflage!" he exclaimed, causing others to turn. He immediately subsided and looked embarrassed. He said it again, more softly, but with no less intensity. "Camouflage! If you can get people to think their children are more valuable if they're albinized, you can move much more freely among the population. If you can attach status to albinization, you can elevate yourself in the process – put yourself in a position both of power and relative anonymity in just a few generations. When I was Eridu's so-called guest, he used to talk about, 'Them'. There was always this intimation that he knew strangers were afoot amongst the native population, but I never got the sense he actually knew who they were. This would explain it."

The comment jolted the Firstlord a little. He'd almost forgotten that Konik had been the prisoner of that madman, Eridu. He'd been treated like royalty one day, tortured nearly to death the next – fed half-raw meat to the point of near starvation – but he'd also sat in council with Eridu, making up fantastic plots to buy himself time and listening to Eridu and others talk. He never mentioned it, but that extra insight had to be there. No wonder he was more attuned to these people than everyone else.

Ardenai caught the governor's quizzical eyebrow and smiled without humor. His head was still reeling with the input. He was trying to sort it by value and probability and still have a conversation, when what he needed, was silence – away from the laughter at the adjoining tables, away from this fascinating distraction. His granddam occasionally joked about her brain being full. Now, he realized, it was no joke. No matter Muru's comforting words, Gideon had disappeared yet again, Bona was off in the unknowns, Ensharra was beyond his immediate grasp, and Nik was too thoroughly engrossed and exhausted to notice. He wondered how much he could look around before it became rudeness.

Muru caught Ardenai's posture and said, "I am not being a very good host. Is everything to your liking?"

"Given that we popped out of the sky with no warning of any kind, I think you've been more than gracious. I do think we've outstayed our welcome, and our governor has an injured companion to get back to."

Despite his kind words, Muru sensed Ardenai's unease and rose immediately, bowing slightly in his direction. "I'm sure Garash and Gideon are with either the newest litter of puppies or bottle-feeding the baby goats, and Bona is most likely just inside the mushroom beds, or out in one of the closest gardens. Let me show you where they are. You can retrieve your anchoress on the way back."

He gestured in the direction they were to go, and both Ardenai and Konik stood up and followed, nodding to Ensharra as they passed. If she was in any way concerned it was not apparent, and that comforted the Firstlord – that, and the fact that he was quite sure Bonfire Dannis and her companions had sniffed out their location and told the Master Captain.

They made their way through the main dining and living areas, through a large communal kitchen which reminded them of the kitchen in the Great House, and then outside, into a deep and sheltered canyon with towering, naturally terraced walls of pale pink stone which appeared to curve in slightly at the top.

Trees of various kinds were everywhere, some within orchards, others growing wild. There were pleasant grassy areas, and long narrow fields blessed with running water. Dotting the walls of the canyon were caves, many with beautifully sculpted entrances, most with terraced gardens, and all of them buzzing with the evening's activities. They could hear instruments and singing, the laughter of children and the barking of dogs.

"Welcome to the world of the Darans," Muru said with an outward gesture. "You are looking at the collapsed ceiling of an enormous prehistoric cave system nearly six thousand feet deep in most places. It runs from northeast to southwest for over a thousand miles, and it is one of the ancient wonders of our planet. In this place live more than two hundred and fifty thousand souls whose lives are now in your hands."

"How can this be?" Ardenai breathed, looking around. "We have absolutely no sense of any of this."

"Good. The web-weaving song is true, then," Muru replied. "We are thriving, albeit on a relatively small scale. We have to control our population in order not to outstrip our resources, and we've tried to leave plenty of room for the many thousands of trees as well as other vegetation we are propagating, and for breeding those animals which are left to us."

"If you are thriving, and propagating trees to plant on a large scale, then you have plans to try to take back your world," Konik said quietly, and his words made Muru turn and stare. Konik flashed his beguiling smile and continued, "To thrive, implies growth, both physical and intellectual. Surely, with the anchoresses making forays to Namen you must have a network of resistance. What's stopping you?"

Without hesitation the man replied, "Religion," and there was defeat in his tone. "Not faith, which is a wonderful thing, but religion. You're right, of course. We'd planned to help our world correct itself by simply employing the truth – letting the people know there were those amongst them who were out to exploit and destroy, who had created an artificial system so people would aspire to wealth beyond necessity and embrace greed, which makes people distrust those above and below them and gather into castes. That, we thought we could overcome. Then, as if they knew, they created this fear-based religion and made people afraid to think. You cannot reason with religion, and you cannot reason with fear, especially when it is clothed as self-righteousness. It is a double curse from which we have not been able to recover."

"Sometimes the truth needs a little help getting told," Konik said, laying a hand on Muru's shoulder, "and there are many ways in which to tell it. We will help you, and together we will succeed. I promise." His eyes narrowed as he looked out over the valley, and Ardenai could see him working on a thought.

"What's bothering you, Governor?"

Konik shook his head. "Nothing's bothering me, but…something unbidden is intriguing me, and it goes back to that cursed ballad we've been mired in for thousands of years."

"Now I'm intrigued," Ardenai said. "Uneasy, but intrigued."

"Remember the line, 'Pallid Death on hooves of darkness'? It makes me wonder if we've found Pallid Death – if maybe the Priestesses hopped on the legend with everybody else over the years, and the real threat yet awaits us on the world of the flamen."

Ardenai shuddered. "Precious Equus, I hope you're imagining things, Governor. Remember, you can wring any confession you want out of literature if you torture it long enough."

"I hope you're right," Konik said, and clapped Muru's shoulder again before releasing it. "I'm sure you're right. In any case, this particular incursion is about to end for them, and not well."

CHAPTER 10

Partly because he was exhausted and sound asleep, mostly because it didn't make a lot of sense, the message came through twice before Ardenai heard it at all.

"Your wife is here."

Well, of course she was. Maybe not sprawled beside him with her fingers in his ribs and one leg thrown over his knees, fetching bed-snatcher that she was, but somewhere on the planet, or the dome or maybe Dragonhorse Thirteen. Maybe the lavage. He'd managed to blink a couple of times and take a deeper breath when it came a third time.

"Your wife is here." This time there was an addendum. "Dragonhorse, Primuxori Ah'riodin is here." Now he was at least conscious.

He sat up, realizing he was in his apartments on the Jocundome, and that he was alone in bed. He'd been with Muru. Had dinner with the Enki-Darans and talked late. Managed to get Gideon away from the baby goats, Bona from the farmers…Ensharra…wasn't sure what he'd done with her … couldn't persuade the governor to go to bed; had looked in on Swift and left Nik there… not that long ago. That's why he was on the dome and not in his own forested bower on Lebonath Tras. The message repeated itself a fourth time. "Ah'riodin is here."

"Coming," he croaked, not sure to whom he was speaking. He was so tired, and so starving hungry he could hardly think. What time was it?

How long had he been asleep? He managed to get his feet over the side of the bed and his head under some unpleasantly cold water before he could really make sense of the message. Io was here. Dread washed over him just as surely as the cold water running down his back. He let it run until he was gasping and shivering and his eyes were wide open, then warmed it a little and rubbed himself all over with foaming rosemary and scrubsand. There was a spot on his back he wasn't used to washing by himself, and that's when he began to wonder where Ah'ren was.

He wasn't worried. She was always busy – with maps, with people, probably just now with Ah'cora, maybe even with Nik. Ardenai realized he was lucky to see her at all, but right now he wanted her company. Maybe she was already in her chambers. He'd stop by and check on the way to the sanecere. Part of him knew he should hurry. Part of him desperately wanted food. Part of him wanted to kick himself for sending for Io. The rest of him wanted to crawl back in bed and pretend like everything was perfect.

He listened to the dithery sub-entity which dragged him out the door at a trot and over to the administrative chambers in the hope Wren would look up from her maps and smile at him. She didn't. He turned without stopping and went on to the sanecere, half afraid that if he let himself lose momentum he'd freeze in place like a terrified fleeter. He was in the corridor heading for Pyrgus' office before he allowed himself to slow down, and by that time, he had an escort.

"This way," one of them said, and he found himself in a small, private dining room where breakfast was laid and Pyrgus looked up and flashed him a tentative smile.

"Please, eat something before we go in," he said, gesturing to the chair across the table, and Ardenai sat down. Just the look on the man's face told him things were not good, but he dutifully sat and made himself reach for the tea pot.

"I'm assuming she's worse than you expected," Ardenai said, wondering if his voice was steady. He'd discovered a lump the size of a polo ball bobbing between his guts and his windpipe and tried unsuccessfully to wash it down with tea. The first bite of food had no flavor and coated the polo ball, making it bigger than ever. Why was Pyrgus not speaking? But … he had. He'd said one word:

Yes.

"I cannot do this alone," Ardenai managed. "I have been through this with her once too often."

Pyrgus nodded. "Pythos is with her," he said. "Now, don't give up hope. She's worse than we expected, but she is not dead, and where there is life…"

"There is hope, I know," Ardenai muttered. "Whoever said that should have his ass kicked."

"You do need to eat something," Pyrgus insisted. "Your physician has chosen that breakfast for you, and I have orders not to budge from here until you have finished. So please." He followed the request with a gesture.

Ardenai wondered just how far away Ah'ren was. If he tried to contact her, would she respond?

Of course I would. I'm your wife. What's wrong, Ardi? You sound half-hysterical.

Only half? Where are you?

Sitting with Swift. What has happened? Where are you?

I'm in the sanecere. Io is here, and I guess she's not good.

And you're panicking before the fact. Your sire's right.

What does that mean?

Ardenai heard the sigh of resignation. *Nothing. Keep an open mind and I'll find you in just a few minutes.*

Knowing that made breakfast slide a little easier, and Ardenai managed to make himself get up and walk with Pyrgus, berating himself all the while for harboring this terrible weakness. Even when Gideon had been missing, Criollo with him, he had not felt this depth of panic. He wished he could tell himself that it was because his baby girls were in jeopardy as well, but it wasn't the truth, and he knew it. He loved the idea of them, but he wasn't in love with them – not yet – and hadn't allowed himself to become so, not after losing Ah'leah.

It was Io. It was Io at three, standing in that lavage basin, cutting her hair off with Ah'ree's weaver's shears. At barely twenty-four, telling him she was pregnant with Salerno's baby. At thirty-six with an arrow sticking out of her belly. Io, hating him because he'd somehow lost the essence of their infant daughter. Io, choosing life over certain death for their twins. Io, the eternal crisis, whose very name evoked a choking sensation. Io, whom he adored and couldn't stand to be around half the time. Io, braver than he would ever be, and more complex than he could ever comprehend. Io, to whom he might never speak again, whose last words had been for him to take care of himself and come home to her. What if Abeyan was right? What if Ardenai's radically-altered relationship with Io had gotten her killed?

"Stop that right now," said a soft, growly alto, and Ah'ren had his arm, her head against his as they walked. "Making yourself crazy does nothing for Io and it does you great harm. Be prepared for whatever lies ahead and stop looking back."

Ardenai nodded and smiled without humor, took a deep breath, and walked through the door Pyrgus was holding open and into the dim interior. When he fully realized what he was looking at, he managed to land in a chair without screaming, but that was about it. "What...?" he gasped. "This is not...how...I...what happened? How did she come to be..." there was a weak gesture, "...like this?"

"And now thee knowss why thy old friend and physsician wass sso upsset when thee ssent for her, doess thee not?" Pythos hissed, turning from the glass bubble, and Ardenai could only nod.

Io was no longer lightly asleep in a comfortable crèche pod, but in a fetal position, bobbing in a yellowish-orange fluid at the far end of an umbilical tether, head shaved, skin wizened, belly protruding grotesquely past the thin frame.

It took the Firstlord a few moments to get enough breath to speak, and when he did his tone was uncomprehending. "What...possessed them to do this to her?"

"Thee would not choosse when thee wass assked," Pythos said reasonably, and he seemed almost to smile. "Thee ssaid to ssave all or none. Thiss, then, iss our feeble attempt to do thy bidding, oh Wissest of the Wisse."

"I did this?" Ardenai whispered. He got his legs under him and walked over to put his hand against the bubble. "They only asked me, if the situation should arise, whom they should…oh, Eladeus. I did not mean for this to happen. I didn't even understand that this could happen. I just meant…." The sentence ended with a groan and his forehead came to rest beside his hand.

"Do not put this on my husband!" Ah'ren said angrily. "No one told either one of us that this is what would ensue, or that it was even a remotely possible scenario. You gave us no chance to discuss it with you, with the other Achernarean physicians, or with one another. We are laymen and you knew that. You should have sought him out. You should have sought both of us out, Pythos. Io is an integral part of our family. You owed us that much."

Pythos shrugged as best he could with no shoulders. "And what iss owed to poor Ah'riodin in there? Thiss one," he jerked his head at Ardenai, "could have ssaid, 'Let me think about my ansswer.' Or he could have assked hiss own physsician what the ramificationss might be of hiss decission. But no. He grieved only to be disstracted from hiss work, then buried himsself in it with no further thought for hiss wordss. Perhapss now that will change, yess?"

Ah'ren's glare did not diminish. "You could have prepared him for this, even after the fact. He has worlds on his shoulders and the lives of billions in his hands! Holding him accountable for every word he speaks to someone who supposedly has his back, is evil. And you, Pyrgus, you could have prepared him for this! Pythos, you allowed him to walk in on this simply because you were miffed, and you enjoy the power that comes with shocking and punishing him. I've seen you do it before. This looks more like your revenge than Ah'riodin's advantage!"

"No, it doess not!" Pythos retorted. "And how dare *you* sspeak to me in that manner, Daughter! Thiss lookss like the doing of ssomeone who lovess Io as much as he lovess the Firsstlord, or nearly sso. Thiss lookss like the doing of ssomeone who knowss that Ardenai and hiss beloved Ah'ren could raisse thesse beautiful little girlss without Io, but that Io would not want to live knowing sshe had again losst a daughter. Two daughterss! That iss what thiss lookss like, Misstresss!"

"He's right," Ardenai managed, laying a calming hand on his wife's forearm. "I never asked a single question. I trusted Io's judgment and that of my physician. I…trusted the judgment and professionalism of others without questioning, and this is the result. Apparently, I can't trust many of those I assumed I could."

"Thiss iss not ressult, but processs. Rebirth, and birth within rebirth," Pythos hissed. "They told thee, Ardenai. That first night thee wass told, the babess could not, by anccient law, be allowed to live outsside their mother'ss body. Io knew thiss wass a posssible sscenario. Sshe ssaid if it sshould come to passs to tell thee, 'It grew back oncce. It will grow back again, Beloved.' And sso it might. We musst have faith now, for that iss all that iss left."

By now Ardenai's shock was turning to anger, and he fought to keep a level tone. "We? We? Why didn't you tell me what condition she was in? Have I become so arrogant as to be unreachable and unreasonable?"

"Neither, Hatchling. But thee iss, as alwayss, frighteningly vulnerable where Io iss conccerned, and again as I have ssaid over and over, thee did not assk. I would have preferred the decception, yess. With everything elsse thee hass to do? I would have allowed thee to sspeak to that comforting image on the sscreen until ssuch time as there wass a final outcome. Thiss – sseeing our little Io like thiss – thiss iss ssomething thee will never be able to erasse from thy tender brain nor will I, ssince I'd not sseen her, either, until now."

"And yet, shocked as you apparently were, you did nothing to cushion the blow for him," Ah'ren said. "Why is that?"

"Assk thy hussband, Lovely One."

There was a long pause before the Firstlord could unclench his teeth to speak. "Because, by my actions, or lack thereof, I chose this result for both of us." Despite the fact that he was shaking with pent-up fury, he turned from the bubble, put his hands together and bowed in subservience. "Forgive me. Father, Mother. Please forgive my thoughtlessness and my arrogance. By wounding you, I have wounded myself, as well, since we are one."

"We are one forever, no matter what," Pythos said soothingly, and Ardenai felt like a mollified child. For the first time in his life, he disliked Pythos, and the knowledge made him sick to his stomach. He felt like he was being torn in two.

"Thee is exhaussted and overwrought. Go back to bed and resst a while before the day beginss in earnesst. Pyrguss and I will keep ssafe the bubble and itss treassure. No one will know. No one will ssee." He embraced them, and flicked Ardenai's face with his tongue. "I forgive thee, Dragonhorsse. And thee musst forgive thysself...for all the sseassons passt with Io, for all the yearss to come with Ah'ren."

He forgives me? Why was that almost funny? Ardenai just nodded, feeling too boneless to do anything else. His head felt like an overripe melon, speared on a twig. He spent a long minute more, studying the small figure bobbing on its tether – wanting to see Io, and not finding her there. He put his arm around Ah'ren's shoulder and steered her out of the room, back to their apartments with never a word between them.

He stood in the middle of their bed chamber, staring at the rumpled bed and fighting the urge to scream and pound the walls. There was probably a metaphor in that bed, but what it was escaped him. He wondered, if he could take that rich, maroon sheet and dry Io, would she look like Io again? Even as a newborn, bloody and slick, she hadn't been bald. What had Pythos meant by his seasons past and years to come comment? When had he started speaking in riddles?

Surely Pyrgus couldn't have known Io's condition or he'd never have asked to have her sent here. What good could he do at this point? What good could anybody do at this point? Why hadn't Pythos told him, prepared him, sheltered him, just a little? Ardenai squeezed his eyes shut, trying to rein in the headlong gallop of thoughts, and there was slimy yellow Io – what was left of Io – maybe the very beginning of a new Io… bob, bob, bob. How could she not be suffocating? How could that skinny, naked, unrecognizable apparition be Io? The whole room…reeling from anger and confusion, and he was in the lavage with breakfast pouring through his fingers, which made him angrier than ever, and weightless. For a brief second, he prayed he'd just pass out…please…just long enough for his coping mechanisms to reset.

He became aware that Ah'ren had one hand on his shoulder, and in the other she was holding a towel, which she proffered as he stood up. "Handling this with my usual grace," he muttered. "Thanks. Sorry."

He went to the basin, washed his hands, rinsed his mouth and splashed cold water on his face. He looked up into the reflector and turned quickly with the towel still in his hand. Ah'ren was sobbing – huge tears streaking her face and dripping off her jaw onto her tunic. "Aw, Sweetheart," he murmured, catching her in his arms and kissing her hair as she sobbed against the side of his neck. "Wren, I'm so sorry. I should never have sent for Io."

"So we wouldn't know? How would that be better?" Wren cried angrily. "What if she dies? What if that's our last image of her? Of that beautiful, funny woman? Oh, I'm so mad at Pythos I could just…" nothing appropriate came to mind and she pounded his shoulder for lack of words. "I just want to…" again her fist connected none too gently with his shoulder. "What if those babies have to grow up without their mother?"

"They will have all of us," Ardenai said softly, rubbing her back. "They will have Ah'rane, and Ah'din. Mostly, they'll have you and me. We'll put them in a backpack like Lionel's and cart them around with us. Besides, she might just make it. Io's a fighter. I've known her all her life, and I've never seen her walk away from a challenge."

"Maybe if she had a brain to fight with," Wren muttered, her sobs turning back into anger. "What if they've stripped her of everything but her reproductive intelligence? What if there's no Io left?" Again, she began to cry. "What if that's just a shell? What if, after the babies are born there's nobody there but another infant? Or nobody at all? Ardi, I'm so scared for her, and for our family, and I'm just so KRAALING ANGRY!"

"Me, too," he said, and smiled a little, realizing that there was a certain bravery to be gained in comforting another. "So, let's ask Pythos. When we're both rested, and well fed, and open minded, let's ask him exactly what's going on in that amniotic bubble."

She nodded against his neck, and after a few minutes she helped herself to the towel he was holding. She scrubbed at her face until her cheeks were as purple as her bloodshot eyes, blew her nose on it, then spun on one toe and tossed the towel across the room into the hamper. "Well then, off to work," she said cheerfully. "I need to look in on Swift, check on Ah'cora, try to find the governor and have a meaningful little chat with him, Oh, and I plan to kill Pythos in some horrible, lingering manner and then get back to my maps. See you for lunch?"

"Ah…sure," he said, then pointed at her front. "Tears on your tunic. Maybe a little snot."

"And I've earned every bit of it," she said firmly. "Wash the side of your neck before you leave. It's pretty nasty." And with that, she was gone.

Kehailan had heard rumor that the Papilli ship in the Jocundome docking ring had brought Firstwife Abeyan Ah'riodin Ardenai Morning Star. No one had seen her. Rumor was, she'd come in a box under heavy Papilli escort. Rumor was, she was dead. Knowing his sire was probably stressed nearly to breaking at the moment, and wanting to stay close in case he was needed, Kehailan paced restlessly into his ship's document room, hoping to occupy himself with some of yesterday's amazements. There were people on Enki-Dara! Smart, forward-thinking, agrarian people. People with whom the Equi could identify. It was all very secret, lest knowledge of their existence put them in danger, but it was also exciting beyond anything they'd encountered so far in this campaign, at least to Kehailan's way of thinking.

They'd debriefed over a very late second dinner, and then, after he'd given his little brother a good shake and scolding, he'd sat for another couple of hours with him, listening to his tales of wonder. Of course his brother was a civilian. His brother could sleep in. Kehailan hadn't been so lucky, and being tired on top of all the worry of the last two or three days, made it hard to focus for very long.

He was trying to place the canyon on the continental map, wondering if the alien ship of which the song spoke really was in the water off the northeast end, trying to plot a possible trajectory, when there was a tap on the door frame and Gideon stepped into the room. He looked tired and worried. "You heard?" was all he said.

"Um hm."

"Our sire looked completely exhausted last night, mostly because of what I've put him through lately. I'm not sure he has the reserves for this kind of added trauma," Gideon said, staring with glazed eyes at a little buoy tender scooting by outside the window. "I was in his chambers when the Achernerians contacted him to let him know she was slipping. I saw what even that news did to him."

"I just wonder if there's any truth in it," Kehailan said.

"There is, at least part of it," said a third voice, and Kehailan and Gideon turned to see Eridi standing in the doorway. "That is, if you're talking about Ah'riodin. She is indeed here, as am I."

"Princess!" Kehailan laughed, taking a step forward. "You're back! You look...wonderful!"

She was more than wonderful. She was gorgeous. She'd sent crystels often, telling him of her studies, and mentioning that in order to relieve some of the boredom while her neck mended, she'd requested that her physicians reverse as much as they could of her extreme albinism. In that, they'd had stunning success. She was no longer pallid, but fair skinned and rosy cheeked, with the golden blonde hair and sparkling hazel eyes which would have been hers under normal circumstances. She was dressed in trousers and a tunic which hinted at the figure underneath, and her smile took Kehailan's breath away.

"I should go," Gideon said hastily and would have made for the door but Kehailan stayed him with one hand.

"Wait," he said, bending to kiss Eridi's forehead. "Princess, what do you know about this thing with Io?"

Eridi sighed and hoped she was hiding her disappointment at not finding Kehailan alone. Had that been the case she was pretty sure she'd have gotten considerably more than a self-conscious peck. She'd had several very involved dreams about what he might do, and this wasn't it. But she smiled and planted one hip against the corner of the map table, delighting in his strength as Kee lifted her easily to sit and then leaned close. "I came on that same Papilli ship, and from the same facility as Io, so we've been together without seeing each other. I know her condition has deteriorated, but I also know she's not dead, and that the twins are very much alive – rumor has it at Io's expense, which isn't going to please their father, or I miss my guess." She stroked Kehailan's hand with hers, and he returned the gesture, allowing his fingers the barest travel up her arm before dropping his hand again.

"Nothing about this has been pleasant," Gideon muttered. "Really, I should leave you two alone to catch up."

"I thought we were going to breakfast," Kehailan said suddenly, and Gideon caught the barest hint of panic in his voice. He didn't want to be alone with this girl, or didn't trust himself. Either way, Gideon rose to the occasion as one does to save a brother in need.

"I suppose we should, despite Eridi's arrival. We've still got a lot of details to go over from yesterday's explorations."

"We do, don't we?" Kehailan sighed, and gave Eridi an apologetic smile. "You are more than welcome to come along, Princess. I'm happy just to look at your beautiful face."

"Thank you," she grinned, "but I can tell when I'm in the way." She caught Kehailan by the nape of his neck, leaned in and gave him a firm and lingering kiss on the lips. "Not sure where I'm staying yet," she said, leaning out again. “When I know, you’ll know, too. I’ll be catching up with Priestess Ah’nis if you need me.” She hopped off the map table, gave a quick flip of a wave, and hurried off.

Kehailan stood with his mouth slightly ajar for a few heartbeats, then caught his breath and said, “She makes me crazy. I mean that quite literally. Just the smell of her, the feel of her makes me crazy. How in kraa I’m going to last five years without…” he glanced at his amused brother. “Are we going to breakfast, or not? I mean, not that you asked in the first place, but thanks for agreeing anyway.”

They walked in silence until Gideon got over the urge to laugh. “I know what you mean,” he said at last. “No, I really do. Whatever she was exuding that first night gave even me a headache, in more than my head, and our sire was aroused to the point of being physically sick, so I get it.” As they turned in at the dining room door Gideon mused, “I wonder if they’re all like that.”

“Like what?”

“You know. Can they all make males…feel like that?”

“I don’t know,” Kehailan muttered, “but if they can, Criollo is in for a miserable ten or fifteen years, because his parents are not going to let him marry Jasreth until he’s of a suitable age to do so.”

They spent breakfast visiting quietly. First, they talked about the poultry that Gideon and Ardenai had found mummified, and that the Darans raised and called flockins. They talked about dogs, goats and other farm animals which the Darans had preserved, and how careful they were not to allow bloodlines to cross – and how careful they were to control their population, and both of them agreed that Krush would be the one to fully explore that aspect…now that he’d taken on the school lunch program in addition to his mapping duties with Ah’ren and Ah’cora and had barely enough time to sleep. Still, he was the one with the best credentials for the job, being a bloodlines specialist.

“And too, we’re going to be thinking about going back to Equus in the not-too-distant future,” Gideon said. “The time here is flying by so fast.

So much exciting stuff is happening, and I love being with you and Dad, but…part of me really wants to go home. I think some of the rest of the family is homesick, too."

Teal was coming to that same conclusion, propped up on one elbow on their fleecy bed, watching Ah'din yank a tunic over her head and stomp into her sandals. "Dini, are you going to tell me what I…" but the flap on the pavilion had already closed on her retreating backside. "Not helpful," he called, but there was no response.

Teal heard her snap, "Don't you dare take his side, either!" and his father-in-law's half-amused, half-confused snort as his daughter blew by on her way to the bathing facilities.

He tossed the covers aside and crawled out of bed to don a brief-cloth and running shoes. He was too tired to run, and even before sunup it was already getting hot. Still, it was called an exercise routine for a reason, wasn't it? He opened the tent flap and shook himself all over, loosening up his muscles for what felt like it was going to be an effort. Maybe he could sneak a day off for both of them and take Ah'din to their apartments on the Jocundome. There was a beautiful park nearby with swans and the ducks she loved. Maybe next week, when the overview of the continents was done. No, he'd be on Equus, looking for a new cavalry captain, wouldn't he?

He was meandering toward the trailhead at the far end of their encampment and trying to figure out what he'd said to set his wife off, when Krush's voice came from over his shoulder. "What did you do to my daughter, you beast?"

Teal turned and watched him approach from the direction of the horses, and just shook his head. "If I say I don't know, I'll come across as unthinking. If I say I do know, I'll come across as uncaring, so I think I'd better keep my mouth shut and hope she enlightens me. How are you this morning?"

"About like you," Krush admitted, "afraid to open my mouth. Ah'rane has snapped at me more in the last three or four days than she has in the last hundred and twenty-three years."

"Maybe they're both coming into a dragonhorse heat," Criollo observed walking up from the river and shaking the water out of his ears. "That is the prediction from Mountain hold, isn't it?"

"Precious Equus, I cannot believe that just came out of your mouth," his father admonished. "You are far too young…oh, that's probably what set your mother's face against me. We were talking about you, young man."

"Or, more likely, Jasreth and me?"

"How do you know these things?" Teal growled. The first rays of the midsummer sun hit him in the face and he squinted and turned away. "See? Now I'm late for my run."

Criollo shrugged and looked innocent. "I know you wanted me to marry Ah'brianne and not Jass…"

"It's not that."

"Let me finish," Criollo said gently, holding up one hand. "I know you wanted me to marry Bree, and now along comes Gideon and she's in love with him, and along comes Jasreth, and I'm fine with Gideon and Ah'brianne being crazy over each other, because I, too, am in love with somebody else. But look, this is how it's going to play out, and I'm surprised you haven't seen it by now, because Ah'brianne and I have already figured it out and agreed – in secret, of course. Gideon is seventeen. Even being one quarter Equi he will live another ninety to a hundred years at the most. Jasreth is sixteen. She will live another seventy years or so. Ah'brianne and I are both twenty-four, and we will live another two hundred and twenty-six years, give or take. We can have it all, Sire. We can marry the people we love, have a family with them, and then marry each other as the best friends we are and have plenty of time to raise children of our own if we want. Am I still grounded?"

"Yes!" Teal snapped. "You're grounded until your wedding day."

"Which one?"

By that time they were both laughing, and Teal dropped an arm around Criollo's shoulder as they walked. "You were never grounded. You were in protective custody. You can go back to the expedition with me if you choose, or help your grandfather, or work with the governor on whatever he's doing, though that may be severely curtailed with Swift so sick. Your choice, just whatever you do, let somebody know where you are, and don't go strange places alone, hm? Oh, and don't talk about dragonhorse cycles. You're much too young and it makes me sad."

"I promise," Criollo said. He nodded respectfully to his grandsire, gave Teal a lingering kiss on the temple, and trotted off toward the tent he shared with Gideon, calling over his shoulder, "I want to go see how Jobie's doing, and then I'll catch up with one or the other of you."

Teal gave Krush a searching look. "Were you that smart at his age? I wasn't that smart at his age."

"I was, and you most assuredly were," Krush chuckled. "You just didn't out yourself quite so readily, because your sire was stricter and less understanding than Criollo's." He gave Teal an affectionate thump on his bare shoulder and then added, "You do know the boy could be right about his mother and his grandmother, and if he is, we could be in for some excitement – and some pain, and not necessarily in that order."

"I could be in for more than that," Teal sighed. "I have to leave for Equus in three days. I've asked Ah'din along and she's refused. She says she's here to work. I told her she could go check on things at home while I'm interviewing candidates, but she says five days each way to spend five days at Canyon keep, is a poor trade for what she's accomplishing with Ensharra. Ah'ren says I have to be with my wife this time around because of the whole Imperial Dragonhorse – whatever the kraa – plus I've promised her a baby this cycle, and if I'm not here to give her one, I may as well just stay gone."

Krush shrugged. "Tell her she has to go with you."

"I have never dictated to my wife, and I'm not going to start now, Sire. I'm sorry if that sounds weak."

"It does, but then I've never dictated to Ah'rane, either, not that it would get me anywhere if I did. Come on, I'll run with you," Krush said, tossing his tunic over a convenient limb and pulling off his boots and britches. He reached into their pavilion and grabbed his runner's shoes, hopping into them as he walked. "So, what are you going to do?"

"Run," Teal grinned, and they were off at a fast trot down the sandy path beside the river. "I suppose I could set up interviews via crys-tel, but I really want to see each of the candidates on horseback – see how they relate to their animals – be able to smell their sweat and that of their horses. That tells me a lot."

"Well, you're no closer to them than they are to you, Son. Have them come here, work with strange horses in a strange environment, ride a few days with the expeditionary forces on Tras. That will tell you a great deal, as well."

Teal nodded and smiled. "That it would, and I've let it cross my mind more than once. What it leaves out, is how they relate to their fellows."

They ran for a bit in silence, picking up the pace and moving up slightly away from the river. "Do you trust Tarpan?" Krush asked, running easily beside the taller man.

"I do. I think he has excellent judgment for his age."

"Then send him to Cavalry headquarters on Equus as you send for the candidates," Krush said. "Have him stop at the Great Stables and pick up Landais and Seglawi, or Jomud, or all of them, and have them mingle and do the secondary interviews informally. Once you pool your information, you'll have the most solid replacement."

"I think you're right," Teal said, glancing over at his father-in-law. "Thank you, Sire. I appreciate your clarity, and I do think it's the best solution in these circumstances."

Krush nodded and smiled without letting his eyes leave the path. "I'm only sorry you have to do this – to replace Abeyan. The three of you were close as boys, and I loved all of you. He was slightly to the arrogant side, but he got that from his sire. I never saw it come out in his relationships with people or horseflesh. He was an insuperable cavalry captain. But when Ardi married Io…"

"I think it was before that," Teal said. "I think Abeyan rather hoped to rise as Dragonhorse. Whether his father put that in his head or not I don't know, but from that first day, I never heard another civil word out of his mouth, much less one spoken in real friendship."

"And now he's leaving Equus and taking the son of Io and Salerno with him, whether Jilfan wants to go or not. I wonder what his mother's going to say about that when she wakes up."

"If," he sighed. "I guess I should ask at this point. Have you..."

"Yup. Just a rumor. Are we going to trot the whole way like a team of draft horses pulling a stone sled, or can you move those ridiculously long legs a little faster without getting tangled up in them?"

"I can, of course," Teal said, looking surprised. "But I'm being respectful of your advanced age and your much shorter underpinnings. If you collapse and I have to carry you back, my wife is going to be angrier yet, so let's just stick with a pace you can manage, hm?"

"Which is just your pathetic way of admitting you don't have what it takes to get your over-muscled ass moving, Master Captain. I'll see you back at camp." With a jaunty wave and a wicked cackle, Krush lengthened his stride and very literally left Teal in the dust.

"I could catch you if I wanted to!" Teal yelled after him, and slowed down with a gasp of relief to put his hands on his knees. "Ordinarily that would not be an idle boast," he panted, and wondered at his lack of energy. By the time he got back to their campsite, Krush was finishing his swim and Ah'din was once again emerging from their pavilion.

"I thought you'd already gone," Teal smiled, not sure what else to say.

"I had to come back," she said, then giggled a little and added, "I forgot my underbodice, and if I perspire, or get wet, not much is left to the imagination. If I were working just with Equi, who don't necessarily associate nudity with sex..."

"But you're not," Teal grinned, "So?"

"As the wife of the Master Captain, I must set an example," she finished, looking up at him and shading her eyes.

She was smiling, but it still made Teal wince inside. Here was this shy, soft-spoken woman who had traveled far from home and loom to be with him and she felt she had to set an example? When he actually thought about it, which he hadn't until now, of course she did. She was sister to the Dragonhorse, wife of the Master Captain. She knew exactly what was expected of her – not by her family, but by the society into which they had asserted themselves. How much pressure was that adding to her decision to be in a strange place with strange people? And, he asked himself, why had he just assumed she was having fun on holiday?

"Teal, have you stopped speaking to me?" she asked. "I'm sorry if you feel I was short with you earlier."

"Not at all what I was thinking," he soothed. "I was thinking about how amazing you are. You have given up so much for me. I'm worried that my choice of reality might be smothering yours."

"I'll tell you when it is," she said. "Meantime, thanks for being the family protector. I know it's a big job and it makes you say strange things." She wrinkled her nose at him, and trotted off, holding on to her wide brimmed straw hat against a freshening breeze. No intimate whisper. No kiss.

Teal stood watching her until she stepped onto the small scramble-shaft pad they'd installed and vanished in a blue and maroon convolution, then he turned and waded into the river, wishing with every fiber of his being that he was home at Canyon keep checking on his wine vats, getting ready for his parent's return to Equus, and getting his wife pregnant.

Ah'cora, too, was wishing for the stars of home. Sitting in Padmar's stall, wiping at fruitless tears and trying to convince herself to stop her self-pity and get back to work mapping those empty cities and empty continents. Lonely, forlorn, forsaken places. Still, a hug would feel so good right now, or the warmth of Padmar's nose on the side of her neck. But there was no-body. Ah'ren had stopped by – knowing where she'd be, which was kind. Ah'cora had told her she was fine and that she just needed some time alone. Ah'ren had nodded and left with a comforting pat. Nik had stopped by, as well, and while his words were kind, his eyes were filled with a different sadness, and he'd left without offering a hug. She dropped her head to her knees and took a few deep, straw-filled breaths before a warm body came down beside her and an arm came around her shoulder, pulling her close.

"Don't you worry," said a gentle voice. "We will figure out who did this to Padmar, and when the time is right, we will find you another horse who will be your friend for many long years. I promise."

Ah'cora looked up and smiled rather tearfully into Krush's craggy, good-humored face. "I have made such a mess of things!" she moaned.

He replied by tightening his grip a little and kissing her temple. "I want you to tell me all about it," he said, and she knew he meant it.

"I should never have brought Padmar," she said, wiping at her nose, "and when your son came to tell me about it, I acted like a complete idiot, and I think I made him angry."

"You scared the pants off him," Krush chuckled. "He's a little bit afraid of women in the first place, and the last thing he wanted was for you to be afraid of him. He meant it when he welcomed you into the family, Ah'cora."

"I just didn't know how to take that whole…"

Krush held up a hand. "Say no more. Neither does my son. He's struggled mightily with the idea of having multiple wives, much less dealing with arranged matings to produce offspring. He's really quite stodgy in a charming sort of way. He's very sorry you were told in a letter, and both he and Ah'ren are trying to get to the bottom of who sent it."

"I don't want him not to like me."

"No chance of that," Krush smiled. "He likes you very much. Now, do you want some breakfast before we go to work, or would you like to sit here and just sog for a bit?"

She sighed and leaned deeper into him, allowing herself to relax, and Krush leaned against the stall wall, extending his legs and laying his cheek against the side of her head as his arms enfolded her. "Tell me the story of your friend Padmar," he said quietly.

CHAPTER 11

Ah'ren could tell by the light, spicy male scent which was the essence of Konik that he'd been in to see Swift in the not-too-distant past, but where he was, or was headed, nobody knew for sure. Sanecere day shift had not seen him. Evening shift had not seen him. Dining room staff could not remember seeing him, though someone who worked the wee hours had affirmed his presence once or twice. He had been to the cottage he shared with Swift, but he had not slept there, and Ah'ren was wondering if he'd slept at all anywhere. His work was getting done, so he had to be in his office at some point during the day or night – but when? When could she catch him to try reasoning with him?

Ardenai was worried that Nik would push himself until he got sick or his heart gave out again, and while Ah'ren had said soothing things, she, too, was worried. She knew all too well that if Konik was anything like Kabardin – really like Kabardin – he could be dangerously overstimulated, or just plain dangerous at this point. And who did they have to thank for that? Kestrel, who never wanted to tell anybody anything about what they were actually getting into.

Why that was, why people were never told these things in front of a crisis was a mystery to Ah'ren, and one she didn't appreciate. What good, exactly, was the shock value if and when they did find out? Why, especially, hadn't Konik been told? His unwitting ancestors had been married off to

Androtech mates by the dozen and had been perfectly happy, which might have brought him both comfort and acceptance, but no, Kestrel wouldn't hear of it. She wondered if it was because it hadn't had the desired effect of eliminating Kabardin's bloodlines from the gene pool, as evidenced by the governor himself. Kestrel prided himself on his thoroughness at such things, and wouldn't appreciate the reminder of his failure.

Ah'ren had to smile. She adored Nik – charming, sexy and self-effacing – a brilliant governor and stalwart friend of the Lebonathi people. What if they'd actually managed to eliminate his bloodline? There would be no soft-spoken man to kneel shirtless and barefooted in the dust and free the slaves and the prisoners. Of all the people the Lebonathi seemed to love and respect, Nik was at the top of the list.

As Ah'ren sat beside Swift, listening to the soft beep of the machines cleaning bloodstream and cells of poison, she wondered why that was. Maybe it was his size – powerfully built, but small for an Equi at barely six feet, just under a hundred and eighty pounds. More likely it was the voice, that gentle purr that made one want to curl in his arms and sleep. Hypnotic, persuasive, reassuring. The prematurely grey hair signaled an age advantage he didn't actually have, but the illusion was near perfect, and it gave him credibility.

Ardi was as much their savior as Konik, but the people didn't seem to recognize it – a fact which annoyed Wren just a little. Her husband was a brilliant and graceful statesman with a gentle smile and peaceful demeanor which revered him to the Seventh Galactic Alliance, but he came across as...young, to these people, and because he was the absolute ruler of eleven planets, he was frightening to them. Because they knew nothing of Equus and her morals, those things like justice, mercy and humility which had been bred into him for ten thousand years, their image was of a towering demi-god who could crush them with the wave of one hand. Since the Lebonathi knew only oppression, they assumed that at some point, Ardenai, too, would become an oppressor, and they held him in a kind of terrified awe. At the same time, because he had not yet chosen to oppress, they considered him a little weak. The Firstlord realized this, and it made him laugh in private moments and then kiss the irked look off his wife's face.

Swift stirred a little and moaned, the poison making every move a physical shock as it lingered in her body – muscle, tendon and bone. Ah'ren shifted her thoughts back to Konik and wondered if he realized that's what she was made of, or if he considered her a Practibaby – one of those dolls with an amazingly real feel, real program, but no reality beyond it. Children loved them, had for years. Adults, had no delusions about what they were.

The first night Konik had returned from Enki-Dara, Ah'ren had held him close and tried to speak words to quiet him, to ease the trembling that passed through him in waves. She could still feel his heart, thrashing in his chest like a marchling trying to escape a snare.

Swift was asleep and would remain so for a few days yet. Swift, Ah'ren wasn't worried about – at least not physically. She stood up, wondering if Krush and Ah'cora had gotten to the offices yet. If they had, they could get things started while she checked scrambleshaft signatures – discreetly. Nik already felt betrayed. The last thing he needed was to feel spied upon. She thought a moment, then said, *Kehailan? I need a favor.*

Konik sat on one boulder, hiking boots braced against another, and watched the pair of raptors circling high on the canyon wall in the fading light. He could hear their calls to one another, and the tipping of their wings in the twilight became a dance, mesmerizing after another long day.

"In answer to your question," Ensharra said, "Muru thinks a great many of the people they took were herded into the big cities. I'm sure he's told us that. More than once."

Konik raised an eyebrow. "Muru this, Muru that. Honestly, you've known the man a week and you can't string a sentence together without his name in it." Ensharra caught the grin where she sat and gave Konik a punch on the shoulder. He rocked to one side and then back, still staring at the birds. "What are they harvesting, Anchoress? Why was that first family we found cut open? What are they getting from these people and how are they doing it?"

Ensharra looked at him with a mix of annoyance and concern. "You do know you've asked me that a hundred times in the last few days?"

"I'm asking me. You just happen to be in earshot all the time – your choice, I might add."

"I'm afraid to leave you alone," she said with some exasperation, "you haven't slept, you've hardly eaten. You're so worried about Swift…"

The footsteps behind them ended the conversation, and Muru joined them, carefully balancing three mugs of hot tea.

He settled himself beside them, distributed the tea and followed Konik's gaze skyward. "Perhaps one day they, too, will be free to fly above the canyon's rim," Muru said. "Careful, this is unusually hot."

"Thank you," Konik responded, blowing on the smoky liquid and smiling over at Muru. "You've been most gracious, hiking all over this part of the valley, making hundreds of introductions, answering thousands of questions. You must be thoroughly worn out by now."

"The pleasure has been mine, and continues to be," the man smiled, glancing sideways in Ensharra's direction.

"Solving weighty problems while the civilized people sleep has ceased to be much pleasure," Ensharra said smothering a yawn and trying not to spill her tea. "I know I'm supposed to be part of the team, but I've been up every morning before dawn and I really want to go to bed at a decent hour tonight." She fixed her eyes on the governor and picked up her train of thought. "You haven't slept in a week," she observed, and Konik shrugged.

"There are many fascinating things to do in the dark around here," he drawled, giving Ensharra a knowing glance which caused her to squirm with discomfort. Konik wanted to ask Muru if he was making any progress with the woman. If not, it wasn't for lack of effort on his part. "Besides, sleep is overrated." A lie on his part, and by now rather an obvious one. He was desperate for sleep, but every time he closed his eyes one of two things happened – he found himself trying to wake the boys, or he found himself with his face under that rock, the serpent beneath it striking at his open eyes. Even now it made him jerk a little. He closed his eyes and took a deep breath to allay the image, and when he opened his eyes again, Ensharra was beside him, one hand on either side of his face.

"Nik, are you having nightmares? You have that same haunted look the Master Captain had when he couldn't get Eridu out of his head."

Her touch was pleasing, and stimulating, but it was also disturbing, and he reached gently to take her hands in his. "Don't do that," he whispered. He caught her momentarily with his eyes, then raised his voice and continued. "I have many duties as governor. While you and Muru sleep each night, I go and take care of some of the most pressing. I don't want you to worry about me, Anchoress."

"You're not answering my question," she smiled, looking up at him.

Konik sensed as much as saw the sudden slump in Muru's shoulders as he watched the anchoress, and guessed at what was going through his mind. "You're being a big sister again," he said firmly. "Don't you have somebody else to fuss over these days, my friend? I know I do."

"Stop deflecting, Nik. It's a bad habit. You're going to be sick if you don't sleep. I can give you something that will make the dreams and the images or voices or whatever is eating at you, go away. I gave it to Teal, and it works wonders for him."

"Maybe I'll borrow some of his."

Ensharra stared at him in disgust. "Yes, do that. You're so close to the same size."

"Fine," Konik sighed, "Get out your cauldron and mix something up, but please, in the meantime would you let me do my job without fussing like an old mare with a new foal? I'm fine, really I am."

Muru chuckled, and Ensharra turned to smile at him. "Sorry," she said. "It's a lovely evening and I'm spoiling it with my obsessive need to protect these stubborn Equi who have chosen to dwell amongst us."

"Our governor is lucky to have you to watch over him," Muru said quietly. "We have been up early and late these last few days, and I, too, am tired. I think I'll go to bed." With that he nodded graciously, gathered his tea cup, and wandered forlornly into the cave.

"You do realize he's crazy about you," Konik hissed.

Even in this light he could see her blush and drop her eyes. "Yes…

I mean…I rather thought so," she said, then looked up again with some annoyance. "Are you going to lecture me about greater duty, or my advancing years? Old mare indeed. That was mean."

"Nonsense, both of them, and the old mare thing is just an expression. You're fussing over the wrong person, my dear, and in that, I am going to lecture you. You just made him think you're in love with me. I thought the poor man was going to break down and weep."

"Well, that's just silly!" she spluttered. "I don't…I'm not…even if I were in love with you, I know I can't have you, and besides, you're an alien species, you're in love with someone else, and you're stubborn as the boulder upon which you sit. What would I want with you?"

"Good girl!" Konik laughed. "Wise choice. Now, go to bed, and say goodnight to Muru on the way by. Nicely. Lingeringly."

"Nik…"

"I'll be fine," he smiled, "and so will you." He took her hand in both of his and held it against his chest. "You need to go in that direction," he murmured, gesturing toward the cave's entrance with his chin, "and I have to go another." He kissed her lingeringly on the forehead, and trotted off north toward the top of the cliff, a mile or so away.

He'd been informed in the course of their ramblings that many of the caves high on the canyon walls opened out on the other side of the glastaline web, and relatively few were inhabited. By threading his way through he could relay to the dome, get some work done, and be back by dawn the next morning. He'd spotted this particular cave earlier in the evening and it held promise without having to cross the canyon floor, which was at least two miles wide at this point. If he was right, he could save himself that extra two miles.

The cavern seemed unoccupied, and he turned on a light, flushing some bats and causing a large white bird to rustle its wings and chirp sleepily with annoyance. Several hundred yards on he found the walled opening and the closed door which kept the animals safe and unnoticed within the canyon, and beyond that, the mouth of the cave itself. He took his crys-tel between thumb and forefinger, said, "Jocundome, continuous relay," and relaxed into the push and glide, spin and slow, like ice-skating, which put him on the main scramble pad of Papilli Jocundome Three.

A blazing hot bath and a change of clothes woke him enough to find the dining room, where different shifts came and went at all hours, and a meal was always available. He ate quickly and went, with his usual sense of dread, to look in on Swift. Not that he expected to find her dead, or gone. She would be there, recovering, and when she opened her eyes, what was he going to say to her? He got out the list of possibilities and shuffled through them yet again:

I was in love with my wife for a hundred years. A hundred years. From the time I was eighteen and assigned a sexual trainer, Ah'davan was my life. I adored her. And yet when I woke up in the sanecere after having my heart fail, or so the story goes, I have been in love with you. I watched you walk into the room, and I knew with surety and a very relaxed kind of comfort, that I loved you and wanted only you – despite my grief, despite having met other attractive women...one in particular...I was drawn to you. Almost against my will. Why is that, exactly? What did Pythos do to me, really? Am I what I was before, or am I...? No. Too long. Too convoluted. Too much about him and not enough about her. Much too angry. Plus, he wasn't sure he wanted an answer. The thought of immortality and an endless cycle of loss was not in the least appealing.

Why wasn't I told? Was I so unaccepting...unworthy...was I such a monster that you were afraid to be honest with me? Truthful, but still angry. Allowing hurt to become anger was never productive.

I love you. Does that compute? Probably not a good choice. Sarcasm was not his best sport.

Did you think me unable or unfit to make my own decision regarding our relationship? Too harsh. Maybe it wasn't her choice. Then again, maybe it was accurate, which was unsettling.

I was married to Ah'davan for ninety years, and there is not a day I do not love her and think of her. But she's dead, and you're not and I know for sure I won't outlive you, so... Still working on that particular variation of number one. Somehow it wasn't very flattering as it came out his mouth, though it made perfect sense in his head.

Do we have a relationship, or is it a specific program beyond which you cannot go – a program designed to keep the governing diabolyte in check and keep him satisfied? No. Too self-pitying. Too whiny. Too self-absorbed. Not that he wasn't all three of those things at this point, but he didn't want to broadcast it by word or deed.

Do you actually feel, or do you just respond to stimulus? Could be accurate. Could get him slapped. Even that would be a comfortingly human response.

Amazing program you have there! Who's your puppet master? Again, too sarcastic – satisfying, though. Nobody likes to be toyed with.

I love you. Every warm, caressable inch, every intellectually stimulating nuance, and I don't give a shit what you were, or are, or will be, other than my friend and lover. Needy. Very needy. And accurate to a fault. Too accurate. Made him shiver and doubt his moral core.

Now what? Not terribly supportive, but open for suggestions. Had possibilities.

Have you actually felt love in the pit of your stomach - had your breath catch and your heart beat faster? Because you do that to me, and I am grateful to feel so alive again. Sounded like something a schoolgirl would say, not a grown man. And if he tried to say that, he'd cry like a schoolgirl. Thinking it made him want to cry. Standing on the rocks at the old watchtower, looking out at their future and feeling all that hope. With her beside him he could do so much for the world of the Lebonathi. If he didn't do anything else in this life, he was going to find that snake and choke the life out of it with his bare hands.

Are you really as sick as you seem? In as much pain? Or is it something being generated so that you can retain the illusion of being...a real woman? Totally unworthy of either of them.

And...what did you mean when you told me not to be afraid? He had the answer to that one. She hadn't said, don't be angry. She'd told him not to be afraid. An impossible request.

He kissed her forehead and very gently ran his thumb over the two tiny holes, side by side, where the venom had gone in. Swelling was down. The hand and arm looked less painful and bruised.

What if she'd been...what was the word...real? Mortal? What if, like Ah'davan, she'd not awakened, but grown cold and stiff in his arms despite the heat? Would that have made a difference, caused a different grief than the one he felt – deeper, less self-centered? No, he thought, all grief is self-centered. Then again, so is love, isn't it?

Ensharra was in love with him and he knew it, though he'd done his best to spare her the embarrassment of an affection he would never allow himself to return. Still, when she'd touched the sides of his face, there had been a definite pleasure – a sort of electric tingle that made him want to kiss the pulse-point on her wrist and the bend in her elbow...and so on. He could take her from Muru if he chose. Knowing that made him feel both comforted and powerful – and lousy about himself. Ensharra wasn't a polo trophy, she was a person. And what was Swift? She was breathing. He could feel her heart beating – just like his. Her eyes had fluttered and reset – just like his. Took having them to recognize how they worked, he reckoned. What would he be with no eyes, no heart? Blind and dead, that's what. Certainly, he was in no position to cast aspersions.

He wondered if knowing what she was, would ever fade enough to be able to appreciate again who she was. Maybe that wouldn't be a choice for him. She was outed. Maybe she'd be sent back to Mountain hold. She said she'd come from there...when Ah'ren...had been sent as companion wife to the Dragonhorse. Sent?

The shock of realization was physically painful, and he caught his breath. Were they the same then? Was Ah'ren Androtech? How many of the people he cared for were manufactured beings? He felt like a miniscule pawn in some universal chess game.

His Androtech heart thudded in his chest, and there was a chilling, prickling weightlessness that made him feel like he had bugs under his skin. He pounded his knees with his fists and came snarling up out of his chair to pounce across the room, fighting the urge to scream and throw things in a fit of absolute powerlessness and frustration, and that's when he realized he was no longer alone.

"I was just thinking about you," he managed, coming up short an inch or two from a head-on collision.

"Let's go outside on the patio," Ah'ren smiled. "It's a lovely evening, and Swift is no longer deeply asleep. In case you actually need to scream and throw things and not just think about it."

He followed her through the double doors and into the fragrant night air with its drifting blossoms and brilliant stars and stood with his eyes closed, palms out, taking deep, even breaths and quieting the shrieks still trying to escape. Wouldn't do to lose his temper. Not here. Not now. Not ever.

Ah'ren went to a nearby bench by a trickling fountain and sat patiently. She'd made up her mind that no matter what he said, what he asked, she was going to be honest with him. He was in torment, and nobody deserved that, least of all him.

He came and stood for a moment in front of her, then took a deep breath and sat beside her instead, dropping the confrontation before it ever got started. After a few moments of silence he asked, "Are you Androtech?"

Not at all the question she'd been expecting. The startlement registered on her features, but the pause was negligible and the voice firm. "Yes."

"Does Ardenai know?"

"Yes."

"Did he know before he married you?"

"Yes."

"That was easy."

"Was it?"

"No."

There was a long silence between them, filled with the chirping of tiny blossom bats and the soft splash of the fountain. "Has it…made a difference between you two? You seem very much in love with one another."

"We are," Ah'ren smiled. "It was a little awkward at first. He wondered if I was programmed in some way. You know, like I had to love him and had no will of my own. Once I convinced him that I am not even aware of the parts of me that aren't hominoid, that I am much more flesh and blood than machine, and that I think of myself as a person, not a machine, things got easier. Now, I'm not sure he thinks about it at all. He does remember once in a while that I am an ancient being and my head is full of history, but it's an easy remembrance, if that makes any sense. He's comfortable with it, and it has made for some fascinating if very private conversations."

"No one else knows?"

"Teal has the actual knowledge. The whole family met me at Mountain hold, though they don't remember it. Before I was Ardenai's wife, I was his hetaera. When Mountain hold and the Great House realized they weren't going to be able to push Ardenai into another marriage – he called back his proposal to Ah'nora because he found out she was marrying somebody else." she chuckled and shook her head. "He has the worst luck with women. Anyway, Io got sick trying to carry the twins, and Ardi was overwrought, and I was sent back into the world to be his companion wife. I was delighted to do that, and I think he came around pretty quickly, despite his fears about what Io might say." At that point Ah'ren sighed and looked sad, and Konik wondered if there was any truth to those rumors he'd heard whispered around the dining room the last few nights.

"I do have some questions," Konik said, carefully not grinding his teeth as he spoke, and Ah'ren recognized the enormity of the understatement.

"Of course. That's why I'm here, now that I've actually caught up with you. Where have you been, or is it any of my business?"

"Walking the world of the Enki-Darans. Fascinating folk, and much like us. Seemingly content to be agrarian, largely classless, well-educated, endlessly curious. All hidden away like seeds, waiting for the right conditions to sprout and produce fruit. They make some amazing goat cheese. Can she, can you, taste things, or do you just pretend?"

"Absolutely we can," Ah'ren laughed. "She has spoken of how good you…taste to her."

Just the way she said it, the slight movement of top teeth across bottom lip, and Konik knew. Another tingle of shock went up his spine, along with a muted shudder of disgust.

"You and Kabardin? Really," he grimaced.

She challenged his eyes for a moment, then looked away and shrugged with shoulders and eyebrows. "It was my job, you know. Wife to some, hetaera to most. Kabardin did have that same wonderful spice about him that you do. Not just a fragrance, but a taste, as well. It was one of his better points. You look ready to collapse, Nik. When did you last sleep, or even lie down for a bit?"

"I thought it was my turn to ask questions," he countered. "May I ask questions about Swift?"

"She is her own person, of course, but insofar as I have knowledge, I will answer. I owe you that much and more. I never thought keeping this a secret from you was a good idea. But I followed instructions from someone at Mountain hold, and I shouldn't have. What do you want to know?"

There was a momentary pause while Konik sought the exact words he wanted. "Did one of you do something to me to make me fall in love with Swift? Because as much as I valued her and liked her, I was not in love with her. And then, all of a sudden, like magic, I was crazy about her. Did Pythos fool with my brain?"

He sensed a momentary discomfort. "Pythos? No."

"Did you or Swift put it into my head?"

"Absolutely not," she said with some heat. "Neither of us would do that. That would be cheating. What else?"

"Chiefly, why wasn't I told she's a manufactured being?" he purred, and Ah'ren could sense the anger, bubbling near the surface.

The last thing she wanted was for this man to lose patience. In many ways he was the spitting image of Kabardin – silky, hyperphilic, and obviously possessed of a simmering temper. Where they differed was in the fact that Konik rarely if ever lost his. Right now, he was as close as she'd seen him get. His voice was just above a whisper, his eyes were a cold, blue flame, and his whole body was vibrating as he stared away across the garden. She could feel the little shock waves coming off him. And he'd asked her the one question for which she had no answer.

"I can only guess," she said. "I've been at this several thousand years and the policy hasn't changed. For some reason the whole society of us who are, as we like to say, mechanically inclined, are a deep and well-kept secret. Maybe it's because people have always had a fear of machines taking over. I personally think it's because we know so much. We are incredibly sophisticated andro-organisms – the only ones in all of known space. Maybe if we were dissected in some manner, we could be copied? Made into slaves or war-machines, just like brain-washed people with really long lifespans? I don't know. I have decided one thing, since Pythos is already thoroughly annoyed, I might as well ask him the same thing you just asked me. All he can do is twist my head off." She shifted on the bench and laughed uncomfortably. "Nik, listen – I never think of myself in these terms, so I'm hedging and meandering and you think I'm trying not to answer, and that's just not the case."

The chiseled profile turned very slowly in her direction. "Would I ever have been told?"

"Probably not. Why would you need to know, unless you wanted children? The only reason Ardi knows is because he already knew me, and I wouldn't let anybody else have him. I'm in love with him and I made that very clear to the ancient dragons of Achernar."

"Could Swift have told me?"

Again, he sensed discomfort on her part. "Something you'd have to ask her. What her personal instructions were regarding you, I do not know. Maybe she was just waiting for the right time, maybe she'd been told not to tell you. Whatever it was, she didn't share it with me, and I didn't think to ask her."

Konik nodded and it seemed he'd relaxed a little. "Is Swift an ancient being, like you are?"

"Yes, though she is younger. She was created to be hetaera to, and then became wife to our old friend, Kabardin. Ask her about those years and you'll have no doubt that we're capable of real dislike – even hatred."

Konik looked at his hands – the palms, then the backs. "You knew him. In more than one sense. Was he as horrific as legend has it?"

"If anything, he was worse. That vast energy you have channeled charitably and creatively and magnanimously, he poured into power and conquest and this penchant for inflicting pain on things and people. His reign truly was the time of calamity. If the priestesses could have figured out how to kill him in the first ten minutes without it being obvious, they would have and nobody would have cared. Accomplishing a coup with any degree of subtlety cost many lives over many years."

"I see," Konik said, and his grandfather's hard face passed in front of his eyes.

"You're nothing like him," Ah'ren stated, reading his body language. "Either of them."

"At least Kabardin died young. Really young."

"That he did," Ah'ren muttered, and Konik let it alone.

They watched one of the bats disappear into a trumpet flower, like a little grey flickernick in a huge yellow hat. He crawled back out, wiping his nose with his paws, and took flight a foot or two over their heads, his squeaks of delight filling the night air. It made both of them laugh, and when Konik turned again to Ah'ren, his eyes had softened, and she began to relax.

"Was she forced to marry him? I can't imagine anyone marrying Kabardin of their own accord."

Ah'ren waggled her hands. "Like most sociopaths, he had some exceedingly charming moments. He was incredibly handsome, and sexually very talented. But forced? Not really. She was persuaded in the sense that it was her job, her duty. Something that had to be done to protect other people, and she was created to do it, given a whole childhood history and upbringing to prepare her for it."

"You aren't just…programmed with a personality?"

"Oh no. Our brains are born into a virtual reality. We grow up with parents, and schooling, and hobbies and passions and opinions. We live twenty-six actual years before we are given a physical body and sent off to Lycee with others our age. In that sense we are absolutely normal Equi. When I said she was created to do that particular job, I meant that she was created, and the *hope* was that she would be willing to take on that job. And, being as brave as she is beautiful, she did it, for the glory of Equus and the good of her people, just like you do your job and Ardi does his."

"The glory of Equus and the good of her people. Is that why she's still around even though my heat cycle is long gone?"

Ah'ren just laughed. "She's still around, because she adores you, silly boy. She wants to be with you and share your life, and she's free to do that. She believes absolutely in what you are doing here, and she's so proud of you. She talks about you, the things you say, the things you do, like she's a schoolgirl with a crush. She asked a hundred years ago to be your hetaera when you were ready, because in you she saw a positive reflection of Kabardin's blood. She's dropped whatever she's been doing to be wherever you were when you needed her. She embraces being here on the dome, having a medical practice and a home with someone in it that she loves and has loved for over a century."

"And all that time I was in love with Ah'davan," he said thoughtfully.

"When you love the conductor, just being in the orchestra is enough. Not all of us can sit first chair, Nik. I certainly can't. Io is Firstwife. I know that and I accept it. When she is well again, I will find my own niche and enjoy the moments I get to share with Ardenai and his amazing family, and I will be happy in doing it."

"Because your job is to make him happy."

"No. You have to make yourself happy. That's ancient wisdom. But to make things better for him, yes. That's any wife's job. To make things better. It's a husband's job to make things better, just as you did for your wife, for as long as you could."

"As she did for me. Eladeus, I loved her, and I miss her so much." He looked far away and twisted his mouth to one side. "And, as much as I cannot fathom why or how, Swift has given that feeling back to me." The blue eyes met Ah'ren's full on and looked right into her. "Is she real? Is she a person beyond a program?"

"Absolutely," Ah'ren nodded. "She's as real as you and me." Then she laughed and reached to pat his hand where it rested on his thigh. "Or at least as real as me. I, too, chose the man I wanted to be with, and I love him with every fiber of my consciousness, which is all any being can do – as horses love their foals, as birds protect their fledglings, as a tiny fleeter will fight a protoped to protect her fawn. Love is a function of consciousness, a choice of both mind and body."

Konik was silent. "I know both of you were sent by Mountain hold. What if…I wanted to marry her someday, as Ardenai married you? Who would I ask? To whom does she belong?"

"Swift, belongs to Swift," Ah'ren said, rising and extending her hand to him, pulling him up off the bench. "She is yours for a lifetime, Konik. Whether you choose to benefit from that, is your prerogative. Do bear in mind that she is very real, and very much her own woman, and though she will always serve you as hetaera, she is capable of being just as out of love with you as she is in love with you, so don't say or do anything stupid, like asking her if she can taste things."

"Who, me?" He laughed softly. "She knows how flawed I am. I only hope I'm man enough to get past…." He stopped and made that little whuffle which so endeared him to Swift. "Probably not a discussion to have anytime soon."

"I thought you were worried about the image you're presenting to the Lebonathi people," Ah'ren grinned.

"I am a mere mortal," he sighed. "Give me time." He realized the anger draining out of him was making him wobbly in the knees; revelation or exhaustion, or both. Weak with relief. He felt transparent, like Ah'ren could see his heart if she opened his shirt – his lopsided heart that had the names of two women scrawled on it in green colorwax. "When is Pythos going to wake her up, do you know?" he asked, casually steadying himself against a trellis.

Ah'ren nodded. "In the morning. You should try to get a little sleep first."

"I have work to do," he responded, then gave that slight smile and courtly nod of the head which signaled most departures. "I need to find someone who is awake at this hour, who will take my place tomorrow morning. The Anchoress will worry if I'm not there when she wakes."

He'd walked a few steps toward the gate when Ah'ren said his name and he turned back. "Being out in the world is a precious thing," she said quietly. "Those of us who are privileged to do so, rejoice in it every day. But if anyone were to find out who we really are ..."

"I would never put you in jeopardy," Konik said.

"Then I will take your place tomorrow."

He gave her a slight smile, said thank you, and disappeared onto the dimly lit cobblestone street outside the sanecere.

It was that moment where Swift asked herself if she was alive or dead, awake or asleep. What had seemed real was fading fast, sounds were adjusting themselves, colors becoming less vibrant, losing their taste and their smell. Everyday fragrances were reasserting themselves. One brought a smile to her face even before she opened her eyes. She hesitated, just in case it, too, was fantasy. It was not. "Nik," she whispered, "You're here."

"Yes," he said, covering her hand with his. "I am."

CHARACTERS FROM THIS BOOK

Abeyan – *Equi*. Master of Cavalry. Ah'riodin's father.

Aga – *Lebonathi*. Captured with Eshkar by Teal and Ulric Hamar.

Ah'brianne – *Equi*. Daughter of Timor and Ah'mae. Love interest of Gideon. Criollo's best friend.

Ah'clare – *Equi*. Mother of Teal, wife of Gidran. She is a teacher.

Ah'cora – *Equi*. Stepdaughter of Saremanno. Archeological Cartographer.

Ah'davan – *Equi*. (Addie) Konik's sexual trainer and later his wife. Deceased.

Ah'din – *Equi*. (Dini). Wife of Teal, sister of Ardenai, mother of Criollo. Physician/Master Weaver.

Ah'krill – *Equi*. High Priestess. Ardenai's birth mother.

Ah'leah – *Equi/Papilli*. Unborn daughter of Ardenai and Ah'riodin. Lost before birth.

Ah'nia – *Anguine Equi*. One of Konik's twin daughters. Wife of Tokara. Mother of Ah'sienna.

Ah'nis – *Equi*. A priestess. Governor of women's Affairs, guardian of Lebonathi Princess Eridi.

Ah'nora – *Calumet Equi.* She bore Ardenai a High Equi son against his possible demise in the battle with Sarkhan and the Telenir.

Ah'rane – *Equi*. Sister/mother of Ardenai. Wife of Krush. Mother of Ah'din.

Ah'ree – *Equi*. Deceased. Beloved first wife of Ardenai, who raised Ah'riodin in her father's absence.

Ah'ren – *Equi*. (Wren). Ancient and beautiful Androtech being. Ardenai's Companion Wife.

Ah'rika – *Anguine Equi*. One of Konik's twin daughters. Wife of Eriskay. Mother of Nokota.

Ah'riodin – *Equi/Papilli*. (Io) Abeyan Ah'riodin Ardenai Morning Star. Wife of Ardenai, Primuxori of Equus. Daughter of Abeyan, mother of Jilfan.

Ah'sienna – *Anguine Equi*. Konik's seven-year-old granddaughter. Parents are Tokara and Ah'nia.

Akadia – *Lebonathi.* Wife of Telloh. Naram's lover.

Amir Cohen – *Terren/Demetrian.* Computator Technologist aboard Belesprit. Father of Yussef.

Anmar – *Lebonathi.* One of the boys playing Lightning. He later guides Kehailan and Jobie.

Anshra – *Lebonathi.* Older brother of Anmar. His life is saved by Kehailan and Ardenai.

Ardenai – *Equi.* (Ardi) Ah'rane Ardenai Krush, who becomes Ah'krill Ardenai Morning Star, the Thirteenth Dragonhorse. Firstlord of Equus. First wife, Ah'ree, deceased. Second wife, Ah'riodin, who is his Primuxori. Third wife, Ah'ren, his companion wife. Fostered by his half-sister Ah'rane and her husband, Krush. Birthed by High Priestess Ah'krill.

Ashte – *Lebonathi.* The older of Kish's grandsons. Son of Temen. Works in the family wood shop.

Ashur – *Lebonathi.* A scientist living at Stone Spring.

Aurus – *Amberian.* Rescues Konik and the boys from the sewer tunnels.

Bona – *Lebonathi.* Rescued from the mushroom tunnels by, and devoted to Konik. Loves raising bees.

Bonfire Dannis – *Phyllan.* Captain of ISTC Nine. "The Dragon's Tail."

Brak – *Lebonathi.* Standard Bearer. Husband of Phaedra, father of Rakba. brother-in-law of Naram. Deceased.

Cadence Holofernes – *Corvi.* Captain of ISTC 5, "The Dragon's Hide" Wife of Merrilina.

Casey – *Demetrian.* A first grader in Orlov Teacher's class aboard Belesprit. Pal of Yussef.

Chirion – *Equi Androtech.* Eldest of the denizens of Mountain Hold.

Coral – *Menorquin.* A first grader in Orlov Teacher's class aboard Belesprit.

Criollo – *Equi.* Age twenty-four Equi years. Ah'din Criollo Teal. Only son of Teal and Ah'din. Nephew of Ardenai.

Cutter – *Equi.* Communications officer aboard Dragonhorse Thirteen. Borrowed from the Great House.

Drena – *Lebonathi.* Eshkar's sister-in-law.

Elam – *Lebonathi.* The youngest of the male scientists At Stone Spring. Father of Umma, Husband of Larsa.

Ellsbeth – *Demetrian*. SGA trooper. On special assignment from Ardenai

Ensharra – *Lebonathi*. An Anchoress. Priestess of the ancient city.

Eridi – *Lebonathi*. Princess. Child of Eridu and Lulana. Given to Ardenai as a flesh-gift. She is about seventeen years old.

Eridu – *Lebonathi*. Ruler of the Lebonathi Worlds. Father of Eridi. Murdered by his sister-in-law.

Eriskay – *Anguine Equi*. Husband of Ah'rika. He is an Intergalactic Communications specialist.

Esha – *Lebonathi*. Youngest grandson of Kish. Works in his grandfather's wood shop.

Eshkar – *Lebonathi*. Brother of Ensharra. Taken by Teal from a mock battle.

Etana – *Lebonathi*. The older of the two women scientists living at Stone Spring.

Gallios – *Menorquin*. General Manager of the terraformers turned farm ships.

Garash – *Daran Lebonathi*. Son of Muru. He is about seventeen years old.

Gideon – *Declivian/Terren/Coronian/Equi*. Gideon Ardenai Morning Star. Adopted son of Ardenai. Brother to Kehailan. Age seventeen.

Gidran – *Equi*. Teal's father. Husband of Ah'clare. Newly appointed Master Vintner.

Gilim – *Lebonathi*. School master.

Hadrian Keats – *Terren*. Former Chief Physician aboard Belesprit. Currently under house arrest and working with a research team on Declivis.

Harrier – *Androtech*. One of the most ancients of Mountain hold. Chef extraordinaire.

Isin – *Lebonathi*. One of the five scientists now living at Stone Spring.

Jasreth – *Lebonathi*. Niece of Girsu. Love interest of Criollo.

Jilfan – *Equi/Papilli*. Son of Ah'riodin by Salerno. Grandson of Abeyan. Ardenai's stepson.

Jobie – *Taraxian*. Son of Ambassador Dahman and Kerala. He is about sixteen years old.

Jomud – *Equi*. Master of Drums for the Great House of Equus.

Josephus – *Terren*. Captain of "The Grand Old Rust Bucket" and dear friend of Ardenai and his family.

Joss – *Amberian.* Rescues Konik and the boys from the sewer tunnels.

Kehailan – *Equi.* (Kee) Ah'ree Kehailan Ardenai. Eldest son of Ardenai. Captain of ISTC Thirteen, "The Dragonhorse."

Kerala – *Taraxian.* Wife of Ambassador Dahman. Mother of Jobie.

Kestrel – *Androtech.* One of the most ancient of the Androtech beings. Supervises much of what goes on at Mountain hold and beyond. Roundly disliked by all who have to deal with him.

Kish – *Lebonathi.* Owner of the woodworking shop in the old city. Father of Temen, Grandfather of Ashte and Esha.

Konik – *Equi.* (Nik) Ah'ria Konik Nokota. Military Governor of the Lebonathi worlds.

Krush – *Equi.* Foster father of Ardenai. Husband of Ah'rane. Father of Ah'din. Father-in-law to Teal.

Landais – *Equi.* Master Smith for the Great House of Equus.

Larsa – *Lebonathi.* The younger of the two women scientists at Stone Spring. Mother of Umma, Wife of Elam.

Lillahn – *Daran Lebonathi.* A young Anchoress. Daughter of Muru.

Lulana – *Lebonathi.* Firstwife of Eridu. Mother of Eridi. Murdered by Eridu.

Luna – *Papilli.* Abeyan's late wife. Mother of Ah'riodin.

Marion Eletsky – *Terren.* Captain of SGASV (Seventh Galactic Alliance Science Vessel) Belesprit.

Merrilina – *Corvi.* Technologist aboard ISTC 5. Wife of Cadence Holofernes.

Muru – *Daran Lebonathi.* Leader of the people hidden on Enki Dara. Love interest of Ensharra.

Naram – *Lebonathi.* Lebonathi Regent after Eridu's death.

Nokota - *Anguine Equi.* (Ah'rika Nokota Eriskay) Grandson of Konik. Age six.

Nokota – *Anguine Equi.* Konik's father.

Oona Pongo – *Terren.* Communications Officer aboard Belesprit.

Orlov – *Equi.* Teacher aboard Belesprit. Former student of Ardenai.

Pen Darus – *Demetrian.* He arrives with the newest Stormclass Tactical Cruiser.

Phaedra – *Lebonathi.* Brak's wife. Mother of Rakba, sister to Lulana and

Naram. She kills Eridu. Deceased.

Pythos – *Achernarean.* One of the serpent physicians of Achernar, personal physician to Ardenai and his household, and one of his closest friends and advisors.

Rakba – *Lebonathi.* Small son of Brak and Phaedra. Deceased.

Reynalda – *Equi/Terren.* Precocious first grader aboard Belesprit, and a thorn in Yussef Cohen's side.

Salerno – *Equi.* Ah'riodin's first husband, killed in battle.. Father of Jilfan.

Sardure – *Telenir.* Right hand to Sarkhan until replaced by Konik.

Saremanno – *Telenir.* Father of Sarkhan and Sardure, stepfather to Ah'cora.

Sarkhan – *Telenir.* Deceased. Sought to overthrow the government and kill the Thirteenth Dragonhorse.

Seglawi – *Equi.* Captain of Arms for the Great House of Equus.

Squire Fidel – *Demetrian.* Owns the horse farm where Ardenai finds Gideon, and who tries to turn Ardenai in for the ransom.

Sura – *Lebonathi.* Eshkar's sister-in-law.

Swift – *Equi.* Konik's Hetaera. Her specialty is Juvenile Cardiopathy. She practices on the Jocundome.

Taki – *Equi/Telenir.* One of the elders who spoke for peace.

Tarpan – *Equi.* Commander of the expedition cavalry contingent assigned to Lebonath Tras

Teal – *Equi.* Ah'clare Teal Gidran. Master Captain and Ardenai's closest friend and advisor. Married to Ardenai's sister, Ah'din.

Telloh – *Lebonathi.* Husband of Akadia.

Temen – *Lebonathi.* Son of Kish. Father of Ashte and Esha. Works with his father in thc wood shop

Timor – *Equi.* Master Farmer. Leases Lea keep from Krush. Father of Ah'brianne, husband of Ah'mae.

Timothy McGill – *Demetrian/Terren.* (Tim). Botanist aboard Belesprit. Kehailan's friend and lover.

Tokara – *Anguine Equi.* Husband of Ah'nia. Father of Ah'sienna. He is a master farmer.

Ulric Hamar – *Amberian.* Captain of Imperial Stormclass Tactical Cruiser One, "The Dragon's Teeth."

Umma – *Lebonathi*. Infant daughter of Elam and Larsa.

Vanner – *Equi*. Master Vintner to the Great House. He has asked to retire, and is being replaced by Gidran.

Winslow Moonsgold – *Declivian*. (Winnie). Chief Medical officer aboard Belesprit.

Yussef Cohen – *Terren/Demetrian*. In the first-grade class aboard Belesprit. Son of Amir Cohen.

THE NAMED DRAGONHORSES

The first Dragonhorse ~ Tersk, a soldier

The Second Dragonhorse ~ Warlander, a farm machinery engineer

The Third Dragonhorse ~ Hirzai, a senator and cavalry officer

The Fourth Dragonhorse ~ Galician, the Captain of a great stellar ship

The Fifth Dragonhorse ~ Timor, a farmer

The Sixth Dragonhorse ~ Carthus, an orchardist

Killed by insurgents his first day in office

The Seventh Dragonhorse ~ Vanner, an interstellar navigator

The Eighth Dragonhorse ~ Balearic, a time-whip engineer

Who was grievously injured, and his wife and children killed by insurgents at Mountain hold

The Ninth Dragonhorse ~ Kabardin, A bloodlines specialist

The Tenth Dragonhorse ~ Ardenai, a master composer and musician

The Eleventh Dragonhorse ~ Asturian, Master of Cavalry, and a botanist

The Twelfth Dragonhorse ~ Kehailan, a bloodlines specialist

The Thirteenth Dragonhorse ~ Ardenai, a teacher

HISTORY AND ACCOMPLISHMENTS OF THE DRAGONHORSES

From the most ancient annals of the Awakening, as recorded by Kestrel, Master of the Fortress of Mountain hold.

This document is for general reference by scholars and interested parties. An exhaustive entry is available for each Dragonhorse under his name at birth, and the years of his reign, and kept in the Great Library of the Dragonhorses for the personal use of its physicians and bloodlines specialists.

Because I appreciate absolutely clarity, I am including in this list the first two princes whose bloodlines were specifically selected, who were incubated by a dragon-physician, and born of a High Priestess for the express purpose of being the sole secular ruler of planet Equus, even though they did not survive.

Kestrel, Master of Mountain Hold

The first ATTEMPTED Dragonhorse was Moorland, of the Waterfowl ~ approximately ten thousand years ago ~ five hundred years after the calendar change at the dawn of the Awakening. Despite careful monitoring, He died of heart failure during his third Imperial Dragonhorse Cycle at the age of one hundred and one. A fine Architect and stone-structure engineer, it was Moorland who designed and began shaping the modern and expansive facility which became the Great House of Equus.

The second ATTEMPTED Dragonhorse was Teal, of the Waterfowl ~ approximately nine thousand five hundred years ago. While relatively more robust than his predecessor, and despite advancements in breeding, he died of bloodboil during his fifth Imperial Dragonhorse Cycle. Teal was the first Captain of the Horse Guard of the Great House of Equus.

(Following this second, tragic loss of a prince, there followed nearly a thousand years of intensive research and experimentation, during which time it was discovered that by bringing the more robust though less intelligent Equine characteristics to the fore in combination with carefully selected but limited ophidian genes, a more rugged individual could be produced. In combination with that increased vigor, experimentation with quelling potions and advancements in medical practices made it possible for a Dragonhorse to survive Imperial cycles.)

The first Dragonhorse to survive and fulfill his term in office, was Tersk, of Equine Lineage ~ eight thousand five hundred years ago. Tersk was a soldier in the Equi cavalry, and an accomplished fighter on horseback. With his reign came the final phase of construction on the Great House of Equus, and expansion of the city of Thura as the planetary capital. During this time Menorquin allied itself with Equus, and began aiding the Equi in the terraforming of the Anguine moons in order to allow for dispersion of a rapidly growing population on the surface of Equus. Because Tersk was not, shall we say, sublimely intelligent, he was not given full rule, though he was bred for that purpose.

The second Dragonhorse was Warlander, of Equine Lineage ~ seven thousand eight hundred years ago. Warlander was a farm machinery engineer. During Warlander's reign, following years of mutual posturing and aggression, Equus subdued the Amberians and made them a tribute world of Equus. Warlander quickly recognized their genius with machinery, and invited them to become a sister world. Under his reign several cities increased exponentially in size, and with an emphasis being put on progress and the components of a modern society, the citizens of Equus began moving away from their agrarian heritage. Air quality began to suffer planet-wide. Warlander was not deemed ready to accept the full responsibility of rule, and remained a figurehead and hinge-pin of the Great Council.

The third Dragonhorse was Hirzai,of Equine Lineage ~ seven thousand two hundred years ago. Hirzai was a senator, and an officer in the Equi cavalry. By this time the Anguine moons were being populated and coming into acceptable levels of production, and it was decided in open council to form the AEW, the Affined Equi Worlds. Hirzai emphasized the importance of industry, and allowed the mentality of the planet to shift completely away from agriculture to manufacturing. A consummate politician, Hirzai was engaged in constant disagreements with both the Great Council and the Eloi, and there was much dissent and bickering at the expense of the population and the environment. While civil war did not break out, nor were there any revolts nor withdrawals from the Great Council, Hirzai did not move Equus forward, and he is recognized more for the lessons he taught about what not to do as Dragonhorse, than by anything he actually did for the people of Equus. Because his personality became obvious in early adulthood, he, like his predecessor, remained a figurehead, but greater efforts were put into breeding an individual who could assume the position of undisputed leader.

The fourth Dragonhorse was Galician, of Equine and Waterfowl Lineage ~ six thousand five hundred years ago. The first Dragonhorse to be given full authority to rule, Galician was the captain of a great stellar ship, and it was he who commissioned the construction of the Great Andalese Shipyards. He emphasized the importance of science, and during his reign the University System of the Affined Equi Worlds was incorporated and gained great status. It was Galician who discovered the devastated world of the Papilli, and brought the full force of the Affined Equi Worlds down upon Tarkelia, Potami, and what is now the Eighth Galactic Alliance planet of Bargul. He then spent the shank of his reign rebuilding Papillia and re-establishing commerce. Before his death he saw Papillia become an Affined Equi World, and called it his finest accomplishment. Galacian is one of the most revered of the Dragonhorses and considered by many to be the true father of modern-day Equus. By the end of his reign Equus was the wealthiest and most powerful planet in what would become the Seventh Galactic Alliance; a position which she has consistently occupied in the millennia since.

The fifth Dragonhorse was Timor of Equine and Arboranthus Lineage ~ five thousand eight hundred years ago. Timor was a farmer, and had a Secundoctora in herbal medicine. He saw no need for conquest, and focused his reign on improving Equus and returning the planet to its agricultural past and simpler wants and needs. It was he who began to enforce the strict birth quotas suggested earlier by the Eloi, and to move Equus away from headlong progress and back into a more proactive, hands-on and agrarian lifestyle, which included phasing out currency and focusing on need, while emphasizing progress in medicine and social services. He never lost his passion for the soil and spent much of his energy on improving alcibus varietals, and increasing crop yields to better support neighboring planets. He said that hungry people made for uneasy neighbors. Industry began moving underground, combustion engines were finally phased out entirely, and Thura became a walking city, full of parks, trees and community gardens. Agriculture saw new birth with Timor, and he is often bantered about as the patron saint of farm folk. He reigned for an exceptionally long time, one hundred and sixty one years.

The sixth Dragonhorse was Carthus, of Equine and Arboranthus Lineage ~ five thousand one hundred years ago. Carthus was an Adjudicator and Senator, and well respected in his profession. He had been through the ceremonies marking him as Dragonhorse, and he, his husband and his personal physician were on their way to Mountain hold when their ship suddenly and mysteriously exploded in mid-air, killing all three of them instantly. Though nothing was ever found to indicate that the explosion was more than a tragic accident, two stories abound to this day ~ one, that he had fallen to the Wind Warriors, and two, that he had been killed by the Eloi because he was homophilic, and they feared he would not properly participate in the breeding programs of the Great House. The High Priestess immediately picked up the reins of government, and within two days it was as if Carthus had never existed.

(Herein lies a span of eight hundred and fifty years while adjustments were once again made to ensure that, by necessity, the Dragonhorse would henceforth be born and remain heterophilic.)

The seventh Dragonhorse was Vanner, of Equine Lineage ~ four thousand, three hundred years ago. Vanner was an archeologist and deep space navigator of exceptional ability. He knew the Corvi well, they trusted him, and under his reign Corvus asked to become part of the AEW. Vanner mounted the first of the Equi Probative Interpositions, this one aimed at the Terrenes and he controlled their world very tightly for nearly one hundred years. It was Vanner who took up the proposition Carthus had made as a senator before the Great Council centuries earlier, and began the actual work of forming the Seventh Galactic Alliance. His only diplomatic misstep was in seizing a fleet of Fifth Alliance cargo vessels transporting cleomitite ore across AEW space, and refusing to negotiate for their return. When the two Fifth Alliance planets involved lodged a protest, Vanner destroyed the ships, sent their crews home in an Amberian prison ship, and issued a public decree stating no AEW planet could trade with the Fifth Alliance. Though the decree was later lifted, it caused several Fifth Alliance planets to bear a lasting grudge against Equus.

The eighth Dragonhorse was Balearic, of Equine and Waterfowl Lineage ~ Three thousand, six hundred years ago. Balearic was a time-whip Engineer and his greatest contribution to Equus was made before he ever rose to be Dragonhorse. It was he who designed the system of high speed tube-trains and the technology which allows the friction of their passing to be used as energy. Balearic and his entire family were in their initial residence at Mountain hold when usurpers penetrated the fortress and attacked them. Balearic lost his parents, his beloved wife, and his small sons. He was grievously injured, and was never again physically strong. Nevertheless, he was an excellent diplomat, and made appropriate overtures and apologies to the Fifth Galactic Alliance which led to a final and secure peace. Under his reign goods moved ever more freely throughout the Seventh Galactic Alliance, and closer economic bonds were formed with SGA planets which were not AEW. Because of his infirmities he had to rely on both the Eloi and the Great Council for their help in the demands of his office, and from a governing standpoint, his reign looked much like those of the first three Dragonhorses. He governed only one hundred and twenty years before passing.

(Again there is a gap before the next Scion is born. This one spanning eight hundred years)

The ninth Dragonhorse was Kabardin, of Equine Lineage ~ two thousand eight hundred years ago. Kabardin was a bloodlines specialist, as well as a paleo-anthropologist and computator engineer. Undeniably brilliant, he was hyperphilic and mentally unstable, given to fits of rage and overweening ego. Within five years of having risen to govern he had threatened the Sixth Galactic Alliance with open warfare over what he saw as trade inequities, and Amberia with expulsion from the AEW for the same reasons. He opened mining operations on the unclaimed planet of Calumet under less than ideal circumstances for those sent to work there, and seized two moons from Taraxia because he felt they were not being utilized to their full potential. When he was challenged by the Great Council, he dissolved it to the last member, forbade the Eloi from any activities which involved governance, and declared himself free of any encumbrances to his authority. There ensued a time of chaos, when to question the Dragonhorse was to court death, and he not only killed political rivals but his own personal physician, one of his wives and his unborn child. At nearly unbearable personal risk, the Great Council reassembled in secret, to be joined by the Eloi and the Physicians of Achernar. Fearing that destroying the Dragonhorse would undermine the entire foundation upon which modern Equus and the entire AEW was built, they sought answers in more clandestine and probably less than honorable ways, which were nonetheless essential to the survival of Equus. Unbeknownst to either the Eloi or the Great Council, three women, each an elite warrior from Mountain hold, were introduced as residents of the Great House – two as hetaeras, one as wife, to Kabardin himself. Despite his continued abuses, and his near-killing of one of them, they remained close to him, and finally, when the opportunity presented itself to make it seem a completely natural death – for the good of the planet, the AEW and the SGA, and with deep personal misgivings about the morality of their act – they assassinated the man by smothering him during sex. His death was declared natural, and there was no investigation.

(At this time there arose hue and cry mostly amongst the Eloi, that the Dragonhorse had outlived his worth and, as a whole, had never lived up to his potential, though the people of Equus insisted that the Dragonhorse was an integral and indispensable part of their heritage. After a lengthy debate and some serious readjustments to both the rules and the bloodlines, another Dragonhorse was conceived.)

The tenth Dragonhorse was Ardenai, of Equine, Waterfowl and Arboranthus Lineage ~ two thousand, one hundred years ago. Ardenai was Master Composer to the Great House, a fine musician and a brilliant scholar.

His first official act as Dragonhorse was to return the moons which Kabardin had seized, to the people of Taraxia. He brought the force of Equus down upon those persons who were systematically pillaging Demeter, and those planets that were benefiting from it, most especially Tarkelia. That Probative Interposition was coupled with the colonization of Calumet, the gridding of vast tracts for settlement, and the establishment of keeps and townships. For those two reasons, Ardenai was absent from Equus for much of his first four decades in office. Of all the Dragonhorses so far, he was the most active off-world. His time on Equus was spent composing, and teaching Lycee. He was, in the opinion of this writer, approaching the perfection which we had so long sought in a Dragonhorse.

The eleventh Dragonhorse, was Asturian, of Equine and Water-fowl Lineage ~ One thousand, four hundred years ago. The second Dragon-horse to approach perfection, Asturian was Master of Cavalry for the Great House of Equus, and is considered the greatest Ethno-Physician and Epide-miologist Equus ever produced. His research during his travels with the cav-alry led to the complete elimination of Firethorn's Disease on both Demeter and Declivis, saving the needless suffering and disfigurement of countless newborns. During his reign Calumet became a tribute world, and it was un-der his direction that the Controlled Atmosphere Corridors were developed so that people could more easily come and go. It was he who invited the Amish-Mennonites of Terren to join the Equi on Calumet, and the success of that planet is largely credited to his sage management. He bound himself very closely to, and improved relations with the Eloi and the High Priestess, which brought added stability to Equus.

The twelfth Dragonhorse, was Kehailan, of Equine Lineage ~ Seven hundred years ago. Kehailan was a bloodlines specialist, and, like his predecessor, a very fine physician. He was also an historian of some note, and, having researched the devastating effects of Dragonhorse cycles in males, most especially Imperial Dragonhorse Cycles in Dragonhorses, spent a great deal of time and effort trying to eliminate heat cycles altogether in both males and females. He turned his attention to Declivis when her plight became obvious, but he arrived too late to prevent the extinction of the orig-inal inhabitants. It was something he regretted to the end of his days. He was an extraordinary diplomat, with a fine sense of humor and a generous heart. He homogenized the Seventh Galactic Alliance into a single force, and expanded trade in both the sixth and eighth alliances. During his reign Demeter became briefly a Tribute World, and then an Affined Equi World, bringing the number of Affined Worlds to eleven.

The thirteenth Dragonhorse, is Ardenai, of Equine lineage~ One year ago. While serving as an ambassador to Terren and designing computators of dizzying capability, his service of choice has been as a creppia-nonage teacher; Children roughly five years old. In his first year as Dragonhorse he has unraveled the millenia-old mystery of the Telenir, killed their leader in open battle, and brought their insurrection to a standstill in a most unusual and merciful manner. He is now applying that same mercy-based tactic in a probative interposition to the Lebonathi worlds. He has applied to the Seventh Galactic Alliance to colonize Lebonath Tras, and is attempting to civilize Lebonath Jas. He is so far a most unusual individual, and amongst the eloi he is spoken of as "the perfect Dragonhorse." We shall see.

THE AFFINED EQUI WORLDS OF WHICH THERE ARE ELEVEN

By Gideon Ardenai Morning Star

A paper For Master Breton's GeoSociology class

Equus ~ More water than land, Equus consists of three large continents, Andal, Benacus, and Viridia, plus the warm island chain of Achernar, several inhabited islands and two large, uninhabited ice caps. All three continents are more or less bisected by the equator, which helps temper the generally cool climate. Viridia is the longest continent, if not the widest. It is the smallest, and has the oldest life-signs. It has vast plains and grasslands, several large river systems, two mountain ranges of modest elevation, some large and many smaller cave systems, and about half the population of Equus. Benacus is highest in elevation and least populated. The major crops are ice pomes and very fine wool. Andal is cool, mountainous, and riddled with huge cave systems which have been carved out to accommodate homes and industry. It is the industrial center of the planet, with most of the industry being subterranean, and most of the surface being keeps and well-ordered villages.

A cool world and relatively new geologically, Equus is rich in geothermal, solar and hydro-energy sources. Equus has wild seasonal swings, and in winter the surface of the planet, most especially Viridia, can be swept by terrible storms. There is nowhere except Achernar that it does not snow. Equus is primarily an agricultural planet and the people are by nature vegetarian. Equus has a small population relative to its power in the Seventh Galactic Alliance. Its government consists of a Great Council, a Guild of

Masters, a Guild of Crafts, a High Priestess, and every seven hundred years, a Firstlord, traditionally referred to as Dragonhorse, who is the only truly secular leader.

Amberia ~ having joined with Equus almost eight thousand years ago during the reign of Warlander, the Second Dragonhorse, Amberia is the second oldest Ally of Equus, and its denizens are closely related to the Equi. Amberia is a large, warm planet, with huge, tangled jungles sprawling across parts of all of its eight continents. It is laced with deserts and dry places, but also with lakes and rivers, which are characteristically gentle flowing and tepid. By contrast its oceans are very deep, frigid and perpetually stormy. Amberia is densely populated in the more hospitable areas and heavily industrialized in those which are not. Huge tracts of land have been left open for purposes of conservation, and agriculture, and despite having a large population, Amberia is clean of air and water, and a prosperous partner in the Affined Equi Worlds. Like the Equi and the rest of the AEW they are vegetarian, and produce more than enough food to feed themselves and their neighbors. They also manufacture most of the farm equipment used in the Seventh Galactic Alliance. Though they were and remain a society that loves war and war games, they have the same government as Equus, and come under the rule of the Firstlord, or Dragonhorse, when he rises to power.

The Anguine Moons *(Anguine Prime and Anguine II)* ~ both planets are close moons of Equus, and were terraformed approximately nine thousand years ago, over a period of about five hundred years, to be agricultural hubs as Equus spread its influence into the spatial extension which later became the Seventh Galactic Alliance. Populated mostly by Equi, the moons are alike in having rolling hills, a few deep craters, and vast expanses of both forest and cultivated farmland. They have large, man made lakes, but no seas. While Anguine II has more water than Anguine Prime, they are both considered agricultural powerhouses, and have served as examples to several emergent agrarian societies. Like Equus they are largely divided into agricultural keeps and clustered townships, and, like Equus, keeps cannot be bought or sold, but only handed down, across or out, thus guaranteeing generations of farmers, horse breeders and silviculturists. Each of the moons has two or three cities which can be considered large, and each has huge ports of entry for shipping agricultural commodities out into the SGA. Their planetary capital, however, is Thura, which is on Equus itself. Anguine II is especially renowned for the quality of its education, most especially history and music studies. Every year it hosts an Enalios Lycee, which engenders fierce competition for seats. Less than an hour's travel from the main planet and from one another, the moons have no national government of their own, but belong in every respect to Equus, and are considered states, rather than sovereignties.

Calumet ~ a planet of five continents and eight oceans, and among the most beautiful of the Affined Equi Worlds, Calumet is a world entirely apart from everyone else in both mindset and lifestyle. While Calumet is capable of generating power, it cannot transfer it. For example, a millwheel powered by water, can grind the grain brought to it, but it cannot send power forth by any means or in any manner to be used elsewhere. Ships cannot operate within its atmosphere and friction fires will not burn. Calumet exists perpetually in a distant past, where wagons and horses hold sway on the roads, and oil lamps and candles light the night. Nevertheless, Calumet is a fully contributing partner in the AEW. The planet produces some of the finest wool in the galaxy, highly sought-after Calumet mahogany, beautiful horses, and precious Cleomitite gemstones, which are coveted throughout the Sixth, Seventh and Eighth Galactic Alliances. Goods are brought to one of several CACs (Controlled Atmosphere Corridors), lifted into ships, and moved out into the galaxy. Calumet is populated by the Equi, who discovered and colonized it nearly three thousand years ago under the reign of the Tenth Dragonhorse, Ardenai. Following the cataclysms on Terren, they were joined by most of the Mennonite-Amish from Terren. In comparison to its size and its bountiful landscapes, Calumet has a tiny population. They are governed on all levels by the laws of Equus and the Dragonhorse.

Corvus ~ One of the most unusual planets to produce a thriving and intelligent population, Corvus is so high and so jagged as to resemble a round pinecone revolving in space. The sides of its impossibly tall, slanted mountains have been masterfully terraced to produce all manner of fruits and vegetables, and beautiful cities, carved into the native stone, gleam forth from the promontories. The fierce winds which whip through the canyons have been baffled by a series of ingenious wings, until they are no more than gentle up and downdrafts upon which both people in their small gliders and birds upon the wing soar effortlessly about on their daily business. Their water supply runs in narrow, fathomless rivers which encircle the planet, and the planet's core is water, heated by geothermal activity. They have a stable population of moderate size and are capable of feeding themselves, though they do not contribute foodstuffs to the AEW. No planet in the galaxy produces finer pilots than does Corvus. They asked to join the AEW, along with Terren, under the reign of Vanner, the Seventh Numbered Dragonhorse, and immediately began to contribute pilots and navigators to the newly formed Seventh Galactic Alliance. They answer to the Dragonhorse when he rises, and their government resembles that of Equus in most ways, though their property laws do not.

Demeter ~ Sister planet to Declivis, and as beautiful as Declivis is ugly, it is Demeter's agriculture which keeps both Declivis and Tarkelia fed and well nourished. This planet most closely resembles Equus in size, though it has considerably less open ocean and more fresh water in the form of glacier-carved lakes and the rivers which pass through and feed them. Demeter has five large continents, several island chains and a small polar ice cap. Like the Anguine moons, Demeter is an agricultural powerhouse, and nearly devoid of industry, having counted for eons upon Declivis to provide her with equipment and technology. Like Equus, the people of Demeter have chosen to remain agrarian based, and eschew many so-called modern conveniences. Because of its location as "The Crossroads of the Alliance," the planet was fiercely contested for much of its early history, and was the site of many bloody battles. Parts of the landscape still bear the scars of near-annihilation. Upon rising to be Firstlord, the Tenth Dragonhorse, Ardenai, brought the conflict to an abrupt end, then annexed and repaired Demeter, making it a tribute world of the AEW. Demeter is most famous for its endless plantations of tea and coffee, and its unique varietals of chenopodium quinoa. It has many small towns which retain their reputation for being brawling backwaters, and it has many larger settlements built around the ports of entry from which goods are shipped to the Great House and other alliance destinations. Their government closely resembles that of Equus, and they fall, like the rest of the AEW, under the reign of the Dragonhorse.

Menorquin ~ The oldest of the Affined Worlds, and an older race far than the Equi, Menorquin consists of an endless scatter of meticulously terraformed islands in an equally endless sea, with no mountains of any size above the tideline. There are no continents at all, and oddly, no seasons. Its people live with equal comfort on land, or in huge and ancient cities beneath their various seas and oceans, where they farm the many kinds of seaweed and kelp which form the basis for their diet. Like the Equi they eat no actual flesh, though they enjoy a type of krill in season. They also eat various cereal grains and are especially fond of berries, which they grow in profusion on their island farms. An ancient industrial power, and by necessity accomplished terraformers, it was they who terraformed the Anguine moons for settlement by the Equi. As a member of the Affined Equi Worlds, their government closely resembles that of Equus, and over many thousands of years the two planets have shared and blended their political and religious beliefs until distinguishing features have all but disappeared. Every seven hundred years they, along with all of the AEW, fall under the rule of the Dragonhorse.

Papillia ~ Being on the border between what are now the Seventh and Eighth Galactic Alliances at a time when both spatial extensions were in a frenzy of acquisition, the people and the planet of Papillia were nearly destroyed. The surface was stripped of resources by the aggressors and largely denuded by the war moving back and forth across the planet. Galician, the Fourth Dragonhorse, discovered their plight and brought the might of the AEW into play to protect them. Having moved many of their resources to deeply sheltered caches beneath the surface, the Papilli were able to utilize their incredible building skills to create a sphere around their ruined planet and to rebuild it as a biosphere. Now considered the most beautiful of the Affined Equi Worlds, Papillia is a small planet consisting mostly of elevated cloud forests enveloped in endless mist. The lowlands boast extensive marshes rich with plants and wildlife. Being lovers of the light, the Papilli build almost exclusively with a form of sheet-crystal, and their sparkling cities are admired throughout the galaxy. They pledged their allegiance to Equus during the last days of Galician's reign, and further repaired themselves to become one of the richest and most productive of the Equi worlds. Their form of government does not differ from that of Equus, except that they have no Eloi (the cadre of ruling priestesses) as a separate entity.

Phylla ~ The coldest of the Affined Equi Worlds, Phylla is also the oldest planet geologically, and its fires are slowly dying, forcing the people underground, closer to the heat source at the core of the planet. Much of their industry and living space is subterranean, and they have beautiful homes and large factories chiseled from the grey native Gyrstone. Phylla is made up largely of expansive tundras, which are chilly and damp most of the year, thawing briefly nearest the equator, where they become impassable bogs. There are arboreal forests spilling north to south across both continents, which host the largest trees in the Seventh Galactic Alliance, and many Phyllans make their homes in or amongst them. Phylla is one of only two AEW planets, Amberia being the other, to engage Equus in open warfare. They were taken into the AEW as a Tribute World under Asturian, the Eleventh Dragonhorse, and became an Affined World about one thousand years ago.

Terren ~ An extremely old, warm planet, Terren once had continents which shook apart in a series of cataclysms both natural and manmade, followed by volcanic activity which nearly destroyed the planet, leaving several dozen convoluted islands, some large, some small, stretching north to south in an endless, single sea. Following near annihilation and facing starvation, Terren came to the attention of the Menorquins, and they began terraforming the continental fragments that were left, creating soil and farm land on the surface. Vanner, the Seventh Dragonhorse, mounted a probative interposition involving the warlike Terrenes, and controlled their government very closely for about one hundred years. At the end of that time Terren became a Tribute World, and during the reign of the Eighth Dragonhorse, Balearic, they finally became an Affined World. Modern Terren actually refers to a conglomerate of terraformed moons and planets in a single orbit, though the original planet has been restored and is home to a modest population and the Terren government, as well as a fascinating collection of plants and animals, several fine universities for studying biological diversity, a whole series of enormous archaeological digs, and a huge SGA park system.

A BRIEF PHYSICAL DESCRIPTION OF THE VARIOUS RACES AND PEOPLES OF THE AFFINED EQUI WORLDS AND THE SEVENTH GALACTIC ALLIANCE

In Alphabetical Order

By Timor Ah'brianne Ah'mae, for Master Breton

Let me just say as I begin this list, that we have much more in common than we have differences. Even though the Sixth, Seventh and Eighth Galactic Alliances occupy a huge section of cosmic space, we were all seeded by a common ancestor in the distant past, and although we have adapted in some interesting ways to our various planetary environments, most of which also closely resemble one another, we retain many traits of our original ancestry. This assignment will focus on the best-known races in Seventh Galactic Alliance space but it is not all-inclusive.

Respectfully,

Timor Ah'brianne Ah'mae

Achernar ~ While not a planet in itself, the islands of Achernar on the planet Equus host a race so unique, and so different from those we think of as Equi, that they deserve special mention. The denizens of Achernar are referred to variously as serpents, dragons, and sea dragons. They are a race old beyond reckoning. Extremely intelligent beings, they have flat, snake-like heads with tiny soft teeth and constricting bodies averaging twenty-eight hands (seven feet) off the floor with another fifteen hands (five feet) or so devoted to their powerful tails, which they use to balance themselves on their short, hipless legs. They have thin, powerful arms and frond-like hands with multiple fingers, and no external shoulders. They have smooth scales of emerald green, and there is no way for an outsider to tell one from another or male from female but by their voices, which vary in timbre and sibilance. Lifespan: approximately one thousand years.

Amberia ~ an AEW member. Very closely related to Equi, both male and female Amberians tend to be tall, broad shouldered, and athletic. Their skin shades from deep peachy gold through orange, and their hair is usually black or dark brown. Their eyes are slightly oversized, almond shaped and range from pale orange to true black. They have large, tapering ears with external ear-bones. They have one set of slightly rounded cuspids. Most Amberians are elaborately tattooed, a process which begins in childhood. Average lifespan: 200 – 250 years.

Anguine Prime ~ an AEW member, has no "native" population. Inhabitants are Equi

Anguine II ~ an AEW member, has no "native" population. Inhabitants are Equi

Aranea ~ no affiliations. Small people related distantly to Menorquins, more closely to Nargawerlders, the Araneans have spindly arms and legs which allow them to climb quickly and efficiently around in the enormous cave systems which they inhabit. Extremely intelligent and task-driven, they are secretive and suspicious of outsiders, and have no strong alliances. They tend to be pale of skin and eye, with thin, wispy hair, lantern jaws, needle-teeth and whispery voices, which has led some to describe them as spider-like. Average lifespan: 50 years.

Calumet ~ an AEW member, has no "native" population. See Equus or Terren for denizens of the various sectors.

Caspia ~ an SGA member. Closely related to Menorquins, distantly to Araneans, Caspians are small, swimming folk who occupy a world largely covered with water. They are elongated of limb and spend much of their time in a watery environment. They are pale of skin, tending to a greenish or bluish cast, with slightly bulbous eyes, small ears covered with a fine membrane, and very short, needled teeth. Like Menorquins, they are unable to mate outside their own race, and show no interest in doing so, being a solitary and solemn people. Average lifespan: 100 years.

Coronia ~ an SGA member. Closely related to both Tarkelians and Terrenes, Coronians are amply proportioned with a tendency to be thick-set, and stand on average seventeen and a half hands (or about five feet six inches) for males, and slightly taller for females. Their skin tones range from fair to dark brown, their hair from blonde to black, and their eyes are generally some shade of brown. They have a single set of sharp cuspids, or tearing teeth. Average lifespan: 86 years.

Corvus ~ an AEW member. Handsome and brilliant, the Corvi look much like their Terren cousins in general height and build, but because their planet is cool, they are lighter of both skin and hair. They tend to be slightly taller, and marginally slimmer than Terrenes. Corvi are almost exclusively homophilic in their pairings, and belong to deeply-bonded groups of eight for purposes of reproduction and companionship. Corvi are excellent parents and fiercely protective of their offspring. Average lifespan: 100 years

Declivis ~ an SGA member, (has applied for entry into the AEW). True Declivians no longer exist as a race, having been overrun by and then interbred with Coronians, Terrenes and Tarkelians. Of their original heritage a certain lankiness of frame remains, along with the dominant feature of brilliant gold eyes, occasionally flecked with cider brown or deep green. The most remarkable remnant is a bony, dual chin resembling two small, knobby horns extending about an inch and a half below the lower jaw, which marks those carrying the heaviest Declivian blood. It is bantered about that Declivians are stupid, which is not at all the case. They were true pacifists and had no way of defending themselves and their agrarian culture from invasion. Average lifespan: 70.5 years.

Demeter ~ an AEW member. Because of its location, Demeter has been a true "Crossroads of the Alliance" since ancient times. Because of this, Demetrians, much like Declivians, are a mix of many races and are therefore many colors, shapes and sizes. The original denizens of the planet were believed to be refugees from either Coronia or the Lebonathi worlds, and legend says they fled the Telenir before the First Dragonhorse appeared ten thousand years ago. There is no genetic evidence to indicate that they are from anywhere outside Alliance space, and the general population most closely resembles Corvi, Coronians and Terrenes in a mix. Average lifespan: 85 – 90 years.

Equus ~ an AEW member. The Equi tend to be tall and slender with broad chests, sloping shoulders and long legs. The taller males top out at around twenty hands (six and a half feet), females at around eighteen hands (six feet). Skin tone ranges from pale, which is rare, to dark olive, with light olive skin and black or dark brown hair being the norm. All High Equi have large, slightly almond-shaped eyes some shade of green, or mottled green and gold with ophidian pupils. Because they have never been flesh-eaters, Equi have large, white, flat teeth with no pronounced cuspids. Their ears, having been described variously as "ram horn" and "chambered seashell," are large, and delicately fluted with external ear-bones which give them extremely acute hearing. Like their Amberian cousins, male Equi have a phallic sheath and tuckable phallus. Both males and females are telepathic; some extremely so. Average lifespan: 200 – 250 years.

Hector ~ no affiliations. The true native population of Hector consists of desert nomads, who stand on average twenty-eight hands (seven feet) tall and who are primitive in the extreme. Almost nothing is known about them. They have rudimentary vocal chords but very little language. They live in scattered tent villages and survive by hunting both large and small game with crude weapons, and by trading with the expatriate Corvi and a smattering of Demetrians, Terrenes and Tarkelians who eke out an existence on the fringes of the planet. Average lifespan unknown.

Kohath Zadok ~ an SGA member. The Kohathi are small people. Standing about twenty-one hands, or just over five feet tall, they are very round, with seven pudgy fingers on each hand, and seven elongated toes on each foot, all of which they ornament extensively with rings and jewels. They have small, bright eyes of various colors, and fluted noses with five small nostrils and four septa, which they pierce at the columella and decorate with rings and gems of various kinds. They have large, flat teeth which they have fitted with permanent, jeweled caps, and their hair is kept long and worn elaborately twined with ornaments and rich fabric. Average lifespan: 125 years. (I must say from personal experience, their personalities leave something to be desired.)

Lebonath Jas and Tras ~ no affiliations. Because of their extreme xenophobia, not much is known about the Lebonathi. From our very limited contact we have observed a people with pink or colorless, slightly bulbous eyes, and white or blond hair. They have two sets of sharp cuspids. The males tend to stand well under twenty-four hands and are stocky in build. The females are smaller, but built on the same, square frame. Apparently there are examples of darker Lebonathi, but, again, there is no hard evidence. Average lifespan unknown

Menorquin ~ an AEW member. Historically an aquatic people of ancient lineage, Menorquins are small and exceptionally graceful, with slender, elongated bodies which allow them to move, eel-like through the water. They have elongated eye sockets, bright lavender or purple eyes, and almost no external nose or ears. Their voices gurgle as though they were speaking underwater, and they can hold their breath for over an hour even at considerable depth. Though they are garrulous and expansive by nature, Menorquins rarely marry outside their own people, and cannot bear children except within their own species. Average lifespan: 200 – 250 years

Nargawerld ~ no affiliations. Disproportionate people with extremely short, thick arms and legs, the Nargas stand no more than twelve and a half hands (four and a half feet) tall. They are uniformly blue-black with black eyes and thick black hair. When clothed it is difficult to tell male from female. Xenophobic and jingoistic, they have a well-earned reputation for being savage and untrustworthy. Next to the Nomads of Hector they are considered the most primitive people in SGA space, though they have space-faring technology and a solid if limited economy. Average lifespan: 45 – 50 years, so far as we can tell.

Papillia ~ an AEW member. Papilli are a slim, graceful and elegant people with beautiful, chime-like voices. They have very large ears which resemble the wings of a butterfly. Both sexes range in color from pure white to jet black. Their hair, which tends to be very thick and curly, ranges from white, to yellow, through every imaginable shade of brown, red and gold to blackest black. Their large eyes come in many shades of blue, green, purple and brown, and many Papilli tint their hair with flower-dye to match or compliment their eye color. They are relatively small and appear fragile, though they are not. They are considered among the most beautiful and intelligent of the races of the AEW, revered for their love of beauty and renowned for their sensuousness. Average lifespan: 150 years.

Phylla ~ an AEW member. A handsome and intelligent, if slightly intimidating race, Phyllans have bold, wolfish faces marked by bright yellow eyes, large, heavily boned noses, and pronounced fangs in place of modified tearing teeth. In males the chest hair climbs the neck to become a heavy beard, which is usually kept short and fastidiously groomed. Hair color is usually grizzled grey or brown – occasionally black or white. They have pointed and sensitive ears set high on the head, and both males and females have four heavily clawed fingers and toes, including opposable thumbs. Average lifespan: 85 - 95 years.

Potami ~ an SGA member. Tall, very heavy-set and coarsely built, the appearance of their race belies their intelligence and ingenuity. Their heads tend to be broad with flattened foreheads and large eye sockets, their jaws jut forward and their thick lips and heavy teeth protrude slightly, giving them a rather bellicose look. Their hair tends to be long, wiry, and some shade of red. Because of their thick, hairy skin, Potami are able to withstand uncomfortably high temperatures, and have colonized worlds upon which others could not thrive in a natural state. Average lifespan: 95 years.

Taraxia ~ an SGA member. Kind, curious and energetic, Taraxians are perhaps most noted for their tails, which they have encouraged as a sign of beauty from vestigial stumps to the luxuriously long, elegant appendages they exhibit today. They are tiny people, with twelve hands (four feet) being about average. They have bright black button eyes which show no white, flat teeth, and small ears set high on their heads. Both males and females have considerable facial and body hair which they keep fastidiously groomed, and they speak with quick voices. They are considered amongst the best parents in the SGA, and make fine teachers, creppiatricians and nurses. Average lifespan: 100 years.

Tarkelia ~ no affiliations. Closely related to Terrenes and Coronians, and for the most part resembling them in height and coloration, Tarkelians are long, loosely boned, usually double-jointed people who seem more to shamble than to walk. They are largely a seafaring folk, and use their long, thin arms and legs to good advantage in the rigging of their ships. They have a bad reputation for general sexual promiscuity, and have actually been observed perpetrating that most vile crime of child abuse, for which there seems to be no real punishment in their society. For that reason alone they are shunned by the AEW, and they are considered by many in the Alliance to be an invasive species. Average lifespan: 75 years

Terren~ an AEW member. Terrenes range in color from olive to black; those fair of skin or hair are rare indeed. The average Terren male stands at twenty-four hands (six feet), with the females being a hand or two shorter. They tend to be dense-boned, with square shoulders. Their arms and legs are proportionate to their size. Most are brown eyed, with hair color ranging from light brown or red to the most common shades of dark brown and black. They have one set of pointed cuspids, referred to as canine teeth. Average lifespan: 90 – 95 years.

PLANET EQUUS

General statistics as affirmed at the Rising of The Thirteenth Dragonhorse, Ah'krill Ardenai Morning Star ~ The Arms of Elohim, etc.

Kestrel ~ Mountain hold

Planet Equus is 26,206 Equi Statute Miles in Circumference ~ no change

The planetary capital is Thura ~ no change

There are now 384 full days in one year (up from 383.96.6 at the Rise of the Twelfth Dragonhorse)

Six seasons of 64 days each, does not need to be adjusted at this time.

48 weeks of equal length remains valid.

Eight days in one week is traditional and remains valid.

The population of the planet is holding steady at 1.1 billion inhabitants, with males and females being about equal in number. Births are averaging two children per family, with twins slightly on the rise and single child families slightly in decline.

The population remains in balance with consumption. Exports are 9.8 times greater than imports. Major cities remain steady in population, with keeps and small villages still the most popular places to live and work. The largest segment of the population is still agrarian. Relative wealth remains steady.

40 percent of the planet's landmass is currently suitable for agriculture, with 18% being cultivated for crops and 13% used for managed grazing. 10% is untouched. 38% of the planet's landmass is forested, 20% heavily so. 10% is managed forests. The remainder is protected. Mariculture remains steady at .05%.

Seasons are unchanged, ice sheets are holding, surface water and underground aquifers are well within acceptable parameters. Sea levels have not changed.

Animal populations both domestic and wild remain steady and within acceptable parameters. No extinctions reported. No significant imports of alien species.

A CHILD'S CHANT FOR LEARNING THE SEASONS

We have six seasons of sixty-four days
Each of them different in so many ways.
There's icy **Aellaeno,** our Season of Storms
Then blustery **Omphas,** when animals are born.
Sweet **Segens** is next, it's when everything grows
Then sun scorched **Enalios,** when the sailing wind blows.
In **Oporens** we harvest, preparing our keeps
For snow white **Chionos,** our season of sleep.

DAYS OF THE WEEK -- A SCHOOLING CHANT

Hormigyre, starting day (Pretend to get ready for a race)
Humilgyre, low day (Bend toward the floor)
Drasterigyre, active day! (Pretend to go to market)
Scoligyre, turning day (Hands out, hop in a circle)
Hyphogyre, weaving day (Pretend to use loom and shuttle)
Hoplegyre, blacksmith's day (Pretend to shoe a horse)
Hesychgyre, quiet day. (Sigh and close your eyes)
Hiergyre, sacred day. (Open your eyes and raise your hands.)

Both of these are lifted from: The Equi Primer for Creppia Nonage
And reprinted by permission of the author

ABOUT THE AUTHOR

I am now and have ever been a country girl. I was literally riding horseback before I could walk. I grew up an only child on huge cattle ranches in the company of horses, dogs, cattle and wildlife. The only person I had to talk to, was me. I got very good at it. I could escape to anywhere and become anybody in an instant – when my mother told me we were moving again, when I was the new kid again, when I was the half-breed kid before it was fashionable to be of Native American heritage, I could just vanish. I still can.

On my knees in a glaring white gully of eroded sandstone, I created whole cities and civilizations, with fields and orchards, and horses, of course. There were always horses. Horses that flew even as they patiently pushed cattle along a dusty track in the middle of nowhere. Fiery steeds that I rode into battle as the conquering hero I became. I wrote florid poetry in relentless iambic pentameter, and I could talk for half an hour during sharing time – always my latest wild fantasy. The teacher would smile and everybody else would smirk. I was – just for those few minutes – oblivious. I'm not sure I had a happy childhood, exactly, but it sure set me up to be a writer. I endured high school. There were ninety-six kids in the whole school, eight in my graduating class. I wrote florid prose. I sang in the choir, acted in the plays, played in the band and sucked at tennis, which was my best sport. After school and on weekends, I rode horses and drew maps of far off places, and made lists of all the supplies I'd need to make a go of it there.

Then there was college. My world opened up. There were people from other countries, people in rainbow shades of skin and clothing – people who had these amazing ideas, mind-blowing slants on life, love and politics. At last, I was popular. I acted in plays, wrote plays. I learned how to control my temper and my tongue. By learning those things, and in praying my way through the toughest English class of my entire undergraduate career, I learned how to control my writing.

I fell in love with a young man of brilliant artistic talent and temperament. We each married someone else, and remain to this day fast friends who remember and cherish that initial spark. When I write about intense love … that's him. It always will be him. When I write about tender, submissive love that becomes intolerable after a while, I draw on my first marriage. When I write about love that becomes affection, and tolerance, and grows immeasurably rich through all the manifestations and perturbations of an enduring friendship, I'm writing about my good and patient husband of the last four decades.

Through jobs and children, backpacking and horseback riding, I wrote. Researching, honing and putting it away for that time when I could devote myself body and soul to its art and its joy and its demands. Being a high school teacher, the enduring joy those kids have brought me as they moved through my classes to become successful, loving, thoughtful adults with jobs and children of their own … when I write about the wondrous order of things … it's them. And the high Cascades on a midsummer's day. And the sweet breath of horses.